THE

SITUATION

Graeme Daniels

ISBN: 978-0692213322

Cover design by Don Mathews

The Situations:

Survival

Nightmare

Comeback

The Game

SURVIVAL

1

I'm alive, thinks Weed, though it's not looking good. Considering the pain, a certain intense heat in his chest, living is not his favorite thing at the moment. But what else can he do but flail his arms and learn to swim—on the fly, so to speak. It's not as though he can just give up and wait for death to happen. That said, what do others do in these kinds of situations? If things are futile, do they stop fighting for their lives and instead spare precious seconds to think about life itself? Do they reflect on a few memories, the highs and lows of their particular biographies? Thinking about it, Weed realizes it would suck if his very last thoughts were about his legs feeling heavy, or the sinking truck beneath him, or his lame attempt at a breast stroke. Gazing upwards, his blurry vision barely making out a cruel, shapeless mass of grey, his face crumbles. Is it possible to cry underwater?

Anyway, it's hardly consoling, this notion of being alive. He censors emotion, as if preparing himself for a dignified end. He exiles hope as if already dispatched to some lonely place that his embryonic self once knew and then soon forgot. Briefly, his mind empties and the thudding in his chest stops. This is it, he thinks, now floating peacefully. From this place beneath the surface of the water, he is in a deep place, his mind calm and clear. Up above there's only noise. What he assumes are his last thoughts are about the lightness that he feels in his legs and the sudden conviction that he could swim if he really wanted to—that is, if it wasn't too late. Suddenly, in his peripheral view, something corporeal creeps into view and jolts him. Feelings return as Weed instinctively latches onto this thing. Seaweed. The thing he's clinging to is a thick trunk of seaweed.

Blame is next, self blame. Terror is what Weed gets for taking unhealthy risks, for not living a normal life of working hard, paying bills, for not settling down to marry a nice girl and creating offspring. Twenty seconds, he thinks, steeling himself for a last ditch effort at life: just twenty more seconds. He climbs the seaweed like it's a beanstalk that stretches up past the water's surface, attached to some indestructible foundation. The beanstalk of life, he wants to call it. It feels slimy, grotesque and coarsely textured, like a creature about to awaken and devour him. Its core feels easy to grip, enabling a quick ascent.

He didn't know it would hurt this much, this drowning. He wants to yell out a fighting noise, but the water won't let him. He wants to call out for help, but he dare not open his fulsome mouth. How long had he been underwater now? How many seconds, or minutes? He'd lost count. Bolinas Lagoon, dark muddy green and ridden with particles of something like rust presses against him, ready to burst down throughout his insides. Any moment now it will drown hope for good, and funereal music, adagio something for strings, will swirl about him, making beautiful this otherwise grisly end. His lungs feel as though the bottom is about to give out. As he climbs, he imagines the flood crushing lung tissue, his stomach, smashing his heart aside, and draining its way past holes ripped through the souls of his feet. Renewed hope rekindles panic. There is nothing to distract him from the horrible thumping his lungs are performing against neighboring organs. But panic or no panic, he is close to passing out.

Bryan Tecco, aka "Weed", next feels his head pop above a membrane and into a hairy expanse. He's caught in a swamp-like mesh, still holding his mouth closed, still believing himself trapped and dying. Now his body tenses, bracing for some other kind of attack: maybe a jerking, pulling under by a wrathful undercurrent. Paranoid fantasies assail him now that survival looms, about his ruthless followers lurking above the surface, looking pitilessly down and whispering, *gotcha*. He looks up, sees black sky above drifting fog, dotted with stars. Now his eyes are stinging from salty water, and there's a burning that hurts him, like the hell of his irreligious mind will hurt him. Is this real? Weed opens his mouth with a daring gasp and lets the night air rush in. Water streams away from his face and time stands still. The world slowly becomes clearer; crystal clear, in fact. Now it seems dark and arbitrary in its judgment. Now clear above the surface, Weed lets out a single, enfeebled cry. He maintains his hold on the branch that is saving his life, rests his cheek against its repellent texture, and murmurs thanks to nature after a guttural expulsion of water and muck. Another spasm of pain radiates up through him like an aftershock. He licks his lips clear of oily liquid, hoping to learn breathing again. This isn't near death, he thinks. This must be what being born was like.

Weed was born twenty seven years earlier. He was the beloved, adopted son of Jim and Sonia Tecco, and before that, of God knows who. He was a video gaming star, some say genius, and part-time drug dealer. That was the obituary Weed had been imagining some minutes earlier, before he'd climbed his way out the truck. He used to wonder about his biological parents, whom he learned were not his "real" parents when he was fourteen, though the adoption occurred when he was four. Weed doesn't remember anything from his life before age five, nor does he recall much about the disclosure from Jim and Sonia. He can't even remember why they chose to tell him about his adoption when they did. At the time, he was preoccupied with other things: his sense of belonging with peers, the company of girls. At seventeen, he started expressing himself through writing. Often, he wrote diatribe-filled essays, interspersed with bathetic poetry—stuff people might dislike or not get, but couldn't dispute. His favorite piece, published in his high school's newsletter, was only two sentences long, but still a hit with readers. It was an imagined rejection letter from his biological parents, fashioned after an editor's rebuff: we're sorry to say that after careful consideration your existence doesn't fit with our needs. We wish you the best of luck with your future goals.

Soon Weed may be free to bemoan his lot for the usual reasons: that people are against him, don't like him, or worse, that they just don't care. Not that he blames them necessarily. His gaming skills notwithstanding, there isn't much to admire as far as he's concerned: he's never won awards, hasn't ever saved a child; he didn't grow up with apartheid or get shot in war-torn country X, and he hadn't survived cancer or anything like that. Well, so far he's survived this ordeal. That's about it. Ten minutes prior survival wasn't his priority. Ten minutes earlier he was feeling good, was full of verve if undefined mission, and on the cusp of a heady escape. Then suddenly he was dying, or anticipating death since he can't swim; and before dying, he found time to reflect on one or two things: Questions, like *who am I, really? how will I be remembered*? Or more ordinarily, *what was my plan here*?

It was a mistake to bring Chris Leavitt along. Chris, his friend from the Oakland hills, was meant to be his chauffeur and then the keeper of his electronic stash when he—Chris—heads back to the East Bay. That was the deal—the quite simple deal from Chris' point of view, as Weed had said little if anything about the stash's importance. Thankfully, or not—Weed wasn't sure at the time—Chris was having his own problems; problems he wouldn't stop talking about. On the long drive out to Marin from West Oakland, Weed got Chris' story: Of his problems at work, as in his suspension from a job at a local hospital; of his problems with his bitchy but hot girlfriend, whom Weed had met briefly earlier that evening, only to get a hit of something not quite right with her. It was a foreboding, like the ones he gets from seeing what he calls Shadows, the same Shadows that Chris Leavitt sees; that a lot of people see these days.

The plan, half-baked as it was, was for the two guys to reach Bolinas, where Weed's parents' live. That's where they were headed. That's where Weed hoped to stay for a weekend, after which he would hitch a ride, head up north to some other hideaway, and then head back down to the Bay Area once things had settled down. He'd done one or two things that no longer seemed worthwhile, like a fledgling piece of corporate theft, for example. That's when more Shadows appeared. These Shadows: different people have different ideas about them, but for the most part they are ghostly figures—humans—that stand silently next to real humans, as in living humans, sometimes indicating their culpability in unseen crimes, or else their impending defeats, possibly deaths. Weed doesn't like talking about Shadows. He doesn't like it when others talk about Shadows either, for he gets little change from such talks—just a sense that others think him anti-social, crazy, or both.

Halfway to Bolinas, a chase followed, one instigated by Weed, who demanded that Chris, his driver, hit the gas and lose their followers, some corporate heavies that were also Shadows, Weed insisted. Corporate America, he said, had unleashed its pack dogs on him. Chris didn't get it because for him Shadows and humans are segregated entities, not co-conspirators, as Weed sees it. Supposedly, most Shadow seers can't see those who might victimize them. It's a problem Weed doesn't often share, largely because he suspects most people of victimizing him, or trying to. It's his default position, his signature cynicism. Chris more or less did as he was told, though the chase ended badly. At some point they pulled off the road to Bolinas, onto to some gravely path that disappeared into a black hole: a shaky, unknown foundation which felt about as strong as balsa wood and which collapsed in seconds. Moments later the guys and their truck—actually, Chris' truck— were sliding down a watery incline, watching the water levels rise up their bodies, hearing it creep through the truck's engine and locking systems, and debating who was being the bigger pussy about it. Weed did the manly, fraternal thing and told his panicky friend how to stay calm, get out and get clear to the surface. Don't panic. Chill out. Get mad. This is Weed's mantra, a phrase he thinks he might brand some day. He was meant to follow Chris as they sprang free from the sinking vehicle. Chris burst out like an Olympic swimmer propelled from his blocks and within moments he was reaching the surface, free as a bird, or a man without a life. Weed, the clumsier of the two in any circumstances, felt the currents of water push him back. It took nearly a minute for him to gain his bearings, point himself in the right direction even. In retrospect, he should have said something about the swimming problem. He should have known that necessity is not the mother of invention, and that swimming is actually harder than it looks. The escape wasn't supposed to happen like this. They were supposed swim alongside each other and survive together.

But they weren't together. Weed and Chris, like many who see Shadows, aren't very organized: they don't really talk. Instead, they banter or jab, or else plainly speak past each other on a regular basis. On the whole, Shadow seers are distracted from their quasi-spiritual purpose, as if God had once decreed that all those who aspire to foreshadowing visions should be otherwise burdened. So the Shadow-seeing types that Weed knows all fit a certain profile: they seem troubled, self-absorbed and paranoid, which in turn leads others to diagnose them with various mental problems, mostly along the schizophrenic continuum. As a result, they make shitty friends. They're unreliable, and are therefore more likely to do things like driving trucks into bodies of water late at night. Some give themselves identifying markers, just to make them feel better; to make themselves feel special. Weed doesn't have a particular word for himself, not one related to Shadows anyway. Unlike Chris, he's given up trying to belong.

Still hugging what seems the most precious branch of seaweed ever, Weed starts to think he should move and claw himself out of the mire. Is this a river? He wonders idly. Weed doesn't know, or remember. Disoriented, he barely knows where he's at, geographically speaking, despite being a Bolinas native. Several more minutes pass. Given his general exhaustion, several hours might pass with him stuck in this position. Such is his sodden, relative comfort and weighty feeling that he can just about picture himself sleeping in this wet bed overnight. It feels like a memory from a childhood camping trip: a practical joke in which he'd woken up lying in a drenched sleeping bag, thinking he'd pissed himself before realizing that his friends, so-called, had slipped a hose just inside the bag's zipper. The slick branch of plant-life to which he holds tightly takes on the quality of Linus' blanket from the old Charlie Brown cartoons. He wants to kiss it goodnight, turn over on his side and curl into a hibernating position. He wants to drag the branch over his shoulder and parade it through the village the next day. It's his new best friend, this branch.

Eventually, he pulls himself forward, feeling for either solid ground or another branch. Beneath him, a muddy bottom feels more substantial. He reaches his feet and lurches through plant-life that is sticky, taut, and just about as tall as him. As he turns forward, his shin hits against a grassy barrier: a wall. Weed feels his hands against a surface that is brick-like, only to give way to a bushy overgrowth, as though someone had started but then given up on man-made additions to the local ecosystem. He grapples in the dark and grabs a thick swath of grass, finding that a ledge is there for his climbing. Finding his last reserves, Weed performs a sloppy vault onto a patch of soil a few feet above. He feels the even terrain as his face slumps against the ground. He's alone yet still at risk from malevolent stalkers. Talk about ruthless: will they ever forgive him, give up their chase? Weed knows that in his corner of the world he is a big fish in a small pond. It's a comfortable role for him. But a small pond of sorts just nearly drowned him, and who knows what the big fish have in store for him next.

Take it slow, he thinks. Back on solid earth, he reaffirms the basics: he is alive.

2

In the area surrounding the body of water that nearly swallows up the life of Bryan "Weed" Tecco, there are knotted bales of weed, overgrowth and prickly plant-life that stab, clutch at, or scrape the skin of wayward pedestrians. Humans don't belong here, nature is saying. Weed is likewise fickle and rejecting. Minutes earlier, he'd been singing the praises of nature for presenting a lifeline in the form of a sturdy, unknown school of plant life. Now saved, he is feeling unwelcome. Short memory, some would say. Ungrateful, God might think. Now he is cursing all living things, as if all the thorns, plants and trees that nature offers have tantalized with survival, only to resume spiting him with vengeful tortures. As he staggers through the woods, Weed utters various four letter words, but neglects to call out the one five letter word that decency or common sense dictates that he shout out loud: that of Chris, the absent one.

But this situation is beyond mere common sense, and decency is, well, a complicated matter. This is a time and place for uncommon sense, his thinking of things outside the average man's box; his ideas; his *craziness*. Soon he reaches the first sign of civilization: a path. Looking left and right, Weed looks down a narrow stretch that is unfamiliar to him. It's not the stretch upon which he and Chris were driving down sometime earlier. Weed feels a crisp wind sail over the brush that's all around, and is enticed. The soft flow creates an ethereal, wispy sound that he recalls from times past but has not heard in ages, especially since living within the metallic neighborhoods of Richmond, across the bay. It's like the sound of breathing. I should never have left here, Weed thinks, indulging a rare sentimental moment. The wind thrusts flimsy trees in his direction. It's like they are lashing out, feebly trying to punch him. Get out and don't come back, this wooded community is saying. As for Chris, he's nowhere to be seen, and though Weed doubts his friend has drowned, he figures Chris is lost. But what can he do? Searching for a direction, Weed sucks it all up, the pain and confusion. He elects to worry about Chris later, much later.

The stretch of path leads to a road that will deliver him to the village in no time. That's the thing with Bolinas: once found, it is easy to navigate. It's just that it's not easy to find, which is why Weed has returned. Only two cars pass him as he treks along the road. He is turning his head every other second, checking every hint of a headlight, ready to jump from the pavement and hit the ground, either to blend into the soil or else be engulfed in a bush. The followers: they might be staking out his parents' house, having done their research, having anticipated Weed's original plan. Or, they might be lingering in town, loitering by the grocery store bulletin board, or else scoping out the atmosphere at the old saloon, Smiley's. Somebody wants him. Corporate America: it wants him bad. Weed considers the time, thinking it may be anywhere between ten and one o'clock. Smiley's, the only place in town still open at this hour, would be that way until two in the morning. Gingerly, he enters the lip of the village, which has a look of a sleepy ghost town from an old western. He feels like he should be riding a horse and wearing a gun and a holster. Squinting with native distrust, he should be on the lookout for rifles poking out of second floor windows. He had a gun, actually—or did until about a quarter hour ago. But his gleaming, new Sig Sauer, which he got recently because hookups told him he either needed to add muscle to his game or get strapped, was gone now, down in the river with the truck and the seaweed.

There is music in the distance, though it's hardly the jangly sound of a ragtime piano. Instead, Weed hears the flaccid notes of a squealing electronic guitar being played at low levels. A lumpen base and a clattering drum are straining to keep up, and a growling singer is barely audible over the din. Might be around eleven o'clock, Weed figures, or maybe closer to midnight. Smiley's, or the local ordinances, or both, doesn't let the entertainment continue much beyond these times, especially on weekdays. Last he remembers this was a Wednesday: the last Wednesday in March. Regardless, Weed wants a bathroom, and depending on the atmosphere, he might be able to squeeze in and use one; that is, as long as the bartender isn't uptight about his not ordering a beer while tramping through looking dirty and destitute. Not that he wouldn't want a beer, or even have money for one. It's just that the money he has—that he still has, miraculously enough—is currently fused to the inside of his wallet, which is wedged into the back pocket of his thoroughly soaked jeans. If stopped at the door, he could offer what he's got in exchange for a minute's privacy, the chance to squeeze a pint of swamp water out of his denim. If not, he'll have to find a dry, unused patch of ground for the night, and hope that by morning his soggy currency has not dissolved into bits. Smiley's saloon: Weed trips on a homonym, recalling that the river is not a river, it's a lagoon—Bolinas Lagoon.

A stolid figure at the door sizes up Weed as he approaches the front. His authority is unclear, and Weed tries to ignore him, predicting an unfriendly encounter.

"Ten dollar cover," the man says.

Weed halts, makes brief eye contact.

"Really?" he replies, half in appeal, half with attitude; a comment on the music, someone might think. The man doesn't move except for a sideways glance towards the bar. A muscular server is looking over Weed, whose wet and muddy, not-as-muscular and not quite six foot frame is now frozen under the spotlight of the entrance. Though the music continues, it seems to go quieter all of a sudden, as if the band were now going through the motions, transfixed, like the sparse audience before them by the blighted stranger at the door. Weed pries his wallet from his ass pocket and performs a kind of surgery so as to extract a pair of bills. The amount is not the problem. Weed has plenty of cash after a week of good business: his inventory of pills, including Oxy, Norco; several grams of his namesake product are popular items with regular customers. He sells Molly, but no syringes. None of that black tar shit. It's one of Weed's few semi-ethical rules to not

14

serve any hardcore dope addicts—no one that might die on him. He no longer has any dope of any kind on his body. As for the cash in his wallet, it's the disposition that's the issue. Some of the notes are shredded around the edges. Andrew Jackson's face looks a little blurred on others.

"Sorry," Weed mutters as he hands over his most passable of bills. The doorman collects it with a disdainful snatch that almost tears the note. Begrudgingly, he steps back about a half foot, letting Weed in. Next, Weed heads straight towards the back, to the restroom. Though he can feel the suspicion at his back—the nodding cue that he is to be watched—it's the customers that concern him, not the help. At first glance, they seem like typical locals: Harley-riding, tattoo covered denizens that might work on the nearby farms or as part of the fishing trades along the coast. Weed merits a glance or two as he moves quickly through the ten to twenty people milling around the bar's stage area, a glowing pool table that flanks a dormant jukebox. Who looks out of place? Weed considers as he inspects the bar's interior. Who's dressed in a mint black suit, wearing dark glasses, looking cool and vigilant? Get the clichés out of your head, Weed tells himself. If his stalkers are around, they'll be drawing much less attention to themselves as he is.

The state of the men's room is scarcely hospitable. The black-lit room, covered in graffiti, offers only one stall, and that's maybe five by three feet, tops, with just one sink and a cigarette ash-speckled urinal beside it. Weed undresses while three guys enter and then grumble as they form a line, all for the urinal. Though a wood partition conceals him, Weed can feel the impatience on the other side, others' knowledge that he is dawdling, misusing the space. He has one method of disguising his actions, that of waiting for the urinal to flush before wringing out his clothes with a short, wrist-crippling grip. The covert aspect fails, as the flushing of the urinal is just a lame stream released by a hand-lever. After a few rounds of this effort, the jeans and his shirt are no longer soaked, only damp and cold to the touch. He knows it will be unpleasant getting them back on again. He's half tempted to ditch the clothes and simply run naked through the bar. He sits down on the John, deciding he might as well take care of other business while he has the chance.

Just then the door to the room pushes open and slams against the opposite wall, as if someone has had just about enough of this. A person has walked in and stopped, facing the stall. Weed looks under the door and sees two black and white wing-tip shoes facing him. The urinal flushes, followed by the sound of footsteps hurrying out the door, back to the noise of the bar. The door closes again with a wooden clap. Quiet. Suddenly there are just two people in the room, Weed and this silent, like not-even-breathing somebody—a Breather-type Shadow, Weed assesses. The witnesses have bailed, and for all Weed knows, they have stuck an 'out of order' sign on the outside, leaving Weed to the mercy of this menacing, unknown figure.

Weed looks up from his crouched position, thinks of poking his head over the partition to face the one on the other side, his Shadow and adversary. I'm an idiot, he thinks. After all he's gone through tonight—after the chase on the highway, after escaping the lagoon—here he is, squatting on a toilet, pinned in a trap he made for himself just because he wanted a piss and a chance to wring out his jeans. Stupid. The figure takes two steps over to the sink, turns on the water. What is that? Is he teasing his prey? The water stops. More silence is followed by a pair of taps—the person's short two steps back to the edge of the stall. In this death's grip moment, Weed has associations, considers his place in the world order. He knows that some people with brass balls really do flirt with things that are much bigger than themselves: the government, big business, big money. Not him. Weed never thought he'd be fighting the big fishes of the world.

Soon there's sound of more humanity: Someone else bursts into the restroom, allowing acrid, sweaty air and bad music to pour in. Weed exhales, only now realizing that he'd been holding his breath for the whole of the last minute. This breathing thing: it's like it's negotiable all of a sudden. Next, there's a knock on the stall.

"What's up?" Weed asks sheepishly. It sounds stupid, but it's all he can think to say.

"Hey bro, there's people out here," an irritated voice says.

"I know that, bro," Weed replies, biting down on something more sarcastic.

"I mean, people out here are waiting for you."

"What?" Weed feels his blood pressure rising; a sweat attack begins.

"Look man, this isn't a dressing room." A pair of eyes appears just over the stall door, not quite looking down upon Weed in his disadvantaged position. It's the bartender, that heavy-set ogre with a thick cologne smell that cuts through the aromas of soap and human waste. It's his presence that's nearly penetrating the door, *gettin' all up* in Weed's business. Ah, blessed misunderstanding, Weed rejoices. Ordinary people, ordinary conflicts. Small fish. He stands up, quickly pulls his jeans on, opens the door and apologizes, though not to the bartender—more to the inconvenienced patron standing beside him. Weed edges his way out, his shirt still off, and it might stay that way, he reasons. On the floor of the bar, the air is hot and thick still. Close to the front, a cool breeze shoots in from outside, striking Weed in the chest, beckoning him once again to the outdoors. If there had been any question up to this point as to where he'd be spending the night, this soft zephyr has just answered the question.

For a small town in West Marin with a largely affluent populace, Bolinas has more than its share of vagrants. As Weed steps out onto the main street, he sees one or two competitors for the village floor space. He didn't recognize anyone in the bar. No one loitering outside the saloon or across the road by the public bulletin board looks either familiar or suspicious. For the first time in hours, Weed feels more or less safe in the knowledge that his followers are no longer dogging his every move. It's a reprieve, finally: time to find a reasonably soft, grassy patch of earth and just sink into it. Time to rest up for a chunk of hours, take it easy and procrastinate, like he often does with life's various to-do lists.

Time to kill time. There's much to figure out, actually; quite a lot to decide. But for now, let time disappear. Let time not survive.

3

The next morning, a Thursday, Weed awakens in a grassy vacant lot with a stiff back and a headache. It had been a long night nesting amid the uneven earth and its irritant tenants: the moist, soily molehills that are situated in numbers, about three feet apart from one another; the fluttering gnats, and that sticky grass that makes him itch. The sun, almost directly overhead, signifying something close to the noon hour, now bears down on him like a hot, devilish eyeball. He is slow to rise, feeling resistance in every muscle south of his neck. It's his back crying the loudest, cramping with the first move towards an upright position. Weed's tongue is working hard, performing a reconnaissance mission around his teeth. It collects a thick layer of plaque from the front, pokes its slimy point into the gap behind his right molars, his mouth's very own vacant lot. Weed's sense of taste is gone. He coughs hoarsely and feels gummy and rotten; his teeth, like Weed overall, lack bite.

He spends a half hour pacing up and down the village's one major street, passing and greeting the same backpacked hitchhiker twice before asking for the time. Eleven o'clock says the dreadlocked and barefooted pedestrian, chuckling as though he had his act so much more together. Weed then approaches a payphone near the grocery store, thinks for a minute about who he might call locally. He doesn't want to call his parents, knowing they'd overreact about the accident, maybe call the cops on him. In fact, if history's anything to go by, they're more likely to call police having heard from him than if they don't hear from him. Best not to make contact, he decides. For the time being, he resurrects a longstanding faith in the art of disappearance, thinking people will simply give up on him at some point. As for the accident: no witnesses, no problem, he thinks and hopes. Starving, he enters the store to buy himself a snack. The burritos from the small deli section look inviting, reminiscent of the tasty gems he can get from roaming food trucks back in Richmond.

A couple of things nag at him. What if Chris didn't make it? What if that brief sight of him moving to the surface like Michael Phelps with a shark on his tail was an illusion, a product of his wishful thinking? What if Chris is the one that's laying on the bottom of the Lagoon, drowned after failing to grab the right species of seaweed? On the other hand, what if Chris escaped the water easily enough, but then left Weed for dead? What is this feeling he's not quite having? Is it guilt? Who has time for guilt? More fear? Abandonment? Weed shakes them off, the bothersome questions, the birthing emotion. He doesn't want to think about it. He turns his mind to practical matters, the near future of subsistence; the unwritten chapters of purpose.

Another problem is the status of his contraband flash drives, currently embedded in a pile of belongings back at Chris' girlfriend's apartment in Oakland. Weed had to go along at first to check the place out. He had to scrutinize the makeshift safe that was her one-bedroom unit; the basic trustworthiness of the unwitting guard. Chris' girlfriend seemed like an edgy chick with a sizable chip on her shoulder, but otherwise Weed had little concern about her, except maybe to log her image for a later fantasy. Thoughts of flash drives remind him that there was a bigger point to the last twenty four hours. Meaning. Weed thinks briefly about meaning, but comes up with nothing specific. He exits the store, swallowing down a three dollar, pesto chicken burrito with about two bites in total. He's a beast, he reflects summarily. He stops next to the payphone, sees another antique dangling from its base: a yellow pages.

It's not so much an idea he has as an association. Rosco. Ross. Mr. Rosco, as he was first known to Weed, was a computer programmer mostly, but also a substitute teacher at West Marin High School whom a few students like Weed befriended shortly after their graduations. Weed remembers frequenting Rosco's place back in the day and partaking of his excellent White Widow marijuana. That frequency would pay dividends in the sense that Weed would otherwise not remember where he lives. It's been about three years, Weed figures. Brighton Avenue: Rosco lives on one of the cul-de-sacs connected to Brighton Avenue, or used to anyway. It is a twenty minute walk away, and the fixtures on the crosstreets—the abandoned vehicles in the driveways, the odd skylights with peace symbols projecting out, or that one house with the top room that looks like a watchtower—are all distinctive enough as navigation tools.

As he walks up the hillside towards the avenue, Weed surveys the majestic rows of eucalyptus trees that frame the road, the forest of poplars through which the sun beams angelic rays of sunlight. He notes how they helped the night before: the way they stood like tall shadows and sort of guard-railed Chris as he drove along the unlit roads in the dark. The lights against the trunks were all that marked the edges of the treacherous, winding highway with their steep ditches. Weed was raised among these wooded areas, within this sleepy village and its outlying spread of homes. The bucolic surroundings recall a time when he was better known as Bryan versus Weed. That was his first decade and a half, roughly. The nickname didn't stick until his latter years of high school, for reasons that strike most people as obvious, though privately, Weed has always known that his nickname has layered meanings. Even Weed's parents slip from time to time and use the term. They have no objection to marijuana, the presumed association—far from it. In fact, they'd once been modest growers of pot, as many are in West Marin. Regardless, Weed gathers that his parents adopted the nickname not because of its drug connotations, but rather because they thought it fit him, sort of, as in naturally.

Reaching the apex of a hill, Weed pays close attention. Which house is Rosco's? Briefly, he considers knocking door to door, looking for his former teacher, but then thinks the better of it. Bolinas folk are notoriously distrustful of outsiders, and Weed still looks—perhaps always looks—a bit too vagrant to be anywhere in Bolinas except the area around the post office down in the village. The road flattens out. He recognizes the stretch of gravel that seems blended with beach. The sound of a wave crashing in the distance just about reaches his ears, and he sees the cliff edge, but feels edgy, knowing he must recognize the correct property soon, or else retrace his steps and try again down another cul-de-sac. He scans the area. This is the part that looks like a slice of Hawaii shipped in. It's vague, now—the connection—but promising. A slim, adolescent palm tree obscures a street sign, and Weed knows from that image, which connects to the memory of getting lost the first time he came to Rosco's, that he's nearby.

The next part is more difficult. The gardens are uniformly higher and thicker, concealing the homes from onlookers. Tiny fence doors lead into cottages that are getting smaller, like the dwellings of hobbits. A white picket-fenced property is either Rosco's house, or that of his neighbor. He can't remember. Screw it. He might as well experiment. Pulling the latch open on a three foot high gate that looks ready to collapse, Weed edges inside an area that leads to an equally derelict front porch. The gate conjures the recent memory of balsa wood. Meanwhile, there's a hammock beneath a window that serves as a look-out. Beside it: a dog's empty bowl, but no dog. Sleeping on the job somewhere, Weed imagines. On the hammock there's a plaid, cotton shirt and next to it, an ashtray. Weed looks around, expects to see a banjo, a trunk of wood with an axe embedded in its center.

Weed steps to the door, sees no doorbell, just a foot-wide iron plate set about eye level, with a bullet-sized hole in the middle. The cottage is wood-paneled, with four inch strips of something having Northern California pedigree. The panels are painted royal blue, but their age is showing. Chips are flaking off, and beneath it, dirt, bugs, and a few spider webs have found nooks and made a home. The porch wood creaks as Weed reaches the door. He looks to his right, ducks slightly as he looks into the window above the hammock. It's dark inside. No sign of life. He gently knocks. It's all coming back to him now, the nights when he and friends would drop by, usually late at night. Rosco would open the door dressed in pajama bottoms and a wife-beater shirt. Living in one of Bolinas' small grandfathered properties, Rosco was proof you needn't be rich to own a home in West Marin. Rustic like trailer trash, he looked as though living nearby a refinery or something were more his style. In Richmond his garden would smell less of nearby ocean and eucalyptus leaf, and much more of beer and gasoline. The grass in front would be golden and dead, not green, and the ambience would be metallic, not peaceful and misty. There would be greasy, fierce smells of industry. Less earth.

That's the image Weed held of Rosco when he first met him. Meek-eyed and twitchy, Rosco carried with him a constant air of disturbance which detracted from an otherwise tidy and knowledgeable presence. Weed found him distractible, likely depressed, standing before a classroom of idle students who'd been told by their regular teacher to read MacBeth the week before, only to need a kidney stone removed over the ensuing weekend, thereby missing the follow-up review. That was left to Rosco who, upon being given the task, stood over the text of the Scottish play like someone who thought he could do better than the great bard. Weed loved the way he stopped reading at some point, tossed the play aside with disdain, and then looked to the class and asked them to share tales of paranoia, betrayal, and ambition from their lives instead. Rosco taught only four classes that last year of Weed's high school year, the best four classes of Weed's high school career, actually.

Over the following summer, Weed learned that Rosco otherwise worked as a computer programmer, lived nearby with his parents, would smoke with just about anybody, and most importantly, was developing a video game that would later be picked up by a publisher. *2012*, the game Rosco helped develop to coincide with the 'end of world' phenomenon that gained popularity leading up to 2012, was a big hit. Weed hadn't played it. Prior to the last month or so, he hadn't much interest in games with a political, much less a religious subtext, though he patronized Rosco's thoughts on these subjects when they got high together. That was the price Rosco charged for using his product: his implicit requirement that people listen to his ideas, even if they had nothing to say in response. Rosco didn't seem bothered by critics, nor did he covet admirers especially. On the whole, he seemed indifferent to feedback. He wanted only listeners, or perhaps not even that. Just witnesses. Rosco was a conversation magnet and then hijacker; that is, someone with a knack for turning any subject in the direction he wanted, with conclusions that only he decreed.

Weed takes a nosy look around the side of the cottage. Towards the back there is an entangled hose lying on a path strewn with kicked up gravel. A messy, dense set of bushes is sticking out from a fence like a bad haircut needing a trim. The faint sound of running water is coming from somewhere. He gazes all around checking out more cracks in the wood panels, believing this place a small earthquake away from being condemned property. It's not as though he's at the wrong house, or even that there's no one home on this particular day, at this particular time. He's pretty sure this is the place wherein he'd partied with Rosco on numerous occasions, even if he'd previously only seen it in the dark. It's more like there's nobody home at all, as though the residents had died but the neighborhood hadn't yet noticed.

"Help you with something?" says a low voice from behind. Instinctively, Weed raises his arms, sure that a shotgun is pointed at his back.

"Whoa, sorry. Didn't mean to intrude—"

"Well you managed to anyway, so you must be a natural." Weed smiles, recognizes the voice and the laconic turn of phrase.

"Rosco," he says, turning carefully. "Ross?"

"Shit," Rosco drawls as he lowers his weapon. It's not a shotgun. It's a shovel that he's holding like a baseball bat. Rosco,

Weed recalls, was or is very anti-firearms; had anti-NRA stickers on his refrigerators and on his truck. Self defense with him is old-school: all pitchforks, knives and bare knuckles. Otherwise, Weed's memory had served him well. Rosco stands before him in a faded blue wifebeater shirt, a soft cotton pair of pants that might be his pajamas. He looks just about the same as he did three years earlier. Maybe his belly protrudes an inch or two further outwards. His blondish hair, graying on the fringes, is stringing outwards with hippy shag, and his skin is a tinge more ruddy than it once was. Rosco gives Weed a short, tired laugh and a grin. "What the hell are you doing here?" he asks.

The cottage Rosco lives in, and has lived in most of his life, currently has two residents, Rosco and his father. His mother, Rosco explains shortly, had died a year earlier of a stroke. His father, now in his eighties and suffering from neuropathy as well as circulatory problems, spends most of his time sleeping indoors, nursing a broken heart. Rosco is now his full-time caretaker, having given up work. Weed is not surprised by the latter news: he'd previously thought that Rosco's success with *2012* would land him a windfall of royalties and a ticket to leisure instead of drudgery. His once substitute teacher would have cause to smile and spread his wings, finally. He thought that success would liberate Rosco's hidden vitality, his brooding intellect. He hadn't learned much of Rosco's attachment to his parents. He hadn't known that Rosco's success had soured like this; that it would look and feel this subdued.

Rosco leads Weed through the cottage, gives him a brief tour and a rusty, half-conscious welcome to Rosco's father who sits inertly in a living room chair, like a fixed plant. Next to him is a walker that looks discarded, like it hasn't been used in a while. The room is shadowy and grey, with signs of neglect that mirror the exterior facade. A layer of dust seems apparent on all surfaces. As Weed suppresses a sneeze, he notes the sound of a clock ticking eerily over a fireplace. This home feels like it's in countdown. Meanwhile, the host, Rosco is quietly genial, offering Weed some food from a fridge so well stocked it seems as though father and son are preparing for nuclear winter. Weed declines for the time being, still feeling the aftertaste of the earlier burrito, but he accepts a soft drink. Rosco outlines options: other kinds of food, some herbal tea; nothing medicinal beyond that. Weed feels spontaneously warm, even joyous. Perhaps it's a reaction to being chased, nearly drowned, disregarded, or regarded suspiciously, that he feels so accepted in this moment. He thinks to ask for a smoke, partly as a joke, to lighten the atmosphere. Surely he must, Weed thinks. Maybe the father is…like, right now, he considers.

"You got anything with you?" Rosco asks, though not about having a smoke. By the weary yet clean look in Rosco's eyes, it seems to Weed as if Rosco hasn't smoked anything in a small lifetime. Looking about Weed's person, Rosco becomes curious, inquires further: "What? Nothing? You don't live around here, right?" he says, looking quizzical. Weed shrugs, returns an affable grin, hoping to ward off impromptu cross-examinations. Suddenly, Rosco's nose wrinkles, like he smells something wretched in the house. Weed's thoughts spin quickly on possibilities: has the old man soiled his pants? Is there dog piss in the hallway? Maybe it's a visual trigger: Rosco's eagle eye has spotted a rat dropping or a cockroach swarm. Just then their eyes meet and Weed detects in the host's expression a look of disgust directed at him. As Rosco is opening his mouth, Weed realizes his problem; has just enough shame to speak up and preempt embarrassing comments. Too late. "You know, there's a shower down the hallway, if you want to…ya know," Rosco offers.

Sometime later, Weed settles in for an earnest talk with Rosco. He is feeling refreshed and clean, though his sour taste lingers: a combination of that burrito, plus dregs of the lagoon that stick inside him and now line his stomach like reminders of his near death. As he catches Rosco's shifty look, Weed feels a whiff of quid pro quo in the air. It is already mid-to-late afternoon in this small village by the Pacific. Rosco is out on the back yard, sipping on a cup of lemon tea. He is waiting expectantly, but saying nothing. Weed approaches, gives an awkward greeting whose implication he immediately thinks to second guess. What's the deal here? He asks himself, feeling a twinge of obligation. Weed looks out, towards a balmy sky and a brightly orange sun perched at a roughly four o'clock height.

"I'm surprised to see you," Rosco begins. "And I don't mean you just walkin' into my back yard. Figured I wouldn't ever see guys like you again. Don't know why, exactly. Just didn't think you were the type to stick around Bolinas. Visiting your parents?"

"Not exactly," Weed replies.

Rosco cuts a sideways look.

"You got a problem?" He sounds like the local sheriff.

"Many, as you might remember."

Rosco doesn't laugh as Weed had expected. He stares ahead, takes another sip of his tea.

"You gonna tell me what's up?" Weed pauses, unsure if he's just heard a question or a statement. He bites.

"I don't want…well, okay, I want, uh…"

"Refuge?" Rosco's not a good listener. He's too impatient; too quick to graft his own take on things. However, he's not wrong.

"Yeah, I don't know. You got your dad and everything. I don't wanna put you out."

"Just tell me what's happening. I probably won't care what it is. It's not like I'm gonna judge you." Rosco shifts in his seat, changes his mind. "I don't know, maybe I will. Look at me. But you came here for a reason, and I'll help if I can. Just don't bullshit me."

Weed laughs, embarrassed. He regards Rosco's bearish face, which ever telegraphs his gruff manner; his invitation that feels vaguely like a pair of shackles waiting to ensnare him. He wants to declare his ignorance, or innocence. Would Rosco— would anyone—ever believe he was once an innocent?

"I don't know where to begin."

Rosco, it seems, has a new drug.

"You want some tea?"

4

The two men sit outside for another three hours discussing everything from the accident in the lagoon, the chase beforehand, even the Shadows obsession, about which Rosco is hearing for the first time. Then, on top of that, Weed introduces his next priority in life: that of recovering a stash of flash drives, stolen corporate property, from his friend, Chris Leavitt. Rosco listens patiently but with stirring thoughts. He's aware that Weed once enjoyed minor celebrity in the world of video gaming. But he knows nothing of Weed's subsequent job with Sahi corporation, the telecommunications giant; is somewhat shocked by Weed's slide into a cool-sounding but actually quite dull occupation: a tester of games being prepared for the video game market. Though Rosco had always known of Weed's habits, his tendencies towards fringe criminal activity, the lackluster ambition implied by his nickname, he also knew Weed, or Bryan, to be uncommonly bright. But all this talk of Shadows, of being followed: something went wrong in there, Rosco thinks. Something anciently corrupted in this young soul has returned and stalled a promising future.

Weed at least feels a bit more human after his shower. The clothes he arrived in are being laundered, but are destined for a bonfire given the state they were in before. He sits alongside Rosco wearing a borrowed tank top and an oversized pair of boxers. At eight o'clock the sun will be down.

"You know, you're lucky to be alive after that accident," says Rosco with a critical air.

"Yeah, I know."

"No, I mean you made a mistake. That idea of waiting for the water to rise so you have equilibrium, making it easier to get out: that's a myth. I don't know how your friend was able to open his door so easily. Maybe it was already dislodged. But it might have taken minutes for the pressure inside the truck to match the pressure outside, by which time you might have been dead already. Didn't you try to get out your side?"

Weed gives a shy grin, recalling the moments he'd tried to open the door next to him. It wouldn't open, and the worst of all things happened: he panicked. There wouldn't be time to wait for Chris, he realized. Shame. All that shameless bravado: he'd told his friend he'd follow him out, as if he'd be helping Chris reach the surface instead of the other way around. Humbly, Weed sanctions Rosco's opinion of that situation, but soon turns to the subject of Sahi, to the game prototypes he'd pilfered.

"Why'd you give them to your friend?" Rosco's tone is disapproving, misunderstanding. Weed heaves a sigh.

"Ugh, I needed to stash them somewhere…somewhere they wouldn't be found, with someone that wasn't connected with Sahi. I was only gonna stop briefly with my parents, anyway. I knew the window of time I had would be short. But when I saw that car on our back—"

"You mean, what you *think* was a car on your back. Were you on something?"

He'd actually prefer it if were that simple.

"Sure, anyway, I can't take the chance that my parents' place isn't being watched." Rosco is still-faced. More skepticism.

"Well, okay, but what are you waiting for? Why not head back to Oakland, get your drives back?"

"I have to wait"

"Why?"

Weed wipes both his hands across his thighs simultaneously, and looks away. He doesn't know why. He doesn't have an answer. He doesn't have a rationale. He has a feeling.

"It's hard to explain."

"Sounds like it."

Weed wants to complain that Rosco doesn't understand, but that's not the problem. No one would understand. Weed, suddenly, doesn't understand; doesn't know anything, it seems like. He feels inscrutable, not deceitful. He feels empty of answers, of purpose. He wants to find a console, play a game.

"I know," he says. For a split second, Weed goes dizzy, sways in his seat and deflects with a non sequitur: "Whoa, I'm trippin' here."

"It aint the tea," Rosco says, offering another cup. What's with the tea obsession, Weed wonders. He wipes his eyes, contemplates starting again, from the beginning, but Rosco takes over: "Okay, so you gave these flash drives to your friend Chris?"

"Right"

"Before you left to come out here?"

"Check"

"So, they're at this place in West Oakland, his girlfriend's place. Now, you think that Chris escaped the lagoon, like you did, but you don't know that, and you haven't seen him since the two of you escaped the truck. By the way, does anyone else know that your truck went down in the water?"

Weed goes blank, has no answer.

"I'll take that as a 'no'. So, if Chris reached the surface and left, and he hasn't seen you, then I figure he's called the police or sheriff's department and told them you're missing, maybe drowned."

"Nah, I told him not to say anything," Weed asserts.

"You sure about that?"

"Pretty sure."

Rosco laughs. "You don't sound sure. You told not him not to say anything, but that was before the truck disappears with you still in it. What was the contingency plan for that?"

Weed is stilled. Rosco has a good point. He continues: "In fact, this whole thing sounds kinda shaky. Now, I get it—sort of— that you've pulled off a theft of a game you were testing. I've no problem with that. I read some of that book you wrote. You know more about games than any of those people at Sahi. I bet you play their new product better than anyone—even the original designers—even dreamt of. You're too talented to be working that mediocre job. Those fuckers are monopolizing the market, ripping off developers and artists. So you sell that shit to whomever you like. That'll teach 'em to come up with new stuff. Meanwhile, you make yourself a nice piece of cash."

"It's not about that," Weed interrupts, sounding righteous, quite unlike him.

"Okay, forget that. The thing is I don't get this other thing you're saying. Are the guys that followed you working for Sahi, or are they these 'Shadow' figures you're talkin' about?"

Weed is halting.

"I'm not sure. They could be both."

"What? This doesn't make sense."

"I told you. The Shadows are hard to explain. They're visions. There are others like me who can see them. When the Shadows appear they're incriminating figures, pointing out the future, pointing out what's gonna happen, especially if it's destructive, by the positions they take up. Meaning, they stand next to culprits, and sometimes victims. But sometimes they embody real people. So those followers—those Sahi followers—are just that: guys hired to hunt me down and recover their stolen property. But the Shadows infiltrate them. I call that type Breathers, not that this matters. That's what I think. They sort of hijack real people, take over their identities, so they can get closer, get in my face and then in my head. They're looking to warn me, make demands of me." Weed stops, notices he is shaking as he speaks. "So, does this sound crazy or what?"

Rosco regards Weed with a disturbed air, not that he hasn't disturbed many with similarly bizarre notions. His eyes roll about his visitor, noting the agitation, the pressured speech. It had been a while, of course, since Rosco had seen Weed, much less shared his company with any regularity. His speculations stir again: what escalation of substances had occurred in the intervening years? What manner of mental illness had gotten a foothold and now worsened?

"Relax, my friend. I'm just tryin' to understand. It sounds like you need to find this guy Chris, or else get your drives back before they get lost, or maybe stolen again."

Wearily, Weed says, "I know. I just need to…I need to chill, ya know?" He actually feels chill, though not in a good way. He's about to add that he shouldn't panic, but then recalls what comes next; he hasn't the energy yet for what comes next.

Rosco frowns. "Okay, but I got a feeling that certain things are gonna force the issue here, and I'm not talking about corporate goons, or Shadows, or whatever. Your parents might be more concerned than you think about you not showing up. I mean, I get this isn't the first time you've broken a promise, but that doesn't mean they'll just write you off. They might call the police, report you missing. And if authorities have by now pulled a truck from a nearby body of water because, say, a guy who could be linked to you says his truck disappeared in a river, and that disappearance coincides with yours, then…"

Rosco opens out his arms, making a display of omniscience. He looks upwards, as if to signify an invisible pink elephant floating about the conversation. It all makes sense, but Weed is still frozen, not reacting. Weed can't decide if Rosco gets denial, as in his need to be in it.

"Bro, do you get that I almost died last night? I get what you're saying. Really, I do. But you have no idea how complicated this is, and how fucked up I feel right now. Look, if you don't want me here, if you don't need this, I get it. I'm fine. I'll—"

Rosco reaches out his left arm, touching Weed on his wrist. His voice is low, firm, yet gentle, like that of an apologist priest.

"Hey, I'm tryin' to help. Stay as long as you need. Anyway, you sound sick."

Weed exhales heavily, almost like he did back at the lagoon, right as he emerged from the water. For a nanosecond, he returns there in his mind. In it, he tastes the salt water on his lips, the pain of not breathing. He even looks around for his trusty beanstalk. Next he sits back down. He glimpses Rosco's fixed, steely expression, sees and feels a man changed from the one he'd known years earlier. He seems like a man in retirement, like a man who has grieved one or two things and simply given up on a few others.

Rosco's cottage has two bedrooms, one for Rosco, one for his father. At nine o'clock, he begins a ritual in which he pulls his father's already sleeping body from his chair and carries him to his bathroom to help him wash up and clean his teeth. Minutes later, the elder man is walking gingerly, assisted by his son to the King sized bed he used to share with his wife. He, the father, insisted it not be replaced with anything smaller. He was determined to continue sleeping in that bed and therefore not forget that former place of love. Rosco is fifty years old now. He has never married, never had any children. By the looks of things, it doesn't seem as though either event is going to happen anytime soon. But upon feeling Rosco's hand on his wrist and then watching him bathe his father and later lay him down to sleep, Weed observes the caring, reverent father that is in him. Weed feels awkward as he watches the pair from a discreet distance. It's been a long time since he's seen anything like that.

5

Weed sleeps, awakens late again the next day, as if some kind of jetlag-like phenomenon has taken hold. He feels like he's coming down with something, becoming sick from the bilge water still living in his gut. He spends the day dawdling about Rosco's property, thinking but not getting very far with his thoughts. They seem diffuse, sort of stringing, but not stringing together. They seem tied up in knots, Gordian Knots, with dust particles drying out synaptic connections. He needs some kind of lubricant: something injected into his brain to loosen the fibers, get his gears properly moving again. Afternoon, he walks down to the beach at the end of the road. He stops at the cliff edge, tossing rocks, gazing out to sea. There is no one around. Early on a Friday, in a quiet neighborhood like this, it's as though Bolinas doesn't really exist. Everyone who lives nearby is either ensconced indoors, hiding from civilization, or else they are hours away from arriving for a long, carefree weekend retreat.

And he sees no Shadows; no visions of anyone flashing their creepy appearances and then disappearing just as quickly. Nor is there any sign of his being followed by what he thinks are hired hands of Sahi corporation. However, beyond the rocks studded with shellfish he sees Wharf road on the south side of the beach, just beyond the village. For all Weed knows, there might be men in suits—iconic mint black suits, accompanied with sunglasses— asking after him in the local shops, or near the post office bulletin board where the other transients hang out. Then there is Smiley's. Sure enough, the bartender, if the same guy is working today, would be happy to report on the freak that came into the bar late Wednesday night, trailing mud and Bolinas Lagoon into the men's room and pissing off customers by taking over the toilet stall for something like a dog's year.

Rosco's comments remind Weed that he hadn't thought through all of his actions the night of the accident. That was the exhilaration of being alive. Or, it was an old habit of Weed's: show off what you've done, no matter the consequent spectacle. Be spontaneous: make sure people notice you, what you've been through. Weed conjures the way he strolled through the bar, thinking he might be recognizable to former neighbors; wondering if onlookers might gather that he'd just survived a harrowing episode. These old conceits might catch up with him. He considers the possibilities: that Chris may indeed have told police that he was in the truck as it went down, and was now missing; that his parents, more annoyed than fretful, might be echoing that conclusion, if only in answer to police questions. If people are talking to the bartender, they'll know Weed's alive by what's reported there, and as that search trail opens up, the point of hiding out at Rosco's—that of resting up and shaking off Shadows—will be lost.

In the meantime, much depends on Chris Leavitt, and Weed hates depending on Chris Leavitt. By now he'd known Chris for a couple of years, had once bonded with him over their shared visions of Shadows, though each assigned different significance to their gifts. For Chris, Shadows were basically flies in the ointment of a disturbed and hierarchical world—a system that needed dissembling, whether it was a workplace, a political system, or a familial disorder. Weed argued with Chris' habit of personalizing, his belief that Shadows "assigned" him important tasks, though now he wasn't so sure of that position. After all, what was his theft of Sahi property about if not profiteering? Why sacrifice a stable, if mundane job, if not because of needs not yet defined?

More recently, Weed had become bored with Chris' dilettante ways. Though he'd been stable in a job at a hospital for some time—that of a surgical assistant—Chris seemed destined to fuck it up, like he had most other jobs in his life. This despite having just finished some rigorous coursework at a training college he was in. Chris had a paranoid streak, just as Weed does, but tended to employ it indiscriminately, and pick fights with the wrong people, like the people in charge of things. It was happening in his latest job, Weed noticed. Chris was alienating doctors, arguing over petty matters, for reasons Weed didn't understand. Maybe Chris didn't either. Predictably, Chris was getting written up and then suspended, and boasting about it when they got together, as if competing with Weed over some prize entitled 'the most troublesome kid in the neighborhood'. Then there was that weird diaper invention of his: Chris had this half-ass idea to create a new kind of diaper based upon something he'd heard in one of his classes, and had begun spending his free time drawing up ideas and later soliciting Weed and others for investment. Boredom: it artificializes fatigue, generating weird pastimes. Damned tweaker, thinks Weed of Chris. Despite being neighbors in Richmond, the friendship was cooling; it was *chilling*.

At least as far as Weed was concerned. Of course, that didn't stop him from requesting favors, because only Weed, it seemed, felt the recent demise of camaraderie. Chris would just about do anything for him, Weed thought. So, when he asked Chris to drive him out to his parents' house in West Marin, saying he couldn't take his own truck in case it would be recognized by followers who were like Shadows, Chris agreed like he was ten years old and Weed was a Disneyland dad. Therefore, Weed knew Chris would do as he was told; knew he'd hold onto his stuff, and thereafter follow instructions to not tell anyone, especially the police, where he was going. And he was counting on Chris' discretion now, if not so much his competence.

The pieces might still come together, despite the mistake of entering the bar. If Chris, assuming *he's* alive, doesn't say anything about Weed being in the truck, then police will have no cause to ask about him in town, and nor will they bother his parents, assuming they, too, refrain from making calls about his absence, despite Weed's alerting them to his upcoming arrival a couple of days earlier. But he'd done that before, Weed quickly reasons. In fact, he could think of more occasions when he'd said he'd come by—and then not—than the reverse. Rosco's concerns notwithstanding, Weed worms his way through his dizzying thought maze, but feels less distressed by the situation the more he thinks about it. He convinces himself that Chris is safe, perhaps having hitchhiked his way back to the East Bay already, and that his parents will be nurturing their abundant gardens instead of obsessing—as they once did—about their troubled and self-centered son. He even feels well enough to walk down to the village the next day, albeit with a modest disguise of hat and sunglasses. It's a Saturday and there are visitors about, taking in the genteel atmosphere, getting a late breakfast at Charley's, the local restaurant at the end of the main street. Many others are chasing dogs, throwing Frisbees, and walking along the thin slice of beach around the corner of Wharf Road.

Weed enters the grocery store, buys himself a twelve ounce cup of Columbian coffee, and then steps outside onto a creaking, wooden porch. He leans against the wall next to the bulletin board, and studies a flyer about a blue grass quartet that will be playing at the local townhouse theater later that evening. He is feeling relaxed and cheerful. He feels the spring sun penetrating the cotton shirt borrowed from Rosco's wardrobe pleasantly warming his skin. In the corner of his eye he sees a face he recognizes and, without thinking, he turns his head. At first he misses it, and upon scanning the surroundings for a few seconds more, relaxes again, as the face is gone. Was that a Shadow? He wonders quickly. If it was then it was an unusual appearance, more fleeting than is typical. Weed shakes his head, thinking his mind a kind of pest.

The face appears again just as Weed's eyes cross over a set of boxes containing newspapers, the front pages of which are pressed against a glass partition. Eyes have much to answer for, playing tricks like this. He steps closer, intent on finding the tantalizing image and holding onto it like it was a fly that needed swatting. The first paper is a local rag, a banal distraction with a headline about new proposals for building developments around the nearby Muir beach area. Weed looks hard to the right, sees in an end box the San Francisco Chronicle sporting a picture of the new Bay Bridge span, now just months way from being open, but with problems in its design structure. Then, in between, he catches what he's just been looking for: a smallish yet stand-out image, containing the smiling expression of Jules Grotius.

It's the New York Times, with Grotius' mug up front, flanking an article, the headline of which is partially obscured because of the limited space of the window. "Media critic and 'Omniscribe' founder mis—" reads the bold print. Weed digs into his pockets, finds the necessary change to slot in and grab a copy. Wandering into the street, he reads the story and is transfixed. Grotius, Jules Grotius, the Swiss-born journalist and former computer hacker, responsible in recent years for the leaking of numerous official documents worldwide, thus compromising several governments, and creating turmoil in the streets of numerous countries, especially in Asia Minor, has been reported missing, feared kidnapped, according to sources.

In the picture, Jules looks happy, atypically disheveled, yet vaguely oblivious to pain—not at all what he looked like the last time Weed saw him. Not that Weed was a friend of his, or even a passing acquaintance. It's rather that Weed had sort of infiltrated an inner circle of Sahi—the result, it seems, of impressing his boss, an executive, with ideas left over from his indie book about popular video games—and was therefore granted the occasional peak into otherwise confidential business. He remembers the day Jules Grotius made a surprise visit to the local offices in Emeryville; the warehouse space wherein temporary cubicles had been set up across the floor, terminals in numbers plugged in, and the job of testing his new would-be game, led by Weed and four other testers, quickly delved into. Jules looked different that day: his stand-out white hair combed neatly instead of tousled, he wore glasses and the stubble of an emerging beard. He was relatively new to the world of gaming. His background and training was as a computer programmer, but it was his radical journalism, or rather his playing at being a journalist, searching new mediums through which alternative news could be spread, that was making him famous. That's what Weed admired in Jules Grotius: his daring, reckless passion for taunting big fishes, coupled with a new and mischievous love of games.

But he was not in a playful mood the day Weed walked into his boss' office, delivering notes on the latest glitches of Cyborg 9-11, a mediocre new sci-fi game that exploited associations, but otherwise sought to give consumers an experience of being a robot in a post-holocaust and twenty third century New York City. It wasn't working, thought Weed. It was Weed's job to declare what wasn't working technically with the games he and his colleagues were testing. It wasn't his job to be more global in his criticism, however—not technically, at least. Weed had walked in unannounced, as was his norm, and was taken aback when he recognized Grotius standing across from Weed's boss, Ed Kim. They were not introduced. Instead, Kim was feckless and gave clipped answers to Weed, dithering over details he had dropped by to discuss. Grotius was quiet, uninterested. He turned away, towards a window that looked out towards San Francisco Bay, and faintly sighed. Weed held his tongue about Cyborg 9-11, and more importantly, about the visit of Jules Grotius, whom few in the general public knew by appearance just a year ago. Weed wouldn't have recognized or known about him either but for one of Chris' friends, an anarchist poseur named Gavin and nicknamed Sweet, who'd been proselytizing Jules' government-outing disclosures, and passing on links to his popular blog essays. In a matter of weeks, Jules Grotius was becoming a household name while sneaking around the country, pitching his latest means of disseminating propaganda: his fledgling entry into the market of video gaming.

As Weed hikes back up to Brighton Avenue and towards the cul-de-sac where Rosco lives, he suddenly feels less comfortable in the sunny, relaxed ambience of Bolinas. Soon he is thinking again of who might be following, or else ordinarily recognizing him, since he'd grown up in this town. Tentatively, he places his sunglasses back on his face after reading the Times' article. He turns to the front and then tilts forward a baseball hat he'd borrowed from Rosco. Weed likes baseball hats, and in the East Bay, he fit in well enough with the bill turned fashionably backwards. But in Bolinas, with his own hat missing, down with the truck, he could not have been more obvious about hiding if he'd worn an dark overcoat with an upward collar and then shuffled it up to conceal his face. Still, he reaches Rosco's home without incident, finding him in the front yard, regarding that knotted hose from the side of the house and thinking it a troublesome, Saturday-consuming puzzle.

"I need to talk," says Weed ominously.

Rosco nods, as if he'd already known Weed was stirring with something. He gladly drops the hose.

"Inside," he directs.

The two men settle in the living room of the cottage, several feet away from Rosco's snoring father. The room is aptly dark.

"Something's happened," Weed begins. "I guess I may need to get out of here soon, like you said."

Rosco is silent. He seems unsurprised and looks over to his father, sees his head slump into his chest and winces slightly.

"I saw something on the cover of a newspaper, down in the village. There's a guy missing. He's…I didn't tell you everything, not that—"

"You got yourself a situation," Rosco remarks. Weed remembers the phrase that Rosco and his one-time clique of former students used to throw back and forth between one another, the specific contexts long forgotten.

"You could say that. This guy—you'll have heard of him, Grotius, has gone missing, the paper says. I think he was working for Sahi, secretly. I didn't yet tell you an important part of the story."

"I heard about that," Rosco interrupts. "He aint missing. He's just not available for comment on federal investigations that are now aimed at him. That's a media twist you're reading."

"Well, whatever. He came by their offices one day, made a delivery of flash drives."

"Flash drives?" Rosco raises his eyebrows.

"Yeah, right—the same ones. See, I knew before anyone else did what he was doing there. I knew what the deal was; what the drives represented. There was an opportunity I couldn't pass up. We'd been working on this game, this game whose elements and purpose I—well, I just recognized. I'd been recognizing it for weeks, not sure what to do—not telling anyone about it. Then, when I saw Grotius at Sahi offices, speaking to my boss, I knew it was his game. I just knew it, and I had to take a chance."

"What's so important?" Rosco asks.

"He's a gifted type. A person who sees Shadows."

"A what?"

Weed brushes past Rosco's snarling reply. "That's what the game is. That's what I recognized. In the game, these Shadows appear next to characters that players are meant to select. It's a role-play, so players are supposed to figure out what the crimes are, who's guilty and who are the victims, by the clues in the scenes from one stage to the next. That's the beauty of the game: because of the stages, and the pieces within each scene, there are thousands of clues, but those who see Shadows—what some call the 'gifted'—will have an advantage and know how to progress more quickly through the game. That's what I thought, anyway. I was only just starting to play it when I realized what it meant."

Rosco shakes his head and gives Weed another disapproving look. He is unmoved by Weed's insights.

"I don't see what this has got to do with Jules Grotius' going incommunicado."

"Jules was creating a game through which players in the gaming world would learn the secrets he wants to reveal but can't through regular channels. Not anymore. Don't you see that he wants to circumvent traditional media, and even the social media, and deliver news only to those who are worthy…those who play his game, and play it well?"

Rosco raises his chin and affects concern. He scrutinizes Weed like he might some sinister presence that has just invaded his home. He is without a pitchfork; without a club. He has instead his bare knuckles, his life experience, and the air of a man who has entertained similar ideas and visions as Weed.

"So, what's on the flash drives?"

Weed pauses, becomes circumspect. "I'm not sure. I just had a taste of this game, haven't played what's on the drives yet, but I think what's on them may be some or all the secrets that Grotius knows exist through his network of whistleblowers—that are kept secret by the government or whatever—but which he's prepared to have installed so that those who penetrate the game to the deepest levels can discover what he has."

Rosco nods, but remains unconvinced. "Weren't these drives part of the original program? Why install them now?"

"Because the game—actually called 'The Situation'—was in its last stage of development. I don't think Kim or anyone at Sahi knew until the last week or so that Grotius was planning changes, introducing new elements."

"So what? Why would that be a problem for them? Weed, if you're not doing this for the money, I don't get why you'd give up this testing job—shitty as it sounds—and risk getting charged with theft, not to mention risk your life running from corporate security. Why are doing this?"

Weed can see that Rosco is worried, though not just because of some vaguely paternal fondness that he had once felt for him. Rather, it is about something else, his reaction—his own foolhardiness, maybe. Rosco, the man who had written and helped develop the game *2012*, and who had bent many a person's ear about his own conspiracy theories in his time, seems to not like being on the other side of this conversation.

"Ross, I know you don't get me, but I trust you. I gotta tell someone this. The day I saw Jules Grotius at that office space in Emeryville, I had one of my visions. I saw guys standing next to him as he walked out—Sahi guys, security goons—as he walked out. I knew he'd just delivered software that would complete our development of 'The Situation'. I could tell that my boss didn't know what was going on, that he had no idea what Grotius was really planning. And I knew where he'd put those drives in his office, thinking he'd deal with them later, or not give them to us at all."

"Why not?" Rosco asks litigiously.

"I don't know. Just a feeling. And that's what I acted on, a feeling. I knew that something was about to happen, and that if I was gonna do anything, I had to act. I was in a unique position, so I broke in that night, last Tuesday. I saw what was gonna happen, you get it? It's down to me."

"It shouldn't be down to you," Rosco retorts.

"Whatever. I mean that I saw what was going to happen, not Grotius. It's an irony: I don't think that Grotius knew that my boss might get cold feet, or that Sahi bosses might betray him.

That's the glitch in our Shadow-seer system. You see, the gifted see what might victimize other people, but many don't see what might victimize themselves."

"Jesus," says Rosco, exhaling thickly. Weed can tell that Rosco is getting tired of all this Shadow business. "Okay, so what next?" he asks.

"I'm going back," Weed replies without thinking. "Back to Oakland to recover those drives." Of course, this had been the plan all along, the original plan restored. That was the plan when he first thought he was being followed, sometime on Wednesday, somewhere near his apartment in Richmond. The first time he'd shared a draft of the plan was minutes later, in a text to Chris, who was returning home amidst his own dramatic set of events. Weed saw a suspicious vehicle following him in his neighborhood. He dashed back to his place, hoping to shake it off. Later, he pulled into his complex, left his truck in his spot below his unit, and then managed to give his followers the slip, only to feel them on his back just an hour or so after that. He never once saw them in person. Had they seen him jump into Chris' truck when he arrived shortly thereafter? He didn't think so at the time, but the combination of his sketchiness and that of his friend fueled misgivings, and soon he believed that his place would be turned upside down, and that cold-hearted men working for those who had money and power would search through his wall of games, maybe steal his X-box Live or Wii consoles just to punish him.

The only consolation Weed felt west of the Richmond Bridge came from believing his followers hadn't seen him at Chris' girlfriend's place, a ten-story apartment building near 14th street in Oakland. Or maybe they had, though if they'd seen them enter, and followed them to her unit, then there would have been a chase in the building, and if caught, Weed would have already lost the drives. Maybe the thick police presence that Weed and Chris saw that night deterred the followers from making an approach, or even jacking Chris' truck while they were upstairs, talking to his girlfriend. Yes. Weed sequenced through his logic: his followers were patient, methodical; they had waited out the scene at the apartment building and then pursued the guys' truck all over again as they left West Oakland. But all the way to Bolinas? Weed was no longer sure.

What's the plan? When are you coming back? Those were the questions asked by Chris sometime during the ride. Weed gave an offhand reply, "soon", not knowing when he'd return, and only half-understanding his friend's attachment to him. How would Weed know when it was safe to return? Would a week away suffice? Two? Who writes the books or blogs on these sorts of things? At what point do the traumatized know they can visit the scenes of former crimes and breathe without melting down? Chris didn't know Weed had a firearm. Things had gotten farther out of hand than he'd thought, but that was the price of impulsive decisions, an impulsive life. For his part, Weed didn't like placing his friend Chris in dangerous positions, but he put his guilt aside for the time being. Fear, he notices, makes people put guilt aside. When would he come back? When could life return to normal? He didn't know. When could Weed return to his apartment, assuming its locks hadn't been changed, and not fear that someone might be there waiting for him, ready to…

"Tomorrow," Weed says to Rosco with a blank look. "Can you take me over to Richmond tomorrow?" Immediately, he looks away, knowing he's asking a lot. He looks away and feels the silence, Rosco's reluctance. At that moment, as if on cue, his father calls out a croaking plea for his son. Rosco's father needs a bathroom.

"I would if I could," Rosco says gloomily. He seems genuinely dejected; ashamed even. "Part of me wants to see this game that Jules created." Rosco smiles like an appreciative, familiar rival. "I wanna see what he has to share."

Weed quickly looks around, speaking past Rosco's frozen whimsy.

"You got a vehicle here? Preferably something other than a truck?"

Rosco holds up his hands. "Nah, afraid not. Just an old chevy with a busted carburetor. It's on my list to get it fixed, just like a lot of things around here, but…" Rosco stops, knowing this isn't useful to Weed.

Weed pauses for just a few moments. "I'd better get ready," he then says.

"For what?"

"Well, it looks like I'm hitchhiking." Rosco reaches out that strong arm again; he pulls Weed back to him.

"Stay tonight. Nothing's gonna change in the next twenty four hours," he argues, though it sounds more like a plea than an argument.

6

Rosco convinces Weed to stay the night, possibly two. What's the rush all of a sudden? What's the plan? He asks, even more to the point. Weed thinks through the suggestions, wonders if Rosco has a secondary motive, like wanting real company, for example. But Weed's mind is made up. Just sitting around waiting for inspiration won't achieve anything now. Gotta leave Sunday, not Monday, he later says to Rosco. Who drives away from Bolinas on a Monday? He reasons, saying that hitchhiking will be more difficult after the weekend is over. Fair point, Rosco concedes, though he also thinks Weed is talking out his ass. After all, what does he know about hitchhiking?

Despite this, Weed gets up late again the next day, and is moving slowly. Motivation competes with his flagging energy, though one thing's for sure: he's gotten plenty of rest on this time-out of the last few days. Rosco is fussing, following Weed around, asking if he needs anything: more clothes, something else to eat before he leaves; more money. Weed accepts the offer of a few snacks, a pair of walking shoes with thick soles, and a spare backpack with some tools that might later come in handy. But not money. Weed pulls a face—an I-don't-want-to-impose kind of look, like he has limits to what he will take from people.

"You don't have a spare cell phone, do you?"

Rosco gives him a crooked, you're-joking smile. This is Bolinas, he wants to say. Since when do people here own cell phones in numbers? Instead he shakes his head, feels bad that he can't help Weed with the things he needs most. Weed steps past him, wades into the living room and makes an utterance in the direction of Rosco's father.

"Sir, it was nice to meet you," he next calls out, politely yet awkwardly. He half raises his hand. Farewell. The father nods back with some effort.

"That reminds me, have you called your parents yet?" Rosco asks. Weed suddenly feels like an adolescent hiding something. "Not to sound old-fashioned, but won't they worry about you? Not even a bit?" Weed turns, tries to look at Rosco in a way that conveys gratitude but also warns him to mind his own.

"It's all good, Ross. I know what it looks like—like I don't care about them—but it's not like that. Like I said, it's all down to me, and my friend Chris. If he hasn't said anything about the accident—and I believe he hasn't, and won't—then they won't know any better. Believe me, we've been here before, my parents and me."

"And what about your friend Chris? Have you called him?"

"Actually, I did try. Thursday. You were outside, I think. I used your landline without asking. Sorry."

"Well?"

Weed notices discomfort; more specifically, a feeling of something he routinely resists: obligation.

"No dice. I called his cell phone number, the only one I have for him. I think it was with him in the truck."

"You know that doesn't prove anything, right?"

"I know," says Weed with an irked look—the first sign of impatience with Rosco. He moves to hug him, hoping he'd squeeze him clean of any more fatherly advice. He says "thanks for everything" into Rosco's shoulder. Rosco limply brings Weed in, mutters "call me". Clearly, he struggles with goodbyes. Weed looks over Rosco's shoulder, sees the father one more time. There's another goodbye coming soon, he figures.

Weed hikes along Brighton Avenue, which turns onto the Olema-Bolinas road. He starts to feel nervous, thinking this is where he came in. Of course, he'd have known that all along. Growing up around here, he'd know the only way out of this town was the way he came in. But, as drug addicts like Chris Leavitt are prone to saying, he wasn't thinking about that at the time. He hadn't anticipated the chill, the unpleasant chill he now feels as the events of last Wednesday night all come back to him. He hadn't considered what he'd feel like as he looks south and makes out the lagoon between the trees. Is the truck still there? He wonders. Had anyone heard about this in the town, been talking about it? Pity he hadn't asked anyone, or asked Rosco to ask someone about it; or stayed attentive at the grocery store in case the locals were still gossiping Saturday morning about the tonnage of metal found in local waters.

The pleasant, shady road belies all of this tension. Weed trudges his way to the end of the road that has no street sign. He looks north and south along the road that is now Highway One. Coming up fast is a Land Rover with a pair of surf boards on top. Weed is slow to react; his thumb raises just as the car passes, just as he catches sight of what looks like a smirking driver. More conviction, he thinks: he must show that he wants to get somewhere, and that he deserves a helping hand. It promises to be a long walk otherwise, under a hot sun that will only get hotter as he heads inland, away from the cooling sea breeze. In the distance there are redwoods, and a layer of fog hovering just above the tree-line. But the fog has that west-leaning look about it, as though it's heading out to sea, looking down upon Weed, but leaving him behind.

Weed looks down. When he was a kid, he often looked down, preferring to see the path directly in front of his feet, and to hide his eyes. With his baseball cap turned outwards, his eyes would be un-shadowed, but looking down and away remained habitual, especially when most paranoid; when most sure he was being followed. Cars heading east pass about one every minute or so, with cars heading the other direction just about doubling that ratio. Annoying, thinks Weed. After a few miles of fruitless thumb raising, Weed figures a stop at the Olema hamlet might yield better results. There he might approach someone at the sandwich shop by the hotel, and ask if they are heading towards the Bay Area. He'd done that once before on a trip down to Santa Cruz when his car had broken down. Troubling people up close with a smile and a heartfelt plea worked for him on that occasion. Right now that strategy would seem to have better odds than trying to catch the eyes of blithe drivers whizzing by.

When he reaches the crossroads, he approaches the first gathering of people he sees. Leading with the wrong question, "are you heading towards San Rafael or Oakland?" he speaks to a sparse collection of individuals in a coffee shop, and one or two others loitering by the bar adjacent to the hotel. Some just shake their heads, uninterested; another, a woman, affects sympathy when Weed shifts tact to that of telling a made-up sad story, and offers some change but not a ride. After that, a man emerging from the bar quickly cuts off Weed's pitch for help and suggests he try asking at the hotel, but Weed knows this is a waste of time. He figures he'd not get far in the lobby before hearing the unwelcoming phrase, "can I help you?" only to be ushered out the front door. Weed looks ahead, sees that the road heading east is inclining, and feels an ache in his calf, a foreshadowing twinge of cramp. Around the back of the hotel is a creek with a soft bed of grass by its side. He chooses to take a load off for a while, soak his tired feet and rest.

He naps instead. At least, until one of the hotel employees walks up and asks him which room he's staying in, he naps. A half hour later he's back on the road, hiking up a hill heading east, past a smattering of bed and breakfasts. Weed raises his thumb as a car speeds by; so much for that other plan, he supposes. Meanwhile, it's not hard keeping his mind occupied; it's just difficult keeping it focused, and thereafter making decisions. His thinking swims again from topic to topic, with pieces of memory, of factors to now consider, floating by. Then they drift off, eluding Weed's grasp, his attempt to put things together. He thinks he knows where he's going in Oakland. He doesn't remember all the street names—only the rough outline of the neighborhood and the general look of the drab edifice where Chris Leavitt's girlfriend lives. The more he thinks about it, the less he can believe that something as potentially valuable—something so potentially explosive—as those flash drives are just sitting there waiting for him in that unlikely place.

Or are they sitting there still? Weed is aware that the script he'd sort of written about where the drives would be, who they'd be with, and how he could simply retrieve them later at his convenience, had been torn up by circumstances. It's just that the same script is in limbo, from all sides. He holds to the idea that Chris is alive, and has by now returned to Oakland. Would that mean that he'd reach for those drives in his backpack, show them to his girlfriend and then surrender them to authorities as soon as possible, just because Weed is missing? Weed didn't think so. And sure, it was pretty mean, perhaps callous, to not make a more determined effort to reach him, let him know he's alive, or even determine if Chris himself is safe and sound. But really, didn't that cut both ways? What was Chris doing to establish Weed's survival? Guilt. Weed knew that guilt divided, both above the surface and beneath.

And what about the drives? What is he to do with the drives when he does recover them? What then? It's not as though he'd mapped out this drama. Along that trail of thought are some labyrinthine fears: that he is in over his head, messing with something beyond his comprehension; that he is a flea biting at a dog's ass, destined to be plucked between the pincers of a superior being and then mercilessly flattened. Weed's current situation does little to quell his fears, yet there is pleasure in the thought that as he walks along one of California's great lonesome highways, being ignored by scores of drivers, an important, new kind of weapon is waiting in that drab building in West Oakland.

Jules Grotius will have a different agenda: a social agenda, perhaps an agenda of macrocosmic scale. As Weed allows himself to indulge possibilities, of his current role as a fly in the ointment, he becomes excited. Thinking back, he wishes he'd talked even more about this part with Rosco, maybe with Chris even. He checks a latent hunger for people to think that he is doing something important, living up to his potential, whatever that may be. It quickens his step, these thoughts. That sense of mission, so volatile ordinarily, yet so strident this past Wednesday night, is returning. He's not sure why his drive comes and goes; why self-doubt leads to contrary beliefs, the sometimes deflating notion that what he lives is imagination: sad projections of his fears; mad indulgences, fantasy.

The news about Jules returns with more questions. So what if he's missing, or just incommunicado? Like that's news, Weed begins thinking. Actually, Jules had been in virtual hiding for much of the past year, skipping from place to place, even country to country, staying one step ahead of his stalkers; his quite real followers. While not technically a fugitive within the United States, the feds had been fighting extradition issues on his behalf with some countries, and many believed it was simply a matter of time before he'd blow the lid off a few choice American secrets. Weed didn't understand the ins and outs of Jules' politics, but knew what medium he'd next use to stir an apathetic public. What genius, he thinks, assuming it will all work. The Times article was ambiguous, but seemed to imply that Grotius was at risk from foreign terrorists who thought him a kind of Salmon Rushdie-type figure—people who might soon take responsibility for his capture. If this is true, God knows why Grotius would just show up in Emeryville, talking with a Sahi executive like he'd just dropped by to observe operations and then head out for coffee, without any security. Something about that didn't seem right, even if his Shadows weren't warning him of the dangers to come.

7

      Sir Francis Drake Boulevard is proving longer than Weed remembers. Of course, he'd never walked this road before, only driven it. Most recently, he hadn't even done that. He'd been merely a passenger on the way out to Bolinas. Now the effort is all upon him. A blister on his right foot is beginning to form, despite the newer tennis shoes given him by Rosco. In three hours of almost non-stop hiking, he's covered nearly eight miles, much of it along winding roads populated by the odd cabin between redwoods, and a bait and tackle shop situated next to a gas station. But he has yet to reach a town of any meaningful size. Fairfax, he knows, will be nearby. Over the last mile or so, the attempts to hitch a ride have lessened; his thumb raising has become half-hearted, even disdainful. Weed isn't cut out for this exercise in persistence amid rejection. On one stretch beyond some woods he passes a farm, which includes a field that is home to a pair of Llamas. They stare at Weed as he approaches, only to turn away as he passes their gate. They seem as uncaring as any driver passing by, and as Weed stares back he decides he's had enough of that attitude. He flips them off.

As he reaches the outskirts of the town, he begins to feel hopeful, but also an un-imaginary cramp in his legs, not to mention the cough that's stubbornly parked in his chest. He wants to stop for another nap but knows it's a bad idea, now that he has momentum. The problem of stopping when tired is that of starting up again. Weed flops his feet forward, willing himself to keep going, yet feeling the magnetic pull of the earth. If he falls he knows he won't get up. Instead, he'll just lie on the ground, his body contorted in grotesque collapse. He'll cough as dust and gravel swirl about his mouth, and once again he'll hear the sound of cars passing his body. If he's lucky this downfall will be more palatable than his watery adventure of the previous Wednesday night: not as dark and not as painful, though ultimately just as humiliating.

Weed stays on his feet. He hears the sound of something treading heavily behind him. Its tires or feet are crunching upon gravely road, but the engine, if there is one, is silent. Weed turns to see a beige-colored Jetta hybrid pulling up along the opposite side of the road, its driver gazing from side to side as if looking for addresses. Weed feels a brief, dark affinity for a fellow lost traveler, but has few reserves of sympathy. Quickly, his thoughts shift towards something more useful and self-serving. The car edges forward. The driver, a man in his late fifties, maybe early sixties, is wearing what looks like a golfing outfit, and is still looking from side to side, past and sort of through Weed. The look is strange: it is wide yet still. Unblinking, he looks nervous yet somehow predatory. He meets Weed's eyes, offers a thin, enigmatic smile as he regards the up-raised thumb, but he continues to drive ahead, slowly. His vehicle scratches at the gravel by the side of the road, spits small rocks in the direction of Weed, who now hangs his head again and walks on. He feels his legs gaining weight with each stride and fixes his attention back on the road, having felt teased by the driver. Dejection. "Fuck you," he mutters in the direction of the Jetta.

It's as if the driver has heard him.

Stopping about forty yards ahead, the driver positions the car just off the shoulder of the road, with the left side mirror now pointed at the pedestrian. Weed twitches as he looks forward and sees the tiny image of the driver reflected in the mirror. He thinks he can make out a smile but he isn't sure. The car has a surreal presence: it looks like a runner in a relay race, ready to collect a baton so it can continue on its course. Otherwise, it's as though the car is waiting to collect Weed, as if Rosco had called up a friend in Fairfax, asked him to be on the lookout for a vagrant fitting Weed's description. Upon that supposition, Weed breaks into a light jog, thinking this a logical, if fanciful explanation. He knew Rosco had wanted to do more for him than just bid a fond farewell. He knew he'd do more to help if he could just find a way.

The man in the Jetta lowers his window and sticks his head out. He issues a retailer's 'hi', but waits a few more seconds for the hitchhiker to approach before he speaks further. By the look on his face, a fixed, almost waxy grin, he seems not so much helpful as beseeching, rather like someone looking *for* help. Suddenly, the smile looks too self serving to be that of a Good Samaritan. Besides, who would Rosco know who drives a Jetta and looks like he just came off a golf course? Weed checks himself. Don't look a gift horse, he thinks, flashing on a cliché his father used to employ whenever his son exhibited bad attitude. Whoever this guy is, whatever he wants, he stopped, so it's an opportunity, and he, Weed, is nothing if not an opportunist.

"I know I can really sneak up on people in this thing," the man says, striking a winning smile. Weed is impressed. Smiling like that, keeping it up, keeping it still and wide like that must be uncomfortable. How does he do it? How effortless he makes it look. What good acting. Weed thinks of the contrast with himself: his lazy, dour expression in which his face slackens, exhibiting talent for sulking, and denying joy.

"Huh," Weed replies, having not caught what the man said, but guessing his comment was about the Jetta and its quiet, electric engine.

The man releases a shrill, excitable giggle. "I don't mean to scare people. I guess it's just how I am—a habit, I think."

Weed nods.

"Uh-huh," he says, feeling crept upon by the driver. He looks ahead, past the Jetta, and sees the road stretching out while the day ages languorously. Anyway, it seems time to move on: not sure if this guy is in tune with others' needs, so Weed steps past, making a wary, sideways glance.

"You need a ride?" the man asks. His tone is one of surprise, as though struck by the hiker's reticence.

Weed stops. He regards the beige car and notices how it matches against the white casual wear of its driver: a dress shirt with sleeves rolled up past the elbows; an off-white pair of corduroy pants; a silver cap with tiny holes across the top—vents for a bald scalp that needs to breath. It all looks a bit like a fashion statement, this presentation. A bit gay, Weed further thinks.

"Sure," he says coolly.

The man nods toward the passenger side while unlocking its door. As Weed circles the front he has brief, shuddering associations with the last time he'd been in a vehicle; the last time he'd crossed a threshold of one's door. He gingerly enters the pristine, white interior and surveys its angelic, some might say evangelic cleanliness and slick features. There is a glowing GPS that defeats Weed's initial impression that the driver was or is lost. There are numerous digital displays upon the dashboard which the driver seems poised to explain. By the proud glint in his eye, it seems as though Weed is about to receive a virtual tour of the vehicle before it drives off. It's a further surprise to him that before anything more is said about this man's prize, an introduction happens.

"Dan Pritchard," He says genially, stretching out a hand. Weed offers his in return, doing so rather meekly, mostly because he's not as used to such old school greetings. In Weed's world, young men lightly punch fists and briefly lock fingers. Sometimes they give quick hugs, pats on the back. They used to high five one another, but they don't shake hands. Weed can't recall the last time he actually shook someone's hand.

"We—Bryan," he says awkwardly. That's another thing: he doesn't introduce himself, either. The people he meets for the first time have typically heard about him from someone else already. He thinks of times when would-be buyers checked who he was by querulously uttering his name. These occasions require only that Weed nod or else say something terse and business-like. "Sup," is his most common greeting, even at work, where he is also known as Weed, except by Kim, his boss—pretty much the only person who addresses him with anything like formality.

"Are you sure?" Dan Pritchard asks, displaying a penchant for teasing. The question throws Weed for a moment. This guy, this happy man, has a ready wit and a mercurial manner. Joviality aside, he is cut from Kim-type cloth. He's of upper middle-class stock, living in a million dollar home, nestled in the hills, in all likelihood. He's probably from Mill Valley, or Sausalito, maybe. Hopefully, he's not from Fairfax, as Weed needs this ride to last longer than the next several minutes if it's to be worthwhile. Weed volleys a short, embarrassed laugh in response to the man's question, but quickly turns to business: his need to get as far as San Rafael at least before he stops somewhere for the night. "Uh" is as far as he gets before Dan Pritchard pulls out a silver, six-inch, cylindrical device that turns down at the end like a ball-point pen. His places it in a thin, lipless mouth and a green light goes off halfway down its length. Next, Dan expels a gust of something like smoke, only it's not smoke. It's a vapor.

What the... Weed thinks. He pauses with his mouth hanging slightly open.

"Want one?" Dan offers. "It's an e-cigarette; one of my own. I own a company that sells these." With his other hand he reaches for an I-phone, begins stabbing with some dexterity at the phone's digits, sending a message. Pausing, he reaches forward, presses some button on his dashboard. Multiple actions are happening at once. This man is all business, multi-tasking, and the task of picking up a hitchhiker and taking him to wherever is like an afterthought to this guy. It's like nothing to him, Weed observes.

"No thanks. Actually, all I need is a ride to San Rafael."

For the first time, Dan Pritchard exhibits a frown, which discolors his features.

"San Rafael?" he asks, looking up from his phone. He sounds disapproving, as though San Rafael were an ill-advised destination for a young man on the road. Dan seems poised to share with his younger passenger all of his recommendations for a more suitable getaway. "Whereabouts in San Rafael?" he asks instead.

Weed shrugs. "No where in particular. Anywhere with a motel is fine."

Dan nods and looks up, sort of into his own head, like he's mulling over Weed's answer.

They chat for a while as they move on. Now seated comfortably, Weed feels the soreness in his legs even more. He notices his feet itching; the temperature in the car is making him sweat. He wants to take his shoes off and grind his fingers between his toes, but doesn't want to be rude; not overtly, anyway. Dan Pritchard is a talkative guy. Turns out that his e-cigarette venture is brand new, which makes sense as Weed is barely aware the things even exist. Weed has heard of the newfangled e-cigarettes but never seen one. His regulars talk about them, sometimes snigger about them as they smoke the old school way, even rolling their own. This scoffing at new enterprise is novel, especially as Weed is a smoker. But then, he's not a serious smoker; that is, he's not addicted. He's knows this because he keeps quitting. This is a joke amongst his friends, but on the matter of not being addicted, Weed is quite serious. He can give or take tobacco, he believes—smoke some one day, not touch it again for weeks. It's the same with marijuana, his nickname notwithstanding, and all drugs for that matter. As for this new contraption that looks like a robot cigar, he can certainly give or take that.

Before he got involved in the e-cigarette business, Dan explains, he was a basketball coach for a Midwest University, a local celebrity. Dan loved basketball, and so did his family. He'd been doing that for ten years, he says, but got bored, despite making a lot of money. Before that he bought and sold commercial properties in the Midwest, and got bored doing that also, despite making lots of money. Listening to this is pretty boring, thinks Weed, and he's not making a lot of money. He thinks to ask how Dan first got into all these lines of work, but knows his interest would be false and perfunctory. He could care less how Dan Pritchard came to be an e-cigarette salesman or a basketball coach. As Dan drives, Weed is surveying the road, the passage through Fairfax, and the burgeoning relief knowing he'll soon complete part one of this journey so he can rest for the night.

"Mind if we stop somewhere to eat," Dan asks. Weed's immediate reaction is petulant. Where could this guy live that he couldn't hold out for a while longer and drop him off somewhere?

"Um…"

"My treat. Don't want to keep you from where you need to go. It's just that I'm on this schedule with food, because of my diabetes." Upon this disclosure, Dan breaks out another device while he's driving. He appears to be checking blood sugar levels while his eyes take on that same stilled and unblinking quality they'd exhibited earlier. To Weed he seems like a kind of doll when he makes this face: he looks lifeless and scary. He's a clown, maybe, moonlighting as something else after hours, just like Weed. Regarding the health needs, Weed feels a requisite jab of sympathy but otherwise can't help feeling manipulated.

"Sure. Thankyou," he says.

Minutes later, they're in the parking lot of a Buttercup Café on the east side of Fairfax. More chatter: Dan knows the manager, says this is the best run restaurant of its kind in the area, as if Weed will care about that. He asks for the time as he sees the sun lowering. Seven-thirty, says Dan. Weed nods, calms himself, his growing impatience. At this point, he supposes it doesn't really matter what time he finds a Motel. So, they may need to check out a few places if some are full. So what? Maybe they can check vacancies over dinner, assuming this Dan will let him borrow his I-phone. Weed looks about the diner, remembers he's also hungry. He reminds himself: Don't panic. Chill out. And finally— amending the last part—relax.

Meanwhile, Dan is bantering with a Mexican waiter whom he sees regularly, and patronizes with broken pieces of Spanish. The waiter returns a joke that Weeds thinks Dan doesn't really understand, though he giggles anyway. It's a nerve-shredding, horrible sound, this giggle—the type of sound that would make animals' heads turn. The two men are sat on barstools, flanking each other. Dan looks sideways at his young hitchhiker guest.

"So, what do you do when not hitchhiking?" The question seems silly, but somehow un-nosy. Actually, if there's another quality Weed might assign to Dan, despite the general creepiness, it's his charm.

"I'm a video game designer," Weed fibs. He reflects briefly that he doesn't really think through things: getaway plans, comeback plans; answers to fairly predictable questions.

"Oh, really," exclaims Dan, as if truly interested. "What kind of games: role-play, maybe?"

Weed returns a slightly quizzical look. What might this guy mean by role play?

"Um, sort of," he says. "Action-adventure games, mostly, with interactive features." Weed is struck by his own inarticulacy, which he often shows when he doesn't want to talk but won't say so. Though the question seems innocuous, he remains distrustful of Dan Pritchard, and not just because hitchhikers should feel this way.

Dan gives him the same look he'd exhibited earlier; the one in which his eyes disappear into his head.

"You must have some views on the new Grand Theft Auto game that's coming out soon—version four is it, maybe five?"

Weed meets his gaze for a moment. Is this guy serious? Is he trying to buddy up with him, use some passing knowledge he has of the gaming world? What's this guy's deal? Is he lonely? A weirdo? As the food arrives, Weed's attitude takes another turn. Maybe I'm being paranoid again, he thinks as he regards a plateful of burger and fries and noting the salt-craving that suddenly comes over him. Ungrateful, he thinks of himself even: more looking at gift horses, etcetera. After all, all this guy's done is give him a ride, buy him some food, and try to make small talk. What an asshole, Weed thinks, directing sarcasm at himself for a change. It's all good, he thinks as he takes a voracious bite out of processed meat. Everything is going according to the plan he hasn't really established yet, and he hasn't even seen a Shadow in a while. Meanwhile, he comments disdainfully on Grand Theft Auto.

"That's not my kind of game. I'm more into games like Soulcraft, The Warcraft Universe series—that kind of thing. I like Sandbox technology, not so much objective-based games, though I like Split Second, which is a racing game." Weed shrugs out of habit, and takes note that he doesn't often shrug when talking to people his age. He doesn't feel the implied disadvantage.

"Really, aren't some of those games published by Blizzard entertainment? I think I know a guy that works for them." It seems like a guess, this trailing thought of Dan's, as if he's trying to impress Weed, like it's a prelude to picking up on him. Weed straightens his back, sits upright, like he's straightening himself—figuratively. He shrugs again, thinking expressions of humility will spare him further intrusion. He's wrong.

"So, what games have you designed, or what are you working on?" Dan asks cheerfully.

Shit. Why did I say designer? Weed thinks. He smiles vacantly, trying to muster some boyish charm of his own. He taps his index finger to the side of his nose.

"Can't say," he says. "Secret stuff, ya know."

"Oh, right," says Dan with a laugh—a pensive laugh, not a giggle. There's a quiet, protracted moment between them, during which Dan looks around wearing a new kind of smile: it is warm, yet amused and knowing, like he is waiting on something. Weed swallows a bite of food and then puts the butt of his fist to his mouth, stifling a belch.

"Okay, I'm not a designer; not sure why I said that," he says in a low, conspiratorial voice. Dan is suddenly impassive; his smile disappears, yet he is attentive. Next he says, "I had a feeling there was something, not sure what."

"I am in the business. For real: I'm a tester of games like the ones I described, only nothing as famous as that."

"A tester?" Dan seems more bemused than interested.

"Yeah," Weed replies languidly, "I don't..."

He is interrupted. A flash of something indistinct appears in his peripheral view: it's like a black spot. Weed's head turns reflexively, and his eyes meet the stolid expression of a man wearing a black uniform with silver trim and a cord wrapped over his shoulder. It's a cop walking out of the men's room just beyond the counter, and it immediately chills Weed—again, not in a good way. But it's not the thing that first catches his glance.

"It's like a..." He tries to keep it together; stay focused, answer Dan's question, and not get carried away, either by the cop, or the black flash that's just appeared. No use. The cop gives a second glance in Weed's direction as he walks across the floor towards a burnt orange colored booth in the corner of the restaurant. Weed is transfixed, tracking without guile the officer's slow march back to his table. There another officer is sat nursing a coffee and bagel, leaning back in a leather seat as if he'd been surveying the scene the entire time Weed and Dan had been at the bar. It's barely lit in that corner, and not with mood lighting. The dark, heavy-looking figure that is the second officer makes ponderous movements, lifting a cup to his lips; looking outward like some bear that's hiding at the lip of a cave, spying on prey.

"You okay?" asks Dan, noticing his passenger's sudden fixation elsewhere.

Weed jerks his head back to him. His face is whitening. Dan gives a subtle look over his shoulder, notes the stimulus of Weed's disquiet and calmly says, "Do we need to go?" Weed shakes his head, brushing him off for the moment.

"Nah, I'm good," he replies unconvincingly. Several minutes pass, during which Dan makes more small talk with the

Mexican waiter before receiving the tab. Meanwhile, Weed has abandoned him, gone inward. Police. Hadn't thought of them in a while, he thinks. He hadn't even seen any cops in days—not since that squad car appeared nearby the apartment building where Chris' girlfriend lives. He wants to look over his shoulder and check to see if they're looking over, scrutinizing the juxtaposition of a young man in a baseball cap wearing a backpack sat next to a dapper, middle-aged man all dressed in white. It's like that awful itching from before, this need to see if he's caught their interest. Weed closes his eyes for a moment. He tries to listen through the noise in the restaurant—its steady, dull buzz, infiltrated by the constant clinking of glass—just to see if he can hear what's being said in the corner booth.

"We can go if you'd like." Dan sounds morose, a bit like a spurned suitor who's just noticed that his date is distracted with other prospects. "Just going to the bathroom," he adds, oblivious to the tension this adds. Another five minutes pass. It's a torment waiting for Dan to come out of the men's room. Weed takes a swig of water, and as he holds his glass aloft, he tries to see into its transparency, determine if it might just reflect a watchful pair of eyes from across the room. Finally, Dan emerges and strides towards Weed, past a row of booths and looking like Liberace taking a curtain call. With a beaming smile, he waves at his friend, the Mexican waiter, and giggles again as if he'd been collecting pieces of others' conversations in the men's room and was still enjoying them. That giggle: it will draw attention from the wild; elicit persecution. As he and Weed walk out together, Dan starts talking about an exchange he'd had while at the urinal. Weed isn't listening. For the first time since he'd first seen them near the bar, he's now looking over his shoulder to see if he has followers, both real and imaginary.

Seated in the car, Dan breaks out one of his e-cigarettes and gives it a soft, rhythmic chew. A strange kind of drag, Weed observes.

"You seem nervous. You sure you wouldn't like one of these?" Dan is calm, detached, yet he seems oddly concerned—poised, as if he might prove quite useful in situations like this.

"I am," Weed admits. "But it's not what you're thinking."

"What am I thinking?" Dan asks, not missing a beat. That unblinking look is back.

Weed doesn't know what Dan is thinking. He doesn't even know what *he's* thinking; more specifically, he doesn't know why he keeps opening his mouth before thinking. Flurries of thoughts consume him: about the possibility that he's been reported missing by Chris Leavitt, or maybe his parents, just as Rosco had warned. There are fresh concerns, the chance that officials at Sahi—Ed Kim, for example—have reported the theft at their Emeryville offices, and cited Bryan Tecco as someone who ought to be questioned by police. Perhaps they've gone to Weed's apartment in Richmond and noted his absence and the likely fretting of the landlord. That reminds him: he hasn't paid his rent for April, which would be due right about now. That could be trouble, too, he thinks offhandedly. Actually, that's something else he hasn't thought through: where's he gonna live if and when this situation is over? What about all his stuff, his games? That asshole landlord will throw it all out and rent the unit to someone else. Jesus, why hadn't he thought about any of this? That's the problem with clawing up a trunk of seaweed, surviving, thinking all hope is not lost.

"Sorry," Weed says to Dan. "I didn't get what you said."

Dan doesn't repeat himself. Instead, he nods and looks past Weed's shoulder, towards the front door of the Buttercup Café. His serious, comradely expression seems to suggest that Weed also take a look, but do so carefully. Weed turns to his front, takes a quick glance to his right and sees the two officers posturing like warlords in the front entry area. One is stretching his arms, and yawning, like it's the end of his day and he's heading home to bed. The other has a fixed, guardian look that's staring outwards beyond the parking lot, towards the horizon, like it's pulling at his attention. It seems like a pose. The officer has the stilled appearance of one who knows he's being watched. Suddenly he turns, maintaining the same general stillness, but catching Weed's eye. The black dots from before appear again, this time dancing around the officer like scratches on an old piece of eight millimeter film. The dots congeal for a split second, forming an image of a man just off the policeman's shoulder.

Chris Leavitt.

Weed quickly looks away and toward Dan Pritchard with another wanting expression. He shakes his head. He wishes he weren't being this obvious.

"I guess you got yourself a situation," Dan says with an air of sympathy. He sees the fear in Weed's eyes; the self absorption. He sighs, starts the car, and pulls away like he's resigned to the role of chauffeur. This business is none of his business.

"Do you mind if I borrow your phone," Weed asks, now dropping pretenses of innocence. "I'd like to check some places online, see what's available." Dan passes over his device like someone surrendering a gun to authorities.

"Try hotels.com," he says civilly. As Weed begins a hasty online search, he does a quick double take as he catches Dan's now souring expression. What did this guy want? Catching sight of his own features in an overhead mirror—of his greasy curls of hair, his oddly protruding jawbone—he questions what horny old men would even see in him.

"There's a place called Premier Inn around here—should be coming up on the right side. Rooms starting at seventy-five a night: that's fine." Weed is matching the matter of fact tone. It's almost like he's bossing Dan now.

"Have you seen what's behind us?" Dan replies.

Weed looks up, tilts the overhead mirror so he can see behind him. Following closely, with its overhead lights unlit yet still somehow luminous in the dusk is a squad car comprised of two curious officers, and a dark shadow of conscience sat in between them. Dan sees in large block letters the words Premier Inn up ahead, with a neon sign below reading "vacancy".

"Do you want me to pull in here?" he asks, sounding skeptical of his young hitchhiker's plans. Weed looks again into the overhead mirror, hoping somehow that the squad car will have lost interest, and that the vision he'd seen with it will have evaporated and become meaningless.

The car's still there, tailing them slowly but not making any decisive moves.

"Nah, keep going," Weed says, noting the coldness in his feet. They were telling him something, he thinks. Trust the body, not the mind, he thinks incongruously.

"If you like, I've got a spare room at my place. You can have it if you like, for the night—no strings attached." Dan shrugs off knowledge of being subject to suspicion, or contempt. He seems indifferent to appearances; merely concerned, possibly saddened. Weed hesitates, sees the Premier Inn sign disappear behind them. It's fully dark out now, and the squad car is still following; its intent still unknown. He sits back in his passenger seat, seriously contemplating the offer now that time is pressing. He doesn't want to stay with this creepy guy, wherever he lives. But something else tells him that the wolves are out again, and if he steps outside, if only for a moment, then…

At that moment, the squad car passes them by. It speeds past with what seems like an irritable burst, as if Dan had been blocking their progress all this time with his slow, remedial driving.

"I guess they've got other fish to fry," he says with a wry smile. Big fish, thinks Weed. The old school expression betrays Dan's age. He no longer seems aspirant towards youth with his flashy clothes and newfangled toys. Instead, he seems defeated, as if the pretext for driving around with his young passenger had just left them in the dust. Weed issues a sigh of relief as he sees the squad car speed away. Now his thoughts turn to the other stressor, the one that compels him to think why a Shadow of Chris Leavitt would be standing next to police. I don't need this shit right now, he thinks tiredly. The implications of the vision are just too much for a guy who's walked all the way from Bolinas and just wants a nice bed on which to rest his aching legs, his itinerant brain. Looking over at Dan, at his suddenly unthreatening, unpretentious demeanor, Weed lets the tension of the last quarter hour drain from him. He's feeling indulgent.

"Pull over for a minute. Maybe we can talk."

Dan obliges with a haste that feels almost like reverence. Once stopped, he breaks out his e-cigarette again and starts chewing on it hungrily like it's his pacifier. Aside from the dashboard, the green LED light is all that's illuminating the car's interior.

"Actually, I wouldn't mind trying one of those," says Weed. Dan quietly reaches into a compartment by the emergency brake to his side. From a rectangular space that resembles a cigar box, he plucks a second e-cigarette, briefly instructs Weed on its use, and hands it over. Weed awkwardly takes a drag, smells the sweet flavor of a fruity substance he can't quite identify. He thinks to ask what it is but stops in mid-thought. Who cares? He thinks as he blows out his first wave of vapor. Dan is pulled over on a main stretch of highway with a freeway entrance just a quarter mile ahead. For a moment, he silently watches as Weed partakes of one of his samples. Grinning, he seems satisfied, like he's scored a new customer.

"Like it?" he asks. Weed returns a mild frown, but nods.

"Sort of. Tastes kinda weird."

He opens his backpack, places the e-cigarette inside. It's not so weird it can't be kept for later use. Then his tone shifts; Weed becomes all business.

"Okay, so I guess you noticed that I'm sketchy around police. It's no big thing—seriously. You deal cigarettes, I deal…ya know…" Weed performs a kind of head rotation while extending his arms. It's a solicitous gesture, an instinctive revealing of poverty and surrender: empty hands. He's not asking for anything in particular; just a break of sorts. He just wants to breathe a little air into the mystery, hoping it will preempt further curiosity, keep him free of obligation. That actually works with some people. Dan Pritchard might think twice about offering him a room for the night, but somehow Weed doesn't think so. He thinks Dan Pritchard has pretty much known what he was getting into all along. Actually, he seems like the kind of guy who usually knows what's risky, but chooses to take risks anyway.

"I figured it might be something like that," Dan replies warmly. There's no judgment in what he says. Suddenly, Weed likes him.

"You still offering that room," he asks. Weed's voice is cool and unexpecting, like he could give or take Dan's hospitality.

"Sure," Dan says, likewise cool, but friendlier.

For the next ten minutes or so they head south on the 101 freeway. Dan indicates that he lives nearby, pointing vaguely in an easterly direction as they enter San Rafael. As they turn off on Tiburon road, Weed sees luxurious waterfront properties and anticipates confirming earlier suppositions about Dan Pritchard's social status. The area looks clean and affluent; a few boats in a marina reflect local elitism. With a pang of inadequacy, Weed observes that he is halfway between homes: the utterly dissimilar worlds of Bolinas and Richmond, and not belonging in either place. The car is coasting. Dan looks tired, a bit disheveled even. His home is only minutes away, he says, implying there will be no more stops along the way. It's close to nine o'clock. Sleepy, Weed lets himself slide in his seat. He is comfortable, finally, like he'd just about cope with sleeping in a car.

As he closes his eyes he feels a wave of dizziness. Weed immediately sits up, thinking he might as well hold on until he gets indoors. He looks around, doesn't recognize the surroundings, but sees the blurry lights of San Francisco in the distance. They are on a road heading towards a peninsula; an exclusive set of homes built on a hill. Weed's vision fails again. This isn't sleepiness, he thinks, feeling a hit of panic. This is something else. He turns to look at Dan, who returns another smile. Then those eyes of his turn cold again; they go upward, into his head, as if about to take off and float away from his body. Weed opens his mouth but can't speak. The interior of the car seems misshapen and everything looks distorted, as though being seen through a fish eyed lens.

"What the fuck," Weed manages. Despite his stupor, he manages a snarl in Dan's direction. Dan looks back. He seems unmoved.

"You look a little pale," he says, jutting his head towards his passenger. He sounds distant and diagnostic, but again satisfied, as if something he'd intended were happening right on schedule. "Still a couple of minutes away," he adds, but this time it's not a statement of reassurance. He says something else about making a pot of tea when he gets home, or maybe running the hot tub in his back yard. His place has a great view of the city, he boasts, just as Weed slips into unconsciousness. Now Dan Pritchard, the happy salesman, the confident huckster, has a buoyant quality about him, as if this latest kidnapping had been all too easy.

NIGHTMARE

8

Around noon on the first Tuesday in April, Eric Pierce takes a call from his supervisor at Sahi's Sacramento security office. Pierce has been working for Sahi for two years, investigating cyber theft, mostly: people looking to hack into systems to steal prototypes for the various divisions of their product line. The gaming department, headquartered in Emeryville, had been enjoying tighter security recently; few of its models had been compromised, according to the last quarter's quality assurance reports. That's changed, says the e-mail Eric receives just as he's breaking for lunch.

The message tells him to do some leg work for a change. Some missing software from a testing lab is likely an inside job, says Pierce's supervisor, Dave Gagliano. Leg work. Inside job. Eric Pierce, amused by the old school terms, conjures his boss' east coast accent and gangster persona. He thinks of Gagliano's other typical phrases, which are delivered so earnestly by middle-aged white men: "We're balls to the wall, gentleman" or "we're up to our necks in it"—finds it endearing how the man can utter such clichés like he's invented the phrases. No originality, but no matter. He's the type who says what he likes in whatever company. He's the personality in charge no matter who's in the room. When telling off-color jokes he elicits indulgent chuckles from sycophants, could care less about dissenters who hold their tongues or hide their eyes. Observably well liked and respected, Gagliano is an unimpeachable figure at Sahi, a man at once in his own world yet wholly in touch with everything happening around him.

Eric Pierce is not like the average security officer working for Sahi, and he is neither well liked nor respected, though he is feared, sort of. Despite being only five foot eight, he intimidates most of his peers with his pit bullish aura and driven ambitions. On the job, he spends hours at his desk, doing social media searches, tracking down suspects from unsolved cases while others sit around and chat or waste time on their smart phones and I-pads. What an irony, thinks Eric. Does Sahi know how much its product is undermining productivity? Though he likes the desk work with all its mental challenges, Eric's never far from an outbreak of physical energy. He's ever rising from his chair with a spurt and then dashing somewhere. His head jerks whenever his name is called. Beyond alert, he's twitchy, uptight. Even during his free time he's hyperactive: either down at the gym practicing his Krav Maga, or else he's at a shooting range, practicing that. Not that he needs to, necessarily. In two years, he's pulled a gun once, on an assignment where he was escorting a CEO to a conference in San Antonio wherein free trade protesters marched in front of the convention hall. His team leader reported a disturbance in back of a meeting room. Pierce investigated and drew his weapon, his adrenaline running. But it turned out to be nothing, and Eric Pierce, craving a chance to do something either heroic or extreme, was visibly disappointed, and shaking. As a result, colleagues give him a wide berth, thinking he ought to be in Afghanistan or someplace given how edgy he always seems. Fierce Pierce, they call him.

The message reads: "investigate stolen files at offices in Emeryville. Current employee, missing from work over last several days, is a suspect. Suspicion reinforced this morning by a contact from Oakland police department to our human resources division, looking for the employee: name of Bryan Tecco. Take precautions." Eric quickly grabs a coat, his phone, and a forty caliber P229 firearm, because that's what he infers from 'take precautions'. He devours what's left of his lunch and heads out the door. It's a good thing he doesn't have a partner—not that anyone's asking for that role—because he'd always be leaving that person behind. Moments later he's in his year-old Subaru, speeding down the wide country road that runs adjacent to Sahi's south Sacramento office complex. Soon he's on the eighty freeway, heading south towards the Bay Area to speak to the division executive that runs the Emeryville office. He checks his inside pocket to see that his firearm is still there, its presence a reminder of frozen impulses. His phone, now sat on the passenger seat, is buzzing with a follow-up text message he figures he doesn't need to read. "Drop everything: top priority," says the message from Dave Gagliano.

It takes only an hour to travel down to the Bay Area, during which time Eric contacts Ed Kim, the division executive whose office had been burgled sometime before the weekend. At least, that's the current story. The two men exchange texts and agree to meet ASAP. As Eric drives, his mind fills with questions: what are these files that have been stolen? What's so important about them? What role did this Bryan Tecco have within the department? Most specifically, if he'd been missing so long as to come to the attention of the police, and these files had gone missing earlier, why had Kim taken so long to report the theft, much less the implication of Tecco? Eric Pierce's mind had always worked feverishly. Ever since he was a kid, his brain thought faster than his tongue such that he could rarely articulate what was happening when it was happening. The result was a stutter that Eric, now twenty eight years old, more or less had under control. To calm himself when overwhelmed, he often took time-outs, ignored others as best he could, and imagined his thoughts pictorially: placing bullet points next to each idea, he'd situate them in columns, or sometimes move them around so as to create a map.

By mid-afternoon he is being led by an assistant to Ed Kim's office, a sizable loft space on a second floor, partitioned by a single glass wall in what looks like a temporary set up. The interior of the building is an un-carpeted expanse, with about two dozen cubicles of computer hardware hastily arranged atop a cement floor. As Eric walks in wearing a mint grey suit, he glances over at the team of testers slumped in their chairs, clicking away at their devices like rats running around a spinning wheel. They are all male tweenies, sloppily dressed and unwashed, as though work were a matter of tumbling out of bed, grabbing a coffee each morning, and staggering over to this warehouse for the job that redeems their static, post-adolescent lives. Eric grins, nods as he catches the glazed looks of a few workers, but beneath this slick veneer he feels only disdain. What a bunch of slobs, he thinks.

Inside Ed Kim's office, the executive is sat at the end of a twenty foot conference table, with a hot female assistant who is diligently tapping away on a laptop. As he sees Pierce enter, he immediately dismisses his assistant, plus the taut, similarly hot Asian girl who has chaperoned Eric to this point. He walks over and wearily extends a hand.

"You're Pierce?"

"Yes sir," Eric replies. Kim, a fifty-five year old Asian man who was born and raised in Silicon Valley, sustains eye contact with the cocky young man whose hand shake feels like iron; whose body seems chiseled from the kind of cement block that will soon gird the new Bay Bridge span. Kim takes an instant dislike to Pierce, noting the thin smile that is ever holding back a derisive laugh; the small charcoal eyes that look like a pair of pellets. In Kim's view, only one or two points diminish Eric Pierce's alpha-maledom: the relatively stunted growth, which stalled for Eric around age sixteen after an urgent spurt in his middle-school years. The other flaw is the receding hairline above a protruding forehead. The hair itself is a spiky tundra of whiskers that Eric wishes he could replace with a thick, curly mane or an abundant comb-over. Eric Pierce, Kim surmises, leads with his intelligence first, and secondly, with his envy.

"We have a situation," Kim says grimly.

The two men sit for an hour as Eric gathers information. He takes notes like a psychoanalyst tracking exchanges. Occasionally, he looks up and stares at the ceiling, which has a Spartan design: aluminum ducts, exposed, are set against red brick, reflecting a clean yet industrial ambience. Eric is not really tuned into Ed Kim's neurosis. He finds him reticent, answering questions with deflective remarks; he is dismissive. Eric, however, is in his own mind, arranging the bullet points, noting the glibness but letting Ed Kim sit in his shame about the loss of files delivered by an unidentified yet high level client. He lets silent pauses hang, causing Kim to squirm. Eric feels resentful that he hasn't been told all there is to know, yet knows that revenge is all he has to satisfy him.

"I suppose it doesn't matter that I know who that is," Eric says smartly.

Kim is blunt: "No, it doesn't."

"Were the files stolen from here?" Eric asks, ignoring the rebuke. He looks around and notes the absence of anything that looks like a safe, or even something like a cabinet attached with a lock. He looks over his shoulder, noting the stairway that leads down a single floor from his office to the floor where the testers work. From this office, Ed Kim has an aerial view of his crew, and despite the transparency, one would think that a view of his desk area would be obscured. Kim answers Eric in the affirmative. Eric frowns in return, looking affectedly quizzical. "How would someone know you had files in here? Is it typical to keep files not locked up? Loose?"

Ed Kim issues a thin sigh, not liking Eric Pierce's tone or insinuations. It's known that gaming companies have to keep secure files that contain new prototypes. It's known that theft of new properties is a real problem in the industry, and that some insiders may be profiting by selling flash drives of new files on the black market, thereby forcing gaming publishers to re-think designs and game narratives. Ed Kim, however, has an unblemished reputation at Sahi; has been one of its most loyal employees for over twenty years, and he'd be damned if he was going to let some punk security officer treat him like a novice manager of a retail outlet.

"Anytime we have sensitive files we keep them locked up. I have a lock on my desk in here, plus another in my assistant's office for prototypes that are delivered."

"You mean they go to her first?"

Kim pauses and then says, "typically, yes."

"You say typically, are you implying something different occurred with the files that were stolen."

Kim issues another labored breath. "On this occasion, yes. A client delivered some files personally. It was a late addition to a prototype we had been working on for months."

"I see. And Tecco was one of the testers working on this prototype?"

Kim pauses, unsure. "I believe so, yes."

"You don't know."

"The testers are working on multiple games; I don't keep track of who is working on what."

"Does he have access to this office, ordinarily?"

"No, of course not." Kim is about to ask why that question was asked when Eric cuts in.

"It's just that when I asked the assistant about the break in, I asked if there was any indication that anything had been disturbed, and she said no and—"

"Well, this isn't her office—"

"Right, but she's in here quite a lot, isn't she? In fact, doesn't she open up before you? And anyway, you told me yourself that you didn't discover anything out of place; nothing disturbed, I mean."

Kim's expression hardens. "What's your point?"

Eric Pierce performs a self-satisfied delivery: "My point is that the intruder knew exactly where to look, which suggests he may have had earlier access to this office, or perhaps witnessed where the files had been placed."

Kim looks dumfounded. "I don't see how this is going to help you locate the files?"

Eric averts his gaze for a moment and stares out of an opposite window that looks out towards San Francisco Bay. He laughs peculiarly.

"I'm sorry. You're right. I'm gonna check out Tecco's place of residence this afternoon and see what I can find there."

"Then what?" Kim asks, now sounding nervous yet eager.

Eric returns a wide, inscrutable grin. "Who knows? We'll see, won't we?"

Kim's tone, no longer defensive, instead turns grave.

"Look, those files are important. Time is of the essence here." The executive's eyes flicker up and down the short, stocky frame of Eric Pierce. His future with the company—perhaps his entire career—rests in the hands of this callow yet perhaps formidable young man. Eric stands, stiffly shakes Kim's hand and tells him he'll be in touch. He walks out parking a thought in his mind: that he'd be back, revisiting a belief that Kim is a collaborator, not a victim of corporate theft as he's presenting. He'd be back having done his job; having busted a gut and outthought whatever opponent is against him—ready to confront Ed Kim and whomever else with evidence of malfeasance. Braced for war, Pierce exits the Emeryville office, determined to find Bryan Tecco, and committed to solving what might be the most important crime his industry has ever known.

9

Eric drives north to Richmond, Bryan Tecco's place of residence. It is late afternoon and the weather's good, which means there's barely a cloud in the sky: not atypical for the Bay Area in spring. Eric exits on the Cutting Boulevard exit and heads west, towards 21st street and an address that will be an apartment building unit. He drives alongside thirty and forty year old homes with broken wooden exteriors; creaking foundations. An attractive park with a pair of soccer fields is marred by pockets of trash that are littered across the patchy, unkempt grass. A whiff of cigarettes and dogshit hangs heavily in the local atmosphere. For the most part, the park seems wasted and empty. Nobody jogs here, Eric Pierce figures. People only languish.

As he pulls up to the address indicated in his notes, he pulls a face which furthers his distaste. The apartment building where Bryan Tecco supposedly lives has a dull brown façade with a plain image of a palm tree on the front next to a name: Sunrise apartments, it reads.

He doesn't get very far. The front door is a ten-foot high glass entryway with an adjacent dial pad. He'd need a code to get inside to a quad area that is the centerpiece of about a dozen units. Eric does due diligence and walks around the side, half expecting to find a manager's office, half-hoping he'll find some opening left carelessly unlocked. He gets lucky. Next to a gate that leads to a parking lot area, a fence door is ajar. Eric squeezes in and wades past a bed of ferns that have overgrown into a walkway. The first door he arrives at has the word manager situated just behind a screen, but the unit seems dormant, with nobody home. There's a front porch with a floor mat that is covered with dog hair, so much so that stray hairs are floating about, being a nuisance to anyone with allergies. Beside the mat sits a nearly empty bowl of water and a discarded cigarette butt. The crud at the base of the door looks a centimeter thick. Eric thinks twice about ringing the bell.

He walks casually among the units, taking in the dingy surroundings, the air of easy violence and drug use. Eric figures that in one of these units there's bound to be a meth lab destined to burn this place to the ground one day. He peers inside windows with little or no insulation. No double glazing: must be stinking hot in summer; freezing in wintertime. Eric sees into dark rooms, wandering about as if he were browsing through a pet store; as if those who lived here didn't even merit privacy.

"Who're you looking for?" says a voice from behind.

Eric turns and sees a middle-aged black man with a sour expression which centrally features a protruding lower lip. Eric returns a winning, salesman's smile and strides towards the man, his arm outstretched. The man is pudgy, about Eric's height, yet wearing contrasting clothes, a pair of jeans stained with what looks like motor oil; a grey sweater marked with pinhole burns. Seeing Eric Pierce advance, he steps back like he's about to reach for a weapon.

"Sorry, I'm looking for unit 24. I didn't know the code but the side door was open. I don't mean to—"

"You looking for Weed?" the man mutters.

"Excuse me." The question's a bit direct, Eric thinks, even for this sketchy neighborhood.

"Tecco," the man corrects. Now he sounds urgent, like he'd join the search for Weed if asked.

"Tecco, yes." Eric pauses as he retracts a stupid follow-up. *You know him?*

"Uh-huh," grunts the man. He steps forward carefully, with a limping gait that suggests he'd once been shot in the leg for being his surly, watchful self in a neighborhood watch. "I'm the manager here. Edgar Brinkley." He looks Eric up and down. "You police?" he asks next.

Eric would love to do the move wherein an officer or detective breaks out a wallet and flashes an ID. He loves that part in movies; used to mimic it as a kid when he role-played cop games with his friends. Ironically, that was in apartment buildings that were as tacky and run down as this; in neighborhoods not unlike this.

"Not exactly. I'm representing Bryan's employer, Sahi communications. I'm a security officer looking to investigate his whereabouts. He hasn't been to work in a few days. Have you seen him?" Eric affects a friendly, offhand voice, like the voice of someone who owes twenty bucks to a resident and has stopped by to drop it off.

"You talk to police?" Brinkley responds, his question competing with Eric's. The man seems impatient now. "They been here yesterday. I called 'em again today. Tecco's not here. I don't know where he is, and if he don't show up soon and pay his rent,

I'm gonna give up his unit, throw all his shit out." Brinkley waves his arm out in a grand gesture; stretches out the vowel of 'all' for emphasis.

"Okay. Do you mind if I take a few notes?" He takes his time, notes the threatened and threatening tone of Edgar Brinkley. It's full of suggestion, as if he suspects Eric Pierce of being a friend of Weed's, not a follower. "You say the police have been here. Did they find anything that might tell us where We—Bryan—is?"

"Nah, they just looked inside his place and then left. They don't give a shit."

"You said you called them today also. Why was that?"

"Tecco had a friend who also lives here, or lived here. Name of Leavitt, in 22. He's also gone."

"Really?" Eric raises an eyebrow, intrigued. He stops and thinks. That mind. That fever. He stares upwards, regarding the second floor of units, and has a flash association with the testing offices in Emeryville. He looks back to Brinkley, whose pained, desperate countenance is about as far removed from the effete, moneyed image of Ed Kim as he can imagine.

"Yeah," says Brinkley, continuing. "I thought…I don't know, that they might act on it if they thought more than one guy was gone." He seems forlorn reflecting on a half-measured ruse that didn't work out.

"Did they?"

Brinkley spits air through his teeth, rippling his lips, especially the fat lower one.

"Nah, did it hell. They just take the information, say thank you, and move on."

"You hear anything else?"

"It was only a few hours ago," Brinkley replies, again sounding plaintive. Eric pulls out his phone, checks the time and a number on his notepad: a contact at Oakland police department. He looks around like he's at ground zero of the mystery; that others might show up any moment and hijack some long sought-after secret.

"Uh…," he starts, trying to think and explain himself simultaneously. He holds out a finger and protrudes it towards Brinkley's face.

"What" says the hapless landlord, looking confused, not intimidated. Eric is staring into middle distance, waiting for his own question to arrive on his tongue.

"Just wondering, why so quick to evict Tecco or his friend?"

Brinkley moves backwards, like he's offended by the query.

"Are you serious? I've wanted to get rid of those guys for weeks; months in the case of Tecco. I've just been looking for an excuse. They're both dope fiends. Or Leavitt is, anyway. I think Tecco's more like a pothead, but he's also a dealer. They stay up all night making noise, playing video games. I lost one unit two years ago to a fire; aint gonna let that happen again. So, I told 'em: 'if I catch you with dat shit on the property, you're outta here. If you're one day late with a payment, then same thing.' I warned 'em. No joke." Edgar Brinkley's diatribe continues as Eric's attention drifts away. His head turns slightly askance and his eyes point towards the front entry, and then beyond, towards his Subaru parked in front. The sound of the landlord turns to mutterings; Edgar Brinkley talking to himself, sounding resigned yet disgruntled about the absence of listeners. He's a lonely man, Eric thinks: a man adrift in the cosmos.

"Thanks," Eric says, again flashing his winner smile. Brinkley nods, aware that this gratitude really means goodbye. Pierce is about to head off before he stops and asks, "actually, do you know anyone connected with either of these guys: friends, family?"

"I don't know about Tecco, but Leavitt is from the hills, I know dat." There's a hint of disdain in Brinkley's voice.

"The hills?"

"The Oakland hills."

Before he drives off, Eric stops before his car and dials the number he has for the contact at OPD: an officer named

Armstrong. As the ringtone sounds out he recalls trainings in which he was coached on the matter of cooperation with local authorities. His boss always says to act collaboratively, even if police don't see the relationship the same way. Of course, it's a double standard: Sahi has plenty of things it keeps from the public, and police departments are just an extension of the public as far as execs are concerned. Plus, Gagliano usually issues these instructions with a disingenuous front; a twitchy smirk on his lips. Meanwhile, Eric knows that investigating officers will likely have little information, and what they have they might not be able to share anyway. Nothing to lose, Eric thinks; then a voice on the phone says, "Armstrong".

"Yes, detective. My name's Pierce, from Sahi Telecommunications. I'm following up on the contact you made to our human resource department this morning."

"Yeah?" Armstrong says tersely. Clearly, he's busy.

"Yeah, I understand that our employee, Bryan Tecco, is still missing. We wondered if you had any more information on the case."

"What's your role in this, if you don't mind me asking?"

"I'm with internal security here. Tecco has a sensitive role in our operations. The sooner we know what's happened to him, the quicker we can make decisions with respect to his function with the company."

"It's only been twenty four hours—barely that. We don't have anything yet." Armstrong seems satisfied that Eric Pierce is legit; he sounds pressured, just this side of cordial.

"Does he have family or something? Who reported him missing?"

"His family did, in West Marin. Don't you guys have your own contact information for them? Won't that be in his file under emergency contact information or something?"

Eric bites his tongue, knowing this to be true, though he'd not done his homework; hadn't read that part of the file before making this call.

"Yeah, we do. But…" He pauses, second-guessing the value of contacting family, of making this call to Oakland police department, now that he thinks of it. But the friend? That's another matter. "Listen, we've heard he has a friend named Leavitt that's missing also."

"Don't tell me—his landlord, right?" Armstrong is suppressing a guffaw. What a dick, thinks Eric. Then he thinks, and I thought I was a…

"Sure," he says in the meantime.

"I don't have any information on that. Look, we're checking this thing out—"

"Can you tell me anything?"

"Whad'ya want me to say? We don't have a last known position. Look, I don't know what his role with your company was, but from what we know, he's got a shady record, a few priors dating back years. But you know how it is: he'll probably surface in days."

"So, no leads," Pierce says pleadingly.

"We have information about an auto accident near Stinson Beach. It might be related."

"Related? I just talked to Tecco's landlord, who says another tenant, a friend of Tecco's, is also missing. Does that connect?"

"We have a person of interest, but we're not discussing names."

"But—"

"When or if we find Tecco we'll call you. I mean, we'll call your human resources department like we did earlier. I spoke to Tecco's boss earlier—Kim, I think his name is—he said there was no cloud over his job, except that he'd missed a couple of days of work. So…" the officer trails off with an indifferent strain in his voice, leaving Eric Pierce to consider just how impersonal this whole thing is to some people. He holds his tongue as he thinks to say something about missed work? Shouldn't that tell them something? Eric ends the call with Armstrong, and closes his phone, shaking his head.

"I'll tell you something else." For a heavy-set man with a limping gait, Edgar Brinkley knows how to sneak up on people.

"Jesus," exclaims Eric, caught in a near-trance. He leans against his car and looks at Brinkley like he's a phantom. The landlord is unperturbed.

"It wasn't just the drugs with them two," he says. "They don't know this, but I'd hear the two of them talking together at night as I walk by their apartment, doing my checks of the property. Crazy potheads and tweakers: they think people can't hear 'em as they stay up all night talkin' their shit; thinking what they do is all secret. Man, you should hear the shit they'd be talkin' about."

"Yeah, what's that?" Eric Pierce asks, half-interested.

"They talk about seeing things—ghosts, the future. These guys, they think they got their fingers on the pulse of the world. They'd be talkin' about conspiracies, and then be making up their own. I'm just sayin', the more I think about it, the more I'm glad to give up a month's rent if it means not seeing 'em anymore. But for you, this is a warning: they're crazy. Especially Tecco, or Weed. Dat's his name. I'm just warning you: he's crazy."

10

Bryan "Weed" Tecco thinks he's going crazy. For the last several hours, or thereabouts, he's been tied up on a bed in a basement of…somewhere. There's been no sign of Dan Pritchard since he passed out in the car. Weed is almost naked but for a heavy pair of underwear. Despite this, his body is just about covered: over his chest, across his ankles, over his head and hands is a network of straps fixed to plastic rods, pinned to what might be a bed—possibly a gurney. It's an elaborate system that allows some flexibility, and just about keeps him warm. Weed can move. Meaning, he can wriggle and shake. He can't speak due to what feels like a boxer's mouth guard that is fixed into place by another strap, but he can utter muffled noises. He can thrash about and give the elastic restraints, and himself, a good workout. When he gets exhausted he can fall asleep and pass the time, because the bed is actually quite comfortable, except he's cold. When he awakens, he can start again, hoping that sooner or later his efforts will pay off, and that the restraints will break. When they don't seem to—when the sheepskin-like straps remain untroubled by his thrashing about—he can slump back and rest again for a spell. He can cry.

Weed hasn't cried in years: not since he was preteen. Back then he cried a lot; got it out of his system, he later joked. Now they're back, the tears. They're streaming down his face, running over his lips and into his mouth, which now hangs open in a suspended, distraught howl. Weed can move but he can't get out. He is trapped, yet teased with the ability to stretch. If he could free his hands from a pair of taped-on gloves, he might rip at the material that's holding him down. If he could somehow bump the guard away from his mouth, or move his head such that he could look up and down his own body, he might assess the problem and find a way out. He'd bite, claw, and tear at these straps until his fingernails tore away; until his teeth broke. He reminds himself of the lagoon, of the pain of nearly drowning. In some ways this is worse, he thinks, and there is no special breed of seaweed around for him to reach out to.

He doesn't know what time it is, but knows it's daytime from a shard of light that beams down through a window in the opposite top corner of the room. That is Dan's only act of kindness, or mistake: the likely decision to not cover up the gap. By the level of brightness, Weed guesses that it's morning. The sunlight has a vaguely fresh feeling. Also, Weed feels the way he often does on a weekend morning: it's a pleasant fatigue enabling a lazy sleep-in followed by a dawdling saunter through the day. He feels like a blind man trying to navigate his way through the world from memory and random impressions. The room seems tidy enough: there are no cobwebs that he can see; not a lot of dust. It seems like he's underground, but thankfully, there are no scratchy sounds of rats or any other kind of rodent. There are no creepy inanimate sounds to speak of, and no flies buzzing about his face, tormenting him. Fleetingly, he thinks he could get into an investigatory mood if this were an exercise. It could be like some kind of deprivation game reminiscent of the kind of things talked about in military boot camps, or by martial arts fanatics. Through the clues around him he could construct meanings and strategize: what time of what day is it? What kind of place is he in? What's the likelihood of being rescued?

He figures one thing out through a force of nature. The need to urinate comes on quickly, which in turn alerts his brain to re-evaluate what he's wearing. As his sensation builds he goes through a body check: he fidgets to see what kind of resistance there is in the underwear, and shakes himself to see what degree of give there is in the crotch. His dick feels strangely comfortable; held, even. He can feel it but can't move it, because it's cushioned within some kind of cotton bedding. It's unsettling no matter how good it feels. Meanwhile, the stream is imminent, yet there's no way he can get free. A panic rises. He doesn't remember this feeling; his body and brain aren't on the same page. How can they be? They don't know what to do, and he can't fathom how any living being can get relief without…

"Jesuf…" he manages through the guard. A diaper. I'm sitting in a fucking diaper, he realizes—then he lets go.

This is not an exercise, Weed thinks as his body relaxes. It may be an experiment, but not one of his choosing. Is it a game? He wonders. Dan Pritchard seemed interested in games, in the games Weed plays, and expertly tests. Dan had tried to engage Weed in a talk about games, but Weed wasn't interested. Weed blew him off. Maybe something happened to Dan in those moments; something the older man kept to himself but then acted upon. Then again, he'd likely planned this all along, as soon as he'd seen Weed by the side of road, plodding along; a weary, vulnerable transient. As Weed tilts his head slightly to his right, he can just about make out a staircase leading upwards. Its top three or four steps are obscured by a cylindrical tank that looks like the property's heating system. It seems small—only a few feet wide and tall—suggesting a home, not a commercial piece of real estate. These clues tell a story about what kind of place this is. The meaning is simple and obvious, yet under the circumstances, primitively moving for Weed: this isn't an abandoned room. People either live or work here. They take those stairs, frequent this fairly clean-looking environment. Maybe they hang out down here and play sometimes. Somebody looks after this space. Somebody cares, and that means Weed won't be alone forever.

And, of course, he has a song stuck in his head. It's not a song he likes. Songs that get "stuck" never seem to be ones that people actually like. If that were the case then for Weed it would be something by Led Zeppelin, Metallica, or Korn—something that would keep him fired up, and more. Modern Wagnerian sounds: they sanctify the lives of the wretched, stirring Weed's soul. He'd settle for less. Even a little house music wouldn't be amiss. But no, it's nothing like that. Instead, the song is a childish ditty, practically a nursery rhyme. It's something that Weed sort of remembers his Dad singing with one of his friends at a New Year's party when he was a kid. The worst part is that Weed isn't even getting the words right, which nags at his perfectionism. The first part, the most famous bit, is correct—*Roll out the barrel*—but the second bit—*Roll out the barrel of fun*—doesn't sound right. And it's on a loop. Eventually, the song turns to something else, but though Weed loves Lou Reed and the Velvet Underground, "I'm Waiting For The Man" isn't making him feel better.

At the same time, Weed tries to summon a Dan Pritchard appearance. If he concentrates hard enough, long enough, he can also wear down the resistance of that resilient sheepskin material, and eventually make the straps loosen just enough so that he might free himself. They feel childlike, these regressions and wishes. That's okay, Weed figures. Meaning, it makes sense. It's human. Fantasies are what he has for the moment, and who knows how long this moment will last? So, for as long as this takes, for as long as he is helpless, he'll let himself feel like a child, and act like a child until someone lets him be an adult again. It shouldn't be *that* hard, being a child. After all, though he doesn't remember it, Bryan "Weed" Tecco was once a helpless child.

11

Sleep seems like the best antidote to depression, which follows when fear runs out of ideas. Some say it's a symptom, fatigue, and for Weed, symptoms and solutions often get conflated. One problem with sleep is that it makes difficult the tracking of time. Another is that sleep doesn't quite stifle anxiety like it should. Dreams transform into nightmares, making him shudder and turn. The most recent stretch of REM offers the image of Dan Pritchard's face squeezed into the opening of a fleshy tube. The tube moves like a churning engine: Dan's body writhing within its works, being crushed. Impassively, the late middle-aged man stares out with a pleading expression. "Ow," he mews, his eyes unblinkingly sad. An intrusion occurs—an entry from the side, of an elderly woman moving slowly alongside the tube, with a walker. "What the fuck," mutters Weed in his sleep. Now he's awake. So far he hasn't seen any lights on in this makeshift guest room of his. As long as he sees daylight then he has a clue; otherwise, the time—even the day—is anyone's guess.

After another snooze of indeterminate length, Weed awakens again to find that a single light bulb has been turned on in the corner of the basement, next to the small window that has now been shuttered. In keeping with the childlike feeling of late, Weed has a brief Goldilocks association: someone's been eating his porridge. He feels a spiking chill, knowing this break in continuity means he is not alone. Strange, for only an hour or so earlier he'd been imploring something or someone to come down those basement stairs, assuming he'd be awake for such an event. Now he imagines that Dan Pritchard had either perfectly timed his entry, or else that he had a closed-circuit camera positioned somewhere, such that he could spy on his hostage. Weed pictures the queer older man standing over him, leering over his body, scrutinizing Weed's fleshy imperfections, inspecting prospects for a later penetration.

Weed has never been one for homophobia, not overtly anyway. It isn't his thing, mostly because he thinks himself wrong for either sex, but also because he lacks moralistic objections, from either side of the divide. Morals: they're for moral people, probably. Fags, as he indifferently calls them, are not his problem. They seem more into Jonny Winner types with six-pack abs, not the pudgy tire he sports around his waist; not that Weed has much inside knowledge on the subject of gay. He hasn't known many gay people, despite living in the supposed hotbed that is the Bay Area. Sweet, Chris Leavitt's flaky friend, seems kinda gay at times, though Chris refutes this. None of his other friends, Weed might say, are of the man-on-man ilk. Still, he has his preconceptions, which inform his prejudices, and now his fears. But above all, what he can't quite shake, what gets him more than anything, is the strange aptness of the situation.

Rape. The more he thinks about it, the more he realizes this situation has nothing to do with sexual preference. This is about control, possibly revenge. Weed feels a shudder; he involuntary shakes his limbs against the restraints. The motion transforms into another thrashing flourish that lasts half a minute: Weed imagines, and hopes, that the straps will somehow animate, be caught off guard, having been asleep themselves. In their weakened condition, they will finally loosen and let him go. Meanwhile, Weed torments himself with images, as if this race to freedom competes with the advance of horror. He needs twenty seconds, or a slew of back-to-back twenty second moments. With thoughts of Dan's face nearing his with a protruding tongue, he flinches and whimpers, sounding like a frightened girl. For a moment, he goes with the thought and feels pangs of affinity: I'm like a girl, he repeats in his mind.

Suddenly, there is a brutal sound of a wooden door opening. It's a slow, creaking breach, like that of a vault in a haunted house. The effect seems so trite that Weed believes he'll soon see a bright light pouring in, impinging upon a shadowy expanse, with someone resembling Nosferatu staggering down the stairs. After a pause, Weed hears heavy footsteps thudding down upon aged wood, accompanied by another sound—that of an iron coil: the springs connecting the door to its frame. It's like a howling; like someone is doing harm to the metal. Through a sliver that is his peripheral vision, Weed can just about make out the beige trousers of Dan Pritchard flapping about his ankles. The footsteps stop. Weed flinches back to a still position, braced for an introduction. Instead, he hears the now familiar, horrible giggle.

"Have a good night?" Dan asks like an amiable owner of a bed and breakfast. "Oh, that's right: you probably won't know whether it's day or night." Weed figures that Dan is regarding the shuttered window in the corner. Perhaps he's reflecting on whether that was an oversight of his, to not cover it up in the first place. "Oh well, it doesn't matter. Time doesn't matter that much—not nearly as much as people think it does," Dan comments obliquely. He appears in full view, standing over Weed like a surgeon greeting his patient ahead of a marathon procedure. He looks relaxed, like he's had a refreshing night's sleep himself. "We have all the time in the world," he adds. He is holding his hand over his stomach, looking over the length of Weed's body, either admiring his handiwork with the straps and diaper, or else examining with hunger a forthcoming feast.

Fuck my imagination, thinks Weed.

"Whad ya wan fugger," he manages through the guard.

Dan frowns as though sympathetic to Weed's handicap.

"Here, let me help you with that," he says gently. With a deft, dentist-like touch, Dan reaches in, extracts the guard and sets it aside. For a split second, Weed thinks to bite Don's hand, only to think twice due to his still compromised position. As the guard is pulled away, he eyes one of Dan's fingers and envisions himself gnawing it to the bone while enjoying Dan's squeals of agony. Now free to move, Weed's tongue feels heavy; swollen. The dryness of his lips is more apparent, and due to what feels like a pound of caked-on saliva, he's finding it not so easy to draw breath and speak.

"Water?" asks Dan. Weed has to hand it to him. If nothing else, he watches and listens attentively; he's a tuned-in villain. "Don't worry. There's nothing in this. There's no need." Dan glances over the bed, needlessly emphasizing his point. Weed begrudgingly nods, accepting the offer. "I'm glad you took the e-cigarette eventually," Dan confesses jovially. "I'd have been stuck if you'd held out. That was almost a miscalculation. Still, it turned out well: it's good you didn't take the hit earlier, actually. It gave me extra time to get you comfortable, fit you in here."

"Chloroform?" Weed whispers, like he's making notes for future reference.

Dan nods. "Sometimes Rohypnol. Regardless, I'm glad the days of the cloth method are behind us." Next, Dan proffers bottled water like a smug man-servant anticipating the hangover needs of his master. As Weed takes a swig he keeps an eye on his captor. He swallows once, but with a second mouthful he holds on, contemplating a squirt into Dan's face. As he drinks, he begins to picture Dan dragging him out of his car; carrying him inside this place, undressing him, tying him down. He stops his thoughts. Dan doesn't move as his hostage takes nourishment. He doesn't flinch, blink, or even withdraw his smile. He seems entirely confident in what he's doing; utterly knowing as to what will happen from one moment to the next in his scheme. The reason: he's done it before, Weed realizes. Anger slips once again into fear, though not so much that he cannot muster attitude.

"What's up, bro?" he asks. Dan, he knows, hasn't met this defiant side of him, and he perhaps won't glean the flippant disregard that "bro" conveys. For Weed, "bro" is a versatile pronoun, covering the purposes of casual greeting and provocation—sometimes simultaneously.

"I was thinking that you'd probably woken up once or twice already. I could hear you moving earlier. It seems like you've been testing the strength of my set-up here." Dan looks over the array of straps again like he's proud of his prison system. "You're maybe wondering where you are," he offers. He stops.

"Is this going to be a quiz? For each wrong answer I get a kiss?"

Predictably, Dan giggles. Weed makes another mental note: must refrain from making smart ass remarks if that sound is the cost.

"That's good. I like having someone with a clever turn of phrase. I could tell you were like that, even though you've been kinda quiet up until now." Dan's amusement subsides. Weed goes silent; looks away like a sullen teenager. "I'm surprised you haven't called out, actually," Dan says. "If I were in your situation I'd be yelling my head off as soon as I had a chance."

He has a point, Weed thinks. Perhaps it's the swollen tongue, in combination with the thick cotton mouth that's holding him back. Maybe it's the presumption that this guy Pritchard will have thought of his shouting pleas already; that he thinks of everything—the earlier shard of light through the window notwithstanding. Regardless, Weed notes that *he* often doesn't think of everything, especially not calling out to people, asking for help.

"It wouldn't be effective, of course; maybe you've realized that already. This room is pretty well sound-proofed on the exterior wall, and the guard was just an initial thing to use so I couldn't hear you from upstairs, so I could sleep. I'll tell you this much about where we are: the nearest neighboring property is at least a hundred yards away." Weed doesn't know whether to believe him; not sure that it matters for the time being. Weed's eyes shoot hatred. Dan's face, as if in reply, turns weary and serious. "That wouldn't have stopped me, by the way. I mean, it didn't stop me when I was once in a similar position."

Jesus, now I'm gonna get a story, Weed inwardly groans. Dan's knack for reading Weed's face continues.

"Oh, you might enjoy this. You'll find it interesting. It'll pass the time—again, not that that's important. You see, I'm a veteran. I was in Vietnam, back in the sixties. You perhaps don't need me to add that, but who knows what young people know about history these days. I find that young people don't read; they don't care about history, just games, like your games." Dan's voice shifts, takes on new inflection: a kind of wistful bitterness. "Back in my day, nobody talked about being gay. It was a real taboo. I was able to conceal it well enough. Basketball helped. It gave my family something positive to say about me to their friends. Dan Pritchard, the famous son, who they secretly knew was a fag. But when I was captured, that was interesting. I was held, along with two other American soldiers, by these Viet Cong troops; tied down in this hut out in the middle of the jungle. I wasn't tied up like this—this is all medical supply stuff I got online—but I was being held captive, and threatened with torture. They were going to drive these knives under our nails, said a translator. Then they were going to insert the tips of the knives into the heads of our penises, splitting open our urethras."

Dan looks down, catching sight of Weed's legs moving: the effort to have one leg reach over the other, to protect himself.

"I don't know why you think I'd find this interesting," Weed says.

Dan cogitates. "Maybe 'interested' is not the right word. You're right: I don't think you'll be interested in my story of being tortured in war. I imagine you wouldn't care; wouldn't care at all, like most people. I guess you might have been interested in my captors' other tactic, that of calling us faggots, suggesting we'd get off on the torture. Especially me. They focused on me, as if they could see into me, what I was really like, despite the language barrier. Actually, that was the scariest part of it: being exposed like that; being called gay in front of my peers."

Weed bangs his head against the bed in a feeble display of rage.

"Look, not to sound rude or insensitive, but don't you have friends you can talk to about this stuff. It sounds like you need to get a lot off your chest. I'm not sure I'm qualified to—"

"Hmm…friends? I have friends," interrupts Dan, now scratching his chin musingly. "Everyone has friends. You likely have friends, don't you? But listeners are the thing. Just because you have friends doesn't mean you have people who know how to listen."

"Have you tried therapy?"

Dan laughs. "That's good. Yes, I did, actually—for almost twenty years. I learned that I had different sides to myself, a light and shadow. I admit having some less-than-palatable hobbies, but actually, people often tell me that I'm quite empathetic. So there are two parts to me: the imp and the emp, I call them. But I don't know how much do you know about psychotherapy?" Dan looks at Weed with an oddly bankrupt expression. Weed manages a shrug, expecting a punch-line. "Sociopathy. You see, research has shown that therapy doesn't work with sociopaths."

Weed thumps his head on the bed again. It's his body doing the talking.

"It's quite dark outside," Dan says, looking to his left, towards the shuttered window. Weed's voice now shakes with both fear and rage. Fear is taking lead.

"What do you want, bro? Tell me what you need or do what you're gonna do. Just get it over with."

Dan ignores him. He maintains his sights on the shuttered window like it's reminding him of something. He says, "I know what you're thinking. It's pretty dark in here, too."

Weed issues another whimper, this time involuntarily. Dan places a hand on Weed's stomach; his fingers are cold as they stroke the hair around Weed's belly and then move slowly downwards. He feels a pang of nausea, thinks he's moments from throwing up. Man up, he exhorts. He fails.

"The word 'interesting' just doesn't cut it, does it? It's so vanilla. I hate vanilla." He briefly looks down, regarding his attire with ironic interest. Self hatred? Meanwhile, Dan's sarcasm is a piece of his act. Within his plaintive words, there is no sneer; no hatred towards his victim. Instead, he seems merely talkative, like he's about to cut Weed's hair. He then looks at his hostage square in the face, his eyes widening with impish discovery.

"I know. I got it wrong earlier. You probably *won't* find this interesting, I was actually thinking. 'Terrifying'. That's the word. You'll probably find this terrifying."

12

Despite appearances to the contrary, Dan Pritchard has a thin skin for rejection. Given a choice, he'd prefer compliant, non-paying, even conscious sexual partners. Sometimes, they are anonymous, though particular habits have changed. Gone are the days when Dan would scout public restrooms in libraries or bus stations, searching for that distinctive look from a would-be partner, or just a certain profile of a man walking by. Though he enjoyed the brief encounters he'd experienced, and even the coded gestures, such as the crooked finger come ones that appeared under restroom stalls, Dan longs for bigger and better things: something more challenging, or more elaborate. Something more dangerous.

With only mild disappointment, he walks away from the prostrate, vulnerable body of Weed, deciding his recent young pick-up is too agitated, too non-compliant, to be any fun at the present time. Oh well, he thinks: it was, after all, a long shot to think it would all go down, so to speak, without any fuss. But he still gives it a shot, what he calls "the silent negotiation". All's fair in this off-center midway point between love and war, but before anything is consummated, peace should be given a chance. These days, Dan's twenty years of therapy pays dividends through his belief that anything can be talked about, or at least hinted at with a glancing, feathery touch of his fingers, or a mischievous glint in his eye.

However, with his touch lightly hovering over its destination, the young man begins shaking violently, bucking against the straps like a seizure victim; screeching homophobic vitriol at his host. Weed had changed his mind. Whatever was about to happen, he suddenly did not want it "over with".

"I'll come back when you've calmed down a bit," says Dan. He sounds a bit like a teacher patronizing a pre-school age child that's having a tantrum. As Weed hears him reach the stairs—when he hears the first creak of wood, the first twang of bending iron—he speaks out, in a lower yet still desperate voice.

"What did you expect? Did you seriously think I'd play this just how you wanted it, like it was some kind of act for you?" As if inspired by Dan's words, Weed takes his time and slowly props his head up and turns to his right. The constant thrashing about has yielded results in so far as he is able to see his captor fully, now standing upon the second step of the stairs, waiting. Though he can't quite see his face, Weed knows that Dan is staring glassy-eyed into space, barely taking in his hostage's words. Weed tries again. "I mean, what are you waiting for? Did you think I was gay, or that I might be into this once you got started? If so, I got news for you: this is about as cooperative as I get, unless you Chloroform me again." Weed halts, thinking his bravado might get the better of him. From what he knows about Chloroform, he considers that provoking another dose may prove fatal. Is this what's going through Dan's mind? Is Dan in Weed's head right now, thinking that Weed is worried about what lengths Dan is willing to go to—perhaps a full reenactment of that Vietnamese torture scene he described earlier—should Weed continue to resist? Is there dark synchrony happening between their minds as Dan waits upon that second step?

"Not exactly," Dan says in a menacing, disembodied voice. A pause. Weed is nonplussed.

"What?" he replies, his voice exasperated.

"I didn't think you were gay. With respect to my tastes, I figured you'd choose the path of least resistance, versus the method I implied earlier. That's all." Dan no longer sounds menacing, merely reasonable. "It's your choice, I guess." Then he takes another step up the stairs; a threatening step. Weed is poised to call out, make some kind of plea bargain, when Dan turns towards him as if he's forgotten something. "I did think you were guilty," he says.

"Guilty? Of what?"

Dan shrugs, says "I don't know. Maybe it doesn't matter. I just noticed how nervous you were around those cops." Dan gives another one of his annoying giggles, and then aims at Weed a narrow-eyed interrogator's gaze. "I wonder if you and I have a few things in common, like taking advantage of people, for instance."

"What's that supposed to mean?" Weed's face contorts into a sneer.

"We'll talk more later," Dan replies. Now he sounds like a therapist, like they sound when calling time on a session.

"The fuck we will. Get back here." Weed makes another restive burst against his restraints, to no avail. Dan slowly makes his way up the staircase, straining its aged boards, torturing that old iron. He keeps a watchful eye upon Weed until the last instant in which he can still see him. This has been the first stage of something, it seems. The captor has made his initial assessment, and so the captive is not yet ready for the treatment, whatever that is. An optimum level of fatigue is required—a few more hours of thrashing upon the straps might do the trick; demoralize. Or maybe hunger will be the factor that finally brings compliance. On cue, Weed feels a pang in his stomach, realizes he doesn't know how long it's been since he last took food or drink. Whichever factor proves decisive, weakness will be a key.

"Hey, don't just leave me down here."

Dan's face, placid and patient, disappears as he reaches the last two steps. He opens a door.

"Hey, talk to me," Weed calls out, now raising his voice. The door closes. The footsteps stop and the lights go out, plunging Weed into darkness. It is silent.

"HEY," he screams.

13

Helpless again. Another indeterminate spell follows, during which Weed experiences dozing recall of previous hospitalizations. Bad memories: at twelve he suffered appendicitis and was rushed to hospital one day after complaining of nausea and persistent stomach cramps. Weed's parents, generally attentive as caretakers, had noticed the signs early and acted quickly. Their decisiveness paid off in so far as Weed was able to make a swift recovery following an easy operation. After a mere two days in inpatient care, he was physically active again within two weeks, a remarkable turnaround for a condition that, as Weed's mother then reported, had once nearly killed her. Still, Weed recalls with a shudder the long night waiting for surgery, laid out in a gurney, slowly feeling the effects of a full-bodied anesthetic. He remembers the drifting in and out of consciousness, the floating dread of being under the knife. He recalls especially his desperation as the hours passed—the delays imposed for reasons never explained—when his native fear of being trapped in circumstances reached a crescendo. He aimed tantrums at hapless nurses, alleging cruelty when the effects of a protracted anesthesia made him throw up. Despite the earlier quick thinking of his parents or the subsequent ease of the operation, Weed later attributed a speedy recovery to sheer revulsion—his own need to get clear of sickness.

He was less appreciative of his parents' role in his next and only other hospitalization, several years later. Actually, this wasn't initially a hospitalization. It was a rehab—a drug program. Despite Weed's denials about habits that were already many years old, his reputation both at home and in the tight West Marin community was preceding him. Weed was bluntly informed that his privilege of living at home, which he still sought in his late teens and early twenties, was contingent upon his completing a drug treatment program. But it didn't work out that way. Ultimately to his and his parents' dismay, a bizarre accident occurred that dissolved the plan. So much for plans. It was during the second week of activities that Weed, languidly participating in some group therapy exercise at a Santa Rosa clinic, was struck by an overhead board whose plastic glass cover had been split down its middle. A protruding shard was driven into Weed's wrist, which sent him back to hospital surgery, followed by a quite arduous recovery period of several months. It was a full year before Weed recovered full use of his digits, and not without considerable physical therapy. As to the accident, he and his parents won a civil suit against the drug program owing to its neglect of facility property. Upon collecting a settlement worth thousands of dollars, Weed determined the whole episode modestly profitable, if not quite worthwhile. He still hates hospitals; still reviles doing anything against his will.

The itching is the worst. He feels it in his toes and knows there's no way for him to reach down and grind his fingers through the affected area. Otherwise, it's up near the small of his back, or worse, just beneath his left shoulder blade, towards the middle. Unfortunately, there's nothing even slightly abrasive upon which Weed can wriggle and find relief. The bed sheets, pillows, even the straps, are all smooth to the touch. Dan, in all his efforts to make his captive feel comfortable, if terrified, had neglected the still person's occasional need for friction. Despite this, and despite hunger pangs that come in waves, or the weighted sensation that signals an archaic need for his diaper to be replaced, Weed continues to wade in and out of consciousness. He knows he is depressed; knows this is what depression feels like and that sleep is his only defense against what's happening.

He wakes up and sees Dan sitting backwards on a chair just two feet away from him. Smiling like a gnome, the elder man eyes a tray of food perched on a stool. It looks like a continental breakfast, featuring toast, a bowl of fruit, a cereal that might be Raisin Bran, as well as some jams and butter. Nothing cooked. It all looks like it's been prepared by a caterer, save for the butter, which sits bare, in rectangle slabs versus packets. As Weed sees the food his mouth starts watering. He could devour the bowl of fruit, possibly the cereal too, in a single gulp. The toast: two bites, tops. Into the two jars of jam—one raspberry, the other apricot orange—he'd delve his finger and then lick chunks. Within minutes he'd look like a four year old eating by himself with bits of food smeared across his face.

"I figured it was time you ate something," Dan says. He regards the tray with a grimy leer, seemingly proud of this hotelier impersonation. "Are we going to try again?" Weed's tongue protrudes slightly. He is set to lick his lips when he catches Dan's eye and considers the double meanings. Dan won't care what's real, he figures. It's all part of the fantasy. This time Weed nods, thinking it an ambiguous enough gesture. Words might let him down again, he considers—provoke another leaving—which might do little more than prolong this ordeal. Though Weed supposes he might be on the missing persons radar of many by now, he seriously doubts whether his dawdling hike through West Marin, or even his perverse-looking pairing with Dan in the restaurant will have led to any official sightings. It's ironic that he should now look back on that moment when the cop car passed them by and regret not flagging it down.

Dan pours a glass of water and holds it over Weed's chin, like it's a spiritual offering.

"Try this," he says like a kindly nurse. Weed contrives a look of suspicion—it's almost perfunctory. Dan doesn't bother rolling his eyes. He simply maintains his position. As he boasted earlier, he's got all the time in the world. Weed gingerly raises his head and leans toward the glass taking a sip. After a second, he glances toward the plates of food and then up towards Dan. The faint yet delicious odor of toasted bread is competing with whiffs of Dan's unidentifiable cologne, creating an unspeakable conflict. So far Dan has been darkly attuned to his captive's every move, and so it continues as he drops in Weed's mouth one grape at a time, one spoonful of Raisin Bran; one buttered piece of bread. After several mouthfuls, Weed is relaxing, chewing his food, and already feeling sufficiently satisfied so as to let his mind turn to the matter of Dan's intentions.

"So, what did you mean earlier when you said I take advantage of people?"

Dan is coy. "Did I say that? I was just wondering if we had that in common. I'll speak for myself. I know I use lots of people."

"You make it sound normal," Weed says.

"I don't know about that. I'm a salesman. Aren't you a salesman, also?" Weed reflects, wondering what he's shared about himself that he now can't remember saying. This might be a ruse, he thinks, designed to pry from him personal information not yet divulged. Who knows? Maybe this is an elaborate identity theft scheme. One thing's for sure: Weed's glad that earlier suggestion of shared sexual vices is gone. Especially as the lights went out moments later, that felt beyond creepy; beyond dark.

"Isn't everyone a salesman of some kind?" He answers. Dan smiles like he's appreciating the comeback, but then shoots a critical look.

"Hmm…I think my observation is less banal than that."

"I don't know where you're going with this, bro."

Dan laughs. "Really?" he asks mockingly. "No idea at all?" Weed shrugs and smirks, attempting to mirror Dan's attitude. Dan reaches behind his chair and produces Weed's wallet, still looking sodden after its adventure in Bolinas Lagoon several days earlier. It also looks reflective of its owner, as in thinner. The reason: it's now shorn of the fat handful of bills that Weed had originally traveled with to Marin.

"There was quite a lot of cash in there for someone hitchhiking," Dan comments. "I figure you're either a drug dealer or a pimp. Probably on the run. Don't worry, though. I have the cash upstairs, straightening it out, ironing some of it. You'll get it back."

Weed bursts out laughing. Pimp? That's the funniest thing he's heard in ages. He looks at Dan, sees that he's unperturbed by the outburst, like it doesn't for one moment alter his perception of his prisoner. Suddenly, Weed wants to rip his hands through his restraining straps just so that he might drive a fist right through Dan's smug, grinning face.

"Is that why you're taking advantage? You think I'm a thug and a pimp, so no one will care about me?"

"Am I wrong?" Dan challenges.

"I think I have more friends than a rapist," Weed rebuts, unwittingly conceding a point.

"Yes, but no one in my world knows I do this, whereas you wear your true colors all over you. You see, it doesn't matter what I know about you. I don't have to google your name to find out what you're about, though that did present a surprise.

Congratulations on that book, I mean. Besides that, you haven't done much, have you? I could tell almost as soon as I saw you that you were trouble, and not just to yourself." Dan looks over Weed's bowl and plate, sees that he is just about finished with breakfast. "Anyway, let me clear that away for you."

Dan rises and seems poised to leave when he sits back down again, chuckling. "Actually, thinking about rape, I saw this thing the other day—really funny—I've been waiting to tell someone about it."

Weed looks back at Dan knowing he is about to hear a bedside story. He sighs.

"Anyway, I was up near Petaluma. There are some farmlands near the freeway up there and I like taking photos of landscapes. So, there was a flock of sheep in this field, just yards away from where I was parked, and they were all quietly going about their business, chewing on grass, occasionally looking up to see what's around. I call out one or two things to them. I like that line, 'bah ram yew'—you know, from that movie about the talking pig. Anyway, I see this one sheep sitting in the middle of the field, not eating. And it's seated or laying down in this strange position, on its stomach with its haunches raised, like it's waiting to take it up the ass."

At this point, Dan starts to splutter as he laughs through his own joke. So far, Weed is unmoved, though the next part forces a twitch on the right side of his mouth.

"So I look over to see the face on this sheep, and I swear to God, it's looking around with this bemused expression, like it's been abandoned in the middle of the act. It's looking behind, saying 'what the fuck? Where'd you go?' to its partner. Sure enough, about ten feet away, there's this other sheep, a larger one, shaking itself like it's just finished with some vigorous activity. But this other sheep…the look on its face—jeez, talk about abandonment." Dan's rolling giggle takes over, interspersed with trailing utterances, boorish imitations of the sheepish sound, "baaaar".

The impersonation is irritating, but otherwise Weed can't help himself. The conjuring of ovine facial expressions in the wake of sexual frustration triggers a short burst of laughter. Much more so than the remark about pimps, this is actually the funniest thing he's heard in ages. After several moments rambling about this, Dan's amusement eventually peters out. He rises again, collecting the empty bowl and plate, and motions towards the staircase. Weed, still amused by the fixed image of a sexually misused sheep, nonetheless feels the same twinge of anxiety he'd felt before when he thought Dan was about to leave.

"So, what's up? Are you coming back?" He asks, trying an indifferent voice. Dan turns, regards him with surprise.

"Do you want me to come back?"

Weed recovers a tempered defiance. "Like I said before, whatever you want, whatever you're gonna do, I just want it over with."

Dan tries the same look he gave the last time Weed said something like this. "That's all I wanted too," he says, staring into space.

"Okay," Weed says with an inflection meant to convey impatience.

"What makes you think it hasn't happened already?" Dan asks.

Weed barely registers the words before he feels his stomach drop; his feet instantly go cold. Calmly, he feels for sensations around his body: any feelings of soreness; evidence of penetration. With some relief, he feels nothing unusual, and then immediately stops his mind from considering explanations. Dan looks him up and down, stops his eyes on Weed's midriff.

"I know you were checking for smells earlier. Didn't you notice anything missing? Didn't you notice that I'd changed your diaper?"

14

Eric Pierce is bored and frustrated. After a night of deliberating, he's spent much of his Tuesday making phone calls, thinking some more, pacing about his hotel room, and then thinking he was wasting his time. Eric's last phone call to Doug Armstrong at Oakland police department hasn't been returned, despite his leaving a message several hours earlier. He considers circumventing Armstrong, who clearly thinks Pierce is a pest to whom he is not obliged to give information. When time stands still and nothing in particular is happening, Eric Pierce obsesses. He wonders what others might know, whether they are on the same trail as him, struggling with missing leads, the absence of clues. Are they following the same hunches, creating the same story as to what's happening beneath the story?

Eric is annoyed that he doesn't have the whole story. He knows Gagliano wasn't telling him something about the significance of Bryan Tecco, and felt sure that Ed Kim was withholding. That's the problem with detective work, private or otherwise: people don't always tell you what you need to know. Sometimes that's an important piece of historical background; maybe it's a more immediate context. He knows people in other professions experience this. He knows that doctors have to deal with patients who won't or can't explain all of their symptoms. He's well aware that lawyers and especially police must contend with clients and suspects who lie; who waste time with obfuscations. But do they have to think this about everyone? Do doctors, lawyers, and everyday cops have to concern themselves with their employers' world of corporate secrecy? Do they have to do their jobs knowing they are mere middlemen, pawns between warring parties; everyone guilty to some degree, of malfeasance?

He was given a simple directive: go find Bryan Tecco. He wasn't asked to figure out why this was important, though again, to most investigators this would seem to be crucial. He wasn't told what to do if he gets stuck, especially after just a day or so. Stop wasting time, he imagines hearing from higher levels, should he indulge curiosity. And he is curious: about the significance of the files stolen from the Emeryville lab; about who screwed up in making them so accessible to a guy who does game testing. Eric is curious about details, like why Sahi's human resource department doesn't have emergency contact information for Bryan Tecco. He'd understand if Tecco were a recent immigrant, or even an illegal one—there are plenty of those working for Sahi, unbeknownst to the public—or an independent contractor doing a temp job. But Tecco is or was a permanent employee, supposedly in good standing with his boss, and with no issues at work to speak of. Pierce did glean from the file that Tecco was hired quickly, partly because he held some kind of celebrity in the gaming world, but that shouldn't excuse not doing due diligence and getting proper background information. The celebrity factor might have been a blessing had it led to some bio material. But a Google search brought up little, only purchase sites for Tecco's book; one or two mentions of him in gaming articles.

Eric hears his phone ring and lets it go to voicemail. A text follows a minute later. This will be Gagliano asking after his progress, uninterested in anything whimsical. That means Eric will have nothing to tell him. Eric's boss is only interested in thinking if it translates into some manner of doing. So far, only phone calls fall thinly into that category, and the ones he thought most promising hadn't yielded results so far. Actually, it was the idea which he thought was promising, an idea attached to Eric's hunch that no one investigating this case, including Oakland police, had yet linked Tecco's disappearance to the whereabouts of Chris Leavitt; at least, not as far as he knows. However, the idea, which involved calling the over one hundred people in Oakland and Berkeley who were named Leavitt, wasn't getting him very far. In fact, given that about two-thirds of the fifty people called hadn't picked up or further identified themselves through their greetings, it instead seemed like the stupidest idea Eric has had in ages.

Just before the call, he gets a small break in the form of a call back from Richmond police department. He'd called earlier, thinking he might as well report Chris Leavitt as missing, since he was likely the person Armstrong termed "person of interest". Claiming to be Leavitt's landlord, Edgar Brinkley, Eric spoke to a flat-voiced officer who said she would enter the information into the missing persons data base, research what might come up with respect to Chris Leavitt, and get back to Eric if she had anything she could share. Now it was three hours later and the officer was calling back with some news, and sounding pleased with herself.

"Well, I can tell you that he's not missing," she says with a nasally inflection, "at least, not since the date you told me before."

"Can you tell me how you know that?"

There is a pause, during which the officer is likely reading notes off a computer screen.

"Actually, he was sighted on the date you estimated when we spoke previously—March 28th." The woman stops, though Eric can still hear the faint sound of clicking upon a keyboard.

"Have you got anything else? I mean, it's just that I've got an issue here with his unit. I'm into April here and he aint paid his rent." Eric notes his half-conscious slip into an urban twang, as if there's no other way he'd be a property manager in Richmond.

"Right," says the officer with a rote stab at empathy.

"Now, I know—"

"Seems like he got into an accident in Marin County. Says here his truck went into a body of water, got impounded the next day. But Mr. Leavitt was released, uninjured." More sounds of clicking. The officer now sounds intrigued, like she's reading ahead to finish the story, regardless of Eric's interest.

"Can you tell me whereabouts in Marin?" This should be Eric's last question.

"Bolinas Lagoon," the woman answers.

"Excuse me?" Eric's supposed brother-from-Richmond accent is gone.

"Bolinas," she repeats, and then she's done helping. "You should call Marin sheriff's department if want a more specific location."

Eric soon ends the call and immediately dials Dave Gagliano's number, knowing he's been waiting all this time. Eric feels better that he has something concrete to share: the name of a lead and a location in which that person was last spotted. In one sense, Eric doesn't really need to make this call. He already knows what his boss will say about a guy named Leavitt and an accident near a town called Bolinas. Without an urban twang or a nasally whine, Dave Gagliano will be querulous, but succinct: what are you wasting time for? Get out there and find him?

15

Before Dan Pritchard can even leave the room, Weed does. He leaves the room, his thoughts, even his body—especially his body. He doesn't like it anymore, not that he was ever enamored of his physical self. There was a spell, between ages eighteen to twenty one, when he thought he was not bad-looking. He was lean enough during those days, having somehow burned off some of the puppy fat that sat heavily upon his frame in his mid-teens. But that was a short window, those three years. Outside of that, Weed's body has always been troublesome: uncooperative with physical activity as a preteen; an embarrassment of pimply disarray by age fourteen; nothing to write home about during the best of times. At some point in his early twenties, his face became a jowly, misshapen lump. The weight of his jaw seemed to cause his mouth to slide downwards, yielding a surly bearing. The worst part: not knowing where it all came from. It wasn't as though pictures of forebears adorned his parents' home, manifesting the same features. There was no lineage for him to examine, no portent of the future for him to work against. But all of those episodes beat this. Right now is his bottom-out experience, his body-image nadir. Never before has he wanted a complete make-over, a cosmetic reconstruction that would render him unrecognizable, his body an object of anything but disgust.

As Dan Pritchard climbs the staircase to whatever lair that creature calls home, Weed closes his eyes, hoping that chosen blindness will keep him from disturbing images the same way it kept motion sickness at bay when he was younger. However, despite his best efforts, flash visions still come to him: of snatches of diaper alongside the sight of a hand peeling back layers of cotton. A pair of scissors comes into view for the severing of tape, and a reddened patch of skin is exposed, to which a wretched old man presses his cheek and smiles. Weed lets out a small cry, which dissolves into a coughing fit. It is pain mixed with fury and then saddled with futility. Thoughts of Chris offer moments of reprieve, but also disorientation, because it is the notion of diapers, linked as they have been with Chris' fanciful ideas that are currently teasing Weed's mind.

Humiliation. Weed knows the point is his humiliation; his utter debasement. Though he whispers aloud the question, "why", he knows why. Somehow, without thinking of specifics, the reasons why he'd be subjected to this, he knows this moment is supernaturally just. Now guilt is prevailing, a residue from rage, which for the time being is a spent force, draining him of energy and steering him again towards an escapist sleep. But there are thoughts and images still for him to ponder and endure. Visions of Chris persist, now like the scratchy, eight millimeter images that

Weed sees whenever Shadows appear. In these new visions, Chris is gaunt, emaciated; his skin peeling off him like that of lepers. He is scabby, addled and tweaking, and it was Weed who started him down this path. Not many think this, as far as he knows. Chris doesn't. Most of their mutual acquaintances don't. But Weed does. As for this guy Dan: he could see into Weed somehow, into his dark heart and its secrets, and use them to justify his own actions.

There is no doubt in Weed's mind that had he not taken Chris Leavitt to certain parties, not introduced him to certain connections, or waved the prospect of enhanced sexual performance amongst vast supplies of eager pussy, then Chris would not have become enticed into the methamphetamine lifestyle. He's sure that whatever inclinations Chris had, and whatever circumstances may have placed him in using circles at any other time, it was he—Bryan Tecco, aka Weed—who did the nodding, careless *go-for-it* approval when the off-white lines were laid out and the cut plastic straws were passed around. Weed knows there is no courtroom for such an offense as peer pressure. He knows that in the concrete realms of justice, he has plausible deniability. But in the courtroom of subdued and minority opinion, amongst the company of Chris' friend Sweet, or, in all likelihood, Chris' girlfriend, Weed is a Svengali of license, a Faustian evil.

It's wrong to mix business with pleasure. Stoking addiction is a habit; a mirror to others' habits and it stays that way as long as everyone involved remembers their roles, their habits, and don't let friendship get in the way. Meaning, it seemed a good idea to let Chris join all the parties, cut him loose, and not think of the other side of it: the contaminating friendship. He didn't see it. The problem with illusions is that they seem…they just seem. But they aren't. It's not as though Weed profited off Chris' habit, as tweak isn't or wasn't even Weed's most prominent drug to sell. Nor did he enjoy seeing Chris get so amped as often as he did, and he certainly didn't enjoy watching him chew his nails, become sketchy, or more unreliable with things like money and work; more weird. Maybe it was about power, he thinks dully—the sense that he could get Chris Leavitt to do just about anything, just because

Chris wanted so badly to be a friend. Everyone gets, or should get, their shot at being the coolest kid in class at some point, Weed reflects. For a hot minute he was enjoying his shot. Now he notices casualties. He didn't mean it, the harm. He feels...

The gurney feels newly warm like a couch, claustrophobic like a confession booth. Weed stares up at a grey, concrete ceiling, thinking that Dan is up there somewhere, musing over Weed's demonized psychology like some Hannibal Lecteresque analyst. Weed calls out, trying in earnest to summon him, though he hasn't fully formulated the reasons why. He has no pressing physical need at the present time. However, it's dark, he feels something akin to loneliness, and time is passing by so wantonly that it's losing meaning. What day is it? Weed wants to ask someone, anyone. What's the weather like? Did the Bay Bridge problem get solved? Did baseball season start yet, and does Dan think the Giants can win the World Series again? Whatever the company, or the circumstances, Weed craves normalcy, the grounding and continuity that comes with trite conversations. Who'd have thought that in the direst of situations he'd be this ordinary, this down to earth?

Footsteps have character. From above Weed hears a pair of feet pounding back and forth, coupled with the sound of another pair treading lighter. It sounds like a symphony of stomping amid tiptoeing. This generates some excitement as Weed makes a hopeful interpretation: there's someone else up there besides Dan. His trained reactions would inform caution and stiffen his movements. Ordinarily, he'd be unnerved by the plodding, angry-sounding footwork of an unknown intruder. But while most criminals have friends, co-conspirators, Weed hopes that another of his stereotypes proves true: that rapists roll solo, so the unexpected company promises disapprobation of Dan, and thereafter rescue. His fingers flinch. Recently dormant muscle memory: it's reaching for that firearm that went down with the truck. When was that? Weed wonders—must be something like a week ago now.

With a burst, the door atop the staircase flies open and light pours down into the room. As Weed raises his head he just about makes out the figure of a woman with shoulder-length, blond curly hair, clambering down the stairs. Her pace is reckless and her balance uncertain, as if she was also managing to escape the clutches of the villain. For a moment, Weed's hope is dampened as it seems as though she has been thrown into this dungeon, a temporary companion for him, but ultimately, much less a savior than a mere fellow prisoner. As she reaches the base of the stairs, she turns breathlessly and stares with seeming disbelief at Weed's captive body, still laying strapped to a gurney via an elaborate system of sheepskin-covered restraints. Weed looks into the woman's eyes and feels sorry for her, thinking it's just dawning upon her what Dan has in mind.

"Jesus Christ. Dad, get down here right now. Goddamnit!"

Weed thumps his head back down upon his pillow, relieved. Thank God, he thinks prematurely.

"I knew it," says Dan's apparent daughter under her breath. "I should've…ugh!" She starts pacing back and forth. She flails her arms, glares at Weed with an impersonal, malevolent air, as though he were less someone to save than something that her troublesome father has brought into the basement: look what the cat dragged in, and so on. Weed hears the now familiar creaking of the steps, and the bending iron. It's Dan tentatively descending the staircase, stopping at a point wherein his upper half—and especially his shamefaced face—remains concealed. He's muttering sheepish sounds like a teenager whose porn stash has been discovered—something to the effect that he hadn't anticipated his daughter's visit that day. She stretches out her arms, gesturing at his handiwork.

"Yeah, Dad, I figured. You don't usually leave your toys lying around upstairs like that."

Weed is no longer relieved, but rather afraid, not to mention re-horrified by the implications linked to the word "toys". The daughter seems unhinged, raving at her father, and as likely to set fire to the building and destroy all evidence, including Weed, as she is to set him free. Dan tries an admonishing reply, pointing out that it's unwise for her to reference him as her father, as that is information the young man might yet exploit. She shouts him down, gesturing again towards the body of her father's captive. A minute into a shrieking diatribe that will test the sound-proofing of which Dan previously boasted, she is yet to reference Weed as a human being. Weed, it seems, is a "choice", and a bad one at that. His presence represents poor impulse control, bad judgment; the fallout of unresolved "issues", lifelong shoddy social skills. Weed is a thing; a mess staining the household, the family name. He must be cleaned up, gotten rid of.

"Uh," Weed attempts.

The daughter's head spins as though shocked that the creature speaks.

"What's your name?" she asks, surprisingly.

"Bryan," he says, surprising himself.

She nods, but still conveys no warmth, no reassurance; only steely resolve to deal with this situation once she's organized it all in her mind.

"Well, Bryan, I'm sorry about this." Her lips tremble as though about to add something, but can't think what to say beyond her understated amends. There are things to promise, perhaps, but that may be a careless tact, and it's clear to Weed that his problem is far from over.

"I was done with him, anyway," Dan seems to say from the stairs. The sound of his voice is muffled by the barrier that decapitates him from Weed's view.

"Yeah, I bet," his daughter snaps back at him. She has a strident, speak-only-when-you're-spoken-to way about her. She's like a bossy third grade teacher, now in control of this situation, and for that reason alone, Weed decides that he likes her. It's just that she hasn't yet figured out what to do about all this. She's clearly conflicted: disgusted by her father's actions, ready to have him committed somewhere. But there's a primitive loyalty at play also; an Electra bond between father and daughter that is impermeable. Next, she softens and looks at her father's victim with a saddened face. Then her expression transforms even further into a foreboding look. She seems afraid now. What will happen if she releases the prisoner? What retributions await her father, or what is perhaps their shared property: will it be legal, the unfolding of this episode? Is the young captive dangerous? Vengeful?

"I think you're overreacting," Dan calls out to his daughter. He's still hiding his face. He sighs. "You're kind of like your mother in that way," he adds. He sounds like a weary yet reasonable parent of a delinquent teen. His daughter sneers, keeps an eye on Weed.

"Yeah, that's it. I'm overreacting. I come over because you haven't been answering my calls the last two days. I'm thinking you've not been watching your diet and your blood sugar's low and you're passed out somewhere. I get in the front door and I find your clothes scattered about upstairs. Then I find you walking around in your underwear and watching that disgusting video. Now this. I mean, do you know who he is? What if people are looking for him? What if you were seen dragging him in here?"

"It's been two days," Dan answers calmly, "I'd think if someone were suspicious they'd have reported it by now. I'd have cops knocking on the front door." Weed can just about see Dan's smug leer from where he lays. He's living vicariously through the daughter now; wants her to walk over to him and wipe the smile off his face. She does walk over. She strides halfway up the staircase and sticks her face right in his.

"Dad, this is serious. You can't keep doing this. You promised me. Look at him." She practically grabs his chin as she reaches out, touching his face and directing his gaze over to where Weed is laying prostrate, hoping this woman's desperation will pay dividends. "Poor guy," she says, now marching back to the gurney. She starts undoing the straps, beginning with those around the ankles. Weed gets excited, thinking freedom is imminent, though the first sensation is that of a thick recess in his skin being exposed. It's a deep trough that's been forged by the strap that's been tightened over him for days. Weed feels the lower half of his leg move, the hairs stand up. The pores up and down his lower half begin to breathe properly.

"I wouldn't do that if I were you," says Dan. Weed hears the iron bend and the wood creak as Dan takes another step down the staircase. He's at the base now, his face now fully visible. His expression is stern, unapologetic.

"You said you were done," the daughter replies in a mocking tone. Dan takes another step towards her.

Hurry up, thinks Weed. A second strap is released. She moves unhesitatingly towards a third that is wrapped around Weed's knee. He is nearly high with anticipation, as this next restraint has been pinching his hairs against his skin the whole time he's been captive. In fact, only in the last hour or so, ironically, has Weed learned to place this pain out of his mind.

Quick as a cat, Dan stretches out an arm and grabs his daughter's wrist, blocking her efforts to free Weed.

"Wait. We need to talk about this," he says.

"There's nothing to talk about." Weed wants to say something; something like "damn right", but for reasons that haven't quite congealed he thinks the better of it. He is quiet, docile like a child being argued over by squabbling parents. Perhaps he's bought into the idea of being a thing—an idea manifested by the psychotic captor, but not fully realized until spoken by his neurotic offspring. Regardless, it's a self censorship that's taken over for the moment—no one is gagging him any longer. He looks pleadingly at Dan's daughter, hoping to see that steely resolve from earlier; needing her to snatch her arm away, push the elder man to the ground, and continue undoing the straps.

The argument between them continues. As Dan forces the issue, his daughter decides there's much to talk about after all. So she lets him have it, and soon thereafter Weed hears a history lesson about Dan's problems. She alludes to his past drug problems, his tendency to fashion bizarre rationales when either relapsing or not cooperating with treatment programs he was once compelled to attend. Excuses: that's what seems to bother his daughter the most, plus the lying. They always say that, thinks

Weed: it's not so bad, except for the lying. The daughter harps on about excuses. The most egregious example occurred after he'd once failed a urinalysis test for something like the sixth consecutive time. Drug tests don't work for him, he said.

"This reminds me of your story about low calcium levels, saying they contaminated the results," his daughter recalls.

"You know, it doesn't help, just yelling at me," Dan grumbles.

"I'm not yelling. I'm being scathing. It's different."

Weed is smirking in the background, enjoying Dan's dressing down, though his daughter seems reckless and, in self-satisfied spurts, gratuitously insulting. Among other things, this exchange reminds him of his own experience of rehab, not to mention his own penchant for bullshitting loved ones followed by an endurance of their wounded vitriol. The daughter turns to Weed, whose straps she is continuing to untie, despite the pressure exerted by Dan's hold on her. "Where'd you find him anyway?" she asks. "He looks like one of the guys who work down at your shithole warehouse in Oakland." She's on a roll, speaking quickly and past Don's feeble interruptions. His lips move but his tongue flounders, stuck between his teeth as he stands helpless before the nearly hysterical woman. Weed notices the man's jaw tense; he follows what seems like a pulse racing down his arm, transmitting rage. Dan tightens his grip on his daughter's wrist.

She freezes.

"Ow, you're hurting me," she cries, and the untying of straps comes to a halt. Hormonally, she whimpers. The brash diatribe and liberating of Weed's limbs now seems like a false memory. His legs can move and stretch with a tantalizing kick, though a series of cramping spasms stalls their rebirth. Other sensations are unfettered: he feels the freedom of being able to curl his toes properly because he can arch his foot. He notes the pleasure of rolling his ankles, and the feeling of air popping between his joints. Still, it's a limited and therefore token liberty, this newfound litheness. He sees that several straps have been undone, but there are at least as many still untouched, still holding him down. With his waist, arms, chest and head all still pinned to the gurney, the freedom of his lower body feels moot and useless.

He watches as the daughter shrinks under the grip of her father, like a teenager restrained by an overbearing parent. Despairingly, Weed sees her face collapse in pain. She seems on the verge of concession, as if she were about to drop to her knees, or worse, ask Weed to move over so that she might join him on the bed; a victim. She shrieks, though moments later she recovers and tears herself away with an impressive burst of strength. The sight of this stirs excitement in Weed all over again. He feels a rush of blood and a renewed hope, like a sports fan sitting on the edge of his seat, exhilarated to see a hero climb back to her feet after a knockdown, ready to lunge at the bullying adversary. The daughter scrambles away from Dan and climbs the staircase, quickly outdistancing him. She's upstairs and gone from sight in seconds, yet despite the urgency of her escape, something in her movement tells Weed she'll be right back, hopefully armed with something that will put Dan in his place and force an end to this nightmare.

Dan looks like a clumsy ogre clutching at a dashing hare. He staggers over to the base of the staircase, at which point he gives up his chase. He looks up, staring into the light that is pouring down, and calls after his daughter plaintively. He looks frightened—a particular kind of frightened—like it's dawned upon him finally that he's just crossed a line, done something he shouldn't have done.

"Sweetie, I'm sorry. I didn't mean to…I mean, I shouldn't have—"

"Don't call me sweetie," Weed hears distantly. Dan stops and hangs his head. For a minute there is silence in the room. Weed watches Dan from his still entrapped position, eager to jeer him. Then the daughter returns. She stomps back down the stairs with the kind of swagger she'd exhibited when she first happened on the scene. The difference is in her right hand: a steel-grey handgun, now pointed at Dan and motioning for him to get out of her way.

He raises his arms, instinctively seeking the surrender position. As a last ditch effort, he affects that condescending, paternal tone again, saying, "okay, let's relax here a minute. You know you're not going to use that. I have this situation under control. If you'd just listen to me—"

"That's my problem, dad. I can't listen to you. It sickens me to listen to you. You don't have this situation under control, and you don't know what I might do with this. I don't care what rationale you had for picking up this guy. It's wrong. I know it's useless saying this to you because you don't care. But if you care about me, then you should know that I'm repulsed by you doing this stuff to innocent people."

"You think he's innocent?" Dan swiftly rebukes. The daughter brushes past him, unleashing a guttural protest.

"Ugh! Whatever," she utters, anticipating a stream of polemics that she's heard before. Dan again steps towards her, seemingly with intent to embrace. She raises her weapon.

"Touch me again and I'll knock you out."

Dan turns away, backs off.

She is back at the gurney, resuming her previously efficient release of Weed.

"Thank you," he says quietly; still obeying his self-imposed near gag order, even as he feels the last of the straps fall away. Now all of his limbs can move. He breathes in a way that feels different, fresh, and every part of his body seems to stretch in unison. Meanwhile, Dan looks on, directing at Weed and his daughter a skeptical, even contemptuous look.

"He's no innocent. I can guarantee that. He's broken the law, used people; stood by indifferently as others fall down in pain."

"Yeah, and how do you know that?" the daughter absently challenges, hurried and half-interested. "What're you? A mind reader? Did you run his fingerprints or something?" With one hand, she fumbles with the straps. With the other she holds her gun ambiguously between the two men, leaving Weed in two minds: his body is twitching, imploring him to run for the staircase, and thereafter to the front door, and to freedom. He figures the woman, much less Dan, wouldn't catch him if he ran. He'd count on her reluctance to gun him down.

"I just know. I have a gift: I understand people," Dan insists. "Look at him. Can't you tell? He's probably raped, or date-raped, ten times as many people as I have." Dan fixes Weed with a look that is unburdened, daring, and uncharacteristically *man-to-man*. Dan Pritchard is on the edge of something. He's pulling no punches, ready to say anything that comes to mind, and proving that an uncensored life is possible. He looks at his daughter. "All women, of course."

The daughter shakes her head. Her hands are also shaking as she holds her weapon.

"Get out of here," she commands, glaring at her father.

"You might—"

"I SAID GET OUT OF HERE, YOU SICK OLD MAN!"

With a last cold, yet ineffectual stare, Dan withdraws with his tail between his legs. As he plods up the staircase, he is mumbling his bitterness like a child whose favorite toy has been confiscated. He will go to bed without supper tonight, and certainly without a kiss.

Now this affair is just between Weed and the woman. He turns to her, smiles docilely, but then flattens his expression as he sees her position fixed, her gun still pointed at him, albeit shakily. Her job's not over and she refuses to smile back or become civil until this business is complete, and it will likely never be that way. Weed thinks to speak at last: to reassure the woman that he will not seek revenge, or to strike a bargain…whatever. Instinctively, his legs drift off the table, like he's about to vault off the gurney for the first time in—well—he's not sure how long.

"Shouldn't we be properly introduced?" he manages. That he's able to muster any kind of wit under the circumstances pleases him. The woman is unmoved.

"Stay there, and don't try to be cute. I'm not interested," she says. She looks around the room like she's seeing it for the first time: her father's dungeon of horrors. How many people has he brought down here? Weed can feel her thinking this. Otherwise, she's stuck, wondering what to do with this guy her father has picked up from somewhere—this possibly dangerous transient.

"Maybe we can talk. You don't know anything about me," Weed attempts.

"Shut up. I'm trying to think."

Weed shuts his mouth and sinks back into the gurney. He allows himself to pout, as now it's harder than ever to lay still, even with a firearm pointed at his chest. He lets thirty seconds pass while looking around the room. With his neck free to move properly, he can indulge his thoughts about his surroundings of the last day or so. He waits until remembering that unlike Dan, he does not feel like he has all the time in the world. His restraints gone, his mind now returns to the purpose he'd only just consolidated the previous weekend: his mission to find Chris Leavitt, recover the files stolen from Sahi corporation, and then…

Then what?

"Okay, here's what we're gonna do," says the daughter. Her body shifts. She takes a step to the right, as if her lengthy ruminations have dislodged her equilibrium, thus forcing her whole body to recalibrate. "We're gonna leave here, but on my terms." She steps over to what looks like a work desk that is situated behind the gurney. Previously, Weed hadn't been able to twist his head in order to see this piece of furniture, so it's a new vision for him. She performs a quick search of a top drawer while keeping an eye and her shaking, gun-holding hand pointed at Weed. He notes her pressured movements, sees the exhausted trembling of her grip upon the weapon. This is too much for her, Weed thinks. She won't be able to take too much more of this.

"Here, put this on." She's thrown at him a black towel, streaked with a substance that smells like oil. Weed returns a look: a you're-kidding kind of look.

"It has oil on it. It'll be toxic," he appeals.

"I'm sorry," she answers with forced and unconvincing sympathy.

Weed grimaces. Tentatively, he pulls the rag to his face and sniffs the acrid odor. As he holds the fabric across his closed eyes, he feels the damp of the liquid against his eyelid.

"It's gonna get in my eyes," he complains.

The woman seems to have thought of this.

"Then you'd better not open them," she retorts. She orders Weed to lay on his stomach and place his arms behind his back. She sits on top of him, which for a moment feels soft and pleasant, a bit like the sensation of a massage therapist poised to work on his back. But the comfort doesn't last long. Aggressively, she pulls his hands together, quickly whipping around them one of the sheepskin straps, pulled from the gurney. He'd have liked to see the handiwork, as he can now feel the gun against his ribs, sitting rigidly, as though it were being held firmly in place, despite the attention being given to the fastening of straps.

With the blindfold on and Weed's hands tied, the woman pulls him up and leads him away, presumably towards the staircase. He can make out no fixtures, only the light shining through the pinholes in the rag. He imagines what this will look like from a detached perspective. With further horror, he considers the associations traditionally made between objects like firearms and blindfolds. He slumps against the staircase, refusing to climb.

"Wait, what're you gonna do with me?" he asks, now sounding even more nervous than he was when he first woke up to find Dan's perverted face staring down at him. The woman prods Weed in the back, prompting him to move on, but he doesn't budge. He won't be led quietly to the firing squad, if that's what's happening. She hisses frustration through her teeth.

"Okay, here's the deal: I'm gonna get you out of here, let you go. But I'm going to take you away so that you can't see where this place is. If you cooperate and go quietly, then we don't have a problem. You can go back to wherever you came from and we need never see each other again. If you try to break free, know that I'm not afraid to use this, and later I'll say you were an intruder whom I shot in self defense."

Weed waits for a moment, making sure there's nothing more to the proposal.

"Okay," he says. "It's a deal."

The woman's not done.

"By the way, if you report this to the police, which I don't think you will—I think you're too street for that—I'll also claim we chased you away when we discovered you in our living room."

Weed can't help himself any longer. He's been compliant, even agreeable ever since this woman arrived on the scene, thinking, unlike before, that the path to freedom lay in making Dan, and perhaps this woman, think they were in charge, making all the right moves. It's a variation on an old prescription: be passive, wait patiently; shut your mouth, and above all, don't get mad. If he keeps this up, he'll nod, follow orders, and even offer praise for the ingenious escape plan. But there's an obvious flaw in this woman's plan, as well as a problem with Weed's acting abilities. Foolhardy or not, he feels compelled to dissent.

"Don't you think that will look strange? I mean, if I'm the one approaching the police, saying you took me hostage and assaulted me, won't they be inclined to believe me, at least enough to come around and investigate you and your father? And what will you say when they ask why you didn't report this supposed burglary? Would you want that? Would you want them checking this place out, scrutinizing your Dad?"

There's a long pause, during which Weed can feel the wheels turning in the woman's mind.

"I'll take the chance," she says in a low, cagey voice. Then she drops down to the level of Weed's slumped body, and speaks into his ear. Weed feels the hot, sensual air of her breath, and briefly imagines her tongue caressing his lobe. Aroused, he relaxes as she calls his bluff: "I'm guessing you won't gamble making a complaint. I think you don't do things like approaching police. Mostly, I'm guessing you are exactly what my father says you are."

16

Eric Pierce isn't sure which activity is the more tedious, driving or making phone calls. Either way, the best way to counteract their dulling effects is to do them both at the same time. Multi-tasking: he'd been doing it as long as he could remember, as early as second grade, wherein he remembers building Leggo castles with his peers and winning at Jenga simultaneously. In grade school, he did his best thinking on the basketball court, shooting hoops by himself. At sixteen, philosophical insights coincided with his fledgling efforts at martial arts. Aikido came first: all that pushing people away. In college, he'd be on the internet, in chat rooms, one-half interacting with vapid coeds, one-half reading his administration of justice textbooks, and—multitasking researchers be damned—be thriving in all areas.

With his I-pad plugged into his dash, he tries narrowing his search for Chris Leavitt, utilizing pieces of information peevishly given by Edgar Brinkley. Fortunately for Eric, the landlord's antipathy towards his tenants was easily exploited, thus yielding some useful facts: Leavitt is or was a kind of nurse, working at a hospital in Oakland, he'd said. Before Tuesday, Brinkley hadn't known which one, but one of the neighbors told police that it was Alta McMahon, near Piedmont at the base of the hills. Brinkley himself remembers that Leavitt was originally from the hills, as in born there, though he hedged his bets twice when asked by Pierce to specify. First he said Oakland. Then he changed it to Berkeley. Brinkley snarled like it didn't matter to him—they're all rich white people, regardless. Strange, but he knew less about Bryan Tecco.

Didn't know about Sahi corporation; didn't know about his living in West Marin. Nothing. Bryan Tecco, it seems, is better at keeping secrets.

Pierce keeps plugging in the name and hitting search. High school records, college, workplace details: he's looking for anything that creates a match and gives a number, hopefully an address. Meanwhile, he keeps an intermittently glancing eye on the road that is heading over the Richmond and San Rafael Bridge, out towards Marin County. On his satellite map, Bolinas and its nearby bodies of water are shown to be on the cusp of the ocean, a good two, possibly three hours away. From dim memories of a childhood camping trip out near Point Reyes, Eric conjures images of shadowy, redwood-phalanxed roads dropping down into watersheds that seem to stretch unnaturally beyond where they should end.

Meanwhile, he settles into another task, that of piecing together the puzzle that is Bryan Tecco's whereabouts, his reasons for stealing game files from a workplace that until this incident had afforded him stable employment. He opens up another window, types in the word "Bolinas", and checks to see what commercial establishments exist; what places, like bars, or hotels, might be open, with staff able to answer questions about an auto accident of the previous week. It's getting late—dark now as it nears eight at night. Where might he stay if this hastily-arranged trip doesn't bring quick answers? It's a long way to go just to answer a couple of basic questions: had anyone seen a guy matching Tecco's description around about March 28th? Was there reason to believe he was still alive, harboring Sahi's precious product? Or had he passed it off to this guy Leavitt, his unwitting and unknown partner in recreational drug use, or—as Edgar Brinkley would have it—psychotic fantasy mixed with petty dope dealing.

It was a long way to go, indeed. But Eric Pierce doesn't mind going extra lengths to find things that others don't know exist. He sort of likes this plan of drifting towards the Pacific horizon in search of missing clues. He figures that Oakland police department have done a cursory job looking for this guy, not to mention investigating this whole situation. They don't have much to go on: just a complaint about a disappearance, and the testimony of a disgruntled landlord. They don't seem to have sought witnesses to this accident that happened in Bolinas. There's no indication that foul play is being considered. No one seems to have determined if Chris Leavitt was alone at the time of his truck's disappearance, which also hasn't been explained. There's no explanation as to why it happened, or whether there was a chase of some kind, a second vehicle, or more, involved.

Eric Pierce hopes to get some or all of this information on his trip to Bolinas, and then report to Dave Gagliano that he knows something the police don't know, and that Sahi can use. He hopes there will be a reward in all of this for him—not of money, necessarily—but of more information, more inclusion into the company's inner circle. In his recent performance review with Gagliano, Eric got the distinct impression that should he prove instrumental in another assignment, then advancement to a mid-level supervisor position would be a real possibility. Eric doesn't know what's contained in the files stolen by Bryan Tecco. He noted Ed Kim's reticence about their significance also. But if Eric can find those files, or at least detain the guy that stole them, especially given the thin set of facts he'd started with, then Sahi's business park offices, those top floors where the air is rarified and thick with knowledge, will open up for him.

After an hour of driving over winding roads, he begins to wonder if he'll ever reach his destination. It's not even that it's taking longer than he'd expected. Instead, it's that the road's sinewy paths feel like a tease, as though he were being sucked into the world's dead end, to chase clues that are either meaningless, or else red herrings, or simply that which is already known by the likes of Doug Armstrong back in Oakland. It's a cul-de-sac, he fears, as he passes one especially long stretch of redwood-overlooked road, thinking the next turn will be decisive, his arrival in Bolinas Village. The further he goes, the further he drifts from his previously edgy excitement; the more he languishes in dread, clutching at his Suburu's steering wheel yet feeling as though it were driving him versus the other way around.

"Snap out of it," he barks at himself. Finally, he finds himself on a road that is adjacent to what looks like a river. Off to the right, he blinkingly sees another road that looks too long and open to be a driveway, yet it is unidentified. A consolation is his fast brewing idea that West Marin is Bryan Tecco's current whereabouts, his perfect hideout. This must be that turn that was referenced in one of the pages of the Bolinas visitor website. For a half minute Eric idles in the middle of the highway, looking back and forth between this unidentified road and the misty horizon ahead. He gazes at the appearance of a gap leading to vastness. He hears the dim sound of ocean. Tentatively, he edges forward, thinking that if he's taken the wrong turn, he won't lose too much time. His satellite is telling him he's running out of land. If he's not heading towards Bolinas, then it's Stinson Beach that will greet him instead.

Over the next mile, he sees the odd house nestled here and there in the hills, and a ranch with a sunroof framed with a peace symbol that's at least ten feet wide. Eric knows he's in the right place, having done his research on the village flavor. Up ahead should be a few lights, and beyond that, more signs of life. Most importantly, he should see at the end of the main street a two-story building that looks like it's leftover from the gold rush. Smileys, the local bar is likely the only place open for business and Eric's queries at this hour. He doesn't mind the lack of options. If anything, his task is made simpler—in fact, uniquely simple—by the modest needs of the locals. If Leavitt and Tecco came out here on March 28th, and it's likely they did so at night, then Smiley's is the only public place that might offer human contact to someone who'd just left the scene of an accident.

Eric Pierce doesn't go to bars, much less saloons. Back home, in Sacramento, his routine is fairly rigid: up at six, he heads to the gym. Then it's off to work and an eight or nine hour day, followed by another spell at a gym, usually for his Krav Maga class. Office bound investigation of cyber theft dominates his workdays, interspersed with occasional field activities such as this, though with much less intrigue. While others leave for drinks between five and six, and even make cursory invitations in Eric's direction, he typically begs off. Even when it's a lunchtime date with his boss Gagliano and one of his associates, Pierce shuffles in the seats of stylish restaurants, feeling restless. He dawdles over the best salads and filet mignons, and banters awkwardly with managerial company. Their lewd, sexist jokes are met with his thin, forced smiles. Eric's lack of humor will be a major obstacle for him, his superiors think privately.

He exits his Suburu having pulled into a space not obviously allocated to vehicles, but rather motorcycles; formerly horses, he imagines. Eric tugs at his tie and looks shiftily around him. In the shadows by a building that looks like a derelict theater, he sees hirsute figures loitering on a deck. The cherries of cigarettes illuminate lips and the lengthy, straggling hairs sprouting out of nostrils. This is a clean yet unkempt village, Eric observes. The ambience of Bolinas is vaguely nineteenth century, back roads, and secretive. From the interior of the saloon there is a buzz of sound and an orange light shining through the windows and doorway. A man with a bent hip stands at the entrance, his bullet-hole shining eyes piercing through the dark, staring at the man in a mint grey business suit who is striding towards him.

"Excuse me," Eric says, edging past. He looks downcast, embarrassed to be seen. Looking around, seeing t-shirts, Stetsons, plaid cotton shirts and a ubiquity of denim, some of which has been produced locally, he feels warm and tense, knowing his clean cut hairlessness doesn't fit in. The temperature of the room is balmy; a whiff of sweat fills the space, blended with light beer odors, the outdoor tobacco smoke drifting in. The crack of pool balls hitting one another sounds out while a waitress snakes her way between customers, collecting heavy glasses, dodging men with thick waists and broad shoulders, and shimmying back behind a twenty foot long bar. Eric steps on the rail, coughs, and as he catches sight of his misplaced self in a mirror beside a liquor rack, he motions for the bartender's attention. A burly man with a receding hairline but a forested pair of forearms, as though someone had gotten a transplant operation horribly wrong, gives Eric an opaque look but then continues his business. The waitress approaches him, readying another plunge onto the floor. As she lifts a partition that separates the bar from the customers, Eric raises a finger and feebly asks for her time. Obligingly, she smiles, but holds up her own hand, signifying that Eric must wait.

"I'm sorry," he manages as she whisks away.

"What's up, boss?" says a voice now behind him. Eric spins back around to see the burly figure standing inches from his face, wiping the brass of the rail with a cloth and waiting not-so-patiently for an order. Eric falters, stuttering a request to speak to someone who might have worked the bar a week earlier. His question is too long, too equivocal, and the bartender squints at him unsympathetically, losing interest when Eric stops mid-sentence to retrace his thoughts, reconfigure his words and start again. Then he is interrupted as someone known to the bartender and customers passes behind Eric and greets two or three people seated at the bar, each of whom turn and heartily, not to mention loudly, return the greeting. Eric raises his voice at the bartender.

"Were you working here last Wednesday or Thursday?" he manages, turning heads at the pool table that is some twenty feet away.

"Maybe," the bartender says cagily. "You want something?"

Eric regards the man's dull expression and quickly decides that a double meaning is not intended. Proprietarily, he orders Pale Ale and persists. Eric reaches out, grazes the man's arm and fixes him with a hard yet pleading look.

"Seriously, can we talk?"

The man pauses, says nothing as he indiscreetly looks Eric up and down.

"Two minutes," Eric says, motioning outside. The bartender flops down his cloth begrudgingly.

"Gina," he calls out. He flicks his chin, which appears to summon her to the bar. Then he lifts the partition and steps out, still saying nothing and assuming the man in the mint suit is following him.

Surprisingly, that small-town taciturnity ends shortly thereafter. Offering an HR file photograph of Bryan Tecco, Eric Pierce repeats his question from earlier, wanting to know if the bartender or, to his knowledge, anyone else either working at or visiting the bar may have seen the man in the photograph. As the man scrutinizes the picture, Eric adds that the person he's looking for may have been involved in the auto accident at the nearby lagoon, which also may have captured local attention. The bartender nods and returns the photo to Eric's hand after having looked at it for about a half second.

"Sure, I remember him. He used to live here."

Eric stifles a sigh.

"Yeah, okay. But did you see him here recently; last Wednesday or Thursday, for instance—that's when the accident occurred." As he says "accident", Eric considers that he doesn't like the precipitate use of the word. After all, this investigation is just beginning.

The man shakes his head. "Nah, I aint seen him here for ages. He's a pothead, bro—used to go by a nickname, 'Weed'. He's a dealer, too, not that that's unique around here."

"Uh-huh." Eric slips the photo back into his pocket, turns to look around the bar at Bolinas' hairy natives. The bartender checks out Eric again: the thin, tidy hair and clean shaven jaw-line; the dry-cleaned suit.

"He owes you money or something?" the man asks.

"Sort of," Eric replies, now the reticent one in the exchange. The man looks past his shoulder.

"Hey Steve, you're always here on a Wednesday. Did you hear about an accident in the lagoon? Anything weird happen in here that night?"

A man standing by the entrance, chatting with the bullet-eyed man with the rose tattoo, issues a sharp guffaw.

"Fuck yeah," says the man, "some guy who looked like he'd just been for a swim and dried himself with seaweed came walking through the bar, and then holed up in the men's until Mike went in and threw him out."

Eric turns around to face the man at the entrance. He quickly retrieves the photo from his pocket, walks up and presses it close to the man's face, making sure the image can be seen amid the burning light.

"Is this him?" Eric demands, just this side of politely.

The man frowns as he studies the picture. He seems unsure.

"Sure, that's him," he nonetheless says.

"Are you sure?"

"Yeah, it's just…"

"What?"

The man scratches his head. "I don't know. I remember he came in, looking like a wet seal and everything. But he said nothing about an accident, and we heard the next day that the sheriff's department pulled a truck from the lagoon, but had taken the driver to the medical center in Point Reyes Station the night before. It doesn't add up."

Eric Pierce gazes past the man's shoulder, towards the street beyond the light of the entrance. He is thinking.

"Maybe you can talk to Mike in the morning," says the bartender uncaringly. He moves away, heading back to his place behind the bar. "He gets in around ten," he calls out. "Sounds like he was here and dealt with the guy," he adds. The other man shrugs and aims at the bartender a further comment, as if the two of them were the invested party now.

"Like I said, it doesn't add up," the second man repeats. He catches Eric's eye with an expectant glance. Eric taps the photo against his hand, and then places it back in his dark suited, unindigenous pocket.

"Because it wasn't the same guy," he states in quiet triumph. He then strides out of the bar, feeling done with his singular task in Bolinas.

17

Weed can't see anything but dots of light, but he can smell old metal, rust, more oil. He's in a garage, feeling cold, sensing the hour is early morning, and listening to the distinctive sound of a heavy aluminum door being raised. The woman has him standing freely, clothed from the waist down, in the underpants and socks given him by Rosco. Getting jeans on him is a grudging, belabored trial for Dan's daughter; a mixture of naughty pleasure and indignity for Weed. Afterwards, after lowering his head like a trained cop, seating him on the passenger side of a vehicle that feels different from Dan's, she tosses his shirt on his lap. The vehicle feels low, too low to be a truck, Weed thinks. The woman issues a heavy breath, suggesting her burden and Weed's good fortune. He should be grateful, she's saying. She's making him comfortable, giving him a ride and letting him go. As for the shirt, he can put that on himself, later. Weed asks after his wallet, thinking mostly about the money that will come in handy once he's free. She sighs like she's being put out, as if Weed is a noisome child, nagging her with trivialities while she has other, more important things on her mind.

She drops the wallet on top of the shirt, assuring him with attitude that she's taken nothing; that her father took nothing. They're above petty theft, she insinuates; above Weed, generally speaking. He feels an urge to set the record straight. As she fusses about the car, fixing Weed's seatbelt, perhaps contemplating the best way to go about driving a vehicle while holding a gun at a semi-restrained passenger, he thinks to disabuse her of one or two fears. He's also ready to move on from this incident. Right now, and maybe well into the future, he's got no interest in punishing

Dan Pritchard's lechery. He wants to forget this ever happened, much less talk about it. Besides, he's also got other, more important things to think about also. He opens his mouth, prepared to make the statement that will convince this fretful, dangerous woman that he is no threat to her or her father. But he can't. Preempting him, she sticks a ball of not-so-oily cloth in his mouth, stilling his tongue. For what she needs to do now, she wants no distractions.

Or she wants no dialogue. Ten minutes into a drive in which the car's speed doesn't rise above thirty, the woman resumes a lesson about her father. She speaks slowly, and sounds calm, as though the situation—her situation—is under control and she can relax finally. There's one last major thing to do before releasing the prisoner: indulge her own need to convert minds and defend her father's image. She tells Weed about Dan's torture in Vietnam, which he already knows, and explains that due to social taboos, Dan didn't receive the care he needed after the war for his trauma as a torture victim, and certainly not for his experience of institutionalized homophobia. Then she tells Weed something he hadn't heard: that Dan had continued his military service well after the Vietnam conflict had ended and that he'd spent years working with special units in Central America in the eighties. Those units worked in conjunction with CIA operatives when interrogating prisoners, thus placing Dan on the other side of an already perplexing divide. The interrogations were less crude than those which had victimized him. They were less nakedly sadistic, yet more cunning and calculated. After consulting with lawyers, who specialized in definitions of "torture" drawn from international law, operatives devised specialized techniques that exploited grey areas. Gratuitously, Dan's loyal daughter cites examples; most notably, her father's role in forcing detainees into awkward seated positions—not torturous positions per se—but definitely uncomfortable, and more importantly, difficult to prosecute as instances of mistreatment.

Ordinarily, Weed might have been sympathetic with a guy like Dan Pritchard. In fact, were he not dealing with a soiled cloth stuck in his mouth, fighting back nausea, persistent chills and chomping on the bit to run free, he might have found himself nodding flawlessly, listening with a reasonably open heart to Dan's biography. After all, there are aspects to the story that stir his interest. Dan seemed not only alone, but quieted and chronically alien: a man unwanted for decades, perhaps his entire life. So, despite the kidnapping, the disgust with which he envisions Dan's molestation of him, and despite the circumstances which now leave him much further adrift of his destination than he'd ever imagined he'd be, Weed finds himself calming as the drive continues. Feelings of peace and fatigue blur, and all feelings within him are softening.

The vehicle stops abruptly. The driver's side door opens and the woman climbs out, allowing cool, distinctively morning air to rush in, further chilling the upper half of Weed's body, which remains bare. He listens intently for sounds, noting creaks in the chassis, the squeaking of leather seats and the crunching of a lock being released. This is an old car, he deduces. The aggregate of noises suggests something oversized and seventies-like—an Oldsmobile, maybe, or a Chevy, circa 1975, like the first car he remembers his dad buying. Weed takes a moment to reflect on the lesson in sound he's been receiving over the last few days. This education will yield further dividends at some point. All this interpretation of ambience: it'll come in handy if trapped again, or in hiding. Hope. He notices now that freedom is near the tendency to think positive; to look forward to the future and give all experience an optimistic spin.

"Okay, you can get out now," the woman says in a weary voice. Though barely cordial, it's the first time Weed feels properly invited to do something rather than directed to it. The feeling doesn't last long, as moments later he is pushed down to his knees and then told to lay down, his face touching what feels like mud speckled with grass. It's a cold morning indeed, with dew streaking the ground and flirting on the edge of a frost-like existence. The woman places a foot firmly on Weed's lower back, holding him still and pushing his nose into a soft, giving surface.

He grunts as she tugs at the straps holding his hands together. Meanwhile, though he can't see the gun, or feel its metal pressed against his back, he can sense its presence, hovering over him, aimed at his head. The woman's untying is now frantic and tearing of the sheepskin fabric. She is losing patience as she nears the end of what is, after all, their shared ordeal. Weed figures she's taken him to some remote location to drop him off, which will prove inconvenient when his thoughts return fully to the matter of his journey. Regardless, she is distracted as she goes about her business: compulsively looking up and around to see if there's anyone around to witness the incriminating scene.

It's time for last words.

"Now, remember what I said," the woman gasps. "You go to the cops—even if you find us—you remember what we'll say."

Though tempted to argue, because some part of him can't help himself, Weed censors his reply upon feeling the cloth being tugged free from his mouth.

"No problem. You don't remember me. I don't remember you."

He waits, thinking the release of his blindfold is moments away. But first, there are more preparations. Weed remains prostrate on the ground but turns his head left and right. It's a habit, this belief that he has fewer obstacles than is actually true. The woman is back by the car, some feet away. He hears the sound of a door opening, and another faint sound, possibly that of a leather seat being depressed by a driver. Immediately, Weed panics.

"What about my straps? They aren't loose yet."

"Hold on," the woman calls out, irritated. "The knot's tight. I'll release it in a second."

Weed starts to wriggle, not trusting the woman's words. *Release it in a second?* What's the problem, he anxiously wonders. She turns over the engine of the car.

"HEY! DON'T LEAVE ME HERE." Terrified, Weed feels his jaw slacken; his lips quiver and his eyes water. He is about to convulse, reach out to her and beg; learn her name. The car: it's about to speed away while his hands remain tied, his vision still occluded, and as his skin is shivering. At that moment, he hears and feels simultaneously the stomping footsteps of the woman running towards him. He braces, thinking he's about to get a kick in the gut, possibly a strike to the head from her firearm. He grimaces and contracts his body, pulling his knees up to protect his midsection, his groin. Unwittingly, he pins his tied hands behind his back but touching the ground, difficult to reach from above. He feels the woman's arm reaching over him, nearly groping his lower back to reach the supposedly recalcitrant strap. With a quick, pre-planned swipe, she tugs at a loose strand of sheepskin, releasing the knot with a fierce snap. Weed's hands spring apart, after which his arms flail behind him, limbs suffering from amnesia, dangling half numb about his body.

"Stay down," the woman commands. Weed, now habituated to compliance, remains still, though he hears again the sound of running footsteps—the woman's apparent flight. Half realizing what's happening, Weed allows his legs to move. He sits up and feels the sensation of being upright. He rolls his neck, attempting to work out an ache that has been bothering him for hours. The next sound he hears is that of tires screeching. Startled, as if awakened by an alarm clock, Weed reaches up and pulls at the blindfold wrapped around his head. It is too tight and therefore resists being stretched, either above his forehead or below his chin. With his fingers regaining feeling, he reaches behind his head and fumbles with the cruder knot that is holding the blindfold together. As he attempts a nimbleness that for several moments will elude him, Weed swears bitterly, observing the cruelty of someone or thing that would dare foil him now. As he finishes the blindfold falls away and Weed sees a blurred, grey vehicle in the distance performing a clumsy half-doughnut and then thrusting forward along a dirt road. He looks around, takes in a largely barren landscape with pockets of trees hundreds of yards away, and beyond them, a set of homes rising up a hill. He looks back to the car, half-caring about its identity, both personal and generic. The car is too far away now. There's no way for him to make out the manufacturer, much less a license plate. It's an eight-cylindered, gas-guzzling seventies car alright, but there's no telling if it's a Chevy or an Oldsmobile.

18

It's a slovenly, patient walk that Weed makes along a dirt road, through a light bank of fog that will have aided the woman's dumping of him. With his hands free and his eyesight reclaimed, he is able to clothe himself with the shirt the woman has kindly—if kindness even applies—returned to him. A further gift appears in the form of his wallet, similar dropped, like the shirt, in a space of grass and mud decorated by the thread of a fast-escaping tire. Weed sees the beaten, five-inch wide leather item as he wipes himself down. Before this, he'd started walking already, not so much forgetting about his wallet as resigning himself to its absence. Its return to him is like a farewell card—a gesture signifying, perhaps, that his last anonymous kidnapper is a woman of her word: that she'd give him back his means and his identity, gambling that in return Weed would not pursue the disclosure of hers.

To Weed's pleasant surprise, he finds himself amongst civilization within about five or ten minutes. A hundred yards or so down the dirt road, a highway takes over, with what looks like a freeway and the lights of dawn-hour commuters speeding by. The thought of hitchhiking comes to him briefly, but is soon rejected in light of recent events. Instead he thinks of buses, or even taxis, either of which he should have considered much earlier, despite the pedestrian-glorifying mini-culture that is Bolinas. The problem is access. On this seemingly rural passage, with a residential area in sight, but only odd commercial properties—industrial sites— nearby, it's not clear how he might get started. He walks over to the other side of the highway, towards a building with a front door and what looks like a waiting area behind a full-length transparency.

There's no one home or at work yet. Gauging the level of light via the time of year, Weed figures it's somewhere between six and seven o'clock. He thinks, and hopes, that it's a weekday still, such that the gathering numbers of cars passing by on the highway are indeed commuters and not weekend early birds. He hopes that whatever poor, drudgery enduring soul works in this office shows up soon. While preparing to be as personable as he can possibly be, Weed further hopes that whoever works here is sufficiently moved by the needs of an abandoned transient; that he offers Weed a coffee, maybe a snack and, further persuaded by the return offer of a few dollars, allows use of the company phone to secure a taxi or else find the nearest bus-line.

Weed huddles by the front door of the business, holding his knees close to his chest which feels like the most vulnerable part of him. His teeth chatter as he waits, burying his nose into a soft layer of skin just above his wrist. Thoughts of images upon pamphlets designed to promote teen runaway programs come to him. In them he'd often see these hackneyed depictions of down and out youth, crouched along sidewalks, their heads down, staring at their laps, just as he is now. He wraps the t-shirt over his arms, looking to increase his warmth, but he can't prevent the morning chill from penetrating his thin cotton tent. Meanwhile, the pavement feels especially hard on his tailbone, and to his right, alongside a chain-link fence containing an area where some lumber is being kept, there is the smell of a dog's recent business.

A stroke of luck occurs within another quarter hour. The sound of the vehicle pulling into the parking space in front of the business carries with it the languid authority of a police squad car. Weed pops his head outside of his shirt to see who's arrived, friend or not. He sees a white pick-up truck—a Dodge—with a driver who appears to be waiting soldierly, leaning to his right as he collects his belongings for the day. He steps out, regards Weed with a stolid, inconvenienced look, and then closes his truck's door. Weed raises his hand and gives a sheepish wave.

"Hey," he greets without imagination—so much for being personable.

"Hey," the man predictably replies. He steps forward and wipes a swath of dirty blond hair from a pair of clear blue eyes. Around them is the faint evidence of a wrap-around bruise, and adjacent to his right eyebrow is a half-inch wide cut. Weed can tell this guy wants to walk right by him, step into his office, go about his work day, and if possible, pretend this transient isn't trying to sleep on his doorstep. The man stops at the front door, gives Weed another dull look, and then pulls out a pair of keys. He has no idea what to say to Weed, and minimal interest in figuring that problem out.

"Listen, not to be a pain, but any chance I can use a phone, or—I don't know—get a snack or something. I've got money." The man shakes his head almost imperceptibly, like he can't bring himself to make a proper, full-bodied refusal. He opens the door and quickly enters, pulling the door behind him. Weed is tempted to stick his foot in the space so as to try and bully his way in. Only at the last instant does he think the better of it. Instead, he raises his voice: "How about directions then?" he says through the glass. He raises a fist and knocks insistently on the door. "Hey, come on. Give me a break. Please." Inside, the man is already turning on lights, setting down his stuff, turning off an alarm; going about his routine as Weed repeats his appeal every few seconds. Soon the man comes to the door, again with his keys but now with the bearing of someone simply opening up for the day's first customer.

"What do you want, bro?" he asks, as though not having heard any of the previous requests. *Bro.* Precipitately, Weed feels an advantage, thinking that he's in his element with such vernacular. Man charm: a terse yet comradely manner is all he'll really need here. He sees before him a desolate-faced tweenie, a guy just woken up from a night of sleep apnea and who looks as made up for customer contact as someone about to have a mug shot taken. He is correspondingly unfriendly: "I haven't got any food. This aint a 7-Eleven," the man says.

"Fine. Can you just give me some directions at least? Where the hell am I, anyway?"

"Jesus," the man utters. He's about to close the door in Weed's face again.

"Okay, directions to a bus line, maybe? Or tell me where that freeway is headed."

"That's not a freeway. It's highway 131." The man sticks his arm out of the door and deigns to wave it to Weed's left. "You take this road and it turns left onto Tiburon Boulevard. About a half mile down the street is when you'll see the first bus stop."

"Tiburon?" Weed says, sounding lost.

"Yeah," the man says, looking Weed up and down like he's an annoying tourist. Weed stutters.

"Okay...so, where—I mean—how to I? Where does Tiburon Boulevard go to?"

"Where you going?" the man asks, now being useful though still seeming uninterested.

"Uh, San Francisco." Weed is guessing.

"Then it's easy. The bus goes down to the Ferry depot. But it's rush hour, so..." The man shrugs. His attitude has softened.

Weed begins walking again, this time with renewed purpose; a sense of direction if not time. As he hits the road toward the highway, he realizes he'd forgotten to ask what day it is, and thinks twice about rushing back the near one hundred yards just to ask that one reality-consolidating question. On the highway, he's able to view Tiburon all around him. That tiny commercial hamlet would appear to have been an aberration, for now all he can see is homes—affluent homes—shrouded amongst trees, covering the hillsides in the distance and the stretch of road before him. After a few minutes wait at a bus stop peopled by two others, he hops on something called a Golden Gate line and settles down for a short ride. Another stoical working man, the driver, gives him a reflexive nod as Weed asks if the bus will indeed take him down to where the Ferry leaves. Outside, the sun has not only risen, it is warming the bus' interior, soothing the chills that Weed by now takes for granted.

It's all easy now. The bus, the sunlight, the surroundings, all seem to convey a message about how he ought to have kept things simple, used good old fashioned public transportation in the first place. Having dished out a bill for a ticket, he takes time to inspect the contents of his wallet. He looks to confirm, just for the sake of believing in good fortune, that neither Dan nor his fulminating daughter had taken any of his money. In the second pocket he sees familiar items alongside his journeyed wad of notes, including his driver's license and an ATM card. For all he knows, they might have used it; maybe figured out a way, though he doesn't think so. In between the two pieces of plastic is a note on a white piece of paper. It looks clean and dry, like it hasn't been swimming in Bolinas Lagoon recently. Intrigued, Weed opens it up and reads:

"Just so you know, my dad says he didn't kiss or penetrate you. Says you're sick, though not in the way he was talking about earlier. He didn't want to come down with something. For what it's worth, I believe him. By the way, my name's Wendy."

COMEBACK

19

The first Thursday in April is only hours old at the Oakland police department, jail division. Some officers, like Doug Armstrong, senior detective in charge of missing persons, have gone home for the night. Others, like his assistant, Angela Boyd, are still downtown, having taken an hour nap after a testy exchange with Marin Sheriff's department. It's seems their willingness to search Bolinas Lagoon for the body of Bryan Tecco following an auto accident on March 28th is limited. Nothing's gonna happen until daybreak, the Sheriff insisted the night before. He's got two guys in his department qualified to dive, he said. Budget cuts. It'll happen when it happens, he added tautologically. Boyd rebutted that there was a time issue: they've got a twelve hour hold on Chris Leavitt, who is yet to be formally charged with anything. They took him in around seven the previous evening; started the clock around eight. Whatever gets found, they'll need it before working hours begin, or else OPD will have to let him go. Again. She's wide awake now, looking up at the clock and waiting on some news. It's only five o'clock.

Asleep in a neighboring interview room, Chris Leavitt is slumped in a chair fit for a grade school classroom, his mouth hanging open. He dreams about his job, which he has just about thrown away through his supposedly bad attitude. For all his complaining about working in hospitals, or working in any kind of system for that matter, he mostly liked his work as a surgical assistant. He liked the organizational tasks of the job: the routine of setting up instruments for procedures, of being in charge of a surgery theater set-up; of making everything neat and perfectly organized—at least until doctors arrived and did their own thing. He'll miss it, he thinks—the routine, not the doctors. In his dream, the instruments are moving, defying his authority, not keeping in line. It's like they don't trust him, as if they know his way is not the right way, or the established way. Chris murmurs in his sleep. His body twitches in subconscious rebellion. When even inanimate objects are not cooperating, Chris Leavitt knows he's losing control.

Angela Boyd, the deputy investigator in the case of Bryan Tecco, peers through the glass window that looks onto Chris' dozing, vacant face; a skinny, tall body that's covered by a blanket gently placed on him by the attending officer. He looks so—she is about to think *innocent*. He reminds her of her six year old nephew, a sweet-natured boy prone to spasmodic and horrible tantrums that are terrorizing the first grade and fast aging his thirty something parents. No one's quite sure what's wrong with the child. Attention deficit is one diagnosis; reactive attachment disorder, or Asperger's syndrome, are the other labels. "On the spectrum" is the umbrella phrase used to describe a range of afflictions while obscuring an uncomfortable truth: no one knows what to do. Angela often sees the boy in his sleepy aftermaths, looking as Chris Leavitt does now: peaceful and quieted as others absorb the fallout.

It had been no small task bringing him in. After Bryan Tecco's parents had reported their son missing on Monday, a succession of events led officers to Leavitt's trail. First it was Tecco's Richmond landlord echoing the parents' complaint, though mostly for self serving reasons—his need of a rent check. Tecco's place of work hadn't seen him in four days, either, though it hadn't occurred to anyone there to report the absence, strangely enough. A few others were missing Tecco: at least one whom Tecco owed money. As for this Leavitt guy: He was gone, too, said the landlord, and it was this news, linked as it was to an auto accident and a connection to Tecco's missing person case, that really started the investigation rolling. First, it was noted that Leavitt had been picked up the week before after driving his truck into Bolinas Lagoon. He'd been taken to a medical center and checked out for injuries, and then later released, having lied to local police about being the only person in the truck when it submerged—which wasn't known at the time. Then, upon hearing the landlord's information the following Tuesday, police resumed their search for Chris Leavitt, the ball they had dropped and would drop again. His employer at a local hospital said he was suspended; his girlfriend, a nurse who worked with Leavitt, said he'd left her and took off to stay with his rich and aged aunt who lived in the hills. Armstrong and Boyd tracked him down on Wednesday, took him in for an interview, and got the story of Leavitt's itinerant actions of the previous week. Everything was falling apart for him, it seemed: his job was in jeopardy; his friend Tecco had ditched town for reasons unknown to him, though he admitted driving Tecco to his hometown village just prior to the accident. Leavitt said he was out of money and was breaking up with his girlfriend. He said he was without a place to live, which was also a lie, and without prospects, wandering the streets of Oakland. He seemed depressed and pathetic, and likely stirring over events he was keeping secret.

But Doug Armstrong, the guy in charge, didn't think there was much else to the story, so Leavitt was let go, despite Angela's Boyd's misgivings, under the pretext that Bryan "Weed" Tecco, a known drug dealer, was likely on the run, or on the road, and heading north where his product is both plentiful and even more liberally policed than it is in the Bay Area. There was more to the case, Boyd insisted. Leavitt was lying about the circumstances of March 28th, she believed. Hours after the interview, this was confirmed as Leavitt's nervy, ambivalent girlfriend called up to reveal an inconsistency in her boyfriend's story. Addressing what police had earlier relayed to her, she pointed out that Chris had misrepresented to friends where his accident had occurred—quite gratuitously, it seems, in retrospect. Still, it showed he'd been lying about something important. Perhaps that meant he had something to hide; something that was still lying in the mud on the bottom of Bolinas Lagoon.

Angela Boyd groggily looks at the clock and heads toward the break room for coffee. It's five fifteen, still an hour or so from daylight, which will give Marin sheriff's department an hour, maybe two for a search before OPD has to make a decision. She'll need a cigarette as well as coffee before thinking through the possibilities. Doug Armstrong's theory remains that Tecco is somewhere along Highway One, sitting in a diner, preparing a pot grower's license application while his creditors bemoan his absence. Over the last couple of days Angela has thought Doug neglectful and cavalier, if indulgent of her driven suspicions. Now, ironically, his take on things seems the most level-headed and likely. After all, her ideas, borne of vexing questions, are still formulating: if the driving of Leavitt's truck into Bolinas Lagoon was an accident, why would he conceal the true location from friends? And why would he lie to police about whether Tecco was in the truck at the time of the accident? Julius Levin, OPD's consultant psychologist, had interviewed Leavitt at length the night before and relayed the would-be suspect's account: Leavitt's story, as told to him, was that he'd driven Tecco out to Marin, at Tecco's request, alongside a cryptic pretext—because he "needed to get out of town"—but didn't share details as to why. The accident was just that, Leavitt continued to insist, but only he—Leavitt—came out of the water. That corrected the previous story, but didn't explain the lies, at least not satisfactorily. Leavitt told Levin that Tecco, whom Leavitt called by his nickname, was nowhere to be found. He might have chosen to say this to the cop who arrived at the scene, but at the time Leavitt was disoriented, operating on automatic pilot, as well as Tecco's strict injunction against telling anyone about him or his plans.

Plans? Boyd was pretty sure that Bryan Tecco's plans didn't include drowning. Levin seemed more or less convinced by Leavitt's story; that is, he seemed to believe that Chris Leavitt had not meant to abandon his friend per se, much less intend him harm prior to or from the outset of the incident, which he further believed to be an accident. "It's complicated," Levin said, implying lenient judgment, empathy, understanding of an esoteric mental disorder, or some other psyche argument that, according to Angela Boyd, held consequence-mitigating currency. She, on the other hand, thinks Chris Leavitt is at least a neglectful citizen, and an obstructer of a missing person investigation. Worst case: he's a murderer, or an accessory to the possible murder of Bryan Tecco. Angela Boyd doesn't share this latter theory with anyone, not wanting to be scoffed at for her reputedly brash, *out there* ideas. Still, the pressure's on. The clock's ticking, and given Leavitt's latest detention, technically the third in the space of a week, she and her Marin colleagues had better resurface, literally, with something soon.

Shortly after six o'clock, Chris Leavitt awakens and finds himself in an unfamiliar room, with his back aching and a thick blanket stretched across his body. The remains of a dream in which a woman feeds him rope down a hill drains away. Blinking, he turns his head to his right in response to the sound of pages turning. There a man in uniform standing by the door sets a magazine aside and raises a phone to his lips, speaking some manner of code. The phone has a unique sound; that of a crackling human voice strained through an electronic filter. Chris is putting the pieces together slowly: a police officer, a brightly lit room; a table in front of him with an empty cup of coffee, a plateful of crumbs that used to be a pair of bagels. He dimly recalls a sequence of conversations which, despite the air of detention, were cordial for the most part, even caring. He conjures the images of Doug Armstrong, a funny psychiatrist named Levin, and most prominently, Angela Boyd. Initially cold and business-like, she seemed to soften as the night wore on. Her voice lowered and her questions lessened in number. Around midnight, it seemed to Chris that her manner took a turn: there was more encouragement and more appeal; more bidding hospitality. "Tell us what happened to Weed," she asked repeatedly. Chris frowned and was puzzled, thinking he'd answered that question already, like a hundred times.

The follow-up was even more ominous: "You'll feel better," she promised.

He sits up, wipes sleep from his eyes and starts to remember more fully. The situation. Here is the situation: he'd been picked up again by the police, this time only a few hours after the previous interview, while he was hanging out at Sweet's place down on Adeline Street. That was right after he'd finally come clean with his friend about what had happened to Weed the previous Wednesday, the last Wednesday in March. Chris and Sweet worked through the separate stuff that was between them: On the week's anniversary of that accident, Sweet nearly got both of them killed while driving along highway thirteen. It was like Sweet knew what had happened the previous week, like he was reenacting accidents, trying to force a working through of traumas by driving like a speed king. So the truth came out, late afternoon Wednesday, Chris drowsily estimates. Chris revealed the full truth of the accident, at least as he knew it. And now? How many times has Chris had the same conversation about that incident? It seems a bit much, this reaction to the previous week: a week in which he'd either not talked at all about the night in Marin, or else lied about it. Damn, he'd tried, and just about succeeded, in pretending the whole situation didn't exist.

Thinking of Sweet, he knows that he had followed him and his arresting, detaining—whatever they said—officers down to the police station last night, along with his former girlfriend, Jill Evans. Was she a former? Chris asks himself. Who knows? He thinks, imbued with bitterness. It was Jill who'd lead the cops to Sweet's place, albeit with Sweet's help. It was Jill's eyes that he first saw after Angela Boyd called out, demanding, alongside a couple of burly sidekicks, that he open up Sweet's front door and let them all in. Then he saw Jill's eyes. Guilt was battling with anger for position; hate was tempered with sympathy, maybe love. Your eyes have much to answer for, he thought to say, but didn't.

He imagines or hopes that they might still be around, Jill and Sweet—waiting downstairs in the station lobby. Although, if Chris is to be charged with something heinous and then arraigned at some point, then there's not much they can do. Sweet can't give him another ride somewhere, whether he learns to drive properly or not. Jill can't loan him her bike, or tell him he can stay at her place for a couple of nights, or buy him good, wholesome organic food, or nag him to call hospital management, explain his latest catastrophe, but still ask them to hold that other job they'd arranged for him down at Alta McMahon's Stanislaus facility. For some reason, he keeps picturing them lying on a bench downstairs, slumped against each other like siblings, or like a cat and dog; fast asleep yet somehow still with Chris, standing by him. In spirit. Like shadows.

One thing they could do, assuming they really do want to help, is get him a lawyer; a real lawyer. The last one he spoke to was that patent huckster Whitman, who is likely still wondering, like many people in Chris' life, why he hasn't called him back yet. The whole last week seemed like this: lots of people whom Chris didn't want to talk to kept calling or texting him, wanting to talk. "All you have to do is talk to me," he remembers someone saying to him not long ago. Maybe it was his Aunt Jenny—poor, lonely, rich yet frail Aunt Jenny. She's not alone in her assumptions. Lots of people seem to think that talking versus not talking is the solution to problems. Whitman's thing is about the diaper patent application, which Chris has by now dismissed as a bad idea—a joke even. The joke's on Whitman if he thinks there's still legs to the idea. It's time to give up childish things, Chris thinks—even things designed for a child.

The events of the previous evening start to take shape in his mind. He recalls being passive at first, cooperating as he was escorted from Sweet's place and brought to the jail next door from the administrative building. When he arrived, he was led upstairs to this office, just as he had been the previous afternoon. After a half hour wait, the questions started up again: when was the last time he'd seen Bryan "Weed" Tecco, and where? Chris protested that they'd been here already, talked about this stuff. Armstrong and Boyd disagreed. They had new information, from Sweet obviously, and also from Jill, that Bryan Tecco had been in the truck with Leavitt as it went down in that West Marin river which, by the way, is a lagoon, not a river. That dream about the woman and the rope comes back to him as he reviews the exchanges with police. Chris knows he'd built himself a Jenga tower of bullshit over the last several days, and that the job of women like Angela Boyd is to pull it down, one slab at a time.

"You lied to us, Mr. Leavitt," she charged.

"No I didn't," Chris argued, "You never asked if he was in the truck."

"You said you last saw him in the village, in a saloon. Do you wanna hear the recording?" Boyd, flanked by Armstrong but now looking as if she were in charge, pointed to a recording machine parked in the corner of the table. It looked simple and dormant, with only a single green light indicating life. It had been hiding out. "Besides, you also lied to police last Wednesday, the time of this so-called accident." Chris flinched and caught sight of Doug Armstrong giving a twitchy glance in Boyd's direction. What did she mean by so-called?

"No, they didn't ask about it either." Boyd tilted her face to the side and sneered as if to say, *come on*. She changed the subject.

"So, why did you tell your friends that this accident happened in the hills?"

Chris froze and felt a lump in his throat. He looked over to Armstrong, whose arms were folded, affording him a grim, executioner's demeanor.

"I want a lawyer. This is harassment," Chris said.

Problem is he doesn't know any lawyers. He doubted that Sweet or Jill, who were likely elsewhere in the building, perhaps being interviewed, knew any lawyers either. But since they're the ones who ratted him out, the least they could do is some footwork, especially as both are prone to making earnest claims: *we're here for you*, and such crap. Angela Boyd even said as much, with respect to Jill at least. Chris demanded a phone call, saying it was his right. Angela looked at Armstrong like she was seeking direction. She seemed unsure of herself. Armstrong nodded, signifying two things: firstly, that Chris could get his phone call with a landline phone in the room. Secondly, and more importantly, he was declaring it time to get formal. Rights? Right, Chris Leavitt, here are your rights.

In truth, he zoned out as Boyd starting reciting the lines in robotic fashion. He was in denial again—dissociating—as he had been all week; as he has been, in all truth, for much of his life. He just about came back into the room in time to hear the prospective charge: "…on the suspicion of obstructing a police investigation." Lying to police: a misdemeanor apparently. Meanwhile, thoughts of Aunt Jenny flashed through his mind. She'd had cause to use a lawyer or two in recent years, mostly for financial reasons concerning the liquidation of her late husband's clothing business. Maybe she'd know someone. Maybe these cops would know someone, or they should know someone. What the hell? Who carries the name and number of a criminal lawyer in their pocket? Do people really get arrested and say things like "I wanna call my lawyer" as if those persons' numbers are programmed into their cell phones.

None of the cops in the room seemed inclined to help. Instead, they seemed content to let Chris flounder, perhaps hoping he'd fall apart, confess something so they could put him in a cell and then go home for the night. At some point in the evening, Armstrong withdrew like he'd lost interest. Boyd stayed and drove the energy, alternating between personas of bossy sister and doting girlfriend. She tried cajoling him at times, reasoning with him. Otherwise, she tried to nurture him, giving him food, a blanket, and finally, shortly after midnight, permission to sleep. The psychologist, Levin, was brought in like a stop-gap measure; something that gave Boyd a chance to step out, take a break, have a smoke and then make phone calls; organize. Chris kind of enjoyed the talk with Levin—his wandering assessment; his uninvested listening. Jill and Sweet were downstairs, Boyd said, hanging out in a waiting area. Feeling what? Chris wondered. Guilty? Responsible?

Chris called his Aunt Jenny. Or rather, he called her house and got one of her servants who then collected Aunt Jenny out of bed. After a short, testy exchange in which she seemed anything but surprised to hear of her nephew's arrest, she scratchily promised that she'd call someone immediately and have them down at Oakland police department first thing in the morning. Her ill-tempered assurance grounded Chris; made him feel like he had a real bully on his side, someone who'd take these upstarts, Armstrong and Boyd, and string them up by their necks. Chris fell asleep around one o'clock feeling reasonably sure that everything would work out. He didn't think he'd be unduly punished for his little white lies of the week before, or yesterday. He knew, ultimately, that he'd done nothing to harm his missing friend. Accidents happen, he thought with healing purpose.

After being made to wait for yet another hour, Angela Boyd finally returns, offering a plate of breakfast and looking dissatisfied. As Chris eats, she reveals what has been happening concurrent with his detention. Marin County sheriff's department has performed another search of Bolinas Lagoon, she announces, this time with divers. They focused their dive around the area from which Chris' truck was pulled on March 29th. Two items were found: a baseball cap, and more disturbingly, a P229 firearm. No sign of a body though. Upon delivering this statement, Boyd stares at Chris for several moments, studying his response. Chris is chewing heavily, not registering the significance of her news. He shrugs. *So?*

"So, okay. Did anyone come here saying they were representing me?"

Angela Boyd frowns.

"No, it isn't necessary. We're releasing you."

"Excuse me," Chris says, almost choking on a piece of bread.

"You're free to go. You won't be charged. Not now anyway." Boyd speaks slowly like she's talking to someone mentally disabled. She's clearly unhappy, and not in charge.

"Uh, what about…?"

"Your friends are still downstairs. They stayed here all night, I think." Boyd seems impressed by this observation. She rises from her chair, turns to leave, but then turns back again. "In future, Mr. Leavitt, don't lie to the police. You'd save everyone a lot of time and effort."

The good news that he is free is just dawning on Chris; the better news implied by an uneventful search expedition is yet to sink in.

"Wait. Is that it? We're done here. No apology for keeping me here all night, scaring the shit out of me? Nothing?"

Angela Boyd gives Chris Leavitt a disdainful look. As far as she's concerned, she's looking at either one of the most selfish assholes she's ever come across, or one of the most clueless.

"Mr. Leavitt, we found no body at the site of your accident, in a lagoon that's about fifty feet deep. That means your friend is alive as far as we know. What else do you want?"

20

The eyes of Jill Evans open around eight o'clock and flicker as they wander about the waiting room of Oakland jail. As yet, they are not answering to anyone, but they are taking in the surroundings, feeding information to Jill's brain and asking a compelling question: what is she doing here?

To her right, slumped into a dusty leather-backed seat, still asleep with his legs stretched out and touching hers, is one of Chris "Crystal" Leavitt's apparently loyal friends, Sweet. He is the third member of a nicknamed triumvirate that also includes Chris' other friend, Bryan "Weed" Tecco, whose continuing absence is the reason they're all sitting in a police station, whether obliged to or just choosing to. Jill knows Sweet's real name isn't Sweet. She has no idea what his last name is, and considers that Chris won't even know. It fits them, somehow, this commitment to anonymity: each of them is elusive, drawn to the fringes of society, and sabotaging of anything that smacks of conformism. Not that Jill sympathizes. Over the last three months, roughly the period of hers and Chris' awkward off and on romance, she's had her fill of unpredictable behavior, fanciful ideas, unreliability. Yet somehow she remains sucked into this black hole of Chris Leavitt's life. After all, she's spent the night here in this wretched place. Is it caring, what she's doing here? Morbid curiosity?

The waiting room of Oakland jail looks like a tunnel that connects two terminals at an airport. A wall of transparent tinted windows lines both front and back, with rows of hard plastic chairs against the glass. Sweet reeks of Patchouli oil and appears decidedly pedestrian. Thoroughly tanned, his brown curly hairs drop just below his eyebrows, handsomely in line with a long, narrow face and a taut upper body. The rest of him is lanky yet ambiguously fit. Wearing sandals, khaki shorts and a similarly-colored, wrinkled and pinhole-ridden t-shirt, Sweet's feet, legs and midriff are liberally exposed. His attire, in combination with skin that looks dry and sort of windswept, reveals an outdoorsmen's life. Despite this, he appears fragile, like someone who ought to be placed in a soft bed, with clinging blankets tucked beneath him. His face betrays a quieted mind; he seems passive, untroubled, like he's at home resting amid the noise of a rowdy crowd. Jill noticed him falling asleep around two o'clock, almost an hour before she lapsed herself. Occasionally, he asks stupid questions but is immune to ironic comebacks, which generally befits his absentee mind. There are no fretting, conflicted questions dogging him it seems.

The people around them are a snapshot of urban disquiet. Officially, citizens are not supposed to be spending the night in the station's spacious capacity, but due to activity happening at all hours, and the non inconsiderable staffing, the presiding officers behind another glass partition don't concern themselves with hangers on unless they're creating a disturbance. Jill and Sweet hardly fit into that category. If anything, they stick out like lost tourists from overseas; looking bereft and homesick. Some in the area are regulars: they've shown up, first thing in the morning, ostensibly to visit inmates while exhibiting sheepish grins, as if serendipity were the only reason they weren't incarcerated themselves. Young men in floppy sweaters with hoods hide their eyes. Angry, abandoned women shepherd children and strollers, with cell phones pinned to their faces, calling others in order to vent about their situations. For much of the evening Jill and Sweet had been seated in between two factions of protesters: one was a political group who'd been demonstrating down near Frank Ogawa Plaza, becoming unruly with signs that decried U.S involvement in Syria. Another group, more numerous than the first, had concerns focused on native areas like East 14th street and International Boulevard. They were protesting violence that was closer to home, between gang members, and victimizing kids—teenage or tweenie males, mostly—whose photographs they held up for all to see and lament.

As a nurse at Alta McMahon hospital in Oakland, Jill keeps to herself that she lives at ground zero as far as the local problem is concerned. Had she looked closely, she might have recognized one or two of the faces within the photos being waved about by grieving families. She might have treated some of those young men in the ER, or been mugged by them in the street, just as she had been the day before, as it happened. On the whole, she feels sympathetic to these people, the vast majority of whom have little choice but to live within crime-ridden neighborhoods. On the other hand, she is weary of, and somewhat unconvinced by the loud diatribes about the tragedy of street violence; the eloquent, yet haranguing, public pleas from mothers and fathers, local preachers, all imploring disaffected young people to stop their *insanity*. But, amid all that impassioned rhetoric, where are the witnesses for all these shootings? Who is opening their eyes as well as their mouths? And who will replace the false bravery of making speeches, with the quieter yet more dangerous risk of pointing fingers, naming names?

It took nearly a full day for Jill Evans to decide whether to snitch on Chris Leavitt. Since Doug Armstrong and Angela Boyd had first questioned her on Tuesday evening, she'd gone back and forth in her mind, wondering if Chris' earlier account to her about his previous week's accident—hitting a tree somewhere in the hills, he'd said—was worth sharing with investigators. Once she made the call, it all seemed obvious: Chris had been lying about what had happened with Weed; his subsequent wandering about Oakland was the clue that should have struck her immediately. She recalled his reticence upon discovering him on Monday; his slippery air over the next day or so. That avoidance: it was so *like* him. Then again, perhaps he'd fallen apart due to other circumstances: a relapse on meth, she first thought, followed by his calamitous insubordination at work. Then there was that thing that happened between the two of them in a supply room of the hospital the week before. Maybe he was stressed out by that—guilt-ridden, tormenting himself. This is wishful thinking, she realizes.

Right around eight, Chris emerges from a secured door that separates the waiting area from police offices. He is looking about as disheveled as he did the night before, only now he looks even more shell-shocked, more tired. His blue eyes glisten but they seem lighter than usual, like they've been drained of color. An escorting officer trails behind him for a step or two beyond the door, but then slips away, giving Chris the faintest of farewell nods. Chris stumbles into the area like someone unsure of how to walk freely. Jill sees him and stands, whacking Sweet's knee as she rises. Then she walks towards Chris, wading past individuals who seem to look through her as if she were a ghost. Chris is different. He sees her. They lock eyes.

"What's happening?" Jill asks plaintively.

A noisy bark of someone calling out across the room drowns out Chris' answer. "What?" Jill repeats, having seen Chris' lips move. She nudges past a woman whose stroller is blocking a space between rows of seats. Jill makes little effort to avoid contact because she's had enough of Oakland wiping itself on her. The woman gives her a scornful look, but Jill is past caring. She's busy reading Chris' lips.

He's alive.

She reaches Chris, moves to hug him but pulls back, instead placing an arm on his shoulder.

"Wait. What?"

Chris' eyes now show red capillaries streaking from his pupils. They are shaking like he is holding back tears.

"The fucker is alive," he says for a third time. It's an idea that bears repeating. Several feet beyond, he sees Sweet emerging from his sleep and stepping towards Chris. He is smiling widely, having gleaned a release from custody.

"What's up, dude? Are we outta here?"

Chris gives his friend a heavy, tired look. Two guys in hoods exchange amused looks; they don't like people who say "dude", or "bro". Typical Sweet: he sounds like he thinks they're at traffic court and that Chris has been fighting a parking ticket.

"Yeah," is all Chris thinks to say. Sweet glances over to Jill and shrugs. He'd spent part of the evening trying to figure her out, and not succeeding. When she looked sullen, he figured she was pissed, but she denied that when asked. When her head leaned backwards and her eyes closed, he woke her and asked if she was tired—she said no to that also. Go figure. Sweet reflects on different aspects of the night: what was the worst thing about it? Right now he'd say it was the problem of dealing with Chris' girlfriend. But if Chris is being sprung then Sweet will soon be done with her, and if his buddy Chris knows what's best for him, he'll be done with her too.

"Hey, we got your backpack," Sweet calls out as Chris marches to the exit door. Chris halts. A backpack—sounds symbolic, like a stand-in for "got your back". His thinks of his backpack, his stuff. What stuff? He wonders. What does he own that has any meaning? Even his driver's license doesn't tell the truth.

Jill's face looks concerned and sympathetic, if conflicted. She brushes past Sweet, grabs Chris by the hand and leads him outside, onto a path and some steps that lead to 7th street. Her hand is warm. Feeling her touch, Chris Leavitt feels as though he is melting.

"I'm sorry," he says.

"I am too," Jill replies in kind, without thinking.

"No, really. I'm sorry. For everything. No, strike that: I mean I'm sorry that I lied to you about what happened. I'm sorry that I put you in a bad spot with work. I'm sorry that I disappeared, that I'm not who I said I was, and older than I said I was. And I'm sorry about what happened at work between us. I didn't mean to hurt you that day. Seriously, I just—"

"Stop. It's okay." Jill's voice is just above a whisper. Her eyes are looking just past his, into the distance. She's not ready for this conversation.

Sweet steps forward, clumsily intruding.

"So, what's the deal with Weed? Still missing?"

"They did a search this morning," Chris answers haltingly. "They didn't find anything, which means they think he's alive." Chris' voice cracks. Jill and Sweet exchange an unlikely glance of like-mindedness. Sweet speaks for them.

"We kinda knew that was true."

Chris drops to the steps, letting go of Jill's touch and burying his head in his own hands.

"I didn't," he says. His face reddens amid labored breaths. *Breathe*, he says inwardly. And he cries.

21

As Chris, Jill, and Sweet all pile into her car, a quick decision is made: head back to the hills and return to Aunt Jenny's house instead of Sweet's place. Jill drives. Sweet, in the back seat, snoozes, having previously woken up the most abruptly. Chris sits in the passenger seat, pawing through his backpack and fondly noting its familiar articles: the two CDs, a few cords to go with his various electronica; the handful of flash drives that Weed had stashed in there. Inspecting his wallet, Chris counts his notes and change and makes internal calculations. Turning on his cell phone, he checks messages and edits e-mail. He curses the phone's rejection of his fingers' not so dexterous movements, and sets it down. Lastly, holding aloft a piece of plastic plucked from one of the sleeves of the wallet, he regards his most untrustworthy item— his driver's license.

"If it makes you feel any better, I think you look like you're in your twenties," Jill says with a wry smile. "You certainly act like you're younger." Chris rolls his eyes, absorbing the gentle and refreshingly good natured insult. Of all of his lies, this one is perhaps the most benign, the whitest; the most strange. "Why?" Jill asks, seeming merely curious.

"Dunno really," Chris replies. "Sweet asked the same thing: why say you're twenty five when you're thirty three? Because it's what I can get away with, I think. I'm sort of aware of growing down and not up. I got smoothed over skin because of a fire that burned me in my early twenties. An accident." Chris pulls back a handful of his dark brownish hair, revealing old, faintly visible sutures—the evidence of a ten year old, successful plastic surgery that Aunt Jenny paid for. Jill's mouth opens slightly, betraying her surprise. "I wish I could make myself ten or something. Don't ask me why," Chris states. Few prior to this episode knew about his gamesmanship with age, much less the triggering event that was the fire. He quickly gets out his words, hoping a terse summing up of history will put it to rest. He supposes it's better to feel embarrassed about this than guilty about everything else.

As the ride to Aunt Jenny's proceeds, Chris keeps glancing back and forth between Jill and Sweet, looking for signs of twitchy preoccupation. There are none. They seem calm, resolved, as if the truth of this whole episode had been known to them all along. Chris is a latecomer to reality, as in this focused, settled reality wherein sketchy theories no longer have currency. Gone are the thoughts of Weed's malevolent mischief: the idea that he might have faked his own death so as to throw off his followers, whoever they are or were. There are no tracks in water, and so on. Chris had spent two or three days on that theory, riding the idea that Weed will have planned it all out, his disappearance. All he wanted from Chris was a ride, and the less he knew the better.

Chris' anger alternates with guilt. His friend didn't tell him everything; he never did. But regardless of the outcome, Chris Leavitt realizes something else. Knowingly or not, he'd left that friend for dead.

"So, what was the deal back there? Are they done with you or what?" Jill asks.

"I think so," Chris replies, frowning. "If it was up to that woman officer I'd still be there, getting charged. I think it was higher ups deciding not to take it further since there was no body."

"A sort of 'no harm, no foul' thing?"

"I guess." He barely hears Jill's opinion. Instead, Chris dwells on his use of the word "body", his cold reference to his absent friend. Now for the first time in over a week, he is entertaining for real thoughts of Weed's whereabouts and circumstances. Why no call from him, or no text? Why take the ruse this far? Does he trust him that little; think him that unreliable with confidences? Once again, Chris inventories the contents of his backpack and glimpses the set of flash drives that Weed had given him to hold. Weed said they contain the files for a game he'd lifted from work: an important game, so he said. So that's what Weed had left Chris of himself: some game that he'd be great at playing—that Chris might be okay at playing—which he might later hawk underground instead of selling schwag?

"So what's the plan?" Jill is characteristically organized and thinking ahead. Chris figures she'll soon withdraw from this drama, head back to her place, and go on with her life. Soon they'll be at Aunt Jenny's. Jill's last favor, or obligation if that's how she thinks of this drive, will be accomplished. Now she's going through the motions of closure: it's like she's at work doing a discharge plan for a patient. With minimal sentiment, she'll touch a palm to Chris' face, exhibit a shade of longing but then obscure it with affected sisterly concern. Then she'll be swift in her departure, and as Chris is choking on his loss, she'll drive away, escape him. He looks behind his shoulder, gestures to a still dozing Sweet with a nod.

"I'll ask him when we get there. First I wanna talk to my aunt, see if we can stay at her place for a while, maybe get some more money before hitting the road."

"Hitting the road? To where?"

"Not sure. Sweet wants to head to LA. He's got work there, he says. Plus, he wants me to help him with a film he's making."

"Where in LA?"

"Not sure. Somewhere near Hollywood, or that area around UCLA, I think."

"So, you're going with him?" Jill had paused after the first word. The inflection of doubt is unmistakable.

"Sure."

"What about the Stanislaus job?"

Chris sighs; then whines. "I don't know. I'll call 'em I guess, see if there are other options. I don't wanna live in Stanislaus County."

Jill mirrors the sigh but says nothing. She's heard this kind of backtracking from him before and isn't having that conversation again. Not anymore. Still, she thrusts her hand against the wheel of her car like she's urging it forward. Chris notices the vehicle pick up a few miles per hour; he imagines he can hear the dim sound of gnashing teeth. But unlike before—unlike her—Jill holds her tongue and Chris knows why. She's done with him.

"What about Weed?" she asks after several contemplative moments. "Aren't you gonna look for him? I mean, it's not that I care about him, necessarily. It's just that twenty minutes ago you were having some kind of catharsis. You seemed relieved, if frustrated, thinking he was alive. I don't get why you wouldn't follow up on that."

"It's complicated," Chris replies, unwittingly matching the thoughts of Julius Levin. He offers an offhand explanation: "He probably doesn't wanna be found. It's best I let it go."

As they pull into Aunt Jenny's driveway, Jill feels mostly satisfied with Chris' novel wisdom—at least with respect to his friend Weed. As they step out of her car and tread towards Aunt Jenny's front door, past her decorous front porch and the dome of azaleas sat before a bay window, Jill, Sweet, and Chris move awkwardly amongst one another, as if knowing they have only minutes left together.

"Do you have work today," Chris asks, killing the silence after the doorbell is rung.

"Nah, I'm off," Jill replies softly.

"This house is sweet," says Sweet, not intending a pun.

Dufus, Jill thinks.

Moments later the sound of a latch being undone jolts their attention. The door opens three inches, revealing the suspicious eyes of a middle-aged Latino woman. Chris is late in making the appropriate greeting; he is staring at Jill.

"Crisf," says the woman at the door.

Soon they are led through an entryway and living area which is impressively adorned. Jill admires the crown molding, a sideboard with stained glass. Everything is tidied, scrubbed clean, and aromatic of musk. They follow the un-introduced housekeeper, a matronly woman dressed in all white, towards a back porch area that is long familiar to Chris. There, Aunt Jenny is seated in a wheelchair, taking in the morning spring sunshine with a glass of tea by her side. Jill can see even from behind that Aunt Jenny has a classic elegance about her, despite some infirmities: she'll be a frequenter of vintage clothing stores, Jill imagines. Her closet will be filled with sequins; her past calendars like those of a socialite. Aunt Jenny will have heard the bell ringing and then barked out a command for one of her aides to answer. Now seventy five, and despite the phlebitis afflicting her left ankle or the chest infection making her hoarse, she seems quite alert and vital. As she sees Chris walking towards her, following Magdalena, her housekeeper, she lets out an exultant bray, believing the legal imbroglio, about which she'd first heard the day before, is surely over and done with. Nonetheless, she chides Chris, telling him that the lawyer to whom she'd been referred and then commissioned with short notice had just wasted a trip down to Oakland police department, only to learn of Chris' release upon arrival.

"Magdalena, if Mr. Sharp calls about Chris, tell him I'll speak to him," Aunt Jenny calls out.

"Yes ma'am," replies the docile housekeeper.

"Aunt Jenny, these are two of my friends, Jill and, uh, this is Sweet."

"Sweet? What kind of name is that?"

No one answers. Chris and Jill exchange an amused glance before Jill shakes Aunt Jenny's hand, smiles warmly and looks deeply into her eyes. For the first time ever Chris envies his aunt. Sweet leans forward, similarly offers his hand and has just enough presence of mind to say "hello, pleased to meet you" instead of "what's up?" For a few minutes they visit and share pleasantries and platitudes. They've all heard so much about each other which, from Sweet's point of view, is not really true. Aunt Jenny implores them each to sit with her, but to no avail. Jill's the first one to beg off, explaining that she must get back and take care of some errands. Had she said she was disturbed, or just plain exhausted by recent events, Aunt Jenny would have understood. Indeed, the older woman reaches out, just as Jill is pulling away, to express how grateful she is that Jill has gone to such lengths to help her nephew. Chris notes the gestures that uniquely signify Jill's unease. She limply allows Chris' aunt to grip her lower arm; she slips behind her ear a strand of hair that has waywardly crossed her eyebrow. Aunt Jenny seeks to bond with Jill; to convey that she understands how difficult it must be to care for someone like Chris. Jill laughs politely, neither confirming nor dispelling the old woman's assumptions. Soon she breaks Aunt Jenny's grip and backs away towards the front entry. To Sweet, she offers a lackluster wave preceded by a comradely embrace. Chris gets a briefer hug, one that is initially tight but then quickly aborted. Exiting, she unconvincingly promises a later call, and then turns her back. Once outside, she dashes to her car with tears only just forming in her unaccountable eyes.

Aunt Jenny is disappointed to see Jill leave. In their brief moments together, she sees into her and feels the heart within a brittle demeanor. She's been good for Chris, she thinks, but is under no illusions: noticing the subtle distance between her and Chris, she gathers that all is not well. The other friend seems well mannered enough, but somewhat blank; his face is perfectly tanned and his body seems fit. But he appears only half-dressed and smells like some kind of animal that collects the debris of nature and then trails it indoors. She beckons him and Chris to sit, but her enthusiasm for company has waned. With only half the energy she mustered earlier, she asks after drink preferences and then calls again to Magdalena, requesting that she bring them each something from the kitchen.

"Ugh, she's on the phone," Aunt Jenny utters, frustrated.

"Sorry to keep doing this," Chris says, referring to something not obvious. For the moment, his feelings about Jill's departure are put aside. He is cheerful, looking on the bright side of life: he is free, both from the clutches of Oakland Police Department and—now that he thinks of it—of his employer, Alta McMahon Hospital. Unbeknownst to Aunt Jenny, he and Sweet had fashioned a plan for the future in the hours before he was picked up by police the day before. Having revealed that he also sees visions like Shadows, Sweet spoke of others who are afflicted with Chris' same burden—people apparently dubbed "the gifted"—who also congregate from time to time. Sweet knows of a group in Southern California that goes by the name "Cassandra's Children" which describes itself, in loose terms, as a society of Shadow-seers. The idea is for Chris to tag along with Sweet, meet his contacts in this group, help Sweet with his latest film project; maybe get a job; maybe a job in a hospital—maybe not.

Magdalena shows her head at the sliding door to the porch. She is not carrying any drinks.

"Miss Jenny, a man call asking for Crisf."

"For Chris? Is it Mr. Sharp? Did you tell him Chris was here?"

"Yes. I mean, no. I say 'hold on'. I come to find you."

"Well, is it him?"

Magdalena looks flustered. "I make a mistake. I go back to ask who it is. But he hung up."

Aunt Jenny slumps. "Alright," she says disapprovingly. "I'll call him back soon. He's probably just feeling inconvenienced, and will bill me for that. Bring two other teas, please: one lemon, one raspberry." She turns to Chris. "Anyway, what matters is that you're back. Did they find your friend?"

Her question takes him by surprise. Her interest will likely be cursory now that Chris is no longer incarcerated.

"Um, no, but that means we know—well, we don't know if he's okay, but we also don't know that he's not okay."

Aunt Jenny notices that Chris' friend is nodding approvingly, like he understands this awkward explanation. She wants to critique Chris, tell him to make more sense, because it will be good for him. She stops herself.

"I see."

Magdalena returns and sets down the two drinks. Sweet regards his choice, the raspberry, and realizes with dismay that he hadn't asked for sugar.

"Auntie, we're not going to stay for long, but I thought my friend here could use one of the guest rooms upstairs for a night, maybe two. Then we'll be heading out."

Aunt Jenny sips at her now half-hour old and lukewarm tea, looking circumspect.

"Well, that room's used by my helpers, you know—for overnights."

"Right. Then maybe he could use my room. I mean, the room I typically use. I'll sleep on the couch or something."

"Alright."

"Okay." Chris does a double take as he meet's his aunt's eye. She seems skeptical, and hasn't really made eye contact with Sweet the whole time they've been present.

"Are you a colleague of Chris'?" Aunt Jenny suddenly asks of Sweet. Her tone is cool, somewhat clipped.

"Oh, no. I'm just going along. I'm going down to LA after..."

She nods uncertainly in response to Sweet's unfinished thought and then glances back at Chris.

"You have that other job you were telling me about, in that town. What was it? Stan—something?"

"Stanislaus. It's a county."

"You have a job in a county? What city?"

"I don't know yet."

"I see. You also said something yesterday morning about talking to the Dean of students at your school. Have you done that yet?"

"Auntie," Chris utters curtly. Aunt Jenny notes the familiar sound of her nephew's agitation. She feels a chill and recalls that she is not so tough that she can't be unnerved by his penchant for angry displays.

"Yes?"

Chris pauses. "Auntie, if you don't want us to stay, just say so. I don't want a problem."

She takes another sip of her drink, buying her an extra moment in which to think. Sweet looks on, lost as to how the mood has changed so quickly. He's an outsider watching two people speak English to each other, though they might as well be speaking in tongues.

"I just want to make sure you're doing what's best, or at least what you said you'd do yesterday." She shoots a quick, accusatory look in Sweet's direction, which Chris notices.

He shakes his head. "That's not an answer. I'll ask you straight up: do you not want me and my friend to stay here?"

"Answer my questions first," Aunt Jenny replies in a hard voice designed to match Chris' emerging vigor. "Are you going to take that job? Are you going to arrange matters with your school?"

Chris glares back at her and fidgets. He wants to stall, look into his tea, sip on it and buy himself some time. He doesn't sip. He takes a gulp instead.

"No," he says, not looking at his aunt. "I'm not going to take that job, and I'm not going back to school."

"I see," Aunt Jenny says, her face flattening into a grim, darkened expression.

"You see?" Chris replies hotly. "What do you see? You don't *see* anything." To his right, Sweet's back straightens and his eyes go wide. He looks embarrassed as his neck seems to lengthen, like he's taking on extra breath and holding it in. Aunt Jenny ignores this young man's discomfort and meets Chris' now violent-looking gaze. She is glassy eyed but resolute.

"I think it's best you go," she says.

A silence follows. Another standoff.

"Come on, man. We're outta here," Chris announces. He darts away from the table on Aunt Jenny's back porch, grabs his backpack, which he'd set down indoors; he marches through the living room, past the bewildered air of Magdalena, and disappears out the front door. Sweet stumbles to his feet and flops after Chris, making feckless goodbyes as he departs Aunt Jenny's company.

"Nice to meet you, thanks for the tea," he says inanely. He nods passing acknowledgement at Magdalena. Chris faintly hears his friend's words and shakes his head, as though embarrassed for and by him. He has to remind himself that despite the bumbling social persona, Sweet has shown a different side to himself recently—a side he may need to depend on in the near future. Outside, Chris strides away from Aunt Jenny's driveway without even looking over his shoulder. He eschews sentiment as he looks ahead to a street that heads down the hills and into the coarse, metallic heart of Oakland. He knows Sweet will follow.

22

The ferry from Tiburon to San Francisco is like a luxury ride for high end commuters. Twenty bucks gets Weed a space on a ship that takes about a half hour to reach a pier on the north side of the city. He feels relieved and celebratory as he passes a closed bar on the inside of the main cabin. He wishes it was five o'clock on the return commute and there was someone there, ready to pour him a five dollar glass of wine, preferably something red. After days of absurd sidetracking, he'll now make it back to Oakland in just over an hour. Outside of a few bicyclists roaming about the deck, Week looks out of place dressed in just a t-shirt and some denim jeans. Everyone else looks polished and pressed, dressed in black and wearing a shine on their shoes and in their hair. The surf of the bay is kicking up against the side of the hull, creating a windy spray as the boat picks up speed. Weed squeezes indoors and holds himself tightly, feeling chilly but also excited.

Once on land he feels even more driven. In his mind, he distorts geography, believing the nearest BART station to be just blocks away. He crosses over a street, looking around him to see where there might be a bus route. Then it occurs to him that his best bet might be a cable car. Meanwhile, he looks around to see if he can find a newspaper stand. On one level, he'd like to know if there is more news about Jules Grotius. More fundamentally, he'd just like to know what day it is. He could ask passers by this question, such as the many tourists that stroll around by the wharf area. But a firm, vigilant policy is now in place which keeps him reticent.

He heads west for a couple of blocks and soon finds a cable car stop on Hyde Street. It's a bit later than he thought: five minutes until eight o'clock, someone tells him in line. He's still cold, but upon boarding a car, he finds himself within a group, warmed by the collective body heat. The people around him are nondescript as a whole: some are shy tourists whispering to one another, but looking animated; others are jabbering teenagers who'd be rendered mute if the word "like" didn't exist. One or two riders look like students, sporting backpacks, absorbed in their phones or I-pods. The backpacks remind Weed that the one Rosco gave him is still back at Dan Pritchard's place, lost. Too bad. Some stuff in there might have been useful, he bemoans. Around him, there is the odd, business-suited commuter looking disgruntled, like they woke up late, missed their bus or couldn't find a taxi, and have jumped on the cable car as a last resort. Finally, one person, seated, is reading a newspaper that shakes due to the clanging movement of the car. Weed leans over and reads the top of the page, hoping to find a day and date. When the person catches his eye, Weed chuckles and points to the back of paper, gesturing to some item he's pretending is irresistible. With apologies, he then utters "can I just see something real quick?" and gently pulls back the paper so he can see its front. The page indicates a Thursday just before the person snatches back the paper.

Thursday. It's been a whole week, he now realizes. Well, time flies when you're having fun, he thinks sardonically. It feels right, though—not that he's given much thought to how time passage feels. Instead, it's that memories of car chases, a near drowning, a kidnapping, and a likely sexual assault are all sort of coalescing into one floating, ambient nightmare. A week? It all could have been a year as far as he could tell. The cable car drops the passenger load down on Powell Street, right in the heart of the city. There Weed sees amongst the crowd pockets of transients, encircling the BART and Muni station across the street. Weed is on automatic pilot now, thinking the plan will unfold as long as he makes it to his destination. He gets lucky as he walks by a Walgreens store that reminds of missing necessities, and slips inside. After a fast purchase, he continues the journey, which then heads expressly towards the train station. On approach, he passes individuals not unlike him in habit and potential, yet further gone in their situations, and with fewer options short of competing with one another over this dense panhandling territory. Some of these people have been here for years, and may be in it for a lifetime. Time, as in a week of it, has moved ruthlessly on for Weed, but there's a glimpse of a one-time past as well as possible future in the form of a late teenage male, approaching Weed with some vim like he's a kindred soul and asking if he "has any shit."

Weed quickens his step as he heads down the escalator to the underground train. At BART stations there is always the sense that a train is just arriving as riders descend towards the platforms. Everyone breaks into a jog, thinking they'll reach the ticket machines first, and make it to the cars just as the doors are closing. Inside the station proper, Weed slows his pace, knowing he needs time to break out the necessary cash to purchase a ticket that will take him just over the Bay to West Oakland. He looks at the familiar cream-colored and dimpled walls, the handful of street musicians territorially spaced apart at fifty yard intervals down the wide, cavernous corridor. They are a diverse crossection of performers, offering sounds of guitars, violins, a capella voices in the case of one act; what looks like a theremin in the case of another.

Downstairs, Weed finds himself waiting on the platform for what feels like an endless eleven minutes. He thinks about his impending search on the other side, thinking he'll have to feel his way to the neighborhood where Chris' girlfriend lives. Having seen it once after dark, he'll maybe recognize the building from a distance. The problem will be getting close enough to tell, and not getting sidetracked down side streets. As for the issue of what to do when he gets there: he has options, the means to carry out a plan, and he'll deal with it when the time comes. One step at a time: that was a phrase he learned once from a twelve-step meeting within his former drug rehab program. Weed was drawn to this phrase, if not so much its sobriety-supporting spirit. He liked its pithy advocacy of short-term thinking; its catering for brief attention spans and limited energy.

The ride is a comfortable, soporific quarter hour, after which Weed is soon striding along Mandela Parkway, pointing his head eastwardly and moving in the rough direction of 14th Street. He knows he's looking for a building that's about ten stories high, with something like two wings, appearing not quite perpendicular to one another. The parking lot in back will be familiar also, as will the single story set of apartments, a couple of Victorians near the bridge to downtown and what previously looked like a derelict school or a utilities plant on the other side of the street. If he's really lucky, a certain transsexual hooker conspicuous to all the senses will be trolling the area, further marking the correct locale.

The station agent at West Oakland tells him the time is just after nine o'clock. Weed's energy is good, but he'll soon need something more than the snack he got from the Walgreens. Prior to that, it'd had been well over twelve hours, by his estimation, since he'd had anything substantial to eat. Still, he's been getting accustomed to that experience, and as he passes a tinted transparency in an office block, he notes with mild pleasure a degree of gauntness in his mirrored image; a discernible trimness in his face and around his middle. Fasting. One of his regulars told him some time back that he dealt with poverty by fasting two days a week, then eating normally the remaining five days. It not only saves money, it feels great, Weed was told. It sounds great, Weed thinks as he treks along. He can certainly attest that hunger is something that can be manipulated; that it comes in waves, and can be dealt with, traversed, as long as he learns that pain in and of itself won't kill him.

Turning a corner, Weed passes a black woman smoking a black and mild cigarette and wearing tigerskin hotpants—an identikit prostitute look. She looks pretty much like the transsexual he'd seen in the neighborhood the previous week, only this one's heavier and tired and doesn't look like she wants to *party*. For a block or two he walks with his head down, distracted by sideways contemplations. Out of nowhere, he then looks up and sees the burgundy edge to the ten-plus story building with the wing that veers away at a strange angle. He's found it.

Elated, Weed jogs the final fifty yards to the front of the complex. That was easier than he thought it would be. He sees the front double set of doors with an intercom by its side. It's locked but he figures it won't be so difficult getting in as long as he's patient, waits for a resident to show, and then musters some bullshit about his keys being lost from unit twenty seven or whatever. The funny thing is that he knows that whoever he speaks to will know that he's bullshitting, but they won't care. That's the deal here: in buildings like this, just like his place back in Richmond, there's no real community; no sense of neighborhood watch. The reason: there's no endemic wish to stick around long enough to care.

Sure enough, Weed makes his way inside the building within minutes, feigning a dash from the parking lot to the door like he's a resident who's just pulled up and is in a hurry. The exiting person barely manages an acknowledging nod, much less a complaint. Once inside, he tries to remember for the first time which floor he'd visited with Chris the week before. Though it had been only eight days, it seems like a lifetime ago, his slovenly lean upon an opposite wall as Chris negotiated entry into his girlfriend's apartment, only to find her stiff, disapproving, and fearful. It was a good thing Leavitt was feeling bold and wanting to prove himself, because if he'd failed to deal with that nervous bitch, the truth is that Weed—feeling as cagey as he did that night—might have lost it and simply busted her door down.

Weed gambles upon his shoddy memory, dredging up the number eight from some internal crypt. He presses that number on the row of elevator buttons and waits. The vertical movement is slow and halting in keeping with the age of the elevator whose permit, Weed notices, is expired. As it stops abruptly, he exits into a darkish hallway and turns right, feeling just about confident that he's choosing the right floor and direction. He gauges the distance from the elevator, trying to guess how much walking will be necessary before hitting the right unit. The stretch of hall is about twenty, maybe thirty yards long, giving him a choice of two or three units that are the likely home of Chris' girlfriend. It's all good, Weed thinks, trying now to relax. If he gets it wrong and someone unfamiliar answers, he'll say he's a friend of a friend. Jill: that's the name he recovers from his shaky memory, just in time to coincide with a soft knock upon the chosen door.

Either way, there will be no busting down of anything. After a second knock, Weed reaches into his back pockets, plucking his wallet from one, and feeling for a screwdriver bought from the Walgreens in the other. From the wallet, he pulls two keys, both of which came with a padlock he'd gotten from the store and then discarded the moment he saw a trashcan at BART. If neither key fits the lock on the flat panel before him, he'll be pissed, especially as it seems to him that most keys these days are generic: they fit initially in most locks, but they don't turn if they're not right. The first doesn't fit at all, which elicits a hiss of frustration but not panic. The second one also resists at first, causing Weed to stop breathing for a moment. Maybe he'll be busting doors down after all, he thinks. He jiggles and thrusts again, muttering a curse before the lock suddenly cooperates. As it settles in but doesn't turn, he looks about, checking for sights or sounds of other residents. He sees and hears nothing—not a squeak. On the one hand, the shadowy nature of this hallway is an advantage, but in a way it's too dark and quiet; too creepy.

He grabs the screwdriver from his pocket and holds its base against the edge of the key that is sticking out from the lock. Then he gives three light yet firm taps against the back of the tool, which in turn beats the key further into the lock. The last of the taps achieves a fit that releases the door, accompanied by a satisfyingly light clicking sound. The door, which is about two inches thick and which doesn't even feel solid, dislodges with a gentle, inviting sound. Lock bumping, this is called. Weed smiles and enters, assuming he'll find no one home. As he edges inside, he revisits this foolhardy conceit, realizing that many won't answer the door just because it's being knocked upon. Also, whoever is home might be sleeping, even though it's daytime—someone who works night shifts or whatever. Besides that, this better be the right place, as it's not like he can pull the same trick with every apartment. He treads carefully.

Unseen by Weed, a child peers around the corner at the end of the hallway, just as Weed disappears from view. The boy's four foot frame is silhouetted against the light coming in through a single, foot-wide window. The child is still and curious, having heard the sound of a door opening, yet also feeling the different quality of the door's movement. Once inside, Weed scans a room that seems especially blank: there are shades of grey here and there, upon a chair, or at the base of a bed that is a central fixture. A desk table with a computer sits beside a narrow kitchen which is dark and looks hidden to the side. The same light that pierced the blackened hallway outside now dominates this single room unit, with a blinding ball of whiteness coming into the main space through a single, oversized and thinly curtained window. Weed begins looking for signs of anything familiar. He knew this part would be difficult; that Chris, if he had made it back to Oakland, will have done so long before now, and was perhaps long gone, along with the flash drives that Weed should never have given him in the first place. He studies the room, its unlikely bareness, which belies all of Weed's beliefs about feminine tastes. Even the bicycle in the corner suggests a masculine, not-here-very-often feel.

The table upon which the computer lives seems a logical place to start searching for drives. On its underside is a single drawer, which Weed spasmodically opens spilling a pen onto the floor. Besides pens, paper clips, and a blank pad of post-it notes, he finds a stray couple of dollars, plus some loose change. In the back there is a tin of mints: Altoids. There are letters and junk mail, all addressed to "current resident". Weed looks for anything that might identify the occupant, confirming that he's in the right apartment. Soon he moves on to the kitchen, drawn partly by the light hum of an appliance. He feels his stomach cry out in joy as he sees a refrigerator. Again, a bright light pours out over him as he peers inside it, looking directly at but then quickly past a set of peaches that sit temptingly in front. Unfortunately, Weed is not a fruit man, so they are like coquettish ugly ducklings to him, posing under a spotlight but not gratifying the onlooker. The other items are all in plain, unmarked containers. Weed opens one, gives what's inside a smell—something vegetable, he decides—and makes a further decision. Good enough, he thinks as he grabs a peach and then sticks his tongue inside a container, licking up some kind of creamy off-white substance.

Next to the refrigerator is another drawer which is slightly opened, revealing slips of paper inside. Weed pulls open the drawer and discovers two bills with the same address and name typed into the center of envelopes. Jill Evans, it reads on top of both. Cool, he's in the right place. He stares at the wall space above the bed, remembering that when he was last here, albeit briefly, Chris and Jill were arguing about something—quite a few things, actually—like where he'd stash his stuff, including a poster he wanted to hang up. Mostly, Weed remembers how their domestic squabble tried his patience, especially as he was all about getting on the road to escape people he felt sure were stalking him. Recalling the spat between Chris and Jill, he considers that it's something of a stretch to assume the two of them are even a couple anyone, let alone that Chris is still living here, guarding belongings of a friend he likely thinks is dead.

Standing at the open space between the kitchen and the studio portion, Weed suddenly feels stupid for once again not thinking through his plans. He looks under the bed and sees nothing. All about the floor there are stray bits of paper, plus lint hovering above an ugly, aged carpet, but nothing that looks interesting, as in something that's his. Idly, Weed pores over in his mind numerous episodes in his life, all marred by shoddy planning, impulsive decision making; lack of common foresight. Only when playing games is he any different. With a console, a controlling device, or a laptop, Weed is in his element, seeing all possibilities, thinking two steps ahead of the game, ahead of the computer, even. He shakes his head, feeling a wave of defeatist thought coming over him. Noticing another door on the other side next to the bed, he steps over presuming it to be a bathroom. With a dim sense of reprise, he figures he might as well take care of all personal business while he's here.

He gives a cursory look inside a medicine cabinet and within a cupboard beneath a sink. Nothing. He sits down in a tight space in the corner; the roll of toilet paper is behind him and it's an awkward turn to reach it. As he drops his jeans he notices that he has carelessly left the door ajar. Then he hears a clicking sound from outside, one that is similar to the sound made when he first bumped the lock, only this reprise feels less satisfying.

Shit.

The occupant has returned.

23

Jill Evans heads down the Oakland hills in her second hand Honda, wiping tears away from her eyes as she drives. Emotion gets in the way, she knows. Or, emotions other than anger get in the way. Seeing Chris sit with and listen to his aunt, even for just those few moments reminded her that she wasn't the only woman giving him a hard time, trying to stir something different in Chris. Others had been doing their shifts whilst the men folk just shrug, relinquish responsibility, disappear, or show up but still manage to seem absent, like Sweet. Even the police interrogation reflected this trend. Weird, she thinks. Now she needs to be pissed off, and to stay pissed off lest sentiment and old habits lead her to turn her car around and drive back up that winding, if beautiful hillside.

Glancing down, she sees another excuse to stay pissed off: Chris has left his phone in her car. She hisses disgust, remembering that he'd forgotten or lost his cell last week also. Hopeless, she thinks of him. Or maybe it's not an accident. Maybe it's his unwitting method of staying close, by simply leaving pieces of himself behind. It takes a half hour for her to drive back to her apartment in West Oakland. The excursion to the hills might have stirred further envy had she really taken time to absorb Aunt Jenny's world. There were homes and neighborhoods up there to dream of, with lush vegetation, peace and a sense of gentility and affluence that Jill Evans, despite herself, actually longs for. Barely two hours since she'd left the police station with Chris and Sweet, she's traveled back and forth across Oakland's economic divide and allowed herself to wonder where she really belongs or what she truly deserves in life, material or otherwise. She reflects upon her Spartan lifestyle, the backlog of credit card and student debt she must take care of before life really starts moving. Back on 14th, she drives slowly by a liquor/grocery store, thinking it time to replenish her refrigerator, but at this point she's too tired and distracted. Those errands she referenced to Chris' aunt: they were real and immediate, but still depressing.

By the time she reaches her building the tears are gone and her face is dry. Her sense of Chris is already sketchy, and after a lengthy nap in a proper bed, she hopes everything will look and feel different with him consigned to an outgoing folder. She resolves not to do anything about the cell phone—just ignore it. With another two days off after a week packed with shifts at the hospital, free time stretches out in a way it hasn't seemed to in ages. Jill can't remember what she used to do for fun, for relaxation, before doing things for others established such a stranglehold upon her. Maybe a leisurely bike ride is called for, this time on the north side of Oakland, towards Berkeley, around Tilden Park. Later, or perhaps tomorrow, she might get a salon treatment: hair and nails are due some attention assuming Jillian, her regular stylist, is available. There are one or two friends she could call if she wants to hang out, but that's the least likely option. In truth, she knows she's singed a few bridges lately, partly because of Chris Leavitt, but mostly because she's forgotten how to be sociable, especially with women.

The interior of her building looks especially grim in contrast to the verdant loveliness of Chris' aunt's property. It's funny that despite her regular bicycling up in the hills, Jill hadn't experienced the differences quite so much as she had done within the last hour. Maybe it's residual sadness, her realization that what she was letting go, alongside Chris Leavitt, was this potential milieu from which he'd apparently been spawned. Then again, the signs were that he didn't really belong there either, so maybe it's just as well the multi-layered teasing, as it now seems, is over. Inside the elevator, Jill leans back against the unfashionably orange paneled wall, anticipating the lurching motion that should unnerve residents far more than it actually does. She presses the number eight along the column of lights and watches the movement, hypnotized by the not so steady ascent from one floor to the next.

At her apartment she notices the door is unlocked but initially thinks nothing of it. Instead, she sighs in self reproach, flashing in her mind the memory of rushing from home to join Angela Boyd and her posse on a mission to Adeline Street to intercept Chris and Sweet the day before. Oh well, if nothing's missing or vandalized then she'll consider herself lucky, but no more lucky than she deserves considering her recent streak of luck. She'd suffered two assaults in the last week: one stranger, one not. The last one was yesterday, from strangers, the two boys who'd snatched her bag and pulled her off her bike in the street. Prior to that it was Chris—that darker, lingering scene in that closet—that was a week ago now. Anyway, it was surely more than most people's fair share, even in West Oakland. To her right she sees a shadow in her peripheral vision. Turning, she catches a glimpse of a figure sneaking around the corner. It's that feral child from down the hall, the one she'd found playing with Chris in her apartment the day before yesterday.

"I see you," she calls out playfully. Though she can't actually see him, she can feel his impish grin. He also can't help himself: a giggle betrays him a second time before he whips around and points a toy gun at her.

"Ptchoo, Ptchoo. I got you," shouts the boy. Jill slumps against the door in mock collapse.

"Oh, how could you? I thought we were friends," she replies. The boy dashes behind the corridor wall, holding his position while again sneaking a look. He thinks this game's gonna continue forever. "Go home, now," Jill says, smiling placidly.

Inside, she removes a coat and tosses her pair of keys into the drawer that's beside her computer. She'd left that open too, she notices. Next, she gives the place a quick scan but doesn't see anything else obviously wrong. Then she heads into the kitchen and straight for the refrigerator for a snack, possibly something more substantial depending upon what's there. Inside are some peaches and a couple of apricots, which still look appetizing after a week. There's a bottle of milk days beyond its sell by date, and a tub of hummus that's been recently licked clean, as in within the hour. She pulls it from the fridge and holds it up to the light, feeling like an inspecting bear from the Goldilocks tale. She thinks to burst into the hallway and interrogate that boy as to whether he'd been lurking about in her apartment, perhaps hoping to see Chris again, only to get bored and then help himself to her food. There's just one thing that doesn't ring true: would he eat hummus?

Dimly she hears a cough and immediately places the sound near the bathroom adjacent to the bed, not the hallway, as she might have expected or hoped for. For a suspended moment, she forces herself to think the cough is a trick. That sound: it's her neighbor on the other side of the wall, she hopes, only her jumpy brain is saying otherwise. What she doesn't know is that just over twelve feet away, beyond the bathroom door that's ajar, a man once believed to be missing, probably dead, is straining to hold within him not only a stubborn, throaty tickle, but also an insistent stream, all the while trying to pull up his jeans without making a sound. Jill tip toes towards the bathroom, grateful that the one feature of the unit which is solid—the floor—is not creaking and therefore giving away her movements. She positions herself into a fighter's stance she learned in her Krav Maga class, ready to plunge through the door and attack the intruder. Her mind flashes on recent altercations. Not again, she determines. This time she's delivering the first blow.

With a heavy kick, Jill slams the door inwards, crashing it into Weed's left knee.

"Fuck," he exclaims, more out of fright than pain. No longer concealed, he sits haplessly on the toilet, having managed to pull his jeans just beyond his knees. With his left hand, he clutches the top button, hiding at least with his arm everything that's private. His right hand has moved instinctively to guard his face, either from assault, recognition, or both. Past his fingers, he dares to look at Jill, who looks more or less as he remembers her: she is thin, lean, wearing jeans like him, but above her waist only a tanktop that stretches taut over a bony shoulder. She remains fixed in her aggressive stance, staring twitchily at Weed because her class hasn't yet covered how to attack someone on the John. She seems poised to strike again, but seems to be weighing options.

"Do you mind?" Weed asks in a half-dignified, half-affronted voice.

Is he kidding?

"Oh, I'm sorry. You wanna finish up before I kick your ass?"

Weed stares at the wiry, muscular limbs pointed at him, thinking she can likely do what she says.

"Well, since you mention it…"

"Get out," spits Jill.

Weed stays calm. "Seriously? You don't recognize me?"

Jill pauses, like she's stumped by the question.

"I recognize you," she says reluctantly.

Weed pulls the door to his left so as to conceal just his lower half.

"So, why don't we chill out? You can get mad about a bunch of things if you just gimme a minute. What d'ya say?"

Jill is frozen with her arms raised and her feet spread apart like a soldier waiting for an order to stand down. Silently, she appraises Weed, reconciling his compromised position with all of her prejudices. Though she had never contrived an exact notion of him, she had figured that if she ever met Weed properly, then it would be her feeling the disadvantage. He looks different without the baseball cap, she decides. The once greasy hair, which speared out in chaotic directions the last time she saw him, is now somewhat contained in tight curls, looking fairly attractive. His face, now shorn of its previous arrogance, looks sorrowful and wounded. Peering around the door, showing both hands so as to not provoke his latest captor, Weed casts an appealing, desperate expression. "Please," he says, almost sweetly.

Unable to resist, Jill lets her shoulders relax; she drops her arms to her side and brings her legs together in seeming peace.

"You didn't plan this out too well, did you?"

Weed shrugs and continues to look gloomy. Humiliated, he finds little relief in Jill's relenting from overt hostility to caustic humor.

"Can ya…you know?"

"Fine. I'll be in the kitchen, seeing if I have any food left." She turns, half-thinking herself foolish and asking for trouble by walking away. Then again, this is one of Chris' friends—an asshole, no doubt—but not a gratuitous criminal, maybe. Anyway, he's back from the hole he's been hiding in, obviously. Now he wants something; something he figures he'll find in her apartment. Maybe he has a weapon with him and is inclined to use it, but somehow she doesn't think so. Jill Evans is unafraid. "You owe me some hummus," she calls out, entering the kitchen.

"I wondered what that…what that was." Weed grimaces as he rethinks his words. His voice affects familiarity, as if he and Jill have already struck a rapport.

"A new front door lock, too," Jill adds. Weed hears the sound of a liquid being poured into a glass, a cap being tossed across a counter—the milk, he guesses. The sound is brusque, careless and manly. This chick sounds like one who'd break Chris Leavitt in half as soon as fuck him. Weed quickly thinks of Chris. Sweet, the nickname of Chris' doltish friend Gavin and Weed's friend by proxy, also comes to mind. Everyone in his circle has a moniker, he once decreed. Widow. That's the name he'll assign to Jill, assuming this clique has any future together.

As the toilet flushes, he steps to the door and strikes a defiant pose, with both his thumbs tugging upon the edges of his jeans.

"You gonna wash those hands?" Jill asks coolly. Weed blinks and turns without complaint to the sink behind him. As the water runs, he spits up balls of phlegm and appears to study himself in the cabinet mirror. Jill steps forward.

"You gonna tell me why you're here, where you've been the last week?"

Weed looks up and sees his image reflected in the mirror; he doesn't like what he sees. Hearing Jill's question, he reflects upon his own simultaneously reasonable and unreasonable expectations: that he might have hoped, albeit briefly, that upon hearing of his survival, anyone with knowledge of his situation might express sympathy, perhaps even joy. Instead, what he gets is angry questions similar to what he used to hear from his parents; like he's come home three hours after his curfew or something.

"Uh…I'm looking for something. Have you seen Chris in the last week?"

"Maybe. Why ask me? Why don't you call him?"

Weed aims a hard, rebuking look into the glass but towards her, which for the first time sends a chill sensation through Jill.

"You think I haven't thought of that?"

"I think it's a no-brainer. Whether that means you thought of it, I don't know."

Part of him wants to match wits with this girl, exercise his own penchant for sarcasm. He could tell the first time he saw her that she thinks he's just some loser friend of her loser boyfriend; someone she can scoff at and treat like shit. He turns from the mirror and faces her, feeling a rush of blood, like he's about to start spitting the foulest of speeches, climaxing with his fist slamming into her chin, sending her sprawling across the room. He pauses. Seeing her flinch, he catches a glimpse of her slender throat tightening. Beneath her thin top he sees an impression of a nipple shaking slightly. The impulse towards rage mutates into something carnal as a peripheral glance surveys the tidy, untouched surface of her bed.

"Listen, you have no idea what I've been through over the last week."

"Same here," Jill retorts with attitude.

Unblinking, the two of them duel with their eyes. As her face is about to redden, Jill breathes out as Weed turns to his left and peers towards the light pouring in from the window.

"Okay. Here's the deal: Last week I came here with Chris, right? I gave him some stuff to hold onto; stuff he was supposed to leave here." Weed gestures to a spot in the corner of the room beyond the bed, as if indicting that space for not safeguarding his belongings. "It's a long story, but that stuff was important and I'm being followed, or was being followed by some dangerous people. I told Chris I'd be gone for a while and then I'd return to collect my stuff. If you haven't seen him, then you won't know that we had an accident with his truck and I was nearly killed. I don't know what happened to Chris 'cause we got separated and I lost my phone, but I'm pretty sure he escaped the scene. Over the last week, I've nearly drowned, after which I slept a night in a field. I've been traveling for days, during which I was kidnapped by some freak as I was tryin' to hitchhike back here, only to escape from that first thing this morning. Now I'm sorry about breaking into your place and maybe scaring the shit out of you, but I didn't break your lock—it's fine, though it's old and it sucks—and I promise to buy you another fucking tub of hummus. But please, pretty please, can ya help me find Chris Leavitt?"

All of a sudden, like a cop pulling a radio from a belt, Jill wields a cell phone and holds it up to the light, ready to press numbers. She stops as she realizes she's calling a device that at this moment is buzzing within the coffee cup holder of her car.

"Shit." She thinks for a second, and then scrolls down the index of recent calls, looking for the number that belongs to Sweet. Wait, she thinks next. They only texted each other, not called. Anyway, she tries sending a message while informing Weed that she'd just left Chris' company only a half hour earlier, at a house in the Oakland hills owned by one of Chris' relatives. Then she gives a short version of events from Chris' point of view. Weed hovers over her shoulder, nagging for more information. Did he say how long he'd be at this Aunt Jenny's house? He soon asks. He wonders if Chris had shared about anything belonging to him— some flash drives, he specifies. Jill is annoyed by Weed's self interest, but more or less accepts that the time is right for pragmatism, not lamenting. She replies that she saw Chris rooting through his backpack on their way up to the hills, but didn't seem especially anxious or excited about its contents. There's nothing of his here, Jill reports indifferently.

Weed turns and paces, knowing that there would be little reason for Chris to express either excitement or fear upon seeing the drives. Weed couldn't recall exactly what he'd said, but it wasn't quite the guard-these-with-your-life sentiment he might have expressed had he known what was in store for them last Wednesday night. Therefore, Weed now thinks of Chris as a host organism, carrying a disease the effects of which Weed himself doesn't understand, not yet anyway. Now that he's close to reuniting with Chris, the urge to recapture those drives and learn their secrets is escalating. He can see now that he is meant, as in destined, to recover and restore them to Jules Grotius. Meanwhile, Jill looks upon Weed with mixed feelings: on the one hand, she is moderately impressed that he has a mission about which he seems concentrated and serious; that he's not just a sleazy dealer intent on ditching Chris as soon as he's made use of him. On the other hand, this cant about drives, important, dangerous people and so on has the familiar ring of delusion. She flashes thoughts of Chris and his notions of revolutionary diapers. It hadn't occurred to her that Chris' friend might be something more like a kindred spirit than a criminal opportunist.

Weed spins to face Jill and asks her the question she knew was coming.

"Look, can't you just drive me to this Aunt Jenny's house? It's gotta be no more than a half hour to get there, right?"

Jill sighs. Her whole body seems to flatten.

"I don't know," she says limply.

"I'm sorry. I'm sure you have shit to do and it sounds like you've been through a lot already." Nice try, Jill thinks, regarding Weed's generic stab at empathy. He breaks out his wallet and pulls a few crumpled bills from a sodden looking leather sleeve. "Look, I'll pay for gas if that's a problem."

"That's not it. Let's wait. I just sent a text to him—to Sweet."

"Okay, but did he answer?" asks Weed.

"It—he—did before," she answers. She grips the phone, willing it to respond so she won't have to…

"How about a voicemail?"

Jill calls the number while Weed fusses. He's gone from apology to entitlement in about a minute. Jill shakes her head: no answer. She leaves a short message requesting a call back and indicating that she's with Weed. He remonstrates.

"Listen, even if they get that, do they have a car? Didn't you drive them up there? How can I meet them if—"

"Alright, goddamn it! I'll drive you there." Jill snatches at her coat, grabs her keys again, including the one to the apartment, not that it's of use to her in this neighborhood.

24

Sweet is following Chris, but he's also looking back over his shoulder. Like he said, Aunt Jenny's place is sweet, and despite a habit for itinerant living, he does not turn his nose up at the creature comforts of the wealthy. That hot tub in back: it caught his eye the moment he stepped out onto the back porch; he'd looked forward to a nice, leisurely soak in steamy hot water, with a cocktail by his side, perhaps, or even another cup of tea—this time with sugar. Ten yards ahead of him, with thoughts far removed from Sweet's reverie, Chris is keeping up a brisk, angry pace as they head down a road which winds down the hill to the main highway. It's maybe just over a mile away, which won't take long for them to reach given the steep incline. Were they walking in the opposite direction, it might take upwards of an hour. Good thing they're not coming back this way anytime soon, Chris thinks. He's at least a day away from feeling any sadness about this.

"There's a bus route along here," Chris announces, turning to face Sweet having reached a road situated parallel to the thirteen freeway.

"Uh, okay. So, where're we going?"

"What do you mean? We're going to LA, right?"

Sweet looks confused.

"I guess."

"What? What's the problem?" Chris demands.

"You," says Sweet, flapping his arms. "You make these decisions. You don't talk about them with me or with anyone. You just do it. You just do whatever comes into your mind at any given moment and you don't care about anyone else. Sorta reminds me of someone, you know what I mean?"

Chris is taken aback. "So…what are you saying? You wanna go back, stay at hotel Aunt Jenny? Didn't you get it? She doesn't want you there."

"Whoa, don't put that on me. She had an issue with you dropping out of school, clearly. Or she wanted you to take that job you talked about so that you're not dependent on her. She may not have thought me a Joe Winner, but that wasn't the reason she said to take a hike."

"Fine, then we're taking a hike. But we're also gonna use a bus, maybe a train, which you prefer anyway, don't you?"

"Yeah, I do, but that's not the point."

"What is your point, Sweet?"

"My point is that you should slow down, think what you're doing. Talk to me. Don't just…act."

Chris wears a mute look about him, as if Sweet were asking the impossible. This is one of his more strident outbursts, in keeping with the new persona Sweet had sort of revealed the day before, just prior to the police visit on Adeline. Instead of the bumbling, socially awkward front he typically displays, now he's the calm, sage-like companion, keeping a watchful, brotherly eye on things, and capable of astute observations. He's the mysterious friend whom others underestimate and overlook, while secretly he machinates over plans. Sweet has a plan for a job down in LA, near Hollywood; he has separate ambitions to complete his film project, including a set of interviews such as the one he'd made of Chris a couple of days ago. Chris was cooperative, but at least until the last installment, wherein he supplied an on-camera confession of what happened in Marin, he had no idea what the film was about. It is Sweet's creative obsession, this capturing of stories in a random form—an act of faith of sorts.

"Alright, I'm sorry," Chris moans. "I mean, I'm sorry we came here. It was a mistake. And you're right. I shouldn't expect her to subsidize me while I keep changing my mind about shit."

Sweet nods approvingly but isn't satisfied.

"Then why not tell her that, or—ya know—some version of that, especially if she's right."

Chris grimaces. "Her being right makes it worse. She knows me. That's the problem. I know a lot of things said about me are true. I just don't wanna hear about 'em from other people."

"See, this is why it's good that you're gonna meet the folks of Cassandra's Children. They'll relate to you, know you. It'll be okay. I just need to stick close to you in case you get all hot-headed around the wrong people."

"Shadows, you mean?" Chris wears a worried expression. He stiffens like an obedient soldier being instructed by a mentoring officer.

"Yeah, but remember, though Shadows is a common term, it doesn't fit everyone's understanding. It's about the afflicted, meaning the guilty and the victimized. We don't know for sure who is who, so we have to take our time, not be—what's the word—hasty?"

"You know I haven't seen any in a while," says Chris, pleased.

"That's good. I think that means you're feeling grounded right now. Meaning, you're starting to deal with things."

Chris frowns. "I'm still confused. What about the visions—'the gift' you called it. If we focus on ourselves and deal with reality, that's all good. You're saying if we get better, we have fewer visions, less disturbance. But what about the ability to see injustice, the future? Who takes responsibility for that stuff? What's the point of that gift if people stop using it?"

Sweet tries patience. "I'm not saying the gifted stop having visions entirely. It just stops being out of control. The confusion stops because the obsessive part of it stops. At some point you stop feeling dogged by the visions; you learn to separate what's a real event that you can foresee, versus a bunch of shit that's just coming from your own head." He strikes a note of humility. "I'm not saying I know how it's supposed to play out. I'm not the one with all the answers. I just listened to others in the organization who explained this stuff to me, and it helped when I was confused. It calmed me down."

"So what do I do?"

"You live your life, I guess. You come down to LA with me; stay with me and my girl Annabelle, help me with my movie, give it shape, some energy. Maybe you get a job. I don't know. But it seems to me you could do with some time without being followed, or without thinking about who's following you, at least."

At this point, Chris goes blank like an autistic child caught in lights. Anomalously, he brings to mind the image of Annabelle, Sweet's new girlfriend, whose Facebook page Sweet had shown him earlier in the week. Chris thinks she looks strange, and a bit too young. Sweet laughs. "Chris? Don't make me feel like a fool now. You there?"

"I'm good. I was just thinking about Weed."

"What about him?"

Chris squirms. "I wonder if he'll try to find me. Follow me?"

Sweet is dismissive. "Sorry, dude. Like I said yesterday, I think he only cares about himself. I mean, it's good that he's alive, and I could see that was a relief for you to learn that. But it should tell you something that a week's gone by and he hasn't tried to contact you."

Again, something inside Chris bristles at Sweet's biases.

"Yeah, though I don't know why," he says.

"Because you wanna believe he cares about you. Makes sense." Chris feels an agitation rise. Now he's not sure he likes this other, more assured side of Sweet's character. He gestures towards his backpack.

"Well, I still have some stuff of his. Maybe he'll want it back?"

Sweet is unimpressed, distracted. "He'll get it if he really wants it. In the meantime, what bus comes around here?"

"I'm not sure. Let's look up a schedule."

Sweet pulls a face. "My battery's dead. That's why it would have been good to stay at your aunt's place for a while. I got nowhere to use my charger. Where's your phone?"

Chris' stomach drops as though his body knows something he doesn't. Body memory: it's lacking, but it searches anyway. First he grabs the back of his pants, checks the front and back pockets. Moments later, he's pouring out the contents of his backpack, spilling delicate items like flash drives on the curb. Chris knows this poring over is futile. A vision—Shadow-like— enters his mind.

"Fuck. It's in Jill's car still."

Sweet flaps his arms but wears a vaguely satisfied grin, as if this were a predestined victory for a Luddite cause. Behind him, a white Dodge Ram truck, which has just sped past he and Chris, stops abruptly and goes into reverse. As it pulls up just in back of Sweet, Chris catches sight of a logo on the passenger side. Seeing the words "Cost" and "landscaping", he makes quick associations. His eyes pore over the lane-hogging, muscular vehicle.

"Hey, buddy, what's happening?"

It's Costman, Aunt Jenny's mow and blow gardener, calling out from the driver's seat through the now lowered passenger side window. Chris waves listlessly and nods. Sweet turns and squints, looking distrustful. "You heading up to your Aunt's house or what?" Costman asks.

"Nah, I'm heading out—got some stuff to do."

"Uh-huh," the gardener replies. "Hey, what was that all about yesterday, with those two people that came by?" In this, Chris infers his aunt's discretion, as it seems Costman isn't even aware that Armstrong and Boyd were cops.

"Oh, that was some business I had to deal with—still have to, actually."

"Okay," says Costman, looking glassy-eyed and distracted by the road ahead, his blocking of a lane into the hills. Costman isn't ordinarily nosy, but even he wants to know why Chris is back in the neighborhood with a stranger standing next to him, and now saying he's leaving again after the seeming drama of the previous day.

"Say, do you know about the bus routes around here? My friend and I need to get going."

"Where're you heading?"

"Train station."

Costman twists his neck looking behind himself.

"Uh, this is—what?—Mountain Boulevard, right? I'm pretty sure there's a service along here. Don't know if it takes you West, though. Sorry."

"It's cool."

"You coming back anytime soon?" This is unlike Costman, Chris thinks. The detached, free-spirited handyman almost seems worried, lonesome even.

"Maybe. I'll see ya," Chris says, waving again and backing off. As he speaks, Sweet collects the remainder of items from the ground. It's like he's looking for something. He says "ask him for a ride" just above a whisper.

"Okay," Costman says in response to Chris, still sounding forlorn. He's not a complicated guy; he knows when he's being blown off. He drives away, leaving Sweet plaintive.

"What the hell. Why not ask him for a ride?"

Chris' eyes glaze over. "I didn't think of it until you said it—don't know why. Maybe I don't want him telling my aunt where we're going."

Sweet gazes out over Oakland. "Well, we should make our way to a station, but not downtown."

"Don't you need anything from your place?"

"Like what?"

"I don't know—your film equipment, maybe?"

"I got stuff down south, at Annabelle's parents' place."

Chris winces. "She lives with her parents."

"In a guest house. It's cool. It won't be for long, anyway."

The two friends each pull on their respective backpacks and acknowledge the other's readiness.

"So is this it? Ready?"

Sweet gestures towards a narrow pedestrian's path alongside the Boulevard. A bus stop with a schedule is about a couple of hundred yards away.

"You lead," Sweet invites, feeling an ache in his back.

25

As Jill drives along 35th avenue, heading east again, Weed scrolls through text messages and e-mails on Chris' phone with investigatory interest. He finds nothing that suggests contact with anyone at Sahi or anyone from their neighborhood who may also be looking for Weed. According to Jill, OPD investigators were the only ones looking for Chris as far as she knows, though he was jumped by someone from her local park the day before—guys who said they were looking for Weed. Getting jumped: she says it like it's an everyday occurrence where she lives. Weed keeps to himself a sneaking suspicion as to who Chris' assailants were. Rival dealers selling shitty skunk product: jealousy and paranoia; they think he owes them money. Weed pauses. Wait a minute—do I? He wonders. As Jill supplies successive unknowing answers to Weed's questions, she becomes aware of her limited role in this situation. Right now, she's just the driver of a car that, if Weed's expression when getting in is anything to go by, isn't up to his fast and furious standards.

Weed continues playing with Chris' cell phone, simultaneously pleased and chagrinned that Chris hasn't taken precautions and applied a security lock. He'd probably forget the password, Weed figures. Thinking ahead, he knows he'll have to replace his own lost phone at some point. Somewhere out there, hookups, regulars, or rivals, are collectively thinking *WTF* with respect to his absence. Now out of a job, he'll need to get back in touch soon; that is, unless he wants to start building a consumer base all over again. That might be hard, though not too hard, as Weed's dealer reputation is pretty good on the whole. Meanwhile, the alternatives are not great. In fact, that's why Weed started targeting business in Richmond and El Cerrito: the stuff people were smoking there was hella pin as far as he was concerned.

So he makes a call—a quick one, to one of his hookups whose name, if Jill is hearing right, is something like "Scar". The call establishes to someone else in Weed's life that he is alive, not that the person Weed's talking to thought otherwise, and also that Weed will be incognito for a spell, but will be returning soon. There's no problem with that, it seems. Weed learns from his hookup that a couple of homeboys from Oakland were indeed looking for him, and that cops were asking questions, too. Best that he chills, says the hookup.

"Word," utters Weed, using a vernacular that ill suits him, while acknowledging the hookup's news without too much concern. Then his thoughts cloud over. Suddenly it occurs to him that his followers of the previous Wednesday were not who he thought they were. He dwells upon all that he had decided that day: his decision to steal the files, to disappear, to leave the pond of small fish and incur the wrath of big boys, people who do not play nicely. Suddenly, it seems to him that much of this drama has been created in his own head, and that only his conceit has led him to think otherwise. Still, first things first: do nothing, chill out, get mad, but above all, don't talk about it.

Afterwards, Weed touches a finger to the phone's camera roll and flicks through the scores of images, many of which feature him and Chris, as well as some of those hookups, regulars and rivals, staring wide-eyed and intoxicated amid the black background of some party in the area. These were strictly social occasions for Chris, but something like business meetings for Weed. Attending parties was how he scouted product, made assessments, saw opportunities and made cash. Weed hates the pictures of himself. Camera lenses seem drawn to the pudgy girth beneath his chin, the blotches of red on his neck. On most shots he is unsmiling, looking *serious*. Chris, on the other hand, seems to know just how to aim his devilish, seductive eyes into an onlooker; to smile and exhibit his much coveted, dimpled face.

"So lemme me ask you a couple of things," Jill requests haughtily. Weed cautiously agrees. "Do you know much about Chris' aunt? You don't seem to."

Weed gives her a quizzical look. That wasn't exactly the question he expected.

"No. Is there something I should know?"

"I'm not sure. She's been his benefactor, sort of—didn't know if you knew that. I think he depends on her, has done ever since his father died and his mom moved to the east coast. That was over a decade ago. His aunt dotes on him. You sure you've never heard any of this?"

Weed still feels unenlightened; also impatient. "Why're you telling me this?" he asks.

"Again, I'm not sure. It seems to me the kind of thing that he might have told his friends. I guess he kept to himself. It seems to me that people don't really know Chris. Maybe people don't know you, either."

"Thanks."

"No problem. Did you know Chris was thirty three years old?"

"Excuse me?"

"Yeah, weird, huh? It threw me, too. We—meaning, his friend Sweet and I—found out because he left his driver's license somewhere."

"Okay," Weed replies bemusedly. "I have no idea what to make of that."

"Neither does he—not really. He talked about it this morning, said he had an accident in his early twenties, or something. Got burned. Had plastic surgery. He showed me scars."

Weed becomes pensive. "Similar thing happened to me. I had an accident when I was younger, I mean." He shakes his head as though clearing away cobwebs. "Anyway, I still don't get what this has to do with anything."

Jill takes a sharp tone.

"Do you care about him? Do you like him, even?"

Weed thinks she has a helluva nerve asking this question.

"Whoa, where's this coming from? Listen girlfriend, I explained to you what happened."

"Don't call me girlfriend."

"Okay, Jill—my bad—you obviously have a problem with me. Mind telling me what's up?"

"You don't know? You have no idea?" Weed sees her angst-ridden face half-focused on the road, half-flitting over towards him. He has a moment of horror. Hers is a classic provocation to a deadbeat lover, only he hasn't had the benefits.

"I can guess, but I'm told it's best for people to express themselves instead of leaving others guessing."

"Well, I hope your guessing is good, 'cause you know what? I've been going through it, and not just over the last week.

He disappears, hangs out with you and whomever else. He causes havoc at work, which comes back at me. When you came over last week and he was whacked out, you looked like you were enjoying watching us fight. And until I found him wandering the streets last Monday, I had no idea where he was. He could've been dead for all I knew. Plus, he thought you were dead, and was pretty relieved this morning to hear you weren't. You don't seem to care about that."

"Sorry," says Weed, now properly chastened. His mouth flattens.

"Yeah, so what's so important? What is it that you're back for? What do you want from Chris, because as far as I can tell, he's better off getting away from you."

As her voice rises, Jill notices Weed receding into himself. She regards his upper half, sees also that he's shivering somewhat. She notes that he's seemed shaky from the first moment she saw him. Perhaps he's coming down off something, she supposes.

"Well listen, if you think that, why don't you just drop me off right now and we can forget about it. I'll find Chris by myself.

"Because I wanna know what's happened. In case you hadn't noticed, I'm involved. I've just spent the night at a police station, and if you're sorry—really sorry—then you'll tell me more. I deserve to know."

Weed sits back and swallows hard. He coughs.

"Okay, maybe you have a point. Um…" He flounders, not knowing where to begin.

"What are you looking for that you gave to Chris last week? He said nothing about this."

"That was the point. It was confidential. I swore him to secrecy, thinking I was being followed by some corporate security guys. Maybe I wasn't. I don't know. I was pretty whacked out myself, thinking these people were…something else."

Jill nods as she listens, checking off the similarities. This all sounds like something Chris would say. Weed continues: "I had these drives, flash drives that I took from work. They're important, worth a lot of money, but possibly much more than that."

"He told me you tested video games or something. Is that what this is about? You stole some game files from work?"

"Sort of."

"What...sort of. Did you or didn't you?"

"Yeah." Weed stops and coughs again. It's a thick, hoarse sound that Jill recognizes.

"You need to get that looked at, by the way. Did you know you were sick?"

"Kind of. I've had other things on my mind."

"So, I was right, basically. You're a thief, and Chris is like your runner, or something. Jesus!"

"No, that's not why I stole the files."

"Then why?"

Weed glowers at her; then turns away, like he still doesn't know. He draws breath.

"Okay, do you know who Jules Grotius is?" he asks, stuttering slightly on Jules' surname.

"Yes, of course."

Weed makes a move of mock-recoil. While Jules is by no means obscure, Weed didn't think the question merited an "of course".

"What would you say if I told you that Jules Grotius has designed a game, an online video game that is like no other, with a subversive aim that could have wide social implications? And it was my job to check the game out, work out its bugs."

"What are you talking about?"

"So, at my job, I was a tester, like you said. Recently, I was given this game to work on by my boss. So I play the game, looking for glitches in the design—that's my job. Then I notice that the game has elements that I recognize, and I realize that it's special, this game."

"What kind of elements?"

Weed pauses, knowing this is a banana skin question. "That's not that important, actually. But my recognizing the game means I know where it's going—what it's about."

"I'm glad because I've no idea where you're going with this."

"Anyway, neither my boss nor anyone else knows that I'm thinking this, even though I've been entrusted with the program and have to report back to him. Then, Jules comes by the office one day and drops off the remaining files for the completion of the program. The thing is I had this feeling that the people at Sahi might betray him, and that this game might be…I don't know, destroyed maybe, or altered, without his permission."

Jill is shaking her head, looking dubious. "So, you thought, or felt his game might be stolen from him, or destroyed. So what? I still don't get why this was worth losing your job, much less everything you say you've been through over the last week; everything Chris, myself, have been through."

Jill's Honda turns onto Mountain Boulevard. She indicates that they are minutes away from Aunt Jenny's house. Weed slides down in his seat, poised to share the aspects of his story that will really test Jill's credulity. Well, she asked for this, he thinks.

"Okay, you're gonna laugh at this and think me crazy, but there's something Chris and I have in common. Has he ever talked to you about people called Shadows?"

"What?"

"Shadows. They're visions we have, of people that position themselves next to others, indicating crimes committed, or crimes that will be committed."

"Hallucinations?" Jill asks calmly.

"Sort of. Not really. What can I say? Shared hallucinations, maybe." Weed gives her a boyish smile. Kind of charming, she quickly thinks. "I know what this sounds like," he adds. He becomes solemn: "But this is the reason I've bailed from my job, waded through slime, hitchhiked over miles, and gone through hell over the last week. Chris and I are the kind of people who see important things that others don't. I never used to think they were important. Until now, I've never thought I needed to do anything with this disorder, curse, gift, or whatever it is. That is, until this game, which features characters that are like Shadows, came across my desk. Now, I don't fully know what Grotius' ambitions are, and I'm pretty sure he didn't see that Sahi officials were gonna betray him."

"To whom? How do you know they are?"

"Because I saw it," Weed replies with a look of divine knowledge.

"A Shadow, I take it—standing next to Jules Grotius. You're saying he's gonna use this Shadows thing in this game, as a way for whistleblowers to reach the public with disclosures."

Weed touches a finger to his nose and smiles. She gets it. She turns cautiously onto to a road that leads into the hills. Street names don't matter so much, as Jill is feeling her way to the right place. She turns onto a short cul-de-sac, sees the gravel driveway of Chris' aunt's home up ahead, and pulls up behind a huge, white Dodge Ram truck.

"This is it."

Suddenly, Weed is nervous. What will be Chris' reaction to seeing him? What's the deal with this aunt that Jill keeps mentioning, and how long will he have to deal with small talk, happy or unhappy reunions, or currents events before taking Chris aside to see if he has his drives with him? The questions shame Weed. But those questions are just the beginning. Soon he'll have to go about the task of finding Grotius, which is no small task since he's likely gone into hiding, using an alias and wearing a disguise no doubt. Maybe Ed Kim will have contact, which begs another question: does he trust him? Is he a part of this? There are other decisions, other assessments he's yet to make. It depends on how much time Weed has to find Grotius. Doing the expedient thing might be best, but the last thing he knows is just how urgent this whole situation is. For all he knows, he could hold onto those files forever, not say anything. Maybe Sahi wasn't following him after all? Maybe they don't even care, or maybe these drives don't even contain anything important? But then, what about the Shadows? What is their purpose here? Maybe they're destined to disappear, just like Jules' whistleblowers; just like Jules Grotius, maybe, or Weed himself?

Jill leads him to the front door. As she rings the doorbell, she notices Weed is standing back, as if set to run away. He looks about the house, looking uncomfortable. He is still shaking.

"Some time after we're inside, I'm gonna ask if they have a thermometer. The woman who lives here is elderly. She has housekeepers, nurses, I think. They probably have some first aid stuff. We need to check you out."

"Elderly? Is she a great-aunt or something?"

"I don't think so, but like I said, Chris is older than we thought."

The door opens with the same chainy sound it gave the first visit. She could use one of those chains for her door, Jill thinks—not that it would have made any difference earlier. Briefly, she looks back at Weed, seeing his now passive, somewhat diffident demeanor. The bravado or sociopathy she'd once attributed to him seems absent now. There's no doubt in her mind that he would have done whatever was necessary to get into her apartment. But would he have assaulted her?

"Hello," greets the same Latino housekeeper that answered the door the first time. She looks at Jill like she doesn't remember her.

"Hi, I'm Jill. I was here earlier, with Chris."

"He's not here."

"Uh, okay. Did he just go out? I mean, do you know when he might be back?"

"No. I don't know. He say something to Ms. Jenny. She's not happy."

Jill turns, meets Weed's eyes. They look quizzical.

"Do you mean he's not coming back? Excuse me, but can I talk to his aunt?"

"Hold on." The woman closes the door, after which Weed starts to agitate.

"What the hell," he says, exasperated. Jill hushes him, reminding that it's important to chill out and not panic. A minute later, the housekeeper returns. They are invited inside.

"Whoa, talk about secrets," says Weed as he walks through the front entry, staring at the decor. By this point, Aunt Jenny is being wheeled inside by a second helper, a barrel-chested man wearing a maroon shirt. She calls behind her as she crosses the threshold from her back porch to her living room.

"And move that damned monster truck of yours. I've told you not to park in front of my begonias." On a dime, her expression turns as she sees Jill. A skin-cracking smile animates her.

"Hello my dear. I'm pleased to see you, though I'm afraid Chris has left already, as I think Magdalena has told you."

"Yes, she has. Um…I'm sorry, I'm not sure what to call you."

"Call me Jenny. And who is this?" Jenny peers around Jill's body to see the dismal figure that is Weed. He half attempts a smile while hers flattens, like they are meeting each other half way. Jenny regards Weed as if he were something her gardener was meant to snare and then release down by the creek.

"Jenny, this is friend of Chris'—the one who went missing. They went on a trip together and got separated. He was injured and unable to communicate, but he's been looking for Chris all this time, it seems. I said I'd help him."

Weed gives Jill a sideways glance and feels grateful for her charitable description.

"I see," Jenny says noncommittally. Weed doesn't know her, but he can immediately tell that when Jenny Leavitt says something like "I see" it's not to convey goodwill. "Well, why wasn't he with you earlier?" she asks.

"He thought he might find Chris at my apartment. He was there when I returned just now."

Jenny nods uncertainly. "I'm sorry, but as I said Chris has left already. I'm afraid I can't help you."

There is an awkward pause. Jill leans down towards Jenny's face. She whispers.

"Jenny, something's happened, with you and Chris, I mean. Can you tell me? I want to help. Really."

Jenny returns a hard, if sympathetic look. "My dear, what are you mixed up in? Driving back and forth like this, spending the night at the jail: I sent Chris and his other friend packing because he breaks promises, won't commit to anything. As an intelligent woman, you should be wary of such habits, not be taken in by them."

Jill nods like a reverent schoolgirl. Embarrassed, she says, "I know, and you're right. But I think this might be important. We—Bryan has some important information he needs to get from Chris. I think it's something related to Chris' work."

"Work?" Jenny asks. She narrows her eyes at Jill. "Don't treat me like a fool, dear."

The atmosphere suddenly loses its spring-like warmth. Weed steps forward, surprising Jill with the confidence of his movement.

"Ma'am, please understand this is my fault. Last week, Chris and I were involved in an accident in Marin County. I had asked him to take me there because I had committed a theft at my workplace, Sahi communications, for reasons that are complicated so I won't go into them now. But because I was nervous about being caught, I asked him to hold onto some electronic equipment which I promised to collect from him later. If Chris has been withholding this from you or Jill here, it's because I asked him to keep this all secret. Ma'am, he likely is what you say, but to me he's been nothing less than honorable. He is committed to some things. He's committed to friendship, kept a promise between us. He trusted me, and while I've no right to ask this, I'm asking you to help me. Can you tell us anything about where he might be headed now?"

Jenny is reluctantly moved by Weed's speech.

"Well, aren't you the noble savage," she says. "But it doesn't change anything. You see, I am not Chris' friend. I am family, which means I know little. Unfortunately, Chris does not keep his promises to me, and furthermore, I do not collude with secrets. Chris knows this and as a result suffers a terrible conflict. Young man, I could tell you a few things about the secrets Chris has kept in his life. Anyway, the point is he doesn't, and didn't tell me about his plans, about where he was going—"

"Jenny, sorry to interrupt, but Chris was talking about going to LA, with his other friend," says Jill.

"Was he?" Jenny replies, confused.

Weed jumps in.

"Look, Chris knows I'm alive. Sorry, ma'am, that was a piece we left out—Chris might have thought I was dead, because of the accident. But he must know that I'm looking for him. He'll want to see me."

Jill, begging to differ, whispers an aside. "That wasn't the impression I got, actually."

"What?"

A ring on the doorbell interrupts the exchange. At once, everyone—Weed, Jill, Jenny, even Magdalena and her muscular assistant—all turn their heads to the door like a cast in a cheesy farce. The punchline is about to be delivered.

"That'll be Costman, asking after something. I've insisted he use the front door because it has concrete steps that are easier to clean and I'm tired of him parking his awful truck in my driveway and treading dirt on my porch."

Magdalena answers the door and appears to have a conversation with someone invisible to the group. From a distance, the group can hear her thick accent with its truncated vowel sounds straining to get out. Tentatively, she opens halfway the front door to reveal a twenty-something man dressed neatly in a mint suit, with short hair and a winning smile.

Eric Pierce.

"He also looking for Crisf," Magdalena calls out. Pierce tilts his head and raises his eyebrows in support of the implied question.

"Who is he?" Jenny asks, speaking for the assembly. Weed's back is to the door. He feels a new chill, looks slightly to his left to see if Jill seems anywhere near as concerned as he is. She isn't.

"He say he from Crisf's work," Magdalena says next. Weed whispers Jill's name. When he catches her eye he shakes his head. The man calls out.

"Ma'am, if I can just have a moment of your time, we'd like to speak to Chris, but we've been having difficulty reaching him, and we understand you're a relative of his."

"No," Weed gasps, but the effort fails. His presumption about Jenny being hard of hearing: it works both ways.

"Come in, if you like. We've been talking about Chris. I'm afraid we don't have much information. It seems everyone's looking for my nephew. Welcome to my life," Jenny says with a pale and bitter laugh. By now, Jill has caught on to Weed's discomfort, though she is between minds.

"Excuse me, could you tell us exactly who you represent?" she asks sternly. Eric Pierce glances between her and the housekeeper who is just about blocking entry.

"May I?" he asks.

He is cautiously allowed in as Weed closes his eyes for a moment and maintains his position. Eric nods appreciation for his entry, and then asks, "I'm sorry, what was your question again?"

"Who are you and who are you working for?" Jill asks, unsmilingly.

"My name's Pierce. I work for Alta McMahon, of course," Eric says, maintaining his pleasant air. Seeing Weed continue to look as though he's hiding, Jill becomes hostile.

"Really, do you have an ID or something," she asks.

"A work ID, you mean. No, I don't." He says it like it was obvious he wouldn't; as if Jill had asked a stupid question.

"Well, I work for Alta McMahon and I have an ID. Here you are, looking for Chris Leavitt, saying you work for Alta McMahon, but we don't know that. We don't know what your interest is. Jenny, I think you should ask this man to leave."

Eric laughs. "Ma'am—I'm sorry, I don't know your name."

"Right, because I didn't give it."

Eric looks past Jill, towards Jenny, gives a jittery, endearing laugh, and overplays pleasantries. "Ma'am, I'm sorry to trouble you, but I think you know Chris has had some trouble at work, and I've been sent to try and find him, and help him. Like you I'm sure, we have his best interests at heart." Halfway through this statement, Eric Pierce notices the man standing on the other side of Jill and Aunt Jenny. He is one of two other men in the room, the other being a large, mute-looking figure in a dark shirt. But this other man has his back turned; his upper body is visibly trembling, and the head shape, even from behind, suddenly looks familiar.

Eric Pierce instantly connects dots, pulls out a firearm and points it at the group.

"Oh my God," shrieks Jenny as she grips Jill's arm. Weed spins around, smirking at the intruder. Eric Pierce's smile graduates to a triumphant grin.

Tecco—Gotcha.

Instinctively, Jill crouches and leans her body over Jenny. Magdalena slumps into the arms of her assistant and speaks frenetic Spanish. Weed is still. Ironically, even the trembling has stopped.

"Whaddya want, bro?"

"You know."

Weed grins in return. "Search me." He holds out his arms, opening up his body like he's ready to be crucified. "Go ahead, knock yourself out. Take me out of here if you have to. But leave them out of it. This is nothing to do with them. Believe me, they won't do anything. They'll just be glad I'm gone."

"Jesus," says Jill, glaring at Weed.

"Stop this ridiculous bravado," rebukes Jenny, like she's speaking to both men.

Eric Pierce's eyes dart about the room, studying the layout. Moving along a wall adjacent to a kitchen, he treads closer to the group, eliciting panicky moans from the housekeeper. The man beside her tries to shush her. Now Pierce is blunt.

"Okay, be quiet now. S—shut up!"

"Look, what do you want?" Jill asks, her voice shaking.

Pierce reaches an edge to the wall and peers around. He sees a door beyond the kitchen.

"First things first. What's behind that door?"

"Garage," says the man in the maroon shirt. Eric looks at him, at the menacing bulk that envelopes the man's soft brown eyes. Eric nods, appreciating cooperation. Stepping backwards, he moves towards this door, opens up, and surveys the garage. Magdalena's moaning continues. Her body quivers like she's going into seizure. Her midsection writhes, unable to control her bladder.

"Outside, who owns the Honda?"

"Me," says Jill.

"The rusty oldsmobile?" The man in the dark shirt raises his arm.

Pierce takes out a knife and begins a sawing action against something unseen next to the doorway. His witnesses exchange bemused looks, save for the man holding Magdalena.

"He's cutting the line to the garage door," he murmurs.

"Okay," Pierce announces. "Everyone's coming in here. The woman on the floor first, then you, big guy."

The assistant pulls Magdalena to her feet, holds her tenderly, and leads her through the kitchen. Pierce halts them at the door.

"You two next," says Pierce, looking at Jill and Aunt Jenny. The old woman purses her lips, exuding contempt. She wheels herself forward, only to stop right before the intruder. She aims a glance at his handgun, then up at Eric Pierce's face. With these gestures she makes a fierce statement: "That piece of metal is all there is to you, young man." Pierce ignores the remark.

Jill follows Aunt Jenny, solemn and unchallenging.

"You stay there," Pierce says to Weed, who remains standing with his arms out, awaiting inspection and looking as though he approves of all the measures being taken so far. "Alright, everyone inside," Pierce announces. It's a short march forward: Magdalena and her assistant step down three steps into the garage; Jenny's wheelchair stalls at the edge. "Help her," directs Pierce, looking at Jill who is looking back to Weed. Her look is frightened, regretful. She wants to say something to him.

"Don't," she utters towards Pierce as she pushes the chair onto each step. "Just don't…" she pleads, glancing backwards one more time.

26

Two separate busses take Chris and Sweet to Jack London Square in Oakland. Sweet had intended to go to the 73rd street train station near the airport, but as he talks about the plan, some guy sitting next to them leans over and advises that the airport train doesn't have direct service to LA—that for some reason it heads north to Sacramento before turning south. It takes them almost an hour to get to the Jack London station so they can then wait another hour before the train arrives for the journey ahead. It'll be a further nine hours before they reach LA. Not knowing Weed's recent turns as a pedestrian, Chris complains that they might save money and maybe even time by hitting the road and sticking up their thumbs instead.

"No way," jokes Sweet, in reference to recently arduous walking stints with Chris. "I aint walking with you anymore." At the station Sweet plays sugardaddy: he buys the tickets, just as he did with the busses, while Chris languishes on a row of seats that remind him of the waiting area at the jail. On a metal strip between chairs, there are carved-in pieces of graffiti marking statewide gangs' hegemony. XIV: the letters catch Chris' eye and then transfix him for several moments, stirring fanciful thoughts. There are many kinds of secret societies, he muses; many ways in which people without power in the conventional sense congregate, conspire, and rebel in this world. Chris looks forward to meeting those contacts in the group Sweet has called Cassandra's Children. That meeting promises the company of like-minded people at last, though Chris wonders if his and their gifts, their secrets, will prove any more meaningful than those kept by the kids of International Boulevard.

Sweet returns from his task and gives the details of the journey. It'll be a long-ass day, he reports.

"I've been thinking of something," Chris says. "If neither of us has a phone, no one can get in touch with us."

Sweet scratches his head. "Okay…so? I mean, we won't really need one until we get close to LA and I need to call Annabelle. We can probably charge the phone on the train."

"My point is that even if Weed did wanna get in touch, he couldn't."

Sweet sighs like he's bored with this subject already. His tone becomes condescending, which disorients Chris. Somewhere amid the generosity and support—that thing about friends *being there* for him—the dynamics have changed, and Sweet now, as well as Jill, and Weed before them, has assumed authority. Bad move. It's true Chris lied about his age. It's true he's always wanted to be younger than he is. But he never bargained for being treated like this—like a child, and certainly not by Sweet.

"Yeah, well, it's not like he didn't have his chance. Like I said, a whole week's gone by since that accident, from which he apparently walked away."

"I didn't even think he could swim," Chris says wistfully.

"Well, unless Marin County hires blind divers, I guess he can swim well enough. He's probably up near Mendocino right about now, getting a pot grower's license and setting up business. You'll hear from him—like a year from now."

Chris chuckles. "You know, one of the cops said something like that back at the jail, about the grower's license I mean. I don't think they even took the case seriously, to be honest—except the woman, Boyd."

"Chicks," says Sweet with characteristically lighthearted derision. He rolls his neck, turns a greedy eye towards Chris' backpack.

"Hey, you got any more pills?"

Chris roots through the bag but turns up nothing. He thinks he might have spilled them on the side of Mountain Boulevard, or possibly in Jill's car. He apologizes, but as he sees his friend suffer with persistent aches, he considers that his neglect will yield benefits. The accidents: some are good news, some not. Within a week, Sweet will be over these cravings...he hopes.

On the train, they settle into coach class, which is about as comfortable as Greyhound. Sweet falls heavily into a seat, pledging to nap most of the way south. The train pulls slowly away, a lumpen quarter mile of electrified metal that will soon be rolling down California. Chris, reminding Sweet of the phone issue, takes the cell and cord from his pocket and heads down the car's length, checking under seats, asking odd passengers if there are outlets anywhere. Only in the overnight cabins, says someone; maybe in the bathrooms, says someone else. He walks through one cabin, and passes onto the next. He steps over the legs of an elderly man whose body protrudes into the aisle. At the end of the car he waits behind a door marked "occupied", thinking that he and Sweet can take turns using the bathroom to charge the phone. He notes that his energy is good, and that he feels free. No recharging of his mood is necessary. Mindful of Sweet's difficulty, he reflects upon all the drugs he's done over the last year, and the few leftover that he was selling recently, but which are now gone, accidentally or not. Unbeknownst to him, a speeding Subaru is pulling into the

Amtrak station at Jack London Square just as the train is pulling out. Chris Leavitt is untroubled. It feels good to be free and clean, he realizes. Damned good.

27

For one whole day, Eric Pierce's job had returned to normal in so far as he was back on a computer, picking up a phone, doing research. His desk was missing. So too was the rest of his office, the short commute in Sacramento, and his not so friendly colleagues. Out in Fairfax, sitting in a motel, he felt more properly alone, and restless. Mid-day on Wednesday, he called his boss, Gagliano, and informed him of the trip to Bolinas, which revealed that Bryan Tecco had wandered into town the previous Wednesday night and spoken to a few locals. This was something that police, who still thought Tecco was missing, had not established. He further told Gagliano that a friend of Tecco's was linked to an accident that occurred on that same Wednesday—a friend that was also missing. Gagliano approved of Pierce's plan to follow the trail of Chris Leavitt. He could care less about the drudgery that would be involved, the phone calls to individual homes; the social media searches that might uncover personal or employment information of this Leavitt guy. Gagliano sounded uptight on the phone: things were getting urgent, and he was under pressure from higher levels. This situation was important, he said; others were on the case of these missing files, only they were following leads in Southern California. Others were being given similar leeway as Pierce to act upon leads. There were unprecedented instructions, coded statements like "do whatever you need to do."

After an evidence-yielding call to Jennifer Leavitt's home, Pierce was on the road in minutes, in pursuit of Chris Leavitt, and was soon ascending the Oakland hills thinking an interception of his target was plausible. Now he is in that woman's living room, not standing in the company of Chris Leavitt, but instead across from the bonus prize of this whole exercise: Bryan Tecco, the real target. Dave Gagliano would be pleased. Were he watching this scene, Dave Gagliano would swallow any misgivings either he or anyone else within Sahi ever had about Eric Pierce. This kid, he would say, has a head on his shoulders, knows how to plan things out. He's got intuition and guts. He sees things others don't see, is one step ahead of everybody else. That Eric Pierce: he sees through lead.

Feeling the high, Eric turns to Bryan "Weed" Tecco and coaches himself to concentrate and stay calm. Weed has his arms up still. He's looking oddly relaxed, like the pressure is off him for the time being. All he needs to do is cooperate, wait for Pierce to figure things out, and stay ready in case he makes a mistake. This guy Tecco has got it easy, Eric correspondingly thinks. He pushes Weed up against the back wall of the living room and pads him down, looking for the flash drives. He extracts Chris' phone from one pocket and drops it to the floor. From the other pocket, he grabs the much-traveled wallet and empties its contents. There's nothing there to interest Pierce. Show some respect, Weed thinks, thinking of what that wallet has been through. There's banging on the garage door. The women are crying out, though for different reasons. Jill is loudest, pleading for and then demanding that Pierce not do anything to harm Weed. The housekeeper is speaking high speed Spanish; she seems to be praying. Pierce yells out, tells them to be quiet. Then he is still.

"Okay, here's what we're gonna do. You and I are going for a drive. You're driving. I'm gonna have you talk to s—some colleagues of mine and we'll see if we can't work through your issue with S—Sahi."

"So, you're a Sahi lackey?"

As Weed mentally notes the stutter, Eric laughs. It's been a while since he's taken an insult for being conformist. He leans over Weed's shoulder, speaks into his ear while holding the gun a ticklish distance from Weed's lobe.

"If I'm a lackey, what does that make you? A s—slob who got tired of his nothing job so he decides to steal some product?"

Eric has Weed keeping his hands up. He pulls back on Weed's neck and steers him in the direction of the front door which is still open from when he was invited inside. Hearing the commotion that continues from the garage, Eric realizes that time is short; that soon the neighborhood watch will hear the noise, a phone call or two will be made, and before he knows it a squad car will be right on top of them. At the double door entry, he positions Weed against the panel that is closed. He pulls back the half open door and looks outside. Everything seems undisturbed, quiet. The sun is high and bearing down. The Subaru is just beyond the driveway, parked at the end of the cul-de-sac—a mistake, Eric realizes, as it means he'll be in open view as he tries to get both himself and his prisoner into the car. Weed likewise looks out over the driveway and towards the car, and has a flash memory: this will be the second time today that he'll be given police escort treatment while entering a vehicle.

"Take it s—slow," Eric Pierce not so coolly advises. Weed steps out onto the porch with a sigh. The area just outside the door looks wider and longer, like a tunnel. The light pouring down into the space seems deceitful to Weed, as though nature were lying about what this next part of the adventure has to offer. Eric gives him some distance, and Weed feels a brief respite as the sensation of hard metal leaves his back. He wishes he knew the tricks that would disarm an assailant when a weapon's position is known. Violence: something else that others are generally better at. To his left, at ground level, he sees a pair of Terra Cotta pots housing cactus plants. There's movement. Something like a lizard has slipped behind a pot. Then Weed catches a glimpse of a shadow, then an eye. Intuiting something, he keeps his head straight and doesn't react. He keeps his eyes upon the Subaru ahead, reminding himself to not panic. He has time enough for hope.

From behind he hears crunching footsteps against the gravel. He loses count of the steps that must correspond to his and Eric Pierce's feet. In another split second, there is a sharp cacophony of this sound, coupled with a clunking noise of something metal hitting a soft surface. A moment later, the crunching becomes heavier. A weight has slumped over, breaching the tidy expanse of stones on the driveway. Weed dares to look over his shoulder to see a third body—a sliver of arm and shoulder, covered in a dirty flannel shirt. He does a double take, and then spins to find Eric Pierce prostrate upon the ground, his eyes wobbling. He is an instant away from unconsciousness, gazing up at the prize that will now elude him.

"Hell yeah," says a man Weed doesn't recognize. He is holding a spade and shaking with exhilaration. He sees Weed and laughs coarsely.

"I'm Costman. The gardener."

Weed stares back, frozen. He is struck dumb by events, thinks of Rosco, whom the gardener resembles with his spade.

"Weed"

"What?"

"I'm a friend of Chris. I'm…where—"

"He's at the train station."

"What?"

"Chris. I saw him down on Mountain Boulevard, like an hour ago. He and some guy were looking for a bus, and saying they were gonna catch the train."

"Train? What train?"

"Dunno. BART. Amtrak, maybe?"

Weed's head spins. His eyes come into focus as he looks at Eric Pierce's body twitching on the ground, passed out. Weed regains his focus, leaning down to pick through the Sahi man's pockets. He finds his car keys, snatches the handgun of familiar type from his loosened grip, and runs back inside the house.

"Uh, wait…" says Costman, nervously looking down at Pierce, half-wondering if he's caused irreparable damage; half-afraid his victim will awaken sooner rather than later.

Weed reaches the garage door, which Jill and the others haven't stopped banging upon since being locked inside. As he opens the door, he is met with Jill's beseeching face. She smiles, looking relieved. For the first time since he doesn't know when, Weed feels like someone is pleased to see him.

"We're outta here," he says, grabbing her hand. "It's all clear," he calls out to the others. He gallops out the front door with Jill trailing behind him, holding questions she's desperate to ask. Weed jumps over the body of Pierce and sees Costman still standing over his handiwork. "Thanks," says Weed in passing. "That's an awesome gardener," he informs Jill.

"Hi," she says awkwardly. As she steps past Pierce's body she feels a tug on her pants, like she's caught them on something. She stumbles and then stops, looking behind herself. The sensation reminds her of times when snagging fabric upon on a sharp point. It's a nuisance that must be dealt with before anything else can happen. Turning, she sees Pierce groveling towards her, clutching at her ankle. He is half-conscious, fighting his way back. Jill shrieks and kicks out.

"What the?" she utters.

Pierce, blinking wildly, reaches his feet and tries feebly to strike a fighter's pose. Jill mirrors the movement, spreads out her body and positions her legs. Pierce lunges with a forearm. Jill blocks. Costman steps backwards, realizing he's out of his depth. He holds his spade close to his chest.

"You wanna try again?" Jill barks at Pierce, her voice still shaky. He looks weary, barely able to stand. At this particular moment, he is more last legs Pierce than Fierce Pierce.

"Jill," says Weed in a commanding voice. He's watching her, satisfied. He sees the Widow in her. As Jill hears him, she notes that he has become all hard ever since this Sahi goon entered the picture. This is the guy she'd imagined—the Weed that Chris had admired; the cool, reptilian figure she'd reluctantly desired for a hot minute after she'd first seen him a week ago.

Pierce curses seeing Weed behind Jill. The prize is standing just outside his Subaru, with one leg situated inside. He is holding a firearm—Eric's handgun—like an expertly trained gunman, and is pointing it directly at Pierce's head.

"Get in," says Weed to Jill. "You're driving again."

Jill does a stutter step, caught between two minds. Her preference is to get in a swift kick to the home invader, in vengeance for the cruel incarceration in the garage, especially of Jenny Leavitt. Instead, she obeys Weed, running behind him and around the Subaru, and then enters the driver's side. Moments later, they pull away and speed down the cul-de-sac and out of sight. Out of the side window, Weed sticks his head out and gives a taunting wave to his brief captor.

"S—see ya," he calls out.

Back on the driveway, Eric Pierce cuts a forlorn figure. Behind him, Costman starts to edge away, anxious that he'll soon be subject to retributive action. But Pierce doesn't care about him, nor does he feel threatened even. Not anymore. The moment is past. The target, Bryan Tecco, has slipped through his fingers. For the time being, that's all that matters.

Aunt Jenny sits in her wheelchair, poised at the threshold to the front entry with her two helpers, Magdalena and her hulking henchman, flanking her.

"The police are on their way," she announces unwisely. She looks and sounds like a disabled yet sinister figure from a James Bond movie, positioned at the gate of her luxurious lair; menacing him with complacent threats: *Give up, Mr. Pierce. You have no hope of escape.*

Pierce feels dizzy, though even as his head aches, he assesses the diffident figure that is the gardener; the disinterested, if imposing man that was earlier babysitting the housekeeper and who is now holding tightly to Jenny Leavitt's wheelchair. Eric Pierce steps backwards, wearing a scowl that is aimed in the old woman's direction. Her mouth flattens in disapproval at yet another young man recklessly defying her. Resigned, her thoughts turn. She wonders if or when she will see Chris again, as the Leavitt men have a legacy of absence. Within the hour, the tension of the morning will ease. Police will come, make their interviews, and settle everyone down. Soon even Magdalena will relax and have something to talk about for weeks with the congregants of her church. She and Raul, her assistant, will be grateful for common blessings, being alive, being forgiving. But for Jenny Leavitt—Aunt Jenny, as she knows herself—the days stretch before her amid comfort and capable supervision. Besides this, there is little for her to look forward to.

Eric Pierce will not give up. He will stagger down the Oakland hills and make a call to his office with the phone that remains in his suit pocket. It won't be an easy call at first, and he'll need to practice for a minute, make sure he can master those tricky consonants. Dave Gagliano won't be pleased. Hearing of this debacle, he'll call out for reinforcements, send a team to meet Eric Pierce and insist that Pierce follow orders to the letter. Had Gagliano watched the scene of the last five minutes, he might have pulled his hair out in frustration. But if he knew what was still to come—if he knew the fight that was left in Fierce Eric Pierce—he might yet be hopeful. He might be impressed.

28

On the winding roads that lead down to Mountain Boulevard, Weed screams out like a cowboy that's just won a rodeo. Despite feeling undernourished and under the weather, he's on a natural high, reveling in the duel he's just won with a Sahi security agent.

"Hell yeah, I feel like Slim Pickens riding a missile," he exults.

"What?" asks Jill, who also enjoyed the moment, despite herself.

"Nevermind. Look, can you get us to the Amtrak station real quick? We might still catch Chris and Sweet."

"How do you know he's going to Amtrak?"

"That gardener told me."

"How would he—"

"Jesus, does it matter? It's not like he'd make it up. Just go would ya?"

"Okay, fine. Which one?"

"What?"

"Which one? Which Amtrak station?"

Weed squirms in his passenger seat, realizing of course that he doesn't know which one.

"I don't know. Whichever's closest. Jack London Square, right?"

"Maybe, but I think there's one near the airport that's closer."

"Fine. Go there."

As they drive west, the adrenaline subsides though the general goodwill persists. Sideways glances and half-smiles betray an emerging admiration. Jill is impressed with Weed's previously cool head, brave and decisive action, and above all, his gracious comments about the "honorable" Chris Leavitt. It stirs her to re-think matters, partly because the last thing she'd attributed to Chris was honor. Weed is likewise smiling upon Jill's fighting spirit, but is also touched by the caring gestures she made as the garage door closed between them. That she seemed frightened for him did not go unnoticed. Now that dust has settled temporarily, both think the other has stepped up to the plate and done well; both think the other a bit more human than before.

"Look, there's no need for a chase here, especially since we don't know exactly where we're going. Let's just call 'em."

Catching his untamed expression, Jill can see that while his wheels are turning, Weed is missing things. That quality of his, of being ahead of the game, seeing all the tacks on the road, has deserted him for the moment. She notices two things that he hasn't seen—two things, actually. First, neither Chris nor Sweet has responded to either of the earlier messages, which suggests something is wrong on their end. Maybe Sweet loses phones also. Secondly, Jill's eyes have passed from Weed's face back to the road ahead, though not before crossing over the space that is the Subaru's coffee cup holder. The association stabs at her. They aren't the only careless ones, she realizes.

"We can't," she says. She doesn't want to explain why.

"Why not?"

She glances at him. It's a don't-make-me-say-it look. It doesn't work.

"I don't have my phone,"

"Excuse me?"

"It's in my car, back at the house we just left."

Weed glares. "You're kidding, right. You're fucking kidding me." Next he screams. He screams like a cowboy that's just been disqualified from the rodeo he thought he just won. Jill argues.

"Look, it was your idea to take the Subaru. We could've taken my car. Why didn't we take my car?"

"Your car's a piece of shit. I wasn't going to drive all the way down to LA in that thing."

"You're damn right you're not. If you think—" Jill stops in mid-sentence, juts out her chin like she's reaching for some words that are getting away. "Goddamnit," she snaps. The implications of hers and Weed's actions of the last half hour are just dawning upon her. Her car is up in the Oakland hills, soon to be studied by Oakland Police Department. She's in a stolen vehicle, ostensibly on route to an Amtrak station near the airport. Then what? Is she getting on a train? Tagging along with this guy on a quest to find her now ex-boyfriend in order to recover some files for a video game that is about God knows what? Is she hitting the road, giving up her solitary life and not quite satisfactory work, in order to join these ridiculous men on their stupid, adolescent missions?

Weed is waiting patiently, still watching Jill with a what-did-you-think-was-happening look. Jill shakes her head, not knowing where to go with all the thoughts that are tumbling about her mind.

"What about Chris' phone? You were playing with it earlier."

Weed checks his pocket, having forgotten this true piece of information.

"Gone. That guy spilled a bunch of stuff out of my pockets. I don't even have my wallet anymore." Fleetingly, Weed looks away with sentiment. He and that wallet: they'd been through a lot together.

"We sorta know where we're going," Jill says meekly. For a moment, it's as if she's abandoned all doubt and joined the cause.

"What?"

"Chris said they were headed to the Hollywood area, near UCLA."

"Well, that's something at least," Weed says grumpily.

But over the next hour things get worse. They make it to the train station by the airport, only to find the schedules confusing: trains seem to head north to Sacramento before heading south. Someone at a kiosk suggests they try Jack London Square station, at which point Weed suppresses a tantrum as this had been his idea initially. They head north to that station and get stuck in some traffic downtown. More frustration. At Jack London Square they see a train pulling away just as they are approaching. Weed yells to be let out so he can give it a chase, but to no avail. A ticket clerk with a reedy voice tells him the train was indeed heading for LA, not via the so-called capitol corridor, but instead through the San Joaquin Valley and then connecting to a bus in Bakersfield which will stop again in Burbank and then finally in downtown LA. Whatever, thinks Weed, quite confused by Amtrak's checkered system. Walking away, Weed stares down the bare track stretching out into the southerly distance. There is no train in sight, and for the time being, nor is there even a Shadow appearing to tell him he's on the right track, so to speak. Right now, all he has is what he feels: the conviction that Chris Leavitt is on the train that has just left, and that somewhere on his person are a collection of thumb-sized flash drives that will change lives. Weed plods back to the parking area, feeling momentarily defeated. Inside the newly acquired Subaru, he sees an ever truculent Jill Evans sitting quietly in the driver's seat, fiercely gripping the wheel. There's a conversation to be had still with her: about plans, the future; about what it is they really want?

THE GAME

29

Weed doesn't know where or when he first learned that some situations call for no words. People talk too much. He's believed this ever since he was ten years old, when his father used to lecture incessantly about the importance of respecting teachers, adults in general, himself. By the time he was being lectured about drug use several years later, Weed's love of silence was ten-fold. Unlike Chris, who according to his aunt labored under the weight of secrets throughout his life, Weed thought the only thing worse than not talking about things was talking about things. At the Santa Rosa drug treatment program where he injured his wrist, he learned the word "Monads" from staff and peers. Of Greek or Latin origin, the word was defined in the program as meaning "be with yourself". It was meant to stir in patients a meditative silence in times of distress, but was used as often as not to simply stop conversation. Ever since then it's been one of Weed's favorite words.

He gets in the Subaru passenger side, thinks twice about slamming the door, and then leans back, saying nothing to Jill. The word Monads comes to mind as he tilts back, though as usual he keeps the esoteric term to himself. Relaxing, he feels a weight come over him. His eyes flicker and then water like they are stealing resource from elsewhere. His mouth is dry from the static mucous lining his throat and sticking there. He is no more giving up than Eric Pierce is, but something is telling him that if he doesn't rest for a while he'll regret it later.

"So, what next?" Jill dares to ask.

Weed rests an arm over his face. Should his eyes open, he'll still block out the light, as well as her eyes.

"Nothing," he answers petulantly. "Just let me rest here for a minute, then we can...I don't know." Conversation stops.

Jill sighs upon seeing him lapse into a snooze. She'd had the opposite experience in her upbringing. Having grown up around terse masculinity in the form of her own father, she quickly accepts Weed's desertion. Her mind shifts. Not that she's in a hurry, but that salon appointment is calling out to her; so too is that bike ride. The day, her life, is still young. Were she and Weed to separate in the next hour or so, she'd still have plenty of time before returning to work in a couple of days. She'd have plenty of time for herself, she repeats in her mind. She thinks of her apartment, of her car being inspected by police. Then she thinks of Chris and the fresh possibility of chasing him, like she did once before for a hot minute. She can't believe she's going *there,* she thinks. Then again, maybe it's not so surprising. Actually, it's not surprising at all. Finally, a real surprise: her eyelids are feeling heavy also. Momentarily, her eyes close. She figures this is a quick rest. She's wrong.

Napping in a stolen car in an Amtrak parking lot, Weed and Jill lose an hour. First it is Weed who awakens and begins shuffling about in his passenger seat. He opens the glove compartment, notes the ominous presence of Pierce's firearm, and scoops out sundry items, a pen and notepad; some car documents. He feels under his seat like he's searching for something, as though he's forgotten that he no longer has any belongings on him: not any tools, no money; not even a driver's license to identify him— nothing. Without stuff, he's nobody. Then he sees something, and he goes to work. His movements stir Jill, who nearly jumps out of her skin when her eyes open and see Weed just about pressed up against her. He's looking down into a space right next to her thigh, into the gap between his seat and the automatic shift.

"Sorry", he says, noticing her flinch. His voice is monotone. He isn't really sorry.

"What are you looking for?" Jill asks.

"It looks like a cell phone," replies Weed. He's jamming his hand into the tight space, trying to reach something pressed against the track upon which his seat runs. He thinks to remark that losing cell phones must be contagious, but isn't in the mood. Jill's hair touches against Weed's forehead as she aims to get a look. "Don't suppose you have anything with a hook do you?" he asks.

"No," she says. Weed shakes his head. "You're nearly there," Jill encourages next.

"Argh, this is impossible," he mutters as he pulls back, frustrated.

"You're a fatalist. Do you know that?"

Weed pauses and gives her an ill-humored look. "I'll give it one more shot. If I get it, I'm a fatalist. If I don't, then I'm a realist."

"Let me try, or pull back the seat."

"It's not...forget it." Weed decides to ignore Jill for the next minute. "Wait," he then says. His hand stops. He's established some kind of grip, and begins a delicate lift, like he's performing a surgery. But hope is short. He then makes a disgruntled noise as he hoists before his eyes the item he'd spied upon the floor of the car.

"Crap. It's just a case." Eric Pierce's unlikely yet unuseful negligence leaves Weed feeling teased. He looks at Jill gloomily, who instead looks on the bright side, sort of.

"You probably couldn't have used it anyway. What are the chances that guy would be as careless as Chris and not set a password? Besides, you can use Chris' phone. No—sorry—you don't, I remember."

Weed glances at Jill to see if she's mocking him. She doesn't appear to be this time. "That guy was Sahi security. There could've been useful information on that thing, stuff that...I don't know." Weed sighs, abruptly changes the subject. "So, are we going to your place?"

"Excuse me?" Still half awake, Jill wears the shadow of a smirk.

Weed remains humorless. "I didn't mean—I meant do you wanna drive to your apartment? Then I'll take this thing from there."

Jill pauses before answering. "Sure," she says half-heartedly.

The drive to her apartment near 14th street is less than ten minutes, not nearly long enough for Jill to think through the unthinkable: the crazy yet unshakable desire to not separate from Weed just yet; to not be done with Chris Leavitt even; to obey some girlish impulse and join either of them on a foolhardy road trip while totally blowing off the healthy plan she'd previously outlined. The biggest problem at this point would be in explaining herself, to herself. If only she didn't have to. Jill gives Weed a prolonged, assessing look, notes his quieted distraction, his seeming disregard of words. He wears a studious expression, like he's appraising Oakland and ready to bid it good riddance. He's elsewhere already, like he's done with Oakland and done with Jill Evans, and likewise assuming she's done with him. He turns to her, concerned and awkward.

"Hey look, about your car. I just realized you've got no way to get back—no easy way, anyway."

"Don't worry about it. I'll figure something out. I doubt the cops will confiscate it or anything."

Weed nods though he's not sure he agrees with this view.

"It's just a piece of shit Honda after all," she adds with a friendly smile. They laugh together for a moment. Weed recovers some of his humor. A moment of disarmed respite hangs between them as they pull up before her apartment building. "So, what's your plan?" she asks casually, though she's getting tired of asking this question.

Weed shrugs, resuming his cool persona from before. Jill senses it's an act, this offhand, I'll-figure-something-out way of his, though in this brief eye of the storm she's not minding that so much. It turns out that ten minutes is more than enough time to think through matters, because she's already decided what she wants. Meanwhile, despite a resourceful, option-seeking habit,

Weed still hasn't thought through this thing. He's stuck in a sparse dimension to his thoughts, unsure of what he wants. He remains confused, still trying to figure out what's happening—traumatized by everything, just as Chris was. It's just that it seems different, his malady. He needs Jill, he realizes. They'd be a decent team, she likewise thinks, knowing she can be offhand too.

"You should come up for a minute, get an extra layer of clothes," she says. "We should go on the Amtrak website and find out what stops there are in LA, or further north maybe, if you wanna try and intercept them."

"Are you sure you don't wanna come along?" he asks simply.

"Are you inviting me?"

Weed shrugs again. More cool.

"Sure."

30

It takes about ten minutes for the following to happen: for an Amtrak schedule to be studied, if thinly understood; for a coat and sweater to be retrieved from Jill's closet, and for a pair of snacks to be snatched from her fridge, available for a journey. There will be no attempt to intercept, they decide together. The best plan is to head straight for LA, to any one of several Amtrak stops throughout the region, using the GPS software in the Subaru. That's LA for you: a handful of long-distance train stops covering an area that is home to nearly twenty million people. Amazing. They briefly discuss the problem: The odds of finding Chris and Sweet without making contact with them first seem slim. Weed and Jill have just a guess as to which stop Chris and Sweet are intending to hit, and if they choose the wrong one and therefore miss contact, who knows if and when they'll reunite.

"Can you believe this shit? Hardly a day goes by without anyone using phones, text, e-mail, but suddenly, between the four of us, no one can get in touch with anyone. Do you think someone is trying to tell us something?"

Jill thinks twice about answering this budding diatribe. Firstly, she's sort of in the shame box for leaving her own phone behind. Secondly, and more importantly, she knows Weed is really just having fun now. Truth is he's been giddy since learning that she's coming with him. While he notes departure and arrival times, and prints out a back-up map for good measure and thorough planning, she grabs a bag and packs a few essentials. Coming out of her bathroom, Jill sticks a thermometer in Weed's mouth. His complaint is muffled.

"Just over ninety six," she says half a minute later. "Not good."

"How accurate is that thing?"

"We could stick it up your ass if you want precision."

"No thanks. I—" Weed is set to joke about having had enough of that action, but catches himself in time. "Anyway doc, what's your diagnosis?"

Jill turns serious. "Not sure. You might have pneumonia, but we'd need to hear your chest to be sure." She places a hand on his forehead. "You're clammy. You've been coughing quite a bit. I'll get you some cough medicine, which should work on the symptoms at least. We need to keep you warm. You're not in the age group most threatened by this kind of thing. You don't lie about your age, do you?"

Minutes later they are on the road, heading south on the 880, later the 101. Even after an hour's nap and the detour to Jill's apartment, they still figure they can beat the sluggish Amtrak service down to LA, but they'd better start moving. The only factor they can't account for is the notorious traffic jams that undoubtedly await them. It's close to noon. Weed still feels like he's been up for days, though it's likely been about seven hours, maybe eight, since this day began for him. Looking back, he can't believe all that's happened in a short amount of time. In general, he can't fathom how time has worked out recently: disappearing, blackout-style on some days; slowing to an ether-like pace on others.

"I'll drive again," says Jill, pointing out that Weed doesn't have his license. Weed is about to object until she adds that he needs rest—as if she doesn't. He can be equal opportunity on the way back, assuming they take that journey together also. He agrees without a fuss, perceiving a need to make placatory gestures. Time goes by. Weed sleeps for two hours, half-blanketed by a puffy coat Jill hasn't worn since the wintertime. There's a tear on the arm, exposing some lining, but it's thick and does the job of warming him quite nicely. Watching him, Jill sees that Weed looks comfortable stretching back in his seat, his head sliding instinctively towards her shoulder. His mouth hangs open and he lightly snores. Meanwhile, his flickering eyelids suggest a healthy spell of dreaming. No nightmares. Around two o'clock he stirs, coughs, and breathes out heavily.

"Where we at?" he asks thickly.

"We're just south of Salinas. We're doing okay, I think." Weed grunts likes he's discouraged; like he'd hoped to wake up just as they were arriving in LA. He reaches into the glove compartment, pulls out one of the map pages he'd printed out, but thinks the GPS on the car is the best bet. He examines the route, thinking the road they're on is their path for the next two hours, at least. He stares out ahead at the pavement that disappears into the horizon. One thing he likes is the unfettered straightness of this drive. Were he behind the wheel, he'd feel tempted to hit the gas, push this new Subaru over the hundred miles per hour mark. He glances over at the speedometer, sees that Jill is holding steady at about seventy five. He holds his tongue, knowing that if they got stopped for speeding, his plans, still unclear as they may be, would be in the dust. That Sahi goon has likely not reported this car missing, but that won't be much consolation when neither he nor Jill can prove ownership.

"You okay?" Jill asks.

"Yeah, fine," Weed replies. He yawns.

"We're still a few hours away. You might wanna get more sleep."

"I'm good," he says. He widens his eyes and pulls back a swath of hair. It's a crude grooming and waking ritual, somehow intended to rouse him. "Nah, we should talk about a couple of things."

"Glad you think so. You start."

"Well, first of all, just so you don't think I can't plan anything, I was thinking we should ditch this car when we get to an Amtrak station. Assuming we find Chris and Sweet, who are on foot, we should use public transportation. The longer we hold onto this thing, the more we're taking a risk."

"Agreed," Jill answers collegially. "By the way, which Amtrak station are we going to? One's called Union station; can't remember the name of the other one."

"We don't have to decide that yet. It may depend on time, going to whichever station is nearest where you said and hoping it's the right one. We got a one in like five shot, basically."

As they pause for a minute, Weed contemplates other subjects to discuss, assuming he's the only one with an agenda related to the road trip. Instead, she breaks the silence.

"Hey, I wanted to say that I was impressed with how you handled that guy back at the house."

Weed turns and looks at her, surprised.

"Thank you. I thought you were pretty…that you were awesome too." He winces at his choice of words. He looks away, concealing a mouthed expletive; a burst of self-reproach.

"Thanks," she answers quietly. She laughs gingerly. "For a minute there, you had me worried, especially when you told him to take you away and leave us alone, like you were sacrificing yourself."

"Are you mocking me?"

"Not at all. I was, I don't know, touched."

"Touched?"

"Impressed, touched, moved, whatever. Is that okay?"

Weed holds a blank, nonchalant expression as Jill maintains her humor. "Nah, that's fine. It was a bad situation, you know. I felt bad bringing that business into that woman's home like that. I didn't want anyone to get hurt."

Jill keeps her eyes on the road while thinking about his answer. To her it seems that Weed is one of those guys that says "bad" when he means "guilt", but for complicated reasons guilt is a word, a concept, that cannot be invoked explicitly.

"Sure," she replies. "I take it he was one of your corporate followers?"

"Yeah"

"And a Shadow?"

Weed perks up for a moment, recalling something he parks in his mind, maybe for later discussion.

"Nah, I didn't see anything like that—not this time."

Jill notes that he's being short, like he doesn't want to talk about the subject, despite her reverently-intoned inquiry. She notices the way impersonal descriptions obscure truer feelings: instead of "I didn't want you or Jenny Leavitt to get hurt", it's "I didn't want *anyone* to get hurt." A subtlety maybe? Jill wonders. Maybe he's just being democratic, expressing concern for everyone, like a nice guy might.

She shifts subjects: "How're you doing? I can't tell if you're still shaking in that thing. You're not coughing as much since I gave you the Robitussin."

"Shaking? Was I shaking?"

"A little—more so when you're standing still, and not obviously stressed out by something."

Weed frowns, not liking this image that's forming: of himself shaking like a hungry orphan, frail. Jill detects his attitude.

"Is that a problem, that I noticed you shaking? I mean, you might be really sick. You might have an infection, pneumonia—I don't know for sure."

"Yeah, okay. Well, I am feeling better. Thank you." Weed's answer sounds curt. Jill laughs again.

"Jeez, you're kind of a grouch, aren't you? You're like this curmudgeonly twenty-something guy."

Weed stiffens. "Nah, I'm just kinda old school, I guess."

"What does that mean?"

"I don't know. I guess it means I don't like a lot of attention."

"Really?" Jill questions, like she believes him but doesn't all at once. She hangs her head back and howls. "*I don't like a lot of attention*," she mimics, now weaving a series of unflattering sounds into her laughter. "Sorry," she includes, disingenuously.

"Fuck you," Weed says, half-serious.

"Please, get over yourself. So, you don't take compliments. You don't like anyone thinking you're sick, or trying to care about you in any way. I get it. I guess it makes sense that you'd be gone for a week and think no one would notice or care. Well, you got attention, Weed. You've gotten lots of it."

"Look, it's getting old, you sayin' that I didn't care enough to contact Chris. How many times do I have to say—"

"Yeah, yeah, I heard what you said, and I get that you were hurting after the accident, hitchhiking for a day, and then you got kidnapped, or whatever."

"You don't believe me?"

"Yes, I believe you, but that's not the point. I'm sure those things were stressful, but they're also excuses."

"Excuses?"

"Yes, and before you lose your shit, I'm going to say something else. Even though those things would scare anyone; even though it was as stressful as it was, I still think you didn't consider anyone's feelings—that they would miss you, care about you, or anything like that."

Weed shakes his head vigorously. "Girl, I don't know where you get off saying this. You haven't even known me for a day."

"Straight up, Weed—am I really off base?"

Weed makes the kind of face that Jill has seen many times before, especially in men. It's the kind of face that says there's much to say—too much to say—but that none of it is supposed to be said. It's the kind of face that's telling her she's breaking some kind of rule; a rule that's not about Jill Evans; a rule that says, *don't go there*. What she's saying is out of line. It's not even fair for her to say it, because the rules say to not answer back, because then someone will get hurt, really hurt. And it's not right, because she's breaking the rule, and because she is saying what she's supposed to keep to herself—then it's about to be *game on*. Unless she turns back RIGHT NOW, shuts her mouth, and goes quiet, on Monads until further notice, then it's gloves off as far as Weed is concerned. Reciprocity clause: mutually assured destruction. And the hurt that will follow? It will be more than her ears can bear, Weed predicts.

"Maybe not," says Weed, finally. It's a compromise, these two words. They're like emissaries from some deep place, leaking out. Against all odds, they have forced their way through some barrier towards a long sought-after freedom.

31

Treading along the side of the road on Mountain Boulevard wearing a sullied mint grey suit, Eric Pierce looks out of place, like someone who's been beaten up and had his car and gun stolen. He tries to shake off his denial: he *has* been beaten up and had his car and gun stolen. Luckily, he hasn't been arrested—not yet at least—for that would be the ultimate indignity. That's something he wouldn't ever live down at work.

Despite a headache and a pain in his knee and shoulder, he manages to stay upright and look more or less normal. He obsessively wipes dust off his arms and lapels. He scans his body for leaves, thorns; bits of plant life belonging to Oakland hills' residents. Rather than simply walk down the hill, Pierce had sneaked into back yards, leaped over fences and stooped alongside passages, past garbage cans and heaps of compost. At one point he thought he saw a squad car through a bush, heading up the hill towards the Leavitt home. There were no sirens flashing; the car was traveling normal speed. There was no sense of urgency, of a crime in progress; of the danger presented by an at large Eric Pierce.

Reaching a sidewalk leading up to a strip mall, he decides to make that call to Dave Gagliano and tell him the bad news. The conversation is short, and Pierce does okay. Meaning, he doesn't stutter. Gagliano is calm and merely directive as he responds to Pierce's thin report—his pitiful, detail-withholding "I had him then lost him" account. For now, Dave Gagliano doesn't care how it happened; doesn't wanna hear lame excuses, and is oblivious to his own contradictions. He just thinks Eric Pierce shouldn't be alone taking on this job. Actually, he no longer thinks he should be on this job at all, though he doesn't say this to Pierce. He tells him to sit tight, make contact with Jeff Willits, one of the other guys in the department, and then pick up the trail of Bryan Tecco as best he can. There are new developments, Gagliano hints. Pierce asks after them, but his boss doesn't say much, showing he can be withholding too.

Pierce knows Willits though they don't talk much. A call comes in before Pierce can scroll through his distribution lists. Willits, it seems, has been given the same directive as him.

"Pierce, what's up?" greets Willits. His question, not really a question, covers up the kind of fawning laughter he is best known for.

"Sup, Willits," Pierce replies in a miserable voice. He gives Willits his location, agrees to wait until he arrives. Willits is within five miles. That's good, Pierce says. He cautions his colleague to move quickly, as he is only a mile or so from the scene of a home intrusion and near kidnapping that didn't go so well. Pierce adds that he was the intruder and would-be kidnapper, though not quite in those words.

"Okay," says Willits, holding his amusement in check for the time being. He'd already heard most of this from their boss.

As Pierce skulks behind a pillar within the strip mall, he remembers that Willits was among the team that accompanied that CEO to the conference where Pierce once ill-advisedly drew a weapon. He recalls Willits as one of the guys who watched him freak out because of that disturbance behind the main hall, only to have egg on his face when it turned out to be nothing. The last thing Eric Pierce needs is to reinforce a reputation of being trigger happy, but here it is. He hopes Willits doesn't cop an attitude, but even if he does, Pierce is ready, because despite what has happened so far, he hasn't yet run out of ideas. Eric Pierce has at least one more trick up his sleeve; one more resource that smart ass Bryan Tecco doesn't know he's got.

Some time later, Jeff Willits pulls into the mall's parking lot, at first passing Eric Pierce, who carefully steps from behind his protective pillar and gives a subtle two fingered wave. Willits is driving a black Chevy Suburban with an arm hanging out the driver's side window, like he's a teenager cruising down the boulevard on a Friday night. Willits doesn't return Pierce's gesture. Instead he nods, which in their line of business signifies agreement, but also disapproval, basic dislike, or all three. He finds a space, parks the car, and waits for Pierce like a parent picking up a kid from school.

"Hey," says Pierce as he jumps in the passenger side. Willits raises a pair of Maui Jim sunglasses to the base of a modestly receding hairline. It's the only flaw in an otherwise male model presentation. Green eyes stare out from a tanned face that has slick black hair streaming backwards, reaching just beyond the bottom of his neck. His hair looks moist and flowing like a wave. Pierce notes the vain caretaking that must be involved, imagines that when Willits goes to a stylist he likely insists that not a single hair be caught facing forward. Meanwhile, Willits' other features are similarly enviable: as his smile broadens, it pushes elastic cheeks up close to his ears, making taut gradations in leathery skin. Not overly thick eyebrows shaped like boomerangs allow for a wide range of expression above a fixed bedroom gaze. He bears perfect anterior teeth, white slabs of biting strength, completing the Cheshire Cat cum alpha male visage. Above all, it's a joker's face; a face that Eric Pierce wants to smack as soon as he sees it.

Jeff Willits bursts out laughing.

"I'm sorry, dude. I just gotta hear about this from the horse's mouth. What the hell happened?"

Pierce thinks of his sparring partner from his Krav Maga class. He wants to say to Willits the inside euphemism he says to his partner when inviting a fight: come outside and touch shoulders with me.

234

"Look, we don't have a lot of time, actually. We need to get on the road, start following the subject. Once we're moving, if you're cool, then I'll tell you what happened."

Willits' face straightens for a moment.

"You got a GPS device on your car?"

"Of course."

"What if he finds it? He might be checking it out now, at the first stop for gas."

The dubious tone annoys Pierce, so he tells the story anyway. Though he'd prepared to take a ton of shit from Willits, actually, he finds he's not prepared to take any shit.

"Okay, two things: first of all, the tank was over three quarters full, and since I took out the guy's wallet, I figure this Bonnie and Clyde act has likely got little, if any money, so they won't be stopping anytime soon. Secondly, the way they drove off, with his ugly face all gloating, I figure they thought they'd seen the last of me."

"Wait, what do you mean, Bonnie and Clyde? Who's the other person with Tecco?"

Pierce sighs. "Some girl, woman—I don't know who she is. He told her to get in the car with him just before they drove off."

"And he's got your heater, right?"

"Yeah."

Willits scrutinizes Pierce up and down, sees the scratch on his face, a disheveled patch on the back of his head. Fierce Pierce got beaten up, it seems.

"How hurt are you? Tecco get you on the head?" he asks, not so much concerned for Pierce as he is that Pierce won't be useful to him.

"I'm okay, Anyway, it wasn't Tecco who hit me. It was some other guy."

"What other guy?"

"This guy, at the house where I—I don't know, it got complicated. Can we go please?"

Willits pulls out onto Mountain Boulevard, finds a freeway heading south within minutes while Pierce studies his phone, finds the GPS indicator for his Subaru.

"Okay, we're good. They're heading south," he says. Willits is still assessing his new partner. He sees that Pierce's suit is all messed up, with something like white powder up and down his pants. He returns to the previous subject.

"You look like you've been rolling in dirt or something. Your suit's fucked up. Did Tecco do that to you, or was that this other guy also?"

"Maybe, though more when I tried to grab the woman. It didn't work. She kicked out and I hit the ground again. Tecco barely touched me. He just grabbed my keys and my gun and ran."

"Except he took this woman with him, and this other guy?"

"Nah, not the other guy—just the woman."

"Of course, you said—Bonnie and Clyde. Anyway, how'd this all happen? Why'd you pull your weapon in the first place?"

Willits seems vaguely offended by his colleague's mishandling of things. Pierce looks across at him with a quizzical look.

"What do you mean? I'd found the subject. Gagliano said this was top priority and that I—we, I guess—were supposed to do whatever we thought necessary to recover company property."

"Did he say to take a weapon with you, be prepared to fire?"

Pierce feels a stutter coming on. It typically happens when feeling defensive. Voices rise. Complaints multiply.

"It was implied. Gimme a break, Willits, what would you have done?"

"I would have called for backup, that's what. The guy wasn't armed before he met you as far as we know. You likely could have detained him without excessive force, maybe involved the local jurisdiction if he ran."

"That wasn't what this situation called for. You know that. Don't bullshit me, Willits."

"Hey, don't get all mad at me. Gagliano called, said to come out and help you, and when he explained the basics of you breaking into a private residence, holding up the subject as well as four other people, he wasn't pleased, okay? If this gets out it's a real public relations problem for us. So, I'm just sayin' you didn't plan this out too well. And by the way, just because Tecco doesn't have any money doesn't mean the chick doesn't."

Pierce sulks as the drive proceeds. For a half hour he fixes attention on his phone and its GPS application. He's like a teenager buried in a text message, on strike from adult company. Willits glances at him from time to time. His taunting, half-suppressed smile is one that Pierce can feel upon him. The pulsing indicator on his map display moves gradually down a line that is the 101 freeway. It's clear where Tecco and his female friend are going; what's unclear is how fast they're getting there, but so far it doesn't look like they're breaking land speed records. He looks over at the Chevy's speedometer. Willits is cruising at a steady seventy five miles an hour, and there's little traffic ahead.

"Pick it up a bit," Pierce says, gently breaking the silence.

Jeff Willits responds with a light grunt.

"You want a chase?"

"This is a chase."

"Actually, it's not. It's an investigation. We're supposed to find Tecco, detain him if necessary, and question him about missing property from the Emeryville office."

"Are you kidding? Question him? Are we working the same case here? I just told you he's got my piece."

"Which is why I'm taking the lead on this from now on. If and when we find him, I'm going to engage Tecco, try to talk. He's not violent—again, as far as we know." Pierce issues a guttural noise that Willits rightly interprets as dissent.

"Try to talk? Like, gee, d'ya think you might return the car and gun you stole—you mean that?"

"Dude, I don't know where you got your cowboy ideas from. I'm taking orders from Gagliano."

"Me too," Pierce retorts.

"Yeah? sounds to me like you've misinterpreted some things."

Pierce blinks at Willits, baffled by his new partner's attitude. His universe smile and comfortable manner unnerves Pierce, as it suggests he knows something that Pierce doesn't. Typical. Something's being kept from him, he thinks, but in this case that wouldn't make any sense. Why would some on the hunt for Bryan Tecco be given the full story and not others? He's confused. Pierce shudders, opens but then shuts his mouth, knowing he'll stutter if trying to argue when this unsettled.

"Okay, Willits, I'm listening. What has Gagliano told you about this situation?"

"It's not just what he's saying. It's what everyone's saying. Dude, you're such a lone wolf. You don't hear anything that people are saying, do you?"

Pierce can't take much more of this. "Why don't you stop with the friendly advice? Just tell me what's happening."

"Alright, the word is that the files that were taken from the Emeryville office are gaming files belonging to that journalist named Jules Grotius."

"Really? Where'd you hear that? The guy at the Emeryville office told me I didn't need to know who the owner of the files was."

Willits thrusts out his prominent chin. "You mean Ed Kim? I don't know what his deal is. Gagliano thinks he may be looking to cover his ass 'cause he didn't secure the files properly. Gagliano told a bunch of us that this was about Jules Grotius, and that the missing files, according to Ed Kim, are from his game. He admitted that to Gagliano. Maybe that's the piece that didn't get told to you."

Pierce ignores Willits' sympathetic theory. "Who the hell is Jules Grotius, and what kind of name is that?"

"You don't know who Jules Grotius is? He's like this famous whistleblower; a programmer, also a journalist. Anyway, he designed this game in partnership with another established designer, and pitched the game to Sahi some time ago. It's been in development for months and was being tested at the Emeryville office. According to Gagliano, Grotius struck a deal with Sahi execs, assuring them the game didn't contain any whistleblower secrets, at least none that would compromise the company, as a condition of publishing the game. It was a liability issue, maybe a public relations issue as far as they were concerned, but they chose to go ahead due to the buzz that was on Grotius' blog site."

Pierce looks again at his GPS tracker, willing the two pulsing indicators to draw closer. He doesn't like the story Jeff Willits is telling him. He doesn't like the sound of this guy called Jules Grotius—doesn't trust people whose names he can't pronounce without stuttering.

"What's Tecco's part in this? Gagliano have a theory on that?"

Willits pauses, gives Pierce a conciliatory nod.

"We don't know what that's about. Gagliano thinks he's just an opportunist thief looking to sell black market."

"He's not done that before," Pierce counters, like he's Weed's advocate.

"He's a drug dealer. Did you know that?"

"Sort of."

"Well, then it adds up."

Pierce shakes his head.

"No it doesn't. Look, I don't know what his motivation is, but I don't think it's common theft." Willits goes quiet for a moment and frowns, thinking he'll soon be hearing some half-baked theory from Pierce. He's set to brush him off. However, as if in consolation, he's obeyed Pierce's request and upped the Chevy's speed ever so slightly, to nearly eighty miles per hour.

"Well, maybe you're right. Who knows? Hopefully we'll get a chance to ask Tecco about that. But the files, those flash drives, are the thing. Gagliano and others believe there's another possibility: that the game files that Grotius submitted for testing actually do contain whistleblower information, despite what he promised to Sahi execs."

"Like what? Like the fact they hire a bunch of people with arrest records?"

"Cute, Pierce. Maybe that, but lots of other stuff too—stuff over our heads, probably. I don't think they've trusted Grotius the whole time they've been dealing with him. But this guy Tecco is a game whiz, which only a few people knew, like Ed Kim, so he's a fly in the ointment. Some people figure he may have found the whistleblower stuff in the games already, which would make the game extra hot." As Pierce listens to his apparent new supervisor, he takes note of Willits' conformist equanimity, his acceptance of things beyond his situation in life. Pierce can't decide whether to envy the man or else hold him in contempt. Meanwhile, Willits turns away from the road for a moment and looks across at Pierce. His green eyes stare daggers at his passenger as he delivers his own verdict about Bryan Tecco: "He might have been a solid citizen for a while, but a good opportunist always waits for the right time. He gets a little courage and seizes the moment. That's what we think, Pierce. That's what we think."

32

"Okay, my turn to ask a couple of questions." After ten minutes of tense silence followed by Jill turning on the radio and playing Katy Perry and Miley Cyrus songs, Weed has the bit between his teeth. He's reviewed in his mind what he remembers about this chick from when he first saw her. He's ready to ask questions based upon the Shadow-hit he got from her that night of the accident back in March. He's ready, as in feeling entitled, to get nosy about the fractious relationship she and Chris Leavitt had for a while. He remembers feeling like something serious had happened between them, something secret. He's going to act like a concerned friend now; going to show that he cares about other people. Having taken his share of character hits, he's ready to push back.

Jill sort of knows what's coming, and is likewise ready for it. It'll be a good fight, she figures—one that'll pay dividends somehow. She's not quite sure why she thinks this. It's a hunch, a gamble, like this whole trip she's on. She's getting something from all this caring about others. She must be, otherwise it's all just a mindless, nihilistic plunge. Maybe she'll learn something new from someone who appears to have trodden different paths.

"Go ahead," she replies, though it sounds more like, *bring it on.*

"Do *you* care about Chris? If not so much, then why were you with him? What did you like about him?"

"That's more than a couple of questions." Weed tilts his head, looking unimpressed by her bland quip. Jill makes a mental note: her last two or three attempts at humor have fallen like lead balloons: must remember that guys like Weed mostly laugh *at* women, not with them. Mildly flustered, she gives the questions her latest best shot. "Ugh," she begins, as if clearing her throat of distaste would ever be necessary when broaching the subject of Chris. "Well, first of all, I do care about him. I wouldn't be spending my free time in police stations, or going on road trips with you, if it wasn't about your relationship with Chris."

"Why are you breaking up with him?" Weed sounds like a prosecuting attorney speeding towards his main point.

"How do you know I am? Did he say that?"

"It's written all over you."

Jill is jolted by this. Even though she knows she makes negative remarks about Chris, and has likely betrayed a bad attitude about him to Weed also, she somehow imagines that her loyal, loving qualities are what stand out the most.

"Okay, I guess that's true," she answers warily.

"So, how come?"

Now she bristles. "Really? You think that's any of your business?"

"You said I don't care about him. Now I ask if you're gonna break up and suddenly it's none of my business? You can't have it both ways."

Jill squirms. "That's different. That's private between him and me."

"That's a bullshit rule. It's about being concerned for a friend, right?—about seeing he doesn't get hurt. Well, guess what, breaking up with you will probably hurt him a whole lot more than not seeing my ass for a week. Besides, you said yourself back at that woman's house that he wasn't so stressed out about finding me."

"I didn't mean—you misunderstood me. I meant that he thought you weren't interested in him so he figured he shouldn't come looking for you."

"Whatever. Point is he's way more affected by you not being around."

Jill's face is scolding red; she doesn't want to look at Weed. She faces forward, keeps her eyes on the road, and tries to turn the tables.

"Look, he definitely looks up to you. He talked about you all the time, told me you wrote a book, said—"

"You're changing the subject. I don't need my ass to be kissed here. I wanna know what you saw in Chris and why you're not into him anymore. That guy was totally into you. He wanted you bad, but thought you were too good for him. I'll be honest: I warned him not to sweat so much over you. I thought he'd be better off with someone else; someone who didn't make him feel so insecure. I had no problem with you. I just didn't wanna see him get hurt, and it seemed like he didn't know how to please—"

"I lost respect for him."

"What?"

"He's not a man, okay?"

There are two seconds of silence, after which Weed guffaws, half in shock.

"Are you kidding?"

"Kidding, yeah—he acts like a kid all the time. He's impulsive, immature, and lazy. He starts things and doesn't follow through. He's unreliable. You wanna know why I was with him? He's cute. That's about it, plus he was cool at first. We had chemistry."

Weed releases an ecstatic laugh. "Translation—you wanted to fuck him."

Jill reddens again. "Yes," she says reluctantly. Weed stifles a further laugh. "But it wasn't long before he wasn't even doing that right," she adds. She runs a hand through her hair, makes a scornful noise that breezes past her teeth. She regrets saying the last part, knowing it crosses a line; knowing it makes her sound *mean*. She thinks about honesty. She questions its value, and thinks about fairness instead.

Weed is nodding as if the world is making sense; all things under the sun are adding up.

"Don't worry," he says evenly. "I won't tell him you told me this stuff. That'll be just between you and me."

Jill holds her forearm up to her eyes, makes a play of wiping her sleeve across her face. Weed has past associations, of women crying or about to cry; of women crying easily, and then bitterly resenting those who witness the crying.

"Anything else you wanna know?"

Weed knows he's supposed to do a chivalrous thing and say "no", but he's not very chivalrous—never claimed to be—so Jill's half intended ploy doesn't work.

"Was there a final straw for you or something?" he asks.

Jill shakes her head like she's gesturing protest to an inside voice that's about to spill truth. She can't stop it.

"A little over a week ago he was spun at work. He was stressing about this drama between him and one of the doctors. Some of the doctors at the hospital are cool, but the one Chris was arguing with is all ego, just wants people to comply, isn't interested in what others think or anything. I tried to tell Chris this. I pulled him off the floor into a private area to warn him about his conduct because he was being loud and causing a scene. When we got into the room he kisses me like a puppy dog, and I kiss him back, thinking it may calm him down or something. But then…" Jill starts to tremble. Her shoulders quiver and a tear drops down from her right eye, only to stall and evaporate halfway down her cheek. Weed isn't looking but he knows what's happening. He feels the quake of her body; hears her quiet sniffle. "He starts to grab onto me. He pulls at my arms, squeezes me. His kisses start to feel like—like he's biting me."

"Shit," Weed mutters. He closes his eyes, puts his hand onto his forehead.

"Sorry. I'll stop. You probably don't wanna hear this. Guys don't wanna hear this."

"There's more?" Weed asks stupidly.

Jill nods and raises her eyebrows. It's a disdainful gesture, half aimed at Chris, who is somewhere down the path where her gaze is pointed; and it's half aimed at Weed, or at anyone who might exhibit surprise at what she's saying. Weed flashes on the face of Chris Leavitt having fun, looking buzzed but not too buzzed at one of those parties they used to have at their apartment back in Richmond. He sees the devilish smile that women seem to love; the cut body and boyish demeanor that initially draws them in. As he pictures him, remembers him, in this scene, Jill releases her ominous reply:

"You know there is."

33

Still feeling good, but getting impatient: that's Chris Leavitt standing outside a bathroom on the Amtrak train. He's been waiting for over five minutes and has knocked twice. As a skinny guy dressed in black finally shuffles out the door wiping his nose, Chris gives him sarcastic thanks and squeezes in. He is ignored. Inside the compartment, Chris looks about for an outlet, still talking to himself about the quality of people one meets on Amtrak. There's no outlet anywhere. Chris twists and turns, looking behind a towel dispenser, checking under a mirror while bemoaning the lack of a cabinet. He sits down, swears repeatedly and feels dejected. He wonders how much time he'll waste on this trip looking for an outlet just so he or Sweet can make one goddamned phone call. Despite this, he is mildly surprised that the bathroom, which is really just a toilet and a sink plus space to stand up, is tidy and clean, like it had just been wiped down.

Stomping back to his seat, he bumps Sweet's elbow as it sticks out into the aisle, waking him. His eyes flicker above black circles and thick folds of eyelids. He's getting tired of being woken up this way.

"What's up? Where'd you go?"

"Bathroom, dude—looking for an outlet for this thing." Chris' head is darting around like he's hunting for a mouse that's under the seats.

"There's one right there." Sweet lazily directs a finger past Chris' shoulder. There's an outlet near the ground, just behind the swollen limb of a fat, stertorous woman sleeping with her head rested against the window. Though this journey has just begun it seems like half the passengers on board are asleep already. Coach class? More like a hibernation car without beds, Chris thinks. To Sweet's amusement, Chris spends the next few minutes trying to plug in a cord while not disturbing the woman by the window. He kneels down and delicately winds the thin lead behind her ankle. He looks like he's in a movie, playing a hero trying to defuse a bomb or something. As he plugs in the cord and attaches it to Sweet's phone, the woman moves. The snoring stops abruptly and her shin edges forward, bumping Chris' nose. She wakes up, eyes immediately widening, and stares down at what might seem to her an incompetent frotteur. She prepares to yell.

Sweet's laughter beats her to it. Chris raises the cord, indicating his real intent to the outraged lady, and apologizes with a hapless wave. He crawls backwards and slumps onto his seat, avoiding the woman's gaping, incredulous face. Trying to relax, he's glad he's gotten the phone-charging task out the way. Now Sweet gets a share of sarcasm: Chris thanking him for showing him an outlet; Chris thanking Sweet for being supportive, for staying alert and generally helping out. For reasons that are unclear to himself, Chris remains restless. He looks about the compartment some more, wondering if there are better seats on the train, like anywhere. Something nags at him; something nameless. In the distance, he sees the skinny guy from before still loitering about the bathroom. Suspicious, yet drawn like a moth to a flame, he rises from his seat and steps over Sweet's legs, entering the aisle.

"Dude, what's your deal? Can't you relax," Sweet moans.

"I'll be back in a minute. Keep an eye on the phone."

By the time Chris has again reached the bathroom, the skinny guy dressed in all black has slipped inside like he's entering a much frequented office. Chris has a hunch that something's not the way it's supposed to be. Something is right and not right all at once. Something is…he actually doesn't wanna think about it. Were he to be honest with himself he'd follow the thought through to its logical and much desired conclusion, and then he'd have to consider the likely consequences. Without that burden he can float about aimlessly, pretending he's not intriguing on anything; just waiting on a bathroom in a public place, like anyone else would. He is innocent and unawares.

The door to the bathroom opens, this time long before five minutes have past. But it's like a magic trick has happened. The guy coming out is not the guy Chris saw going in. The person leaving is less skinny and has shoulder length blond hair, all knotted and dirty like a bale of hay that has been left out in the rain. He says nothing, like he doesn't even see Chris standing next to the door, though he leaves the door dislodged. No consideration, it seems, because from inside there's a token complaint. Sneaking a look through the three inch gap that's been left, Chris sees curly black hair in the mirror that's adjacent to the door. He hears the sound of fidgeting, of someone cursing, scrambling to recover items they have dropped all over the floor. Chris goes blackout for a moment, makes a brave yet reckless decision, and sticks his toe in the door.

"Dafuk!" says the voice from inside, louder now. Chris sticks his nose inside just far enough to catch sight of one or two telling pieces: he glimpses a razor blade and a hollowed out pen. Beside the pen there is residue of white powder speckled about a small countertop. The guy in black steps to the door and blocks any further viewing of this scene. He stands before Chris, nose to nose, with a nose that is bleeding.

"What d'ya want, bro?" he asks, quickly looking Chris up and down, determining that he is not cop-like. He has a chalk white expression, with pocked skin and a greasy metallic air about him. Chris gives a cordial nod, looks nervously into the mirror wherein he can see exactly what he wants: there are two more lines of white powder neatly arrayed, well crushed though perhaps cut with something unsavory, and best of all, untouched, with instruments laying all around it. While admiring the set up, he speaks in a low voice.

"Lemme take some of that off your hands."

The guy stares woodenly into Chris, with black eyes that look like punch holes. He wipes a tissue across his nose and sneaks a thinly concerned look at his own blood. For this reason alone, it seems that profiteering might take priority over recreation, though otherwise he seems untroubled.

"Twenty for a quarter," he says.

"I just got ten."

"Then get lost."

Chris looks up and down the car to see if he can spot anyone official-looking, like a ticket agent.

"You sure?" he says, trying to act cool and hoping the guy might take a cut price on his leftovers. But the guy is unblinkingly short and steadfast.

"If you don't want it I'll bag it for later. No problem. Problem for you though if you open your mouth." Chris returns a dullish, half-heartedly *hard* look, knowing his negotiation skills would leave much to be desired.

"Give me a minute?" he asks, motioning down the car.

The guy smirks, like he could give a shit; like those two lines might be gone by the time Chris returns, nose bleed or not. As Chris hurries back to his seat, he feels dread and delight in equal measure. He stumbles over a crack in the floor, moving a bit too quickly for his own good. In his mind he's already back in the bathroom compartment, feeling the sour taste in his throat, anticipating the thrilling kick that will come minutes later. He doesn't really want to do this. Every part of him that is him and not the portion of his brain that isn't and can't live without this experience wants him to not do this. He knows Sweet won't want him to do it, despite having his own pill cravings recently, and hopefully Sweet's newfound level-headedness will stop this foolishness. Then again, it's only snorting, which is at least better, meaning safer and less addicting than smoking. Chris recognizes the rationales from months past as they float into his mind: it's a friendly reunion, as if Chris, already high, wants to greet these familiar thoughts, welcome them back into the fold after their roughly three month hiatus, odd slips notwithstanding.

As he reaches the seat, Chris finds that Sweet has fallen asleep again, but this time doesn't wake him. Sweet is definitely not keeping an eye on the phone, which is still being charged, still sitting where it was left. That's a lucky break, Chris thinks, especially given their recent luck with phones. He reaches over and collects it, this time more skillfully than before, and sticks it in Sweet's shirt pocket. The action fails to rouse Sweet, which gives Chris an idea. Across from Sweet, that fat woman with the attitude remains sleeping, and on the opposite side of the aisle there is one other person, a man with an impassive gaze who looks as though he too is moments away from the soporific contagion. Chris spies the wallet that sticks out of Sweet's backside and deftly takes it out, half thinking his careless friend shouldn't be holding the money anyway. Inside there's two twenty dollar bills and a few ones crumpling beneath them. Feeling greedy, thinking that he'll worry about explanations, not to mention other provisions later, Chris takes the twenties, shiftily looks about and catches the eyes of a disapproving little girl two seats away. Guiltily, he looks away from her.

On the way back to the bathroom he starts to sweat and get excited, though he figures it might be a lonely trip tweakin' amongst all these Amtrak zombies. He's not sure how he'll pass the time or what he'll do with his high once it kicks in. Who will play with this lost little boy? The skinny guy in black has locked himself inside the bathroom in case anyone comes looking to make normal use of facilities. He and Chris had briefly worked out a code—three knocks—that would renew acquaintances on his return. Chris squeezes in, hands him the two bills, and looks over the two lines that are still laid out, looking neat and untouched. A part of Chris wants to leave them that way, keep it beautifully crushed, new like tiny shards of fiberglass, and something to be ever anticipated as opposed to finished with. No consummation. The problem with transient pleasures, Chris knows, is that they are indeed transient—that once past they leave behind a broken self that will then have to face all of those children of the world, with their innocent, preternatural faces. For the amount given, the skinny guy supplies an extra one inch by one inch Ziploc and gives Chris a business-like nod alongside a gratuitous promotion of his product: "Shit's raw, bro," he says, though he sounds about as

convincing as a store clerk wishing him a nice day. As for the
accessories, he tells Chris he can use the pen if he likes, but not the
razors, which he's already stashed. He abruptly leaves—no
handshakes or even touching fists—and shuts the door behind him,
leaving Chris alone.

Above the mirror there is a sign that sternly warns
passengers not to smoke. Chris smirks, matching the expression of
the departed salesman. Yes sir, he thinks. No problem there. For a
moment, he lets himself experience another feeling that will soon
take a back seat: shame. He's not proud of what he's about to do.
He looks in the mirror, stares at himself in a solemn way, like he's
ruminating, saying thanks to God for the gifts he is about to
receive. Then he smiles a thin, wicked smile. Time to feel good, he
thinks—time to feel damned good.

34

Compared to Jill Evans' Honda, Eric Pierce's Subaru feels
brand new, like a rental car. It has a new car smell, reflecting the
fastidious touch of its owner. The vinyl-plastic on the dashboard
has an oily yet clean complexion. There is no dust on the surfaces,
no crud layered at the base of a coffee cup holder; no scattering of
change or keys in the palm-sized pocket beneath the handbrake.
Jill, thinking about the circumstances, wondering how her life
might be impacted by this adventure, reflects upon times as a

teenager when she'd borrowed her sisters' clothes without permission, only to give them back later with flaws, like tiny holes in the armpits. She pictures herself talking to police officers, or else being tracked down by the irate and bullish owner whom she'd decked back at Jenny Leavitt's house. She takes her mind off the pain of the previous topic and instead considers a mischievous quip that she hopes someone will think funny if and when caught: she and Weed have not so much stolen a car as rented one.

Weed is rocking slightly in his seat, brooding over the story Jill has sort of told him, about Chris. Every few seconds Jill glances over and sees his jaws moving, like he's grinding his teeth. She starts to worry that she's said too much, given Weed the wrong idea, or rather the right idea, but the wrong prescription for what might follow.

"Sorry. I shouldn't have told you that. It's not your problem."

Weed's response is low, grave and menacing.

"I wanted to know, right? I got what I asked for."

I did know, sort of, he thinks.

"Are you alright?"

Weed wants to glare at her. Were she asking this question in relation to any other subject, he might be glaring at her, in effect saying she should back off and leave him alone. Now he doesn't have the heart to tell her anything. He doesn't feel entitled to tell her anything. He simply feels like asking her questions.

"How come you're asking me that?"

Jill shakes her head, starts to cry again as she mouths the words, "I don't know".

Weed fills his cheeks with air and then blows out. He's at a loss: for lost words.

"I don't want you to get the wrong idea," Jill says, collecting herself. "He didn't quite...I pushed him away. I don't think he meant to hurt me. Really. He was just..."

"Tweaked."

"Right."

Weed nods. Again, much is making sense. He holds a hand over his eyes, concealing a pained expression. He lets the hand slide upwards, stroking his forehead, pushing back his hairline.

"That's my bad, actually," he says. "The day before we took off for Marin I took him on one of my errands. At first he didn't wanna come, but I was planning this thing with Sahi I've told you about and I was running it by Chris already. He wasn't really listening. When we got to this guy's place, I was selling eighths to a group while this other guy was hawking meth. I wasn't interested, but Chris was and ended up getting a teenie and blowing his last set of cash."

Jill barely knows what a teenie is but it doesn't matter.

"Chris told me he was clean," she says absently. "I mean, I asked him. It's so weird that I'd ask him knowing what he was like that whole time."

"I think he tells himself that he's clean when he's not. But he did wanna stop. That part's real, and it was partly because of you that he wanted to be clean. If he hadn't gone along with me to that guy's place, he might've stayed clean that day."

"You don't know that," Jill rebuts, aware that by caretaking for Weed she may block his awkward caretaking of her.

"Yeah, you're right. But I didn't help. That's the point. Jesus, how bad did he hurt you?"

"He didn't—that's *my* point. Well, he hurt my wrists a bit, and my heart; that's all. They've been sore recently, the wrists. But you saw me back there, with that security guy. You think I couldn't do worse to Chris? I got him. I got him you know where." Weed nods like he's accepting her account and its just climax. Afterwards, his jaw stills itself. He seems steely, tough and mad as he looks forward out the front window of the car. Jill regards his dangerous air, forgetting that he's still sick as a dog, holding off needing a bed and a greater dose of meds only because of the situation. Noting his gesture, she nervously asks, "What are you gonna do? I don't want to be the reason there's any drama between you and Chris."

"It's okay," Weed answers curtly. It's strange that his tone seems aggressive, like she's done something wrong or else reported something shameful about herself. The words don't match the feeling. Weed's earlier statements, crystal clear in meaning, were in support of her, and was, if anything, self recriminating. "I'm not gonna do anything to him," he concludes.

"You look angry. Do you hate him now or something?"

"Nah, I don't hate him. He's a drug addict and I've got no business hating drug addicts. But he hurt you, tried to rape you and that's not cool. He's gonna know that I know this and what I think about it."

"Please don't," Jill says. Weed bites his lip, frustrated.

"Why not? Why tell me if you didn't expect a reaction? Do you expect me to not say anything at all about this? You say guys don't talk about this. Do you think we don't have any feelings about rape? What kind of man do you think I am?"

Jill stirs inside with a flurry of thoughts, most of them memories about things Chris used to say about Weed: stories about his charismatic pull; stories about how he dominated at games, and depending upon his mood, either became boastful or else truculent, discouraged by the lack of sound opposition. Some stuff Weed did was questionable, Chris told her: the people he associated with were often dangerous or sordid. The women that clung to him were, well, not exactly empowered types: strippers or drug addicts, sometimes prostitutes. Chris never held any of this against Weed. If anything, the cast and milieu around Weed seemed to Chris a kind of hell's kitchen. Everyone in it was some manner of deviant or sprite, including Weed. He was a visitor, someone who ventured the wrong side of the tracks mostly because it offered liberties, but he could leave it all behind if he chose to, and he did choose to— sometimes. Weed chose his life, Chris more or less asserted. A rich white male's privilege, Jill argued. Chris bristled; thought this a facile, jaundiced view of an individualist. Weed accepted his reputation, a baseline lack of security, as the cost of doing his thing, being answerable to no one. In this way Chris admired Weed.

"I'm not sure, to be honest," Jill replies. "Like I said, Chris seems to look up to you, but the way he described your life wasn't flattering, not to me anyway. And I'll say this: before today, I wouldn't have guessed you'd empathize with a victim of sexual assault."

Weed turns from Jill, his body a step ahead of his thoughts, which strain to note the significance of her detached, clinical terminology. His face heats up slightly, suggesting a blush. Something in his stomach drops. He briefly looks back at Jill to show he's not avoiding her eyes, but her frank expression is hard to take. It's like she's looking into him, about to pry open a dark secret and then comment upon its entrails. Suddenly, the tears, the trembling, and the open frailty are all gone, replaced by the skilled inquisitor and provider of astute observations. Feeling sketchy, even terrified, Weed becomes shifty and searching of his mind: what can he do, and what can he say, to redirect her scent from the truth of recent events?

"I don't really know what to say," he says, rolling his eyes. "Makes me wonder what he told you that would make you think that."

Jill pauses before answering. Caught between minds, she half wants to stoke Weed's budding heroics, his intention of calling out Chris when they meet up later. On the other hand, she doesn't trust them to stay calm, and meant what she said about keeping the boys from fighting.

"Maybe I got the wrong idea, but he said the women you date or hang out with or whatever are mostly…"

"What?"

"Skanks,"

Weed tries to find outrage through a trail of forced laughter. "Excuse me, Chris said that? Chris didn't say that. Guys don't even say that. That's a woman's word: a jealous woman's word."

Jill shoots him a frown. "Okay, that's my word, but I wasn't jealous. That's my word for women who'll sleep with anyone."

"Thanks."

"I didn't mean—shit—Chris said you took him to night clubs and that you got together with whoever smoked with you."

Weed's expression flattens. He no longer looks outraged; merely glum.

"I guess that's true."

For the time being, the hanging question as to whether Weed might confront Chris about Jill is sidelined. For the time being, it feels safer, if girlishly prurient, for Jill to take this highway 101 chat in another direction.

"So, you're not in any kind of relationship then?" she asks.

"No."

"Have you ever been?"

Weed shakes his head but laughs again, snidely. Actually, he snorts. "Unbelievable," he remarks.

"Sorry, am I getting too personal?"

"No, just insulting."

Jill sighs. "Okay, maybe that was bitchy. Again—sorry. I guess Chris will have told you that about me. I'm just tryin' to find out what your deal is."

"Do you think I'm gay or something?"

"Oh…my God."

"What? That's what people usually mean when they ask questions like that."

Now Jill's face turns into a grimace. Weed, she figures, has been smoking his inventory. Ordinarily, she stops short of rhetorical "what's your problem" questions, not wanting to be shrill. But her perplexity with respect to Weed is all over her. She looks back and forth between him and the road. Not knowing what to say, Jill settles upon plain resignation.

"I don't understand you."

Weed looks over at the gas gauge, sees that the indicator is hovering around the quarter tank mark. Up ahead are signs directing traffic east towards Bakersfield and the five freeway, which is a straighter run at this point so they agree that taking the turn is best. Weed figures they are an hour away from the base of the LA mountains, the so-called grapevine. He looks at the clock: just past four, it reads. He yawns. Still mid-afternoon: this has been a long ass day, he thinks.

"We should stop soon," he says. "Get gas, take a bathroom break."

"Sure," Jill replies, accepting the end of conversation. For another quarter hour there is silence as they both gaze up ahead or sideways, looking at misty, distant mountain ranges, stretches of telephone towers, flatlands, farms, and stolid, uninspired cows. Weed dwells on his secrets, feels an odd, dull weight at the base of his stomach, like something's pushing out.

"A lot of people say that to me," he suddenly remarks, presumably in reference to Jill's last comment. "That's partly why I wrote a book," he adds.

"Yeah?" says Jill in a bored voice. She bites. "What was the book about?"

"It was about gaming. I thought Chris told you about it."

"He did but he didn't describe it much."

Weed issues a barely discernible grunt. Disappointment. "Well, in case you're interested it's relevant to what we're doing here. A few years ago I started blogging about games that were available on the market. I made You-Tube videos of myself playing games like *Call Of Duty*, commenting as I played. I got plenty of hits, then subscribers. Soon You-Tube wanted to partner with me, advertise on my site. Then with the blog, people started saying I should write a book or something, and I actually got a publisher a while later."

Weed pauses as if looking for reinforcement.

"Uh-huh," Jill utters.

"People seemed to like what I was saying, which was a full-on review of all kinds of games, but also a general complaint about a games market that lacked imagination. I mean, I was good at COD, and Battlefield whatever version, but these games are mostly about wandering around with a camera on your head, being alert for resources and enemies, and then figuring out ways to kill 'em. I preferred Battlefield to COD, wrote about how lone ranger games weren't as good as those which fostered teamwork. At the same time, I thought more games should be like Soulcraft, which is based on Minecraft—games which find different kinds of goals for players; more creative or complex goals. When I was writing the book, which took about six months—it wasn't long, only a hundred pages—I thought that's what people wanted to hear, deep down anyway. When I presented the book, called *Play Gone Wrong*, the publisher balked, said they wanted something more positive and less weird in the title, though they supported the content." Weed stops again, shaking his head.

"So what happened? What was the title?"

"A bullshit title, *Today's Top Games*. It sold about a hundred and fifty copies."

"That's stupid," Jill remarks awkwardly. "The title change, not the fact that it sold only a hundred and fifty copies."

"Yeah." Now Weed sounds bored. He goes quiet again, and it seems to Jill that talking to this guy, getting stuff out of him is hard work; just as hard as prying stuff from Chris, actually. Several times she thinks to ask another question, kick the pebble that is this exchange just a little ways further. She stops herself, reasoning that at some point Weed will simply resume talking, picking up from where he left off, the context obvious from his point of view. Weed's mind is actually elsewhere, recalling that about a quarter of the books he sold were bought by his dad, and a few others by book club friends of his mom who would otherwise read anything: cookbooks, travelogues; quaint stories about pets named Marvin; pretentious drivel from writers who over-use terms like "personal journey". When that reverie stops, Weed's thoughts turn back to the secrets he's keeping; specifically, the stuff he now feels pressure to share with Jill. "I got something else to tell you," he says.

Jill raises her eyebrows. "Okay," she answers warily.

"What you were talking about earlier, about Chris: I kinda knew about that."

"Really? I'm listening." Jill doesn't sound shocked.

"I don't mean that Chris told me what you just said. Believe me, if he had then I'd have called him out." Weed and Jill's eyes meet. "Well, maybe you won't believe me. Whatever, but that's what I'm saying, anyway. But the thing is this: when I first met you—that night of the accident—I recognized you. I'd seen you before. You know what I'm saying?" He gives her a patient, studious look, the type a teacher gives when hoping a student will get a lesson that's been suggestively imparted. Jill looks at Weed, confused.

"No, I don't," she replies impatiently, "why don't you enlighten me."

"You were a Shadow the first time I saw you—what I call a Breather-Shadow, something that I think…well, I saw you as a vision standing next to Chris, saying something to him. That meant, as far as I was concerned, that something had happened between the two of you, or was going to happen."

Jill's patience, if not something else, breaks. It breaks almost to the point wherein it transfers to her feet, halting the car in the middle of the highway, which is especially dangerous given that traffic is thickening as the afternoon wears on.

"Wait. What do you mean by 'something had happened'?"

"I mean…ya know," he says, because *he* didn't know.

"Didn't you say that Shadow sightings or whatever alerted you to crimes, future or past?"

"Yeah." Weed's agreement is tenuous and foreboding. By the fierce look in her eyes and the jutting of her jaw, he gleans that Jill is about to hit Krav Maga mode with her tongue.

"So if you thought Chris had committed or was going to commit some kind of crime with respect to me, why wouldn't you 'call him out', as you put it?"

Weed looks dumbstruck, caught without a good answer for the skilled inquisitor. That'll teach him not to reveal his secrets. Should've stayed on Monads—should've have seen this coming. Not that he doesn't have anything to say. He has an explanation for her; not a bad one, even, at least from one point of view. But it sounds feeble to him when he thinks about it—it's too personal.

It's different. I know you now. I...

"I don't know. You're right. It's messed up that I didn't even ask him about it."

"Just as I figured," says Jill, disgustedly turning her attentions back to the road. "This Shadow business is just a load of bullshit wasting everybody's time."

Weed sits shamefacedly, his shoulders slumped; his jaw slackened, shorn of the steely mastication that Jill, unbeknownst to him, found sexy not that long ago. Meanwhile, Jill sits in her driver's seat, fuming. The task of keeping her hands on the wheel is all that keeps her from lashing out and flailing her arms at the hapless passenger. Not for the first time with a guy roughly her age, she feels like a big sister driving a delinquent brother home after a disgraced appearance with a school principal. But it's too late to turn back now. She's in this thing, committed. Up ahead, appearing like an oasis in a desert, the outline of the grapevine, with the five freeway snaking its way into the hills, looms fantastically like the land of Oz. A sign by the side of the road indicates that a last chance of gas and food for many miles is coming up. Weed feels like a ten year old boy about to annoy a parent with biological needs that ought to have been dealt with beforehand.

"I really need that bathroom," he says in a pitiful voice.

35

"Do you see it yet?" asks Jeff Willits.

Eric Pierce has seen three white Subarus in the last hour. None have been his car. None have had its distinctive license plate: DPCOGMD. Jeff, his reluctant partner, is starting to pester Eric, wondering if they might have passed them at some point, maybe even lost the Subaru somewhere after the junction at the 101.

"I think they've stopped," says Eric. He sounds gritty as he looks up from his phone and stares ahead. He hath vengeance on his mind. "The gas stations before the grapevine, probably." As they pull off the freeway, they take it slow over the pass, looking between competing oil giants, a Texaco on one side, a Chevron on the other.

"There," says Willits, pointing ahead at a car that's stopped at one of eight pumps at the Chevron. Pierce follows the gesture, sees the car, its make and color, and a license plate from which he can make out three letters that aren't blocked by the car behind it: DPC, it reads. Good enough, thinks Pierce. There's no sign of life in or outside the car, though their view is still partially obscured.

"Can't see 'em," says Pierce. "We should pull up behind and then take 'em." Jeff Willits pulls a face.

"No way. I'm gonna park to the side, spot them first and then approach."

"Approach? You sound like a door-to-door salesman. Look, we need to treat this like a takedown."

"No. Look, cowboy, we need to chill out, approach them in a public scene, with witnesses, and talk to them, like I said." Pierce hisses protest. "This is how we engage," Willits continues. "If they refuse to cooperate then we call the cops. That's Gagliano's call. Remember, at this point it's not even about those files. It's about a stolen vehicle. That's what I'm gonna tell 'em, right now." Willits pulls into a parking space behind the pump towers, right near the air devices. "Do you see 'em yet?" he asks, sounding like he feels: in charge.

"Not yet—wait. There, by the food mart. It's the woman." Eric Pierce points to the woman, Jill Evans, who stands at the open double doorway to the store, about to go in.

"Where's Tecco?"

"Dunno." As soon as the question is asked, Pierce has a horrified thought: Tecco has ditched the woman and the Subaru, knowing he was being followed. He's made the woman a decoy. Willits opens his door and jumps out of the Suburban. "I should talk to her," Pierce calls after him.

"Fuck no. She'll just kick your ass again. Besides, I told you that Gagliano wants you back seat at this point, so stay here." As Willits walks away towards the food mart he wears a cartoon smile. Pierce watches and stirs, feeling helpless and benched by a boss who doesn't explain himself, a peer that's now striding towards a final destination, ready to make a decisive catch. Jeff Willits will soon be having lunch with Sahi bosses, drinking wine and eating filet mignons at stylish restaurants; receiving congratulations for a job well done and generally feeling at ease amongst power. Pierce sits for a few seconds and then exits his side of the Suburban feeling petulant, like a ten year old that's been told to wait in the car but is now rebelling. He walks towards the unattended Subaru that's almost fully concealed by the pump tower, and now also by a pair of monster trucks that have just pulled up to the other side. To hell with Jeff Willits, he thinks. To hell with Dave Gagliano. Eric Pierce wants to see his car. He wants to touch its panels, check for damage, reclaim what's rightfully his and then kick some ass.

He steps between the trucks and in front of a Minivan whose front is right up against the back of the Subaru. Standing beside its back windshield, Pierce looks over his stolen property and smiles. Not overly possessive, he nonetheless takes care of his Subaru. He figures he's never been happier to see his fairly ordinary car. He feels silly thinking that soon he'll be taking this now precious piece of metal home and giving it a deserved wash and a thorough waxing. Around him, three guys, all from the trucks, wearing white T-shirts and backwards-turned baseball caps swarm about him, nudging past as they head towards the food mart. Their chatter about diesel trucks, off-road this and that distracts Pierce and makes him think of the slobs he used to throw out of bars when he first started working in security.

"Excuse me," says the clumsiest one with some kind of southern twang.

Pierce nods and mutters "No problem".

The next person does a lot more than nudge. With a forceful yank, Pierce is pulled backwards, his lower back bumping against the side of the Minivan from behind. He has no time to protest.

It's a problem.

36

Pulling off the freeway ahead of the grapevine, Weed and Jill are not talking to each other. For the time being, it'll be hard for them to plan anything. They'll likely not cooperate on what gas station to use, much less coordinate their lottery approach to finding Chris and Sweet. And for the time being, Weed doesn't even care anymore. As long as they pull into some place that looks like it has a bathroom and a place to buy snacks, he's good—again, for now. Jill observes a Chevron across from a Texaco station, quietly points out that it seems to be less busy. Weed sulks.

Whatever.

Once parked at a pump, they move to exit simultaneously, though Weed pauses. Just to be safe, he opens the glove compartment and takes out the firearm he'd lifted from Eric Pierce back in Oakland. He sticks it in the back of his pants and gets out the car. He wanders off towards what looks like a public bathroom behind a food mart.

"You might need a key," Jill calls out after him. First of all, Weed doesn't think so. Secondly, he's had enough of Jill's suggestions, her motherly pretense.

"Uh-huh," he says, barely looking over his shoulder. Jill follows him, but not to the bathroom. Near the double doors to the store she stops and watches him walk along a wall towards the back of the building. She watches Weed as if making sure he reaches the right door, though really it's another kind of espionage that's under way. Jill shakes her head, having yielded no results from these thoughts.

After pumping twenty dollars worth of gas into the Subaru, Jill looks to see if Weed has emerged from the restroom area. There's no sign of him, though there appears to be a small milling about next to the bathroom; a kind of line. She heads back towards the store. I guess *I'll* get us something to eat, she thinks resentfully. Inside, she buys a bag of chips, two bananas, and a plastic bottle of diet coke upon deciding that all the hot food or sandwich items are substandard. Minutes later she walks out the store only to be confronted by a slick guy in a business suit who flashes bright white teeth, an ID that says he works for Sahi corporation, and who then asks if he can have a minute of her time.

Weed comes out of the single occupancy bathroom to find an effete-looking youth waiting his turn. The boy's vacant look betrays the kind of self-absorption that Weed has come to know and exploit. Briefly, he saddens. As the boy turns into the bathroom he leaves behind him a clear line of sight aimed at cars that are pulling into pump stations or else parked behind, waiting for a space. At that precise moment, Weed sees Eric Pierce sitting in the passenger seat of a black Suburban, about thirty five yards ahead of him. Weed freezes: The vision is unmistakeable. It's him. He shakes his head and closes his eyes, thinking this a Shadow. Nice timing, Weed thinks. He takes a moment and stands up against a wall adjacent to the bathroom, seeking to lean against something. Then he opens his eyes and looks back to check if the vision is still there. Most of the time, Shadows flicker in and out for several seconds, and sometimes make eye contact. But then, typically, they disappear, having done their job. That's how it usually works in Weed's game. However, one thing Shadows don't do is walk fluidly, as in without any break in the continuity of their image.

As Weed watches Eric Pierce exit from his vehicle and edge towards a pump tower, he feels a different kind of chill. This is no vision, he realizes. This is happening. Quickly, his mind puts the pieces together. Of course, the Subaru, a company vehicle no doubt, must have a tracking device on it somewhere. That guy must have followed us all way the down here, Weed realizes. He's followed them to this point, thinking it will lead him to Chris Leavitt and the files that belong to Jules Grotius. Weed bangs his head against the wall, thinking himself a fool for overlooking all of this. In his lower back, he feels the metal of the P229 firearm pressed against him. Quietly, with terminator-like purpose, he pushes off from the wall and starts walking steadily towards the gas pump area. Walking in a semi-circle that veers away from the cars, Weed achieves a vantage point from which he sees Eric Pierce stepping up towards his Subaru, behind a Minivan that is parked up behind it. From the position he's in, Weed knows he will be instantly exposed should Pierce choose to turn. Taking the risk of being heard, he quickens his step so as to hide behind the bulky frame of the van, thereby enabling a sneaking final approach.

"Bend down," Weed says as he grabs the shoulder of Eric Pierce. "Be chill. I got your piece in my other hand," adds Weed in a breathy voice. He's a guy who believes in Breather-Shadows. Pierce nods.

Tecco—Gotcha.

He cooperates, immediately recalling that Weed took his firearm back in Oakland. He grinds his teeth as Weed issues a fuller greeting: "S—say partner, looks like you made a long personal journey. S—sorry for the inconvenience, but I don't think I'm ready to chat with your bosses just yet." Pierce says nothing. For the moment he keeps his wits and feels for the gap between his and Weed's body, looking to see if one of his wrestling-type moves might reverse their positions. No dice, he assesses. Weed is crouched too far back, and is half-standing while Pierce is on his knees. Weed's left hand is stabbing flesh beneath his left shoulder. As for the right hand, Pierce can't see or feel that, yet. "Who else is with you?" Weed interrogates.

Pierce has attitude but no guile. "What d'ya think? My partner, another security officer from Sahi—he's in the store." Weed, holding Pierce by the back of his coat, looks between the Minivan and the Subaru and sees Jill talking to a guy dressed in— he guesses it—a black suit and sunglasses. He checks the area around them, relieved to be camouflaged for the moment by a few sizable vehicles, though he knows he doesn't have much time.

"Okay bro, stay down and move forward. Whatever device you got on this thing, take it off. And remember, take it slow."

"It's under the hood," says Pierce. He gets whacked for giving a wrong answer. He feels dizzy and his nose bleeds.

"Don't fuck with me, bro. It's under the car."

Pierce stalls for another moment and winces. Half of him is waiting for the next blow—the other half is scurrying through the angles in his mind: How's this guy gonna do this? Sooner or later, someone will see him and call out or make a 911 call. Highway patrol won't be far away and will be on him like flies on horseshit. Any moment now he'll have to make a decision, make a move.

Weed eyes the back of Pierce's neck, the soft spot he will strike next.

"Do I need to jog your memory again? I can see your partner through the window and I can feel you twitch. If he turns in this direction and you aint removed your toy, then..." Weed makes a childlike noise. *Ptchoo*.

Internally, Weed has a completely different dialogue running: Come on, girlfriend, he thinks, regarding Jill. I don't care how cute that guy is. Stop yappin' and kick him in the you-know-where. Meanwhile, Pierce is following orders, taking it slow, running his hand underneath the chassis on the driver's side. While he feels about, he regrets not trying a ruse; that of claiming the device is on the other side, in more open view of witnesses. With no ceremony, much less pleasure, he mutely pulls a palm-sized device from underneath the car and holds it aloft.

"Good job," says Weed, patting him on the shoulder. He takes the device, tosses it aside, and breathes out, as if this drama is nearing an end.

At the doorway to the food mart, Jill is nervously fielding questions from a presumptuous, if good-looking guy who seems to want his colleague's stolen car back.

"Ma'am, I think we can work this out so there's as little trouble as possible for everyone."

"Like I said, I don't know what you're talking about and I suggest you leave me alone." One or two people walk by them, taking notice of the curt exchange, but not intruding. Changing tact, Willits matches Jill's terse manner.

"Oh, I think you know."

"Fine, then why don't you call the cops? Go ahead. You think I'm a car thief, take down my license plate and go for it."

Willits looks about himself and smiles winningly. Dealing with women isn't usually this difficult for him.

"Okay, why don't we cut through it? You've driven this car down here from Oakland. I know that; I followed you here. That's a long drive and a bit more than a getaway from danger, if that's what you'd claim. And for what? What are you getting out of this? Now I'm offering you a chance to give up the car, tell us what happened to your friend, and maybe avoid some real trouble. That's if you cooperate with me."

Jill nods sarcastically. "Uh-huh. Avoiding trouble? Yeah, I'm sure you'd like to avoid trouble. I'm sure you'd like to avoid the trouble of some bad publicity, like the story of your colleague, who broke into a house this morning and assaulted an elderly woman. Can we talk about how your company avoids trouble for that?"

Jill's volume begins to rise. Willits ill-advisedly reaches out and touches her arm, looking to calm her.

"Alright, let's take it easy."

"Take your hands off me," Jill snaps. From inside the store, the clerk behind the counter looks up and stares out at the quarreling pair. It's not the look of a man wanting to intervene. It's the look of someone avoiding conflict, hoping that staring alone will deter further unpleasantness. But it doesn't matter, because moments later, beyond this couple and closer to the pump area, there's another piece of unpleasantness, one that will force action.

"Now..." says Weed, feeling momentarily satisfied.

He is interrupted by a scream from behind. Reflexively, he flinches but keeps his head. Every corpuscle of his being is begging him to look behind and see where the scream is coming from. But he doesn't need to. He can picture the woman who's screaming: she's about fifty years old, overweight, with one or two kids. Maybe one's a teenager, the other a preteen. She'll be the owner of the Minivan, seeing him from behind having approached the back with junk goods bought from the store. Maybe the kids are still in line at the bathroom Weed just finished using. Anyway, he doesn't need to look at her. There's no danger, at least not from a terrified woman standing in shock several feet behind him, her hands and limbs shaking wildly.

Eric Pierce is making different assumptions. A split second upon hearing the scream, he decides to seize the moment, take his gamble. Employing a maneuver that seems familiar to Weed, Pierce shoves back his elbow and jumps to his feet. Before turning, he achieves a stance that already has him positioned to strike, though he is yet to turn. Weed recognizes the move from a party he'd attended some time back. A hookup of his was showing off some new moves he'd learned in his beginner's Krav Maga class. Jesus, is everyone learning that shit except me? Weed thinks. He watches unmoved as Pierce reaches his feet. Then, without thinking, he swipes hard the length of the gun across the back of Pierce's head, pistol-whipping the Sahi man.

As Jeff Willits' head turns, Jill seizes her opportunity and delivers a sharp kick to his knee, flooring him. It's a hard blow, strong enough to have Willits howling and clutching at his limb as soon as he hits the ground. Jill stands over him for a split second, unsure as to whether she might give him a second kick, a knockout strike. But it's a luxury move, she decides. Twenty yards away, a drama is unfolding that no doubt involves Weed. Out there by the pump stations, he'll be wielding that gun he took from the other Sahi officer. Any moment now, a fire fight is about to happen and someone's gonna get killed.

Unless *she* does something.

Not thinking, running on instinct, Jill leaps over the body of Jeff Willits, and sprints towards the Subaru that's situated among the middle row of pumps. She doesn't see Weed. She doesn't see the woman who was screaming a moment ago. All around her there is white noise intruded upon by random shouts, the sight of a guy hitting the deck, frightened, and letting his baseball cap fly away from him. Just feet from the car, she stops as she sees Weed rise from the other side of the vehicle. He's rising like a man that's standing over another's body; like he's just killed someone and is contemplating the act. Jill looks into his face to see if there's anything there: fear, sadness, guilt…anything.

"HEY," cries Jill in the direction of Weed. He looks up at her with dead eyes as she sprints towards him. Beyond her, laying on a step beside the foot mart, prostrate across the ground with his mouth open in some kind of agony, is that guy with the black suit and the sunglasses. Right on, Widow, thinks Weed.

"Gimme the keys. I'm driving," Weed says, stepping over Pierce's slumping, concussed body. Jill complies, tosses him the keys and gets in the already unlocked passenger side. As she settles into her seat, she notes her ready cooperation; the automatic submission that relives the similar moment at Jenny Leavitt's house.

"But," she says, and then stops. Weed starts the Subaru, saying, "Yeah, I know—no license. I could be in real trouble now, huh?" He pulls away, screeching the tires as he reaches something like fifty miles per hour even before exiting the station. In the wide street beyond, he performs a gratuitous doughnut and yells out in triumph before coming to a halt. Pinned to her seat, Jill regards his delighted face and feels his blowtorch noise and scorching breath pouring over the car and her. It's a reprise of that Slim whomever character he referenced earlier: a vomit of rage blended with indecent relish. He speeds away from the gas station, maintaining this exultant roar for something like a minute. From deadness to the greatest moment of his life: zero to sixty in less than ten seconds. Gone is the dejected post-adolescent sitting chastened in the passenger seat. Now he seems not only hopeful, but driven and unrepentant, and operating on overdrive. On a high, he imagines the next several hours: there will be everything to fight about and nothing to apologize for. He switches on the radio, smiles as he checks the gas gauge and sees the car has been fed. He finds a classic rock station; an old Led Zeppelin song begins, and Weed cranks up the volume. It's been a long time since he's rock and rolled. Next, he lowers his window and sees that Pierce, passed out for the second time in a day, is starting to move gingerly by the gas pump; that his partner, looking pained and limping in the distance, is only just reaching his feet.

Eric Pierce remains dizzy and his nose continues to bleed, but he's still fighting, trying to get to his knees. He doesn't see Willits and he doesn't see his Subaru, but he can hear Tecco's voice coming from somewhere; could feel everything about his car as it drove off, nearly running over him. Wherever Willits is, he might be pulling out his phone, ready to make that 911 call. Then again, maybe he isn't. Maybe he's lying on the ground, having suffered the same fate Pierce did hours earlier. Now he knows how it feels. Now he'll know what failure feels like. Maybe he doesn't have to make a call to 911 because someone else is—whoever was screaming a few moments ago. The shit's gonna hit the fan now, and suddenly it makes sense why Pierce was told to sit back and not get involved. He didn't plan this out very well. Nobody did, it seems. Sure, there's a stolen car out there, but it's a car belonging to a guy, a Sahi employee, who made a home invasion several hours ago, who just got held up at a gas station, and who probably needs a hospital more than anything right about now. Pierce figures cops will surely be as interested in these events and prospects as they will a stolen Subaru. And Dave Gagliano? He won't be pleased by any of this. As Eric Pierce sits up, he looks out at the road running parallel to the gas station and sees Bryan Tecco waving at him from the driver's side of his car. His car!

It's over. Meaning, his part in the situation is over. Eric is dazed as opposed to panicked, and he's definitely still mad. But above all, Fierce Eric Pierce needs to chill out.

37

It's mid-afternoon on the Amtrak service that runs along the San Joaquin Valley down towards Bakersfield. Sweet awakens from a nap of indeterminate length, not knowing what time it is and further not knowing where Chris has gotten to. It takes a few minutes for him to orient himself to time and place, roll his sore neck, blink multiple times to kick-start his eyes, and to properly assess the ache coming from somewhere near his tailbone. A pain in the ass, he shortly concludes.

From the pocket on his left breast, Sweet feels the vibration of his phone, which he doesn't recall being put there. Must've been Chris, he figures. The buzz is like an alarm, though it's not. It's an intermittent reminder that he has messages—in this case, several messages.

"Shit," Sweet drawls as he checks the face and sees three texts and two voicemails, each several hours old. He recognizes the number on two messages—that of his girlfriend, Annabelle. He sort of recognizes the number on the others.

First he reads Annabelle's text, which is an urgent request to heed a voicemail that was left sometime earlier. As he listens to that message, he sees Chris passing by his seat in a rush. He attempts to flag him down but fails, though Chris looks back at him. There's a watery look in Chris' eye, like he's frightened—panicked even—by a crisis on the train that only he observes. It's happening, Sweet associates. Chris: he's seeing Shadows again. We can't reach Cassandra's Children soon enough, Sweet thinks. Distracted, he misses part of Annabelle's message but hears enough to know that things have changed, and that something important is happening, like hours from now, according to her.

Next he listens to the other messages, both from Jill Evans. The text is short: I'm coming back, with Weed! The words strike Sweet like something spicy that's been spit in his face. He listens to the voicemail, incredulous, but knowing in his gut that Jill Evans, bitchy as she might be, does not play games. And the voicemail confirms the news: Weed is not only alive, he's back, as in back in Oakland, having made his way to Jill's place somehow. He's even audible in the background of the message, though there's no explanation as to where he's been for a week. Sweet feels moved to extrapolate: to assert that Weed had planned this return all along; that he'd been hiding out from the stalkers he'd told Chris about, somewhere in Marin County. He cares, Sweet decides, but it's not enough, this fresh, sanguine thought. He doesn't trust Weed—never has. He must want something? There must be an ulterior, nefarious reason he wants Jill to help him track down Chris.

Looking for Chris, Sweet sticks his head out into the aisle and peers down the length of the train. In the distance, through a transparency in the middle of a door that separates sections, Sweet regards a sloppy phalanx of humanity, with limbs dangling into floor space, heads slumped into chests; mouths hanging unflatteringly open. He gets up, grabs the backpack that he and Chris have been sharing, and which now looks sort of beaten up and deflated. He walks down the aisle, hoping to find his friend. As he rises from his seat, Sweet has an uneasy feeling. Without benefit of a Shadow appearance, he notes a premonition of dramatic events soon to unfold. Meanwhile, there's something creepy and not right about Chris' absence, not to mention that watery look in his eyes from moments ago.

As Sweet steps through to the next train car, he starts looking from seat to seat, as if thinking that Chris is playing a game on him, hiding. It's a brotherly thing, this search: a search for an elusive imp. Sweet can't help taking a caretaker's attitude, despite not having that reputation. Keeping others guessing as to what he's really like is more like Sweet's thing. He's always liked playing life like a dumb blond in a fifties movie. Now he turns the tables, makes his own movies, and depicts others from the position of director in his own casual, itinerant way. But this situation is anything but casual. People like Jill Evans, the folks of Cassandra's Children, and his girlfriend, Annabelle, are all quite serious people who expect things. Above all, Bryan "Weed" Tecco is a serious person. The prospect of Weed's return unnerves Sweet, as does the prospect of informing Chris about the messages from Jill. As to Weed's return, he predicts a serious I-told-you-so is also coming.

Chris is seating on a spare seat at the end of the next car. It's like he's been banished from a conversation with the group of people sat next to him. That doesn't seem to stop him though. From twenty yards away, Sweet can see that Chris' mouth is still moving despite the lack of attending audience; that he's talking to no one but himself and that everyone in ear shot is tuning him out. Not good, Sweet thinks as he approaches.

"Sup, man," Chris calls out. He's not drunk. There's no slur or flopping of body parts. Instead, he merely seems edgy and trembling. Despite the greeting, he's not seen Sweet coming up to him—only felt his presence, it seems. A guy next to Chris, pot-bellied, shaped like an avocado and heavily bearded, shakes his head as he casts a disapproving glance at Chris. Across from the man is his wife, a frumpy, sour-faced woman who is preoccupied with their infant child and the changing of a diaper. If Chris makes one more disrespectful remark, then he's gonna get clocked. Chris looks unconcerned about this, though he seems alone and rejected, his mouth down-turned, largely because he'd tried explaining his diaper idea to the initially indulgent couple, only to feel their not-so-polite apathy as his lecture wore on. In the absence of a real dialogue, Chris is imposing his central lesson, talking too fast.

"You see, it's all about urease, which, when catalyzed, is converted into ammonia, which is the cause of skin irritations. I don't know why people aren't interested in this. It's not like I'm just some huckster trying to make millions of dollars here. I care about people, and animals. Actually, I care a little bit more about animals. In fact, I should have become a vet if you really wanna know. That's what I'm about—helping…the living. Anyway, all I'm interested in is how to help new parents, or parents who don't know what they're doing—not that you guys are like this—from unnecessarily harming their children through careless attention to hygiene. I mean, it's fundamental. It should be on every doctor's preventive care plan, every hospital administrator's agenda; every managed care company's list of evidence-based prescriptions for new families. And I don't care if I don't take the credit, or the money. It's not about—hey Sweet."

"What's up, dude?" Sweet replies, trying to look friendly but not annoying. The guy next to Chris sees Sweet, who looks as though he has something to do with Chris so he sports a cautiously welcoming look. Giving Sweet the benefit of doubt the man signals to him, striking a surreptitious whacko sign, which Sweet doesn't acknowledge. Sweet flashes a peace gesture at the desperate-looking man, which is more like his reputation. He affects a caretaking air, like he's an orderly come to collect a wandering inmate. He nods at Chris. "How're you doin', bud?" he asks.

"I'm good, bud."

"Yeah, sounds like it. Can we talk?"

"What's up?"

"You're doing it again."

"Huh?"

"You're doing things without talking to me. You're being impulsive. You disappeared."

"Sorry." Chris' eyes glaze over.

"S'alright," Sweet replies. He lightly punches Chris' arm, gives a sideways, sympathetic look to the disgruntled, bearded figure. Chris thinks he sees a wink between them. "Seriously, let's talk," Sweet repeats.

"Okay," says Chris robotically. He stands and turns at Sweet's direction, and heads through another glass door, leading to an area around another bathroom. A man steps out of the compartment wearing a business suit and carrying a laptop case. He gives a nod to Sweet and Chris and turns away, destined for business class and a higher breed of citizenry. Chris gazes enviously at the man's back and figures this is the clean and sober part of the train—a scumbag-free zone.

"I got some messages on the phone, each left a while ago," begins Sweet, speaking just above a whisper. "The first message is from Annabelle. She says there's a change in plan for when we arrive. She was expecting me today, but says there's a meeting tonight that we should attend."

Chris frowns, straining to keep up. He looks about, distracted by LED lights in the compartment.

"Okay," he repeats.

"It's a meeting of that group I told you about, Cassandra's Children. It takes place once a month in this Masonic Temple near Hollywood. The next one was supposed to be on the weekend—

Saturday, I thought—but Annabelle says they have a special speaker who's only in for one night. She sounds really excited, but wasn't sure we were gonna make it, 'cause…ya know."

"Uh-huh," Chris murmurs. By now he is barely reinforcing Sweet, who continues doggedly.

"Anyway, I texted her, saying we should arrive shortly after eight, which just about works because the meeting doesn't start until ten." Sweet laughs. "Anyway, she was pleased to hear from me, and knows you're with me, and says it's cool. 'Finally', she said, about me answering her." Next, Sweet pauses. "So, are we good?"

Chris returns a staccato nodding action.

"Uh-huh," Sweet says with a knowing look. "Okay, you have obviously taken something, not sure what, though I could guess."

"Nah, man, it's—" Chris feigns argument while swaying like an indolent teenager.

"Don't," says Sweet, waving a hand. "I don't even wanna know why. I do wanna know what, and how, and most importantly, how much."

Chris regards Sweet with short-lived calm. After all the time spent together over the last few days, not to mention over the last year or so, he still can't get used to Sweet's chameleon habits, the way he can seem like a hapless pre-teen one minute, an even-handed adult who sees all the next. Chris tries to be nonchalant.

"A couple of lines, that's all."

"From where?"

"Some guy on the train. What does it matter? Besides, you've been jonesin' for pills the last several days, haven't you?"

Sweet nods. "It's true, though I'm gettin' through it." His voice is paternal, but there's no judgment in Sweet; no superiority. Instead, he's nervous, like a father might be nervous. Suddenly it's as if he is responsible for Chris, and so he is resolute: no more pills for himself. Period. He's lucky, actually. They aren't really his problem. But for Chris it's a different story, and Sweet ponders his role, not to mention the burdens Chris might put on him, perhaps well into the future. Chris has a blank, elsewhere look about him, a look not so far removed from the distant gazes he often exhibits. Sweet figures he should have known better. Anyone would have known better than to think the worst of Chris' habits were behind him. After all, what had been going on with him recently, at work and in his private life? He guesses this explains why Chris' girlfriend seemed so jaded and bitchy; why his aunt was so fed up. It all adds up to what he now sees in Chris' face. "Anyway, there's other stuff to tell you," Sweet prefaces, thinking none of this changes what he still has to reveal. "Weed is with Jill."

At first, Chris stares back, half-interested, or perhaps only half taking it in, like a replay of his slowness with Angela Boyd.

"What?"

"Weed. He's with Jill, and I think they're coming down here after us."

"How..."

"It was one of the other messages, left sometime after we left your aunt's house, I guess. That's all I know. Sorry."

Chris looks over Sweet's shoulder, glimpses a Shadow that has appeared but not taken shape. It's no good. It's not processing, this new information. Only images appear, one after another, before his eyes and in his mind: the teasing flicker of a would-be Shadow, Weed's face, Jill's image; the thought of them together. Weird, he thinks. They're probably talking about him, he imagines. After that, thoughts stall. Feelings drown.

"That's cool," is all he can think to say.

Sweet turns his body, gesturing for a return to their original seats. Overhead, there's some kind of announcement that is overloud and distorted. Sweet makes it out but Chris doesn't.

"Come on. Let's head back to our seat, try and chill out for a bit before the train stops."

"We're there? We're in LA?"

"Nah, we're coming into Bakersfield. Sorry, forgot to tell you that. We transfer at Bakersfield. The rest of the way is on bus."

They turn to walk back to their seats. Chris is looking at Sweet's back, at the bag strapped around his shoulder. In a few moments, the two friends will be on the same page, wondering the same things.

"Hey, lemme see the bag for a second," Chris asks with a newfound clarity in his voice. "I wanna check that I haven't lost something."

38

For an hour the ride along the grapevine is a road trip dream. Weed puts his foot down, no longer worried about the consequences of speeding—he's past that now. The grin on his face is fixed and indestructible. He looks over from time to time, assessing Jill's sourpuss frown, her attempt to prove she didn't enjoy any part of what just happened. But for Weed's mania, they might have deconstructed the scene at the gas station, just as they did the altercation at Jenny Leavitt's home. Cruising along the highway's steep gradients, Weed's still on a roll, falling in love with this mission; thinking it's his drug now, this quest to find Chris, recover his drives, and then continue on like a Tolkien character holding precious treasure but not knowing what lies ahead. Meanwhile, he hasn't stopped being curious about Jill. He still has headspace for the questions he had earlier: what does she want? Why isn't she commanding him to stop, if not in some place like Valencia, then why not Burbank? Why isn't she saying she wants off this hellacious ride?

In San Fernando they start hitting traffic and Weed's adrenaline rush finally wanes. It's close to seven o'clock: he's exhausted but barely knows it. A flicker of his eyes warns him that there's a massive weight of sleep coming down that will at some point catch up to him, causing a narcoleptic meltdown. Jill, in one of her few glances over to him, sees the black circles around Weed's eyes, the emergent crow's feet wrinkling the sides of his face. He looks a year older than the guy she met shortly after nine in the morning. She's aged too, she figures, and it's even harder staying alive as a passenger.

"We should pause for a bit. I could drive for a while," she offers.

"Nah, I'm good."

"You don't look good. You should take some more medicine."

"Taken enough—any more and I'm drunk. We can stop if you're done with this, not for long though. I understand."

Jill swiftly rebukes him. "I'm not done with anything, and you don't understand me anymore than I understand you."

It feels unnecessary, her remark about "understanding", but she couldn't let pass the set up he'd given her.

"Fine. Well, I'm heading for Union station downtown. I figure we're about an hour away if we're lucky, with the train due to arrive shortly after eight."

"Fine."

With bumper-to-bumper traffic now thwarting momentum, Weed feels his thoughts multiply and his nerves heighten. The prospect of missing the connection with Chris and Sweet and then having nowhere to turn doesn't bear thinking about. He's got no money, and no place to stay, temporary or otherwise. Down here there's no family home near the coast to which he can retreat—no taken for granted loved ones or old friends and teachers who might take him in and give him a bed. He looks around at the sights, at the endless suburb that is LA. There's no perspective here. The hills around them are giant forested bumps littered with homes. Beside the freeway, the commercial properties are colorful but conform to mass consumerism and lack character. They could be anywhere in America, Weed thinks, but the deceptive pull of one valley after another teases with a promise of nearby arrival. He can't stand the twenty miles per hour pace, and even classic rock radio has lost its luster amid the stalled progress. Only tension will make time go faster now; only an argument or a heart to heart will make the difference.

"Look, assuming we find Chris, have you decided what you're gonna do? I mean, I don't know what their plan is. I figure I might crash on someone's couch, but with you and Chris…I don't know."

"Don't worry about it," Jill says, not unkindly.

"I'm not. I'm just—" Actually, he doesn't know where he's going with this. He stops. "How're you gonna get back to the Bay Area. Are you—"

"Hey, I need to find him too, though not for the crazy reasons you may need to. It's not like I can just look up his aunt's number right now. When we meet Chris, I'll let you have your business with him. Then, when there's a moment, I'll ask him for her number, call her up and ask that she not have my car towed away, not that she'd do that, necessarily."

Weed holds his tongue for a moment and stifles a laugh. Then he releases one anyway.

"You're kidding, right? That can't be the reason you're still on this trip with me—because you need to use Sweet's phone so you can call Chris' aunt."

"No, of course not," Jill retorts.

Weed moves his shoulders. It's not so much a shrug as it is a shuffle that asks, *what gives*. Jill continues: "Listen, I'll take care of myself, find my way to LAX, or whatever, get a flight back to Oakland and then get a taxi back to my place. I'll call up work, take an extra day off, which I have coming anyway. Maybe I'll ride my bike up to Jenny Leavitt's place the next day. No one's stolen my wallet. I got a bit of cash. I got cards. It's not a problem." Jill stares into Weed. She is trembling slightly, but is unblinking. Weed returns a soft nod and a surrendering look. His air is ambiguous, somewhere between respect and disappointment.

"Okay," he says solemnly. Then he turns his attention back to the troublesome road.

"Plus, I wanna see what happens," Jill states. Her voice is hard, determined; her fears seem eclipsed. Her eyes narrow as she looks upon Weed, at once daring him to bullshit her further, but also daring herself to remain credulous. This Shadow business, the matter of those drives: all this had better be about something real, she's saying. Weed takes his time before answering.

"So do I," he replies, trying to sound clever but also sincere. Jill maintains her fixed look.

"I'm saying I'm in this to the bitter end."

"I get that," Weed says, and looks back at her as if to say, *stop now—enough*. He changes the subject.

"Alright then, help me figure out where we need to exit."

Nearly an hour later, they are within sight of the downtown area, but still they cannot get a fix upon their position, and time is running out. By now, the bumper-to-bumper movement has become maddening, and the view of LA, primarily upwards from the trench-like vantage point of the freeway, makes Weed feel small and blind. As the hour approaches eight o'clock, Weed starts to lose it. He starts yelling out every five minutes or so invective aimed at drivers trying to cut in; at California's failure to build reliable mass transit systems; at America's unrequited love of the automobile. Weed's right foot feels leaden and despairing. If it could talk it would beg him to stop asking it to press down, first on an accelerator, and then, repetitively and with mounting frustration, upon a spirit-crushing brake.

"WORST CITY EVER," Weed decrees.

With some relief, they merge onto the 110 heading into downtown, knowing they are close. But there the traffic is even worse, and within a minute they are at a standstill, going nowhere with maybe a mile or two to go. Weed goes apoplectic as he sees the sun going down in the distance, taking hope with it. Twenty seconds, he thinks. I need twenty seconds just to get through this feeling so I can move on. Meanwhile, he regresses to the life of a toddler, thumping his fists on the steering wheel; punching the dashboard and breaking skin on his knuckles.

"Calm down! This isn't doing us any good," Jill screeches at him.

Weed looks over to the downtown high rises. He wants an Amtrak sign to stick out over the city and call him to it. He wants to reach out and slap LA, wipe the taunting smile off its ugly face.

"This is bullshit," he keeps repeating. Ambient thoughts of justice and purpose flutter in and out of his mind. He repeats his profane complaint one more time. Then he turns to Jill and adds a twist to the latest *plan*. "Okay, since this is a stolen car, we might as well leave it behind."

"What are you doing?" Jill shrieks as Weed turns the Subaru hard to his right. Now he is edging over to the shoulder, attempting to cut through two lanes. With his middle finger flailing, he pushes past one car, a measly Toyota. Then he tries to sneak in front of a Ford Truck. Inside, there are two guys who look like they could have featured in that old TV commercial: they are big tough guys. They drive a big fat truck. They don't got no boundaries. They don't give a fuck. Jill creeps down in her seat, wondering when the last time there was a gunfight on one of LA's notoriously violent freeways. She doesn't really want to know. Knowing that Eric Pierce's firearm is still in the glove compartment, she presses her knee up against it, blocking Weed should he get ideas.

There's no getting through. The big Ford truck isn't budging and Weed's middle finger is not persuasive with its drivers.

"Fuck it, we're outta here," he announces. He puts the car in park and turns off the engine, but doesn't bother taking the keys. "COME ON!" he shouts as he opens his door and leaps out. Rounding the front, he's still looking at Jill, still exhorting her to join him on adventures. From her seat, Jill can hear through the window the remonstrations of the Ford truck guys. Ignoring them, she pushes out her door and runs behind their vehicle. It's only about ten yards to the shoulder wherein she and Weed can now run past stalled commuters to the nearest exit. She sees him up ahead, looking over his shoulder, hoping that she's following him. As she runs she thinks of the phrase she'd earlier pulled back and kept to herself, right after saying she was in this thing until the bitter end:

No matter what happens, I believe you'll do the right thing.

39

"I don't get it," Sweet says forlornly. "I've left two messages now. They haven't responded to either." It's like a personal rejection of him.

Chris is biting his nails, half-attentive to his friend. He gives Sweet a what-do-you-want-me-to-do-about-it look and then turns to look out the window by his side. The traffic heading into downtown LA is predictably thick and the Amtrak bus is moving at a snail's pace, though for Chris, everything seems like it's moving at a snail's pace. Since locating the flash drives in the backpack, Chris has renewed curiosity about their significance, still thinking Weed wants to retrieve the drives so he can sell what's on them maybe. But maybe there's something else, he wonders idly. He is pleased he hasn't lost the drives, but that's about all he feels on the subject. Not losing things is a start of something new, he otherwise thinks. Anyway, if Weed is feeling inconvenienced by the absence of his stash, Chris figures this should teach him something about paranoia. If Weed hadn't been so sure he was followed by Shadows that last night in March, then he would have held onto the drives himself, and he wouldn't need Chris to return them now, or deliver them to him, if that's what he's really expecting. That's assuming Jill's message was all about this, of course. On the other hand, if he had held onto the drives then they'd be at the bottom of a West Marin lake with his truck, so maybe—actually, Chris can't decide what may have been best.

Temporarily over his failed attempts to reach Jill Evans by phone, Sweet turns his thoughts to the problem of methamphetamine use. METH = DEATH. It was a public services advertisement that he'd seen somewhere recently. Sitting next to Chris, he can feel his jittery friend stirring in his seat, straining to keep still. Knowing that his thoughts are spinning, Sweet worries what ideas might be feverishly brewing in Chris' head only to arrive at frozen cul-de-sacs; what words might he spit about the hapless crowd on this final leg of their long, sluggish journey. As the bus plods along, Sweet decides to engage Chris for good or ill; to insinuate adult thoughts about money, plans for the future, and the need for clean healthy living—quite unlike him, Chris might soon be thinking again.

"So, have you thought about what you might wanna do down here?" Sweet asks conversationally. "As in a job," he adds lest Chris not catch his drift. He sounds nervous, like he hadn't counted on some of the answers Chris had given his Aunt Jenny back in Oakland; the burden he might actually be now.

"You said I could help you with your film. It's still got a ways to go, you said," Chris replies with surprising lucidity, though it's clear he hasn't caught Sweet's drift.

"Yeah, but…" Sweet stalls as his shoulders drop. His mouth hangs open.

"What?"

"I can't pay you. You know that, right?"

"Duh. I wasn't expecting to get paid."

"Yeah, okay. I just thought…" This habit of not completing sentences is more like the Sweet Chris knows.

"Come on, Sweet. Even if I wasn't tweakin' this conversation would be moving way too slow for me."

Sweet gulps, exhibiting nerves in talking to Chris for the first time since they'd emerged from Oakland Police Department earlier that day. He has the shifty-eyed look of someone about to fire him, or in Sweet's case, of someone about to say he doesn't want to be friends anymore.

"I've been thinking about the job you had, at the hospital. Maybe it's not such a great idea to just give it up like that; at least, not until you get something else going."

Chris returns a sniffling laugh. People have no idea, he thinks bitterly. He softens. People have no idea, he consolidates.

"I can't do that work anymore," he says flatly. Once out, the words feel pure and precise. Chris is calm, as if the stimulant has evened him out, brought clarity and removed the impulse towards slippery answers.

"What do you mean?"

Chris gives a gray smile to Sweet, thinking he might as well tell a story. It's fairly involved story—takes some effort to get out—and it lacks a happy ending.

"I told you all the wrong stuff the other day," Chris begins, wanly. He pauses to collect all the thoughts that have just been passing through his mind's assembly line. He wonders if he can make sense of it all, much less whether Sweet can take it in. If only Sweet, or anyone for that matter, could appreciate what it meant to believe the seeming fact of Weed's death, only to then have that reality stripped away. Could anyone understand just how much it had taken for Chris to get to that point of consciousness, only to now feel disoriented all over again? No wonder he relapsed, he now rationalizes. Still, rationales, whatever gives them birth, feel clear; crystal clear in fact. Which reminds him: he might as well resurrect his old nickname. He looks at Sweet, decides to come clean with respect to the hanging question.

"I can't believe myself sometimes. All that stuff about the argument with a doctor, the one that led to my suspension: I left out the worst of it. You see, I didn't tell you about the procedure we were doing—the one that sent me over the edge. There was this kid that had been brought in after a car accident. It was horrific. He had his head twisted around, like in a whiplash, and the force of an impact broke his Odontoid process. That's the bone at the base of your neck that connects the neck to the spine. If it breaks then you're fucked. Anyway, that's what this kid had, and it was down to me to make sure the right instruments were available for the operation. What we needed was a Canulated driver, which is— anyway, it doesn't matter. That was the tool we needed." Sweet affects a sympathetic air but isn't clear where Chris is going with this. "The reason the surgeon was on my case was because I was so stressed out watching this procedure that I gave him the wrong tool, even though I knew what he was asking for and had correctly prepared all the instruments ahead of time."

As Chris pauses and shakes his head, Sweet attempts a few words of support.

"It was a mistake. Everyone makes 'em."

"Nah, it wasn't that. See, I knew in that moment that I couldn't hack it; that I wasn't really cut out for that kind of work. I didn't belong there—that's what that doctor was really saying to me, and he was right. If it was only about knowing the information—knowing technically how to do the procedures, what tools to use—then I'd be good. But you need more than that to be in an operating theater, which I needed to be. You need to know how to deal with tension, like more tension than you can believe human beings can stand. You need to know how to hang in there when exhausted, when every part of you wants to get out and not look at how the human body can be assembled and disassembled, like parts of a car. It's mechanical and degrading. It's not human, the human body. Did you know that, Sweet? Anyway, doing that work wasn't for me. I wish it was. Really."

Sweet lets his head drop. For several seconds he sort of looks into himself, thinking that some essence of Chris' words might equally apply to himself. He thinks about what he wants to say in response. He thinks about what he'd want others to say if he were sharing similar thoughts.

"I don't know, Chris. I think you give up too easy."

Chris shakes his head again, dismissing Sweet. "You don't understand, man. I guess I can't explain because you don't know what it's like."

"Maybe, and what you describe does sound shitty. But maybe it doesn't matter so much that it was that way. I mean, I understand that job became too real for you, but all real things are difficult. Growing up is difficult."

Knowing he sounds trite, Sweet shuts up. Maybe he doesn't belong in this conversation, he wonders. Chris likewise says nothing, and does nothing but stare ahead, no longer listening. He doesn't even smile or shake his head anymore. He is robotic as he looks about, scrutinizing the same collection of weary travelers that shared the train down to Bakersfield. He wants to exile thought and feeling, study the world from a stoic distance, and not be impacted by life. He sighs as he turns to gaze out the window again.

"Holy shit," he suddenly exclaims.

Sweet perks up from letting his head rest in his chin, but is slow to comment. He looks over and sees Chris, his nose pressed up against the window like a kid trying to catch sight of Disneyland. "It's Weed," Chris is saying. "It's fucking Weed, running along the side of the freeway and—I don't believe this—Jill is right behind him!"

Sweet closes his eyes, thinking this is meth doing the talking. He shouldn't have gotten all teacher-like, Sweet thinks. Now he's made it worse. Now Chris will start acting like a ten year old, never mind whatever age he was perpetrating before yesterday.

"Relax, Chris. We're gonna be at the station soon. Remember we got that meeting later. When we stop we'll get something to eat before heading out again. You don't know Annabelle. She's probably—"

Chris whips around, astonished by Sweet's obtuseness. "JESUS, SWEET, I'M NOT KIDDING. I just saw Weed and Jill running along the shoulder about twenty yards away." Chris looks up and over his seat, sees that he's roused a few somnolent souls with his sudden ranting. He peers beyond the front of the bus, trying to assess the level of congestion up ahead. The traffic is immobile. The freeway might as well be a parking lot. As a live artery within LA's diseased body, it is blocked and in pain, and should be pronounced dead as far as Chris is concerned. Sweet's mouth is hanging open again. He isn't sure what to say or how otherwise to babysit his intoxicated, possibly psychotic friend. Shadows. Sweet reminds himself that Chris is a novice practitioner of the gift; that he tends to overreact to his visions, overstate their importance or their menace.

"I'm outta here," Chris says, stepping over Sweet. He grabs the backpack with the drives, and as he plunders down the aisle of the bus, Sweet rises and chases him, trying to clutch at his back. For about five seconds, Chris argues with Sweet and the driver about the advisability of opening a door onto freeway traffic, but Chris' frantic yelling and kicking at the door soon wins the argument. The door opens and Chris, followed by Sweet, dives onto the pavement, slithers in between honking cars, past drivers envious of anyone or anything moving faster than them. Reaching the yard of space at the side, they break into a steady jog, with Sweet keeping a close distance behind. They move past jeering voices, heads popping out of windows to catcall Chris and Sweet's escapist effort.

"YEAH, GO GET 'EM!" someone shouts, unhelpfully. Chris looks over the barrier separating the freeway from a street down below. He sees the head of a palm tree situated at eye-level. Unbeknownst to him, the bus had been on an overpass that was about to drop down into the downtown area. Up ahead he sees an exit sloping down at a thirty degree angle. Bumper-to-bumper traffic continues, even for those in teasing distance of city streets. Chris hits his stride, not sure how far he has to go. At the base of the off ramp he passes a transient who holds a cardboard sign that reads "Hungry White Trash" and stirs a memory of the previous week's panhandling. Plagiarism, Chris thinks.

"I know where they're going," Sweet calls out after Chris. Sweet's going with the flow, choosing to believe that what's happening is real.

40

Weed turns onto a street called West College, which he remembers from one of the maps. After that, he'll need to turn right onto Alameda Street, Boulevard, or whatever it's called, and jog another several blocks. After that it's—he can't remember what's next—a street whose name he might recognize when he sees it, hopefully. Or maybe Jill will know. He looks over his shoulder again to check whether he's lost her. No sign of her. For a moment, there's a panic-stricken belief that she's stopped and given up, or else been obstructed, struck by a car; maybe assaulted. Poor girl, Weed thinks. She's been assaulted. Don't panic, he instructs himself. At that moment, Jill appears, sidestepping a listless pedestrian that was in her way, but she's still following Weed and keeping up. She's twenty yards behind him.

As he reaches about four blocks down Alameda, he looks right, thinking he should be seeing signs of a train station, or an Amtrak insignia or something. In his dreams there should be glowing lights high above the city, pointing to the spot where he needs to be. The stolid Angelino faces all around should look as though they might conceivably help a lost visitor. Someone or something—a Shadow, or God—should give him a sign and show him where to go. So far, the signs suggest that he's in the wrong place. Looking around at the bland, everywhere and nowhere quality of downtown LA, he sees nothing that suggests train, or train station. Instead, it's all cars, a cluster of high rise buildings, and cheesy billboards. Overhead, a plane is descending, flying into LAX, Weed figures. He feels mocked by these reminders of alternate means of travel.

"WHAT THE HELL!" he shouts, stopping at a streetcorner and flailing his arms. Jill is approaching fast. "There's no train coming through here," he complains at her.

"THAT'S BECAUSE IT'S A BUS, DUFUS," yells Jill, not bothering to stop. He watches her pass him by. It seems she knows exactly where to go.

Five minutes later they find themselves in an area that indeed looks like a bus depot, with blessed Amtrak symbols exhibiting the message that Weed, now winded and coughing again, desperately needs to feel: he has arrived. As he strains to catch his breath, he staggers about a row of overhanging shelter fixtures. They are made of solid steel and plastic, and cover benches that are pock-marked with holes for some kind of aerodynamic purpose that would only be apparent to engineers. The collection of people in the area seem uncohesive: an urban crossection of the blue and white collar workforce; teens from the valleys absorbed in cellular technology, or listening to music through oversized headphones. An androgynous couple of overdressed guys, likely gay, suggest the flamboyance of nearby Hollywood. There's a girl squatting on a plastic bench, looking down and staring at the ground like she can't bear to look up until a bus arrives. Black dots flicker inexplicably about her head.

"What now?" Jill asks, reasonably enough. She circles Weed a couple of times, waiting upon his directions. When he says nothing, she rolls her eyes and heads toward a water fountain nearby. "I'll give you a minute," she says with less attitude.

"We wait I guess," he says as she walks away. He throws up his arms. What else could he say? He ambles towards the benches, thinking he might find one upon which he can lay down for a minute, though he knows this isn't the best of ideas. Got to keep moving now, he commands himself—still can't afford to stop. He mills about the other would-be passengers, or people waiting to collect travelers, assuming that he and Jill are the only ones looking for Chris and Sweet. It doesn't occur to him that he might have something in common with any of the people now waiting alongside him.

Next to the girl that's staring at the ground, the black dots start dancing again. They compel a double take, and moments later, a decided halt to his patrol amongst the crowd. The girl looks up, baring unnatural-looking eyebrows that arch high over a stark, witch's expression. Her body is tiny for a seeming adult, as in that of a preteen, but her face seems peculiarly aged, like she might be forty, or even older. She has an offbeat beauty, a sinister, penetrating gaze. She looks up as though she'd felt Weed's eyes upon her, or else felt something else in the searching quality of his walk.

"You looking for someone?" she asks Weed. From the average person at a place like this, it might have sounded like a provocation, her question. For Weed, who now sees flash images of Chris' friend, Sweet, standing beside this girl or woman, it seems anything but. He smiles, feeling lucky all of a sudden. He got that sign he needed after all.

"Waiting for the same person you are, maybe?" he asks coolly.

Jill saunters back from the water fountain near a ticket office, at first not seeing Weed and therefore feeling annoyed in thinking that he keeps leaving her behind. When she does see him she notices that he's talking to a girl who, from a distance, looks to be no more than twelve years old. Jill has a creepy feeling as she approaches them.

"Hey," Jill says to Weed, somewhat irritably. His head jerks towards her like he's just been caught doing something he shouldn't. He smiles what seems to Jill a guilty smile, and then his expression flattens.

"Hey. This is Annabelle. She's a friend of Sweet's. She's expecting him, and only found out a little while ago that Chris is with him also. She says the bus is running late, stuck in traffic, which means we can chill now." Weed pauses before delivering a conclusion: "We made it."

Jill nods but doesn't feel the elation suggested by Weed's statement. It's not just that she doesn't feel like giving him a high five. Somehow, his mood isn't matching what he's saying; he's holding something back, she thinks. Meanwhile, the girl starts speaking in a whinny, pedantic voice to which Jill takes an instant dislike.

"You say you haven't spoken to Gavin, so you probably don't know that we're supposed to go to a meeting tonight."

"Gavin?" questions Jill.

"That's Sweet's real name," Weed informs her.

The girl continues. "I guess we have time to get a snack, but not much time. Gavin texted saying they'd be starving, but we'll have to move quickly. It's a really important meeting." Weed nods in response to Annabelle's fretting, realizing that she is accustomed to being indulged.

"Uh-huh. Annabelle, what's this meeting you're talking about?"

She is overly serious in her response. "I'd rather not say right now. I'd rather wait until Gavin and your other friend arrive. Then I'll explain what's happening to them and then they can share what they like with you." Jill looks over Annabelle, thinking there's definitely something strange about her. Well, there is definitely something strange about Sweet, she reasons, so it adds up. Still, she notes that Annabelle has now folded one leg over another, and is tapping the ground with her feet. The action seems compulsive. Jill looks back at Weed, raising an eyebrow, thus signifying a freakazoid alert. Weed meets Jill's querulous eyes with an affectedly sincere look that doesn't suit him—or, it doesn't suit the guy she's heard about for months and known over the last twelve hours.

"Annabelle, I hope you don't mind me asking, but how long have you known Gavin?" he asks. Jill gives Weed a quizzical look.

"About three months," Annabelle replies, looking beyond Weed towards the direction from which the bus is presumed to be arriving soon. "Why do you ask?" she follows up. Annabelle randomly turns to look in the opposite direction. She is at best half-listening to the man she's just met.

"I don't know how to say this exactly," Weed resumes, now stuttering. He looks again at Jill, who is still looking quizzical, as if to ground himself before making a dire pronouncement. "I'm concerned that being friends with Gavin might not be the best thing for you."

"What?" Jill interrupts, barely above a whisper.

"Holy crap, it's them! What the hell happened to the bus?" Annabelle has not heard anything Weed has just said. In the distance, from the same direction Weed and Jill had just come from, Sweet and Chris jog limply towards them. Sweet is wearing a victorious smile and spreading out his arms, likely for his girlfriend's benefit. Behind him, Chris Leavitt has slowed to a walk, as if more conflicted about the now imminent reunion. His face betrays a less obvious pleasure.

41

It is night finally. There are several minutes of awkward mingling reminiscent of family gatherings, the coming together of people with not much in common beyond the blood in their veins. The most straightforward greeting is a hug between Sweet and Annabelle, followed by a cordial handshake between her and Chris. It's an untold number of seconds before sustained eye contact occurs between Chris and Weed, or Chris and Jill.

But they do embrace, sort of, with weary, nervous pats on each others' backs. As for Sweet, he gives a polite nod to Jill, a begrudging "sup" directed at Weed. He maintains a cautious distance, waiting to see or hear what this reunion is truly about. Annabelle, the person who knows the least about everyone, does most of the talking. Time is short, she insists. They must get something to eat quickly, possibly on the way to Culver City, where the meeting she described earlier is happening. Then she remarks on the number of people around her; wonders if everyone can fit in her Mitsubishi Outlander, or whether people have somewhere to stay the night. Weed is half-impressed by her caretaking, half-jolted by the insinuation of short-term plans, immediate and commonplace needs. It's strange to be giving thought to the future already. In his mind and in his bones, the future doesn't exist—because today will never end, he reasons.

Jill gives sideways looks to Chris and Weed, wondering what each is thinking as they pretend to listen to Annabelle's fussing. Sweet observes that Weed is eyeing the backpack worn by Chris. Catching the look and forming associations, Chris slips it off his shoulder and passes it over to his friend, smiling thinly and motioning with his eyes: *what you seek is there*. The action is wordless, as in secret and undisturbing of conversation. Weed fumbles through the bag. As he finds the set of drives, his body seems to relax. There is no smile—no joy per se—just a soft look of relief and satisfaction. Following Annabelle's lead, everyone walks towards her car, which is parked on a side street. Her chatter has moved on to esoteric subjects which presumably bond her and Sweet, but to the others it is all white noise. It's like a bad party: none of them wants to be there talking about the things they're talking about, but no one wants to seize the pulpit and call out the various situations.

Once in the car, that changes. Annabelle and Sweet are up front, with Annabelle driving, despite being just a few stray hairs beyond dwarfism. This places Chris, Jill, and Weed in the back seat, squeezed in. Jill is in the middle, aptly enough—stuck there after being suckered by Chris: he'd opened the door for her.

"Are you kidding?" she asks rhetorically, looking between them. "Are you guys gonna say anything to each other?" The guys laugh at first, embarrassed. They gesture, speak haltingly: "I don't…" Weed begins. "I know," Chris replies, as if the meaning is self-evident. They each give Jill a what-are-we-supposed-to-say look.

I'm glad you're alive

Same here

They stop at a Denny's in Culver City, bypassing, at Weed's insistence, the group's first choice, a Buttercup Café. Again, Annabelle is pressing the issue of time, citing this meeting they must soon attend. As they walk into the restaurant, Weed asks his first meaningful question directed at Chris: "What's this meeting she's talkin' about, bro?"

Chris pauses, reluctant to answer. "You're not gonna like it," he says as the group settles at a table, with Annabelle positioned centrally, like she's presiding. "Though I think you should be interested," Chris continues. "It's something called Cassandra's Children, which is the name of this secret society that believes…" Chris is nodding as though appealing to not finish the thought "that believe the kind of things we believe." He knows as soon as he stops that "believe" isn't the right word; that Weed does a lot of things, but believing isn't one of them.

He's wrong, actually.

"What things?" Weed challenges. His expression seems open and stoic. Chris wonders if he might utter an opinion without being scoffed at or summarily rebuked.

"Shadows," he says bluntly. "It's a meeting of people who see Shadows." Weed stares back at Chris with a blank look.

"Seriously?"

"Seriously."

Annabelle cuts in, having heard the word "Cassandra".

"Are you talking about the society?" She has a worried but confused look. She motions to Sweet. "Do you know about the society? Is that why you've come here?"

"It's okay. They know about it. They're similar to us," Sweet says in a soothing, confidential voice. His shoulders drop. He relaxes as though his thoughts have soothed him also. "Except maybe…" he amends, looking at Jill.

"Well, okay, but I think we should be careful in a public place—maybe lower our voices." It's taking all of Jill's strength to stop her eyes rolling. Chris and Weed nod reverently at Annabelle, while quietly hoping the strange girl stops talking soon. No chance: she's like an oblivious guest at a dinner party; the one who doesn't know the family rules and therefore charges forward with awkward questions.

"I'm sorry, but Gavin didn't say there would be three of you. I knew that you would be with him, Chris. I guess I don't understand why you all didn't travel together." Everyone shoots glances between one another, except Jill, who's keeping her eyes to herself. Annabelle laughs nervously. "I don't mean to be difficult, really. In fact, you're all welcome to stay tonight at my parents' house. They have a small guest house with one bed, and a couch. Maybe someone has to sleep on the floor. I don't know. It's just a few miles from here, near Mount Washington." Buoyant smiles erupt, and suddenly Annabelle is not so much weird as generous; her smile is suddenly angelic as opposed to creepy. A ripple of gratitude follows, after which Weed feels obliged to shed some light on things.

"Annabelle, what you don't know is that a week ago Chris and I had an accident in Northern California. It was my fault, actually, and I owe Chris a new truck, not that he's gonna get it anytime soon." A sideways look and grin signifies something in between a promise and an inside joke. "Before that, I had given him something of mine to hold onto—something important." Weed stops. "Fuck, I feel like I'm in a spy novel. It's hard to explain: Chris had—meaning, now I've got—these flash drives that I stole from this company I was working for. But I'm not a thief. Now I've got these, I need to find this other guy, this—" Weed trails off as his thoughts become cloudy. He catches Jill's eye and recovers an idea that somehow had barely occurred to him before this moment. "I've actually given up stuff to be here. I've basically ditched a job. After tonight, I have no where to go, and I've no idea what I'm doing. Thank you for tonight, by the way."

Heads lower imperceptibly, and for a suspended moment no one says anything. Helplessness. Embarrassment. Annabelle, however, feels none of this.

"It kinda sounds like a spy novel," she says, proving she is not without humor. "But Gavin and Chris only traveled down today. You said the accident happened a week ago. What happened after that? Have you—I mean, didn't you both…? I don't get why it took a week to find each other." Annabelle's gaze is fixed and curious; she is neither angry nor worried—merely steadfast and clear thinking. Weed fumbles for words as he responds to Annabelle's questions. Looking around the table, he can see everyone's eager curiosity, especially that of Chris and Jill. Actually, Jill seems even more curious than Chris. She, after all, had gotten more information than the others, about that kidnapping he'd alluded to first thing. But a fuller explanation is not forthcoming. Somewhere after the third or fourth platitude—Weed's "got sidetracked with some business" comment—she turns away, knowing that something happened in that blackout spell of several days, something Weed's just not going to talk about.

They move on. After a round of BLTs with frozen meat hit the spots but presage indigestion, they all pile back into Annabelle's Mitsubishi and drive on to the meeting of Cassandra's Children. In the dawdling moments before leaving the restaurant, as Annabelle and Sweet are settling the bill, Jill walks up to Weed.

"Hey, what was that weird thing you said to her at the bus depot, about Sweet not being right for her or something?"

Weed demurs. "I don't know. I don't really wanna go into it right now. I just got a hit of something, that's all." Jill nods with an ambiguously respectful air. Her face is warm if unsmiling. Weed maintains a hapless demeanor. Somehow he conveys a message that he can't win at certain things, but he'll give them his best shot anyhow. She turns and walks back to Chris. Weed observes the gravitational pull between them and feels several layers of irony weigh upon him. They are whispering, Chris and Jill, though not conspiratorially. Instead, it seems normal, their quiet words and fluid movement around each other—like nothing less than the resumption of a natural, if dark bond. Weed sees how they fit together, physically at least. They look correspondingly lithe and sensual. Despite contrasting personalities, they seem inexplicably well-matched, sibling-like yet not at the same time. Weed imagines their initial getting together. He figures Jill made the moves early on, manizing the ordinarily diffident Chris, persuading him that resistance was futile, and that the two of them were meant to link parts, permanently or not.

Chemistry.

As they drive away, Weed feels weariness settling in again. The day's finally coming to an end, he realizes. Time to rest properly, on a bed preferably, though anything would be better than what he'd slept in the last few nights. In the front, Sweet and Annabelle are exchanging more white noise. Though he looked suspicious initially, Sweet seems to have relaxed and accepted Weed's presence. Annabelle is excited about the upcoming meeting and oblivious to everyone's exhaustion. No one wants to go to this meeting, but it seems the price to pay for Annabelle's hospitality. In the back, also decompressing from her long and traumatic day, Jill leans her head against the side door and closes her eyes. Chris, sitting in the middle, strokes her hair, perhaps having heard by now some details of the various chases, break-ins and assaults. Weed looks away. He doesn't envy his touching of her per se, but he envies that Chris feels entitled to it. Knowing what he knows, he can barely stand that Chris feels entitled to it.

"Hey, did you ever call your parents?" Chris asks him randomly.

"Nah. Didn't get around to it," Weed says.

"Maybe it's time you should," Chris suggests amiably. "After all, it wouldn't hurt now, would it? If you're being followed still, it's not to their place. Anyway, when I was at OPD, they told me your folks were the ones who reported you missing. You probably didn't know that, huh?"

"No, I didn't," Weed replies numbly.

Thankfully, at least from Weed's point of view, Annabelle pulls into a parking lot and gratuitously announces that they have arrived at the meeting place. The Masonic Temple is a chalk white cubicle, two stories high and designed with as little imagination as possible, as if anonymity were the architect's guiding principle. The lot is nearly filled, with a handful of people congregating around a double door entrance, or else lingering at the base of a derelict set of stairs.

"It's a special meeting tonight," Annabelle says as they wait behind one other car. "Usually, we don't start this late, but the speaker couldn't get here earlier. Do you guys follow current events?"

Weed is half listening, half-dozing as the car rides over a speed bump, jostling him. At the base of the stairs leading to the building's entrance, there's a bottleneck of visitors crowded around a pair of individuals. One figure captures Weed's attention, and also Annabelle's. "That's him," she squeals like a clinging teenybopper. The person in the center of the crowd is shaking hands with visitors, greeting them like a pastor who's about to deliver a sermon. And the thing is: he is. The man is thin and tall, and has white but neatly combed hair. The light that shines from the entrance pours down over him, striking the lens on his glasses. He seems to be looking past the visitors who clamor for his attention. Though his eyes are obscured, the glare from his spectacles tracks the path of the just arriving Mitsubishi. He sees something he wants. Annabelle tries to continue: "That's—"

"Jules Grotius," Weed interrupts. He briefly sits up and looks past Chris and Jill, towards where the man is standing amongst the crowd. Then Weed slumps back down in his seat. "I know him," he says.

42

Julies Grotius, aged forty two, unmarried, without kids or any major attachment to speak of, waits outside the Masonic Temple in Culver City, shaking hands and smiling diligently. It's a half hour before a gathering of Cassandra's Children, the local chapter of a nationwide society that offers legitimacy to those who see what they and many others call Shadows, or what the medical or psychiatric establishment would term psychotic hallucinations. Jules accepted an invitation to speak on the grounds that his identity would be kept secret up until ten o'clock, the time of the meeting. At this point it would seem as though someone has let him down, as there are numerous people walking up to the Temple and greeting him, having anticipated his appearance. Jules isn't helping matters by standing out front, gazing around as though he's looking for someone. It's dangerous, his entourage warns.

Despite subtle yet distinctive changes in his features, or his traveling incognito under the name Joseph Greening, he's likely still recognizable to some ardent followers of his movements; still a story for skeptical journalists, and still a target for death threats from foreign exiles living in the US.

But Jules Grotius is being stubborn. He insists he's had visions—seen Shadows—of a guy he'd seen once before, and who has since been in his visions, his thoughts, even his dreams and nightmares. His own visions are changing, he believes. It's a result of his experience and learning, this evolution of understanding. When he was a kid, Jules thought Shadows were like ghosts, the dregs of the dead lingering on earth, struggling to let go of life. As a teen, he nuanced this view as he found others who had what was being called "the gift". From then on and for some time thereafter, Shadows were visions of people with unfinished business, but he bristled at anyone who suggested that psychics were treading along similar territory with their crude beliefs. For Jules and the growing number of kindred spirits he discovered, the meaning of the Shadows was more political, social, and psychological. These Shadows, he and others insisted, had something important to say about the world.

That aspect hasn't changed; just evolved. In more recent years, Jules has even transitioned his belief that Shadows herald crimes in the community, or else in some macrocosmic realm. Currently, the take of those who carry the oral tradition of this underground religion is more abstract, and therefore less consumable by an average follower. What Jules now believes is that Shadows portend simply what is important, whether it be good or bad. Those hungry for leadership, simpler prescriptions, or a clearer purpose may recoil in disillusionment. Perhaps fewer and fewer "gifted" people will subscribe to the understandings that he and some others are espousing, but that's okay with Jules. The movement needs only that which is real, Jules is known to say. It may seem elitist to some, but the last thing Shadow-seers need are idle passengers for a serious cause, hungry groupies who lack the right palette.

One of his remaining areas of weakness is in recognizing those who may hurt him. This is a near mythical flaw, the most resilient flaw of gifted individuals, say self-proclaimed elders— self-proclaimed simply because no one is *proclaimed* a leader of the gifted. Where there is hierarchy there is violence, reads a banner inside the Temple. It's a popular saying within Cassandra's Children, though no one seems to know where the phrase comes from. That's anarchy for you. Regardless, the person Jules Grotius now seeks, whom he believes will soon arrive at the Temple, carrying Jules' property, is a person who at least tried to hurt him, or so he assumed. He stole from him, Jules has been declaring for days. He stole the files that contain the final stages of his game, 'The Situation'.

"But you said those drives don't actually contain any whistleblower information," complains Ed Kim. Ed is standing at the door to the Temple, calling after Jules like he's talking someone down off a ledge.

"He didn't know that," Jules argues, though it's not really the point.

"So what? What does it matter what he knows or doesn't know. There's nothing on that game, in the form he has it, that can be leaked. Look Jules, your little test of Sahi, and of me, worked. So you've discovered we can't be trusted—that we can't secure your files and assure lack of editorial tampering."

"This wasn't quite the security breach I had in mind, Ed."

"Exactly. That's my point. This guy is a wild-card, the factor you hadn't accounted for. Sahi's not even your problem. Don't you realize that's the beauty of your game: by the time they know what's programmed in it'll be too late. But you know what I think? I think this is the thing that's bothering you—that something happened that wasn't in your plan.

Jules is circumspect, knowing he didn't plan this—well, not perfectly, anyway. "Maybe," he says to Ed Kim with a disembodied voice. "Still, I wanna meet him."

"Why?" Kim answers, bewildered.

"Because I want to learn for myself what his intentions are, whether I can trust him. You say his theft is common knowledge in the company, so there's no way you can keep a lid on this anymore, give him his job back?"

"No way," says Kim, not knowing where Jules is going with this.

"But you say he's the best tester you got—the person most likely to reach the latter stages of the game first. Right?"

"Sure," Ed Kim confirms.

"Then I'll hire him. If I like him, he can work directly with me on the final development."

"But—"

"And don't give me any crap about his being a drug dealer or whatever else. That didn't stop you from taking him on. Look, I know you stuck your neck out for me. I appreciate that, but try to see we're in the same boat here. No one gets to feel secure in this thing, including you. Besides, there's a funny side. I don't trust Sahi. You didn't trust Sahi. Now, since it's known you didn't secure the drives according to protocols, they won't trust you either. Maybe that's how things are: nobody trusts anyone."

The exchange subsides as a larger crowd converges on the Temple. Jules Grotius is half-listening to seeming admirers, half-looking past people's shoulders, peering into cars to see if there's a recognizable figure. At two minutes to ten o'clock a secretary who typically chairs the meeting comes outside and politely announces the time. It's the second time this man has come out with an alert, and yet Jules Grotius is still scanning the area, seemingly intent on speaking whenever he feels he's ready. The secretary seems nervous, perhaps because he's spent considerable time calling people up individually and changing the meeting time to suit Jules Grotius. Now he has a room full of expectant, eager listeners, but still people whose patience may wear thin if the meeting is further delayed.

Then a Mitsubishi Outlander pulls up and Jules sees another flash of Shadows.

Tecco—Gotcha.

He tries to see into the car as it pulls slowly into the lot, but it's hard to catch sight of the face he would immediately recognize. Seated at the windows there are two women: one is driving, the other is in the back seat. The two or three people beside them, perhaps male, are all silhouetted and are therefore not distinct. Still, the guy must be in there. The vision can't be wrong. By now, the secretary is inviting all visitors inside, informing them the meeting will be starting any moment. The sly efforts to pressure Jules will at some point work if Bryan "Weed" Tecco doesn't appear, and as the Mitsubishi finds a parking space, Jules still lacks one hundred percent faith in his own visions. Jules Grotius crosses his fingers.

Five people emerge from the car, the last of which is hanging his head like he knows what's coming. It's Tecco, wearing an expression which says there are no surprises left in his life. Up front is what looks like a teenage girl charging towards Grotius like she's craving an autograph. One more person to deal with and then look past, Jules thinks. Three others are twenty somethings, like Bryan Tecco. They all look tired except for the girl leading them, and none beside her looks especially enthusiastic about being there. Jules has been thinking about Bryan Tecco for days; has been wondering what kind of thief he is, what kind of profit he might expect to earn from the game. That was until he had his visions. Ever since then, Jules has been more intrigued than offended. What is this guy about? Is he a Shadow seer? Is that why he stole the drives? And now that he's reached the Temple and found the game's creator, what does he want?

The eager, smiling girl reaches the foot of the stairs and reaches out a hand, introducing herself as Annabelle. Another woman and two guys sort of nod at Jules and then make way for Tecco, who stands behind, holding a backpack. Jules warmly greets them all with nods and handshakes. Weed holds back.

"Mr. Tecco, good evening. I'm hoping you have something for me." Jules Grotius is smiling. Weed is not. He looks up, sees the pale, anxious face of Ed Kim at the top of the stairs, staring down. Weed sighs like he's busted, like it's time for him to come inside after a long day of playing out. "It seems the pleasure's all mine," Jules says in a quasi regal voice. Now Weed looks like he's remembered what he came for. It's an accident, this meeting, but accidents happen and have meaning. He likes this guy Grotius: not just the cocksure vision, but the flippant manner; the irresistible Ivy League charm. Gimme a night's rest, Weed thinks—by morning I'll be matching wits with you. Lethargically, Weed reaches into the bag, grabs the set of drives and places them in Jules' palm. They exchange thin, satisfied grins. Wordlessly, they seem to agree upon something.

"Jules, it really is time," says the officious secretary, now standing at the top of the stairs.

Jules' lip twitches with thinly veiled contempt. "Fine, Philip. I'm coming now," he says, barely looking over his shoulder. "Can we talk after the show?" he asks of Weed.

"Sure."

"Good."

Next they are all led into the meeting hall, with the group now following Jules as if they have all been deputized as part of his entourage. Once inside Weed feels the energy of an anticipating crowd. He feels the coolness of Ed Kim's disapproving eyes on his back, but chooses to ignore him. He listens to an overhead speaker system playing rabble-rousing rock and roll, glances at old photographs of society founders on the walls, and people watches. A disc plays the MC5: Weed has memories of his dad listening to that band. Weed's dad had a thing for hard rock with a revolutionary flavor. He used to play this stuff when he invited his friends over to their Bolinas home to drink, smoke pot, and talk politics. Weed liked the grungy, molten guitars, the wildcat vocals and general primitivism, but he could give or take the Eldridge Cleaver rhetoric. As he watches the near one hundred people cluster in rows before a table with a podium on top, Weed recalls the end-of-days vibe that his dad used to cultivate as he and his guests looked out over the Pacific. As the secretary calls the meeting to order, Weed half expects a familiar, incendiary greeting: *Brothers and Sisters of the revolution, we are gathered here tonight...*

43

Jules Grotius stands before the Shadow-seeing members of Cassandra's Children with his arms folded, looking sage and mystical, like a druid that's about to perform a necromantic ritual. His small eyes make tight, darting movements about the brightly-lit room, taking in the tense ambience, assessing the needs of his audience, in nanoseconds. But there's no danger. If there was he'd feel it, or he'd have seen the images dancing around individuals, implicating them as adversarial, or—in his current parlance of non-judgment—*important*. With no seats left, Weed has seized a spot against a wall, next to a bookshelf with a largely cosmetic purpose. He scans the venerable-looking sets of encyclopedias, embroidered texts containing arcane information. Weed recognizes just one book: an anomalously placed print of *A Hero With A Thousand Faces* by Joseph Campbell.

He is struck by the lack of security in the room, thinks it foolhardy considering how controversial the speaker has become, not to mention how congested the room is. Anyway, Jules looks comfortable enough, and with almost everyone around him capable of spotting an out of place motivation, let alone a would-be assailant, Weed figures the situation is more or less under control. Besides, someone might be packing a heater but just concealing it, just as he had been for much of the day. Besides that, what's preoccupying Weed is the range of reactions to his own arrival: from Sweet's deferential suspicion, to Ed Kim's not-so surprising appearance and not-so-surprised spotting of him, to the strangely blasé interactions with Chris. It's as if he and Chris haven't truly reunited after their near-death adventure of the previous week. Looking at Chris, who is flirting with Jill, looking jazzed by the atmosphere, Weed supposes that only he and not Chris is aware of an unresolved trauma.

Amid the noisy chatter, the secretary that was troubling Jules earlier is still calling the meeting to order. Once a relative quiet is achieved, he makes sundry announcements that have everything to do with the Temple, little to do with Jules Grotius or Cassandra's Children. Then, as he introduces the speaker there's a rapturous applause, a release of built-up energy, plus diffuse anger, and possibly confusion. Jules steps languidly to the podium and keeps his arms folded, as if making a point of keeping focus. He begins his presentation blandly, thanking the organizers for their hard work and patience; thanking the audience for its indulgence of his scheduling requests, their patience with him. Explaining himself, he describes a recent lifestyle marked by fatigue from traveling, hotel hopping, a sometimes reliance upon the hospitality of friends; his staying one step ahead of subpoenas or hostile journalists. Jules thanks the audience for its commitment and then jokes that had he needed security tonight, it would have resulted from society members wanting to hurt him for keeping them up so late. Laughter fills the room.

Then it really begins. Jules Grotius stares out into the heart of the crowd like he's trying to connect with some core entity within its midst. It's a diverse-looking group in front of him: there are Whites, Blacks, Asians and a few Latinos, all sitting in cliques, but nonetheless squeezed into the tight room, rubbing shoulders with long-faced seriousness. He nods at a Middle-Eastern-looking man in front who, moments earlier, had drawn much attention for his particular take on Shadows: they are angels, he insists; specifically, archangels of death, named Azrael in the Islamic tradition. Thankfully, as far as Jules is concerned, there are no other major religious factions in the room, thus containing the indices of diversity. All in all, there are equal numbers of men and women, and maybe one or two for whom either designation may be in question.

"You are all here tonight because you have something in common," Jules calls out. "You believe in something that is difficult to talk about, because to talk about it is to risk being marginalized, maybe ridiculed. Whatever your differences are, wherever you've come from, your shared experience of Shadows, your shared social conscience, bonds you. There may be other experiences, phenomena that bind you—things you may not be aware of. What are you here for? Do you want to know if I see Shadows? Do you want to know if I belong? Well, let me dispel one mystery at least: I do." More laughter, only this time it's gentler. Jules leaves a theatrical pause. "But talking about Shadows is not really why I'm here tonight. So, let me ask this: based upon your experiences, concerns, and what you've heard about me, what have you come to hear tonight?"

Jules steps away from the podium, begins to pace with his arms now unfolded and placed on his hips. Faces in the crowd start looking between one another. They are waiting, and stirring. They are whispering uncertainly. "Come on," Jules provokes, "what is it you wanna know about?"

Many are confused, including the likes of Chris and Jill, who share nonplussed glances. Sweet wears a frown, embodying his brand of confusion. Annabelle wears a beatific smile as if familiar with Jules' presentation style; as if nothing Jules Grotius says could possibly *not* make sense. From the middle of the room, a middle-aged white man, apparently alone, finally raises his hand. He is overweight, heavily bearded, with a stars and stripes bandana around his head. "Yes sir," Jules beckons.

"I wanna know about US involvement in Syria," the man says.

"Good," replies Jules. He looks elsewhere around the room, hoping others feel reinforced. A woman in the next row forward gingerly raises her hand.

"I want to know what countries are uranium-ready," she volunteers.

"Okay," Jules answers supportively, though he's not quite sure what the woman means by "uranium-ready". "Let's keep going," he exhorts.

"Real numbers about Obamacare costs," says a voice from the back.

"Obama's birth certificate," says someone else. There's some more laughter, and some uneasy feeling.

"Alright," says Jules with a disarming chuckle. "It seems we have representatives of varied opinions and interests. Oh well, I didn't say you'd have everything in common. But I think most of you get the point. Most of you know the work I do. You are aware that my interest is in the revealing of secrets—things the public should know. Ever since I was a kid I've distrusted secrets, especially those that are known, or felt, but simply not talked about. In our present-day world, I suggest we come to think of secrets not so much as that which is unknown, but rather that which is known but not talked about. And thus our task is to overcome fear, and especially the fears of closed systems, those in power who control the dissemination of information in our society. It is our task to place faith in the revealing of truth."

At this point, a significant portion of the crowd breaks into applause. They are galvanized by Jules Grotius, and nodding in tandem with words they've heard from him before. The arguments themselves aren't original, but the difference is that Jules Grotius has put his money and his home where his mouth is: he's whistleblown, he's snitched; he's pointed fingers and taken risks, and no less than anyone in the crowd, he's not sure where he'll be tomorrow. Significantly, of the group that is comprised of Weed and the others, only Annabelle joins in the celebratory fervor.

Chris and Jill look stilled and noncommittal. Sweet continues to frown and look confused, not sure where this is all going, but more or less trusting the process. Weed recedes ever more subtly against the wall. He's not exactly sure why, but he doesn't care for the diatribe of Jules Grotius. So far it's all a bit grandstanding and demagogic. When he is going to relate all this to the game? He wonders.

It's as if their minds are speaking to each other.

"So, I have a new way of revealing truth that I wanna talk about tonight." A couple of shouts sound out, people going "yeah" and "right on" as in an evangelical call-and-response ritual. It seems as though a few might know what is coming. "I play games," Jules says next. "I play video games, sandbox games, shooter games—been playin' 'em for years. Anyone here relate to that?" A few hands go up, not exactly the majority of those present. Weed looks around and smirks thinly. He notes the older demographic, figures late nights with inflammatory podcasts are more this crowd's thing than video games. Jules points to one person. "What's your favorite game?" he asks.

"League of Legends," the guy responds. Jules nods, puckers his lips and raises an eyebrow, signifying the coolness. Weed shakes his head. He doesn't like League of Legends.

"Well, as some of you may know, I've recently parlayed my hobby into a new endeavor: I've got a new game for you. I got a new game for the market. Man, I've got a game like no other before it." More noise. More shouts of approval. Weed is starting to get impatient. He wants to stand up, interrupt this cheesy rally and announce that he—his efforts, his ordeal of the last week—is the reason Jules Grotius gets to act like a rock star and move on with his schemes. "What is the point of a video game? What are players' objectives? Is it to kill, accrue money, or achieve power, psychologically, if not in actuality? Is it to win something, create something? My game, which I have been developing over the last two years, will contain all of these objectives to one degree or another. And then, at the advanced levels, it will reveal truths, the secrets." Jules stops for another theatrical moment, leaving some in the room to ponder implications. By this time, some have gleaned the loose, interactive structure to the meeting.

"Why only at advanced levels?" someone asks cautiously.

"Good question," Jules replies, "because only those who work hard, endure the process and achieve progress get to hear the secrets." He looks out over his audience, notices odd murmurings of misunderstanding, or dissent. He presses on. "I can see that some of you are having second thoughts now, maybe not understanding. Let me prevail on your goodwill a while longer and explain. You see, one of the problems with having a whistleblower's resource, whether it's a website, or a network of connections to media outlets, is that at some point you have to deal with the truth that not enough people care about the revealing of state secrets, corporate secrets, or any of the stuff you all shouted out minutes ago. Seriously, that stuff you all mentioned: I've forgotten it already." Jules yawns for effect. "I mean, think about it. You all come here each week, right? You bask in each others' company, thinking you're all special because you have a gift that you think others don't have—that you see things that others don't. And you think that if you share what you see, talk about it, spread the word, then what? The world will change?"

Jules places his hands on the corner of the podium and thrusts out a mocking glare at his audience. People are looking around, speechless. They want someone to stop this. This isn't fun anymore. Isn't there someone in charge?

A man speaks up. "What are you saying, that we should give up, not try to do anything with what we know?" They are the first words said in anger. Weed perks up.

"Does it change anything, speaking up? Has it brought you anything but trouble?"

"But you said it's time to reveal truths," says a woman in front. She sounds hurt.

Jules Grotius is succinct and hard in his response: "I manipulated you, told you what you wanted to hear. I got your attention."

"Why?" asks the woman, looking more like she needs a comforting hug than an answer.

"So that I might then disorient you, prime you for a learning experience." Jules looks into the woman's eyes and sees her pupils constrict. "You don't like me right now, do you? You think I'm arrogant, maybe evil."

"You're an asshole," says the man by the woman's side.

"I can see that time and goodwill is running out, so let me get to the point. I must disabuse you of the notion that whistleblowing, as you currently understand it, will change society. My brave friends, trust me for just a moment longer as I share with you an ironic truth: my secrets mean nothing. The revelations for which I have become famous or infamous over the last year—THEY MEAN NOTHING."

By now the crowd is staring back at Jules Grotius, half in contempt for a shameless poseur, half in sympathy for a man falling apart before their eyes. Jules' voice softens. He sounds breathless and on the cusp of tears. "Please forgive me, I do not mean to only provoke. What I'm sharing with you, what I have still to share with you, I do so because I admire your pact of anonymity; your commitment to the sacredness of a confidence. And so I tell you, and will only tell you—the revelations you may expect to hear are mere decoys, carrots for the average consumer, because the real secret is in the process." Jules steps up from behind the podium and walks along the front row. Now he's in touching distance, spitting distance of his disgruntled listeners. His expression beseeches. "The process," he repeats. "The secret is in the process. In my game, players defeat adversaries, enter portals to next stages, and traverse obstacles, as in many games. But above all, in my game the successful player advances over levels because he or she establishes alliances that belie prejudices. In my game, a player sometimes kills an adversary and manages to survive. On other occasions, a player takes a risk, chooses to trust and even follows an alien other, because that player sees in that other something else…something to connect with. In so doing that player achieves growth. Imagine with me please a contest that rewards growth in terms our violent, material, conspiracy-seeking society still has yet to embrace. You might wonder what traits, or skills might enable such brave yet promising risks: is it intelligence? Quick motor skills? Is it so-called sound judgment, or a well organized mind? Or is spontaneity or creativity the premium aptitudes? Well, again, all of these qualities are important, but none are as important as the following: empathy. Take a moment and imagine with me please a game that has programmed in the capacity to reward empathy."

At this point, the crowd is transfixed. Some are moved, despite not fully understanding what is happening. Weed, Chris, and Jill are gripped. Jules flicks glances about the room. He sees that he has won back the room, for now. He continues: "People, neuroscientists and psychologists are now telling us what we've known all along—that a single glance can communicate aggression, attraction, and many other feelings, in microseconds. We know that body posture, tone, or what is termed prosody, can determine feelings of safety, and can help us feel understood. We know from infant studies and still-face experiments that our capacity for integrating non-verbal forms of communication is present from the outset of life; that we have unconscious ways of relating to others, and that sometimes that primal nurturing process goes wrong." Next Jules makes an extravagant gesture with his arms, pointing beyond the walls. "Out there is the target audience for my game: people are chronically traumatized, mindlessly, if intelligently reacting to their fears instead of fully using their minds, learning to use—you guessed it—empathy. And they play games instead of becoming involved with the world. But we should not give up on them."

Next, Weed has a moment not unlike many from his school days. Teachers, sensing Weed's distraction or resistance, would synchronously pass eyes over Weed, implicating him while ostensibly provoking the whole class with pious pronouncements.

Someone calls out a challenge. "So, let me get this straight. You're saying your game has the unique feature of rewarding play strategies that exhibit player empathy, even though the game may otherwise resemble other games on the market."

"That's correct," Jules answers. "And allow me to break it down for you with some specifics and at the same time demonstrate how the game's development has been influenced by our shared preoccupation." He jumps back to his podium and clicks on a laptop on the desk next to it. On an overhead screen, a blue background appears, marked by white bullet points, sentences with highlighted words. Among the boldfaced words are terms like Creepers, Endmen, Nether-terrain, and most notably, Shadows.

"These are some of the characters and features of the game. A player is situated in a pixilated world, charged initially with a basic task: survive. At his or her disposal are weapons menus, resource menus, which graduate in strength as the game proceeds. A player can, through vanquishing others and building tools and infrastructure, gather materials, more sophisticated weaponry, build a home or a swimming pool, even a business. A player has access to basic resources, such as water and coal, and can later make use of more efficient energy devices if he or she advances. A player can fish, though he or she can gain credit if recognizing endangered species and leaving them alone. There are recreational menus, opportunities for players to indulge in vices such as drug use, sex, even eating, though the catch is that such behaviors may render players vulnerable, because players' rivals, like Creepers and Endmen, never stop playing the game. They never stop competing."

As Jules pauses again, he looks around the room to gauge reaction. There are still quite a few bemused expressions; a few others are stilled. Some are nodding, clearly intrigued. One or two are looking away, perhaps disturbed. But no one's leaving, nor has he been chased out of the building. This is going well enough, Jules thinks—more or less how he'd hoped it would go.

"All characters in the game may appear as monsters and enemies, or friends, depending upon players' prejudices. But as a player, you don't get a long time to decide what you're experiencing. You may kill enemies, like Creepers and Endmen,

313

and survive, perhaps even thrive. Those ends may justify your means. But if you kill Shadows, who only occasionally appear and do not herald or preview their appearances, then you do not gain passage into new territory. You do not grow at these watershed moments. You stalemate. And so, my game is one of steady progress, requiring patience and diligence. But at its core it is also a game that calls for spontaneity, inspiration, the capacity to feel into another's experience, based upon a confluence of a single moment, plus the aggregate of moments in a person's life."

Someone raises their hand, suggesting a return to reverent order. Jules wearily nods.

"So, what about the whistleblower stuff, the state or corporate secrets you have? Are you telling us it's not gonna be in this game, but you're gonna say to the public that it is?"

"It'll be there—some of what you expect and along the lines of what we spoke of earlier—but it's not the core of the game. That's what I'm telling you." Jules casts his eyes over the room and holds out his hands like a pastor appealing for a new day of peace and brotherhood. "Look, in the end of the day it's just a game, and I'm a guy who is passionate about games. Despite what I said earlier, I'm not here to stomp on anyone's social conscience. If speaking up about corruption is what you want to do, then fine. I don't want to dampen the courage of those willing to risk exposing themselves, for that is what I have done after all. A mentor of mine once told me it takes twenty seconds of courage to decide on any course of action in life. First, there is the recognition, the bringing to consciousness, and that's what my game, 'The Situation', is really about. But I know that in the real world—that is, in the world outside of games—decisions have to be made, and courage is required."

Standing against the wall, Weed feels a wave of something like nausea. He flushes as something warm, something comfortable and not at the same time, radiates through him.

"Again, people, my game is about the process. At the risk of sounding propagandist, or like someone speaking past their level of knowledge, I believe my game offers an abstraction, an experience that is the necessary precursor to all other actions in life, and I intend to offer this experience to those who don't even know it exists. So please hear me that it's not about the learning of a fact or an event whose meaning in time will dissolve without context because most human beings simply do not carry collective history in a conscious way. We carry our own histories, and we do so, for the most part, unconsciously."

The heat upon Weed is becoming unbearable. It's a fever, he thinks—the pneumonia. The tight crowd and lack of space is getting to him. He makes a twenty second decision. Nudging past a man in front of him, he next steps in front of Chris and Jill, heading towards the double door entrance.

"Weed?" Jill asks softly as he passes. He shakes his head but doesn't look at her. She notices that his face his red and his lips are quivering. As he approaches the exit, his steps quicken. He thrusts out his arms and shoves open the door. As he, his friends or his enemies might say, he's outta there.

44

Outside, it has started to rain. Not much, just a drizzle. Weed looks up, allowing soft droplets to strike his cheeks and run down his face. He walks to the end of the parking lot, considers walking on, disappearing. Moments later, he is followed by Jill, who at first calls out to him from the top of the stairs. He turns briefly, shouts out that he's fine, just needs some air and space. Jill retorts that it's not good for him to be walking out in the rain in his condition. His condition? He dwells for a moment on what that means, as opposed to what Jill means. She hurries down the stairs and strides after him with militant determination. As she approaches within a few feet, her pace softens. She notices that Weed is circling and hiding himself. He seems cagey, vulnerable, and at best indulgent of Jill's need to know what's happening at all times.

"I'm fine. Go back to the meeting."

"Obviously, something's wrong. Tell me what it is."

"It's nothing," he says unconvincingly.

"Look, it's been a long day. A lot's happened. You must be exhausted. I'm exhausted. I know it was important to meet this guy Grotius, but we should get going, and if that stupid girlfriend of Sweet's says any—"

"It's not the meeting. It's fine."

"Well, what, then? Is it something to do with Chris? You guys have hardly said a word since you got here." As she invokes his name, Jill looks over her shoulder, half-expecting Chris to appear beneath the spotlight by the front entrance. On cue, he pops out and stands frozenly at the top of the stairs. "Is it something to do with me, or anything we talked about earlier?" she asks.

"What's up?" Chris calls out. Weed looks at Jill and shakes his head. Jill nods faintly and then turns, facing Chris.

"It's okay, Chris. Weed hasn't been feeling well. I'm just checking up on him." Chris starts descending the stairs. "Isn't the meeting still going?" Jill asks, hoping to deter him.

"Dude's speech is over. He's taking questions now." Chris notices that Weed's back is turned, and that he's looking upwards. What he doesn't know is that Weed loves the rain. It's his favorite kind of water. He loves how it streams down his face, how it obscures his tears but doesn't force him to swim. What he can't conceal is the redness of his features, the quivering of his lips, or the strain of holding back the collapse of his body. Jill steps gently towards him.

"We—Bryan, something's upset you. Please tell me what it is."

Weed issues a short, bitter laugh. "It's okay, call me Weed. That's my name." Jill says nothing. "Nah, it's good—what Jules is talking about. I get what he's saying, sort of. I just wish I had known. I kinda knew when I was first playing his game that I was missing something basic. Now I know. I feel stupid, actually, if you wanna know the truth. I've come all this way, put up with all kinds of shit—put you through all kinds of shit—and those drives likely have nothing on them. Nothing we needed to risk our lives for, anyway."

"We don't know that. I'm sure when Jules finishes he'll—"

"He'll what? Explain? This has all been a huge waste of time, Jill." The use of her name startles her. Her eyes widen, expressing something in between fear and caring. Weed shakes his head again and tightens his jaw. It's taking all he's got to hold off the secret.

"That's not it, is it?" she asks daringly. She stares into Weed.

Weed chokes on a response. He lowers his head, unable to look at her. Twenty seconds have passed: he unknowingly takes a risk.

"Anyway, it was a cool bit about courage, don't you think?" he says in a heavy voice. He tries laughing again, but the muscles in his face stall on him. Jill stays silent. Weed sighs. "It reminded me of something, if you really wanna know. When I was fourteen my parents told me I was adopted. That's not something people know about me, generally, so you're lucky. Or maybe you're not. I don't know. Anyway, that was half a lifetime ago. You'd think I'd be over it by now." Weed gives a nod to Jill and then looks over her shoulder, assuming Chris can also hear him. He can, but only barely, and he remains at a distance.

"I'm sorry," says Jill, trying to be sensitive.

"Don't be. It's not a bad thing. My folks, my adoptive parents, are wonderful people. Seriously. It's me that's the problem. But when I was fourteen, it did throw me, their announcement. I remember my dad taking me for a walk one day, shortly after he and my mom had sat me down at home and told me the news. I guess they were going through difficulty at the time. I don't know what. They didn't tell me, not that they should have. It was all between them. But my dad wanted to tell me that relationships were difficult, that all relationships were difficult, no matter how good they are. In fact, the better the relationship, the more difficult it is, he said. Anyway, somehow we got on the subject of courage. I probably turned the discussion this way, not wanting to hear whatever was going on between him and my mom. I wanted to talk about his favorite comic book heroes from his day—what characters had the most courage, for example. But he turned serious, didn't wanna talk about comic books the way we used to. I kept tryin' but at some point he just shook his head and said, straight up, that the most courageous thing he ever did was…" Weed stutters "… was to adopt me. I remember I just looked at him and said nothing. He started to choke up and tear. Then he said how frightened he was to make the decision, along with my mom. He said he took days thinking about it, changing his mind once or twice, getting cold feet, procrastinating. Then at some point he just decided. They didn't know much about me, except that I was a preemie. My dad said this thing about it taking twenty seconds of courage to decide on anything important in life. That's when—" Weed's face breaks. A broken whimper leaks out of him, uncontrolled. "I'm sorry," he says, averting his eyes but recovering a previous composure. "It was an accident," he barely whispers, "an accident that I'm alive."

Jill reaches out and corals him. Her arms stretch across his shoulders and wrap sloppily around his body. Reeling, Weed attempts to twist free, only to end up pressed against her chest, with her damp sweater absorbing his emerging, quiet sobs. From behind, Chris steps up and tentatively places a hand on the back of his friend's head. He gives Jill a look that briefly suggests jealousy, only to then turn his gaze upon Weed. A gentle, massage-like action soothes Weed's cranium, and the three of them remain locked together for a full minute. Unseen, Chris' face contorts, exhibiting a certain kind of pain that he and Weed share but have never spoken of. Following Weed's cue, Chris and Jill repeat apologies, both to Weed and towards each other, though no one can bear to make explanations.

The doors to the Masonic Temple open up, releasing quieted, disappointed members of Cassandra's Children from the self indulgence of Jules Grotius. The sound of grumbling pours down the staircase and into the parking lot. Those leaving are shaking their heads, not getting this business about the *process*. After about a dozen people file out, Jules bursts onto the area atop the stairs. He is by himself, stood under a spot-lit entrance and anxiously looking around, trying to spot Weed and desperately hoping he hasn't lost him a second time. No one is stopping to talk, to question him further or shake his hand. That rock star thing is gone now. He stumbles down the stairs, more like someone who's been ejected than the recently hailed key note speaker.

"TECCO," he calls out, recognizing the small huddle by the edge of the lot. Weed, Chris, and Jill have by this point moved apart. Wearily, they regard Jules Grotius walking towards them. He is shivering in the rain, which is now coming down harder, but he's holding his head up, making a point of looking dignified. "You left like the place was on fire. I know I'm not the best public speaker, but I didn't think I deserved that response."

But Weed and his two friends have abandoned humor.

"It wasn't you. It was gettin' kinda hot in there and I'm not feeling good," Weed says, half-truthfully.

"Well, I hope you feel better soon because I may need you. Meaning, I have a proposal to make."

Jill and Chris look at each other. "Do you need us to give you a minute?" Chris asks.

"Or maybe just take this indoors," Jill suggests.

Jules Grotius gives a defeated shrug. "Fine with me if Weed's okay with going back inside." He turns and looks up towards the entrance. "I assure you it will be a lot emptier by the time we get up there," he adds. He starts to walk back and the three friends follow him, with arms again around one another, like they're inseparable. At the top of the stairs, Jules meets the bereft figure that is Ed Kim. If Jules Grotius can't pitch the game to this crowd, how will he stand a chance with conference audiences, future investors, the average gaming consumer. "Relax," Jules says to him, smiling and reading Kim's mind. Jules Grotius sounds like a man who's about to place his last dollar on the last bet of a lifetime.

"Let's stop here," Weed says, not wanting to go back inside. Something about the Temple creeps him out, and besides, there is overhang in front of the entrance, a bright light all over them. Inside the door, Sweet and Annabelle are whispering agitatedly. She wants to know what's happening, but Sweet isn't quite the ideal narrator. He needs others to tell the stories.

"Do you—" Jill starts to ask.

"No. Stay," Weed interrupts.

Jules nods, assenting. "Well, to the point. This is a disaster, at least from one point of view." He looks back, implicating Ed Kim's perspective; the Sahi man doesn't contradict him. "But it's not entirely unexpected."

"What do you want?" Weed asks. Jules' eyes narrow.

"I rather thought I'd ask you that," he replies, finding Weed's attitude curious. "I had it in mind to offer you a job, for example. Kim here says you're his best tester. I could use someone to help me finish this thing—someone I might trust."

Weed remains inexplicably difficult. "Why would you trust me? I stole your files."

Jules raises an eyebrow. He's like a supercilious villain: acting all cool, even when things are fucked up.

"You came to the meeting, didn't you? Why would you come here if all you wanted was to steal from me?" Weed doesn't answer. He just looks stolidly at Jules Grotius, still feeling burned by the turn of events. "So, are you interested?" asks Jules, looking humbled all of a sudden.

"I don't think I understand your game," Weed says.

"Really? I think you might. If you're a Shadow-seer, and I think you are, I think you stand as good a chance of beating the game as anyone."

"So, I beat the game. What do I get out of that? A paycheck? Or do I get to learn some big-time secrets?"

"Is that what you're looking for?" Jules asks skeptically.

"It's what I was expecting, like everyone else who came here tonight," Weed replies.

Jules pulls back an inch or two. "Oh, I get it. You're resentful because you sacrificed your job thinking the game was something it isn't."

"My job plus a few other things," Weed says, giving a sideways look to Chris and Jill. "So, those files: there's nothing on them, is there?"

Jules Grotius turns his head shiftily from one person to another. He's trying to be cute. "You mean, is there a stage where players learn what countries are uranium ready, whatever that means? No, there isn't. I didn't even bother encrypting the files. Sorry."

Weed performs a motion that is a half-sigh, half a tightening of his jaw. Chris and even Jill have come to recognize the look. Weed wants to hit Jules Grotius.

Jules matches the expression. "Look, maybe you weren't listening in there, so let me explain something to you. I've done the whistleblowing thing. I've been there. I've revealed a few things, exposed a few bullies, and that has felt good. But I've also been used, especially by overseas groups. A couple of leaks about under-funded relief efforts for earthquake victims were embarrassing for one or two governments, but it turns out the leaks were deliberate. They enabled opposition party principals to announce initiatives they'd prepared ahead of time; financial contributions to victims that ultimately did little more than strengthen those parties' positions at bargaining tables. Know what I'm talkin' about?" Jules' sudden plainspoken twang throws everyone, as if he, like everyone else has been thrown back down to earth with small fish. "I'm as in over my head as anyone in this thing, Tecco. Now I've had a feeling about you. I don't fully know what your deal is, but my guess is you saw a Shadow by me the last time we met—something or one I didn't see myself. Now I'm out on a limb, developing a game for a company, for a market, that I'm sure wants to use me. Ed's on a limb, too. He's just as committed to this thing, even though he lacks the right imagination, bless him. I guess you've been out on a limb also."

You have no idea, Weed thinks.

Jules pushes his head forward. He stares into Weed, his eyes firing bullets. "Think about it, Bryan. What do you want? What's next for you? Wanna sell drugs for a living? Where do you belong? You say you don't get it. Are you sure you don't get it, or is it that you don't wanna stay on the limb?"

Weed pauses and grinds his teeth, making everyone wait. Jules issues one more provocation: "Come on, play the game with me."

Weed is calm all of a sudden.

"I'll need some help; someone else who can play the game," he requests.

"No problem. I'll find someone," says Jules. Weed gestures towards Chris.

"I want him."

"Okay," utters Jules, unsure. "Can he play? Is he a tester?"

"I trust him, so you'll need to. Stay on the limb."

Chris' face goes white. His spun on the run feeling has worn off.

"Fine," says Jules, as if weary of argument. Soon they are shaking hands, albeit limply, as in warily. Quiet words all around now suggest that the business of the day is done. Everyone should go home, or go to whatever nest is home for the night, and reconvene sometime the next day. Arrangements are quickly made. Numbers are exchanged. Sweet, the only one of the group with a working phone, is summoned forward to exchange information with Jules and Ed Kim. Sweet wears a cheerful grin, feeling useful.

"Let's go," says Jill, tugging at Weed's arm. She indicates Annabelle, who is calling everyone to her car and jabbering about the amenities of her parents' home. Chris gives an approving look to Weed. They are all ushering him into the bosom. Weed turns to Sweet.

"When we get to her place, lemme use that phone," he asks.

"You're kidding, right?" Jill remonstrates. "I think you're done for today. Besides, who're you gonna call at this hour?"

She must be tired. Weed tilts his head querulously. He wants to call her *dufus*.

"I'll give you one guess."

45

Apropos of nothing, Chris Leavitt wakes up the following morning, thinking about his age, feeling his age, but deciding that being thirty three isn't so bad. The previous day's spin has left a sour reminder of manic energy and fleeting pleasures, such as wanting Jill—wanting her bad. But it's not to be, and if he's to resume his rehab towards reality, he'll need to let certain things go. Other things, like the chance to feel useful, help others, is being rekindled. So, too, is the promise of finding like-minded spirits, people committed to speaking truth. Last night was a false start, he realizes—must get Sweet, possibly Weed, to go to another Cassandra's Children meeting at that Masonic Temple. Then he'd like to call up Aunt Jenny, tell her he's okay—tell her she's right about a few things. Thank her. Chris feels mature. If he feels old, it's partly because his libido has tanked, as it often does in the aftermath of an episode. Soon pretty faces, eye catching eyes will turn his head, but his lower half, un-distended, will be unimpressed. Also, he has a back ache. In the guest house on Annabelle's parents' property, in keeping with a recent trend, he got the floor, though a nice Swiss army blanket softened his night somewhat. Jill got the couch. Sweet got a guest room in the main house. Weed, one of America's most wanted, the one who is sick, got the guest house bed.

He wakes up last, which is fitting for various reasons, not least because he was on the phone well after midnight, talking first to Rosco, and then, at length, to his parents. By the time he's actually out of bed, it's close to noon. Jill has been up making him tea, taking his temperature, nagging him to make a doctor's appointment, thinking he needs antibiotics. Weed is predictably difficult, explaining he doesn't like doctors, hospitals, rehabs— anything medical. Privately, he knows that being sick keeps others at arms length more often than not and often that's a good thing. Jill is used to such dialogues as she's having with him. So is Weed. On these things, not much is going to change.

Early afternoon, the group, save for Annabelle, travel over to Santa Monica, where Ed Kim owns a home near the beach. This is where Jules Grotius stayed the night, where he'll stay for another couple of days, he'll soon report. The group's plans are up in the air. They can stay at Annabelle's place for a few days, it seems. After that, nobody knows. On the ride over, Jill ends speculation as to what she's going to do. As the next person to seize Sweet's phone, she calls up her boss at Alta McMahon in Oakland, calls in sick for the following day, but then asserts she'll be back for a Sunday shift. Both Chris and Weed are impressed, but also concerned. How's she gonna swing that, they wonder? They'd start managing the problem but for three things: First, they realize they'll soon have a new job to focus on instead; second, that Jill can take care of herself; and lastly, that their track record of thinking through things puts them in no position to judge.

At Ed Kim's place, he and Jules greet them all at the front door and usher them through to a naturally lit room that is facing the ocean. There are two tables joined together, with a pair of computers already booted up and the game downloaded, ready for Chris and Weed. Jules is friendly but all business, talking quickly like a man who's always got somewhere else to be. He pulls Weed and Chris aside, along with Kim, and the four of them appear to go over the particulars, what the guys are gonna get paid, among other things. There's much shrugging happening as usual, the posturing of cool. Later, Jules orients them to the game, or re-orients in Weed's case, tells them he's going to be in and out all day, but that he can be reached by phone or text if necessary. He is hospitable to Sweet and Jill, but is clearly unhappy about hangers on. Jill notices this and makes a point of seeming indifferent. Games: she doesn't play games, she exudes. Sweet, however, promises to be an interested witness, both of Jules' game as well as Jules' life as a whole. Oblivious to distrust, Sweet flatters the former journalist with knowledge about his now famous career.

Satisfied, Jules takes off soon after. A typically important person, Weed thinks—always disappearing. Cheerfully paternal, Jules leaves the group fifty bucks for food, assuming they are all poverty-stricken. With the exception of Jill, they all look poverty-stricken, which is something she points out to them as she volunteers to drive out to a grocery store. The guys agree on burritos as the choice for lunch, preferably from a food truck if she passes one. As she leaves them, they consider her comment and each takes a moment to reflect on the faded, torn and porous fabrics they stretch over their bodies each day. They scoff at Jill, realizing that she will soon be returning to a system that requires uniforms; that she is unlike them—that she is *establishment.* Some more attitudes are entrenched: if they are made men someday, they won't be made by anything as trivial as clothes.

When Jill returns, it seems the game is in full swing. She sets bags of ingredients on a kitchen counter and looks over the shoulders of Chris and Weed. Intrigued, she sees the pixilated, multi-colored world in which their characters, identified by chosen nicknames, roam about. There are flashing images, darting movements, and drop-down menus flitting about the screen to the accompaniment of an already opaque dialogue between the three guys. Besides playing the game and commenting upon it, a relentless bantering is occurring. Comments on each other's performance are interspersed with remarks about each other's life habits—put-downs, mostly.

"This game's gonna teach you a few things," Weed darkly warns Chris. "We're gonna harness some of those impulses of yours." It sounds like an insinuation; the punctuating remark of a concerned earlier discussion.

"How's it going?" asks Jill, hoping to get a gist of what's been said. She imagines Weed has just threatened Chris, in code.

"Well, I'm still alive," says Weed in a gloating voice.

"I've only died once," Chris contributes.

"Uh-huh," says Jill. She notices Sweet looking bored. "How about you, Sweet? How're you doin'?"

"He's got a bug up his ass 'cause I won't do an interview for his film," Weed intrudes.

Sweet is left with his mouth hanging open while others hijack his thoughts. They play on.

"Hey, we need to come up with a nickname for Jules," Chris announces.

Weed nods but keeps his eyes fixed on the game. "Damn right we do. What's it gonna be?"

"Dunno. Let's start throwing out names."

"Why does everyone have to have nicknames?" Jill interrupts.

"Everyone here has nicknames," Sweet declares, sounding prideful, like he belongs to something. "Didn't you know these guys give nicknames to everyone they hang with?"

"I don't have a nickname," Jill argues.

They all laugh.

"Anyway, what about Jules? Make a decision, bro," Weed demands.

"How about Jewel?" offers Chris.

"Too obvious. Or it makes him sound like a girl, which he kinda is. Think of something else."

In the game, Weed has just shot someone or something with a digitized glock pistol. His movement is through a seeming maze, with a camera positioned as if on the forehead of the player. The movement is too fast; Jill can't follow it except for its staccato halts. Otherwise, the game looks more or less like any other video game, not that Jill knows about these things. One difference: there are no cartoon hot chicks. But there are women. Moments later, Weed, or his character stops as he regards a figure that looks exactly like the one Weed had previously destroyed. The character that is Weed, and the target, both freeze and Jill glances at Weed's face. He is still and concentrated. Some kind of stoic assessment is transpiring. Then the character, the target, disappears. Weed's character, withdrawing the pistol, follows. It's a silent move, followed by a disappearance, then a mystery. "Well?" asks Weed, while operating within some other part of his brain.

"Dunno yet. Gimme time," Chris says, regarding the matter of Jules' nickname. He is leaned forward, looking more closely at his video screen, trying harder because he has to. His movements are more agitated than those of Weed, and he is yet to withdraw his weapon. But there is hope: his eyes shine with their light blue color, seeming as carefree and childlike as ever. Weed's eyes are less boyish. Weed's eyes are brown.

AUTHOR'S NOTE

This book is dedicated to those who work hard, even when reading. Especially when reading. Special thanks are due two people whose hard work didn't make this book possible, just better. Probably. Anyway, thanks to Jason Stephens, my best friend, and to my Dad, Tony Daniels, for giving this project their time and enthusiasm, and me their honesty. Seriously guys, I owe you big time. Thanks also to childhood friend Jonathan Tedds for his thoughts, and to a few guys named Matt, Anthony, and Brad for their tidbits of advice. Thanks to my wife, Maria, for once again keeping me company during my after-hours writing habit: for blessed support and good-humored interruption. While much of this was written amid silence or soft instrumental music, sometimes my process blended with her world-observing conversation, plus the relayed concerns of people like Bill Moyers.

By the way, any resemblance between specific people, places and organizations indicated in this novel and those that actually exist is coincidental. No offense. *The Situation* is a sequel to my 2012 novel, *Crystal From The Hills*. Actually, maybe it's not a sequel. It's more of a companion piece. A best friend, maybe.

www.ingramcontent.com/pod-product-compliance
Lightning Source LLC
Chambersburg PA
CBHW060518180626
46817CB00002B/395